D0765281

Cynthia Harrod-Eagles is the author of the hugely popular Morland Dynasty novels, which have captivated and enthralled readers for decades. She is also the author of the contemporary Bill Slider mystery series, as well as her recent series, War at Home, which is an epic family drama set against the backdrop of World War I. Cynthia's passions are music, wine, horses, architecture and the English countryside.

# The Affairs of Ashmore Castle

## Cynthia Harrod-Eagles

SPHERE

SPHERE

First published in Great Britain in 2022 by Sphere

3 5 7 9 10 8 6 4 2

A CIP catalogue record for this book is available from the British Library.

ISBN 978-1-4087-2530-6

Typeset in Plantin by Palimpsest Book Production Limited, Falkirk, Stirlingshire
Printed and bound in Great Britain by Clays Ltd, Elcograf S.p.A.

Papers used by Sphere are from well-managed forests
and other responsible sources.

MIX
Paper from
responsible sources
FSC® C104740

Sphere
An imprint of
Little, Brown Book Group
Carmelite House
50 Victoria Embankment
London
EC4Y 0DZ

An Hachette UK Company
www.hachette.co.uk

www.littlebrown.co.uk

*To Tony, as always*

# DRAMATIS PERSONAE

## AT ASHMORE CASTLE

*The family*

Giles Tallant, 6th Earl of Stainton
— his wife, Kitty, the countess
— his eldest sister Linda, married to Viscount Cordwell
— his brother Richard
— his sister Rachel, aged seventeen
— his sister Alice, aged sixteen
— his widowed grandmother, Victoire (Grandmère)
— his grandfather's half-brother, Sebastian (Uncle Sebastian)
— his widowed mother, Maud, the dowager countess,
  — her brother Fergus, 9th Earl of Leake (Uncle Stuffy)
  — her sister Caroline, widow of Sir James Manningtree
    (Aunt Caroline)
  — her sister Victoria (Aunt Vicky), married to the Prince
    of Wittenstein-Glücksberg (Uncle Bobo)

*The servants*

Moss, the butler
Mrs Webster, the housekeeper
Hook, valet to the earl
Speen, valet to Mr Richard
Crooks, valet to Mr Sebastian

Miss Hatto, maid to the countess
Miss Taylor, maid to the dowager countess
Dorey, sewing maid
Mrs Oxlea, cook
Kitchen maids Ida, Brigid, Aggie
Footmen William, Cyril
Maids Rose, Daisy, Doris, Ellen, Mabel, Tilda
Frewing, hall porter

*In the stables*
Giddins, head man
Archer, groom to the earl
Josh Brandom, groom to the young ladies
John Manley, Joe Green, coachmen

*On the estate*
Markham, land agent
Adeane, bailiff
Moresby, solicitor
Saddler, gamekeeper
Cutmore, woodsman
Gale, carpenter
Porson, head gardener

## IN THE VILLAGE

*St Peter's Church*
— rector, Dr Bannister
— choirmaster, Mr Arden
— curate, Anstruther
— sexton, Gomperts

*Doctors*
— Dr Arbogast
— Dr Welkes

Tom Holyoak, policeman
Persons, station master
Albright, postmaster
Eli Rowse, blacksmith,
Axe Brandom (brother to Josh), assistant blacksmith

## NINA'S FAMILY

Nina, Mrs Joseph Cowling and Kitty's friend
— her Aunt Schofield
— her friend, Lepida Morris
— Mr Cowling's amenuensis, Decius Blake

# CHAPTER ONE

January 1903

Maud Stainton was feeling discontented. It was not something she was used to. She had no truck with feelings, her own or anyone else's: they were a self-indulgence. Likewise with illness – admitting to feeling unwell showed a lack of character. There was no excuse for it.

She was the eldest child of the 8th Earl of Leake, brought up at Cawburn Castle, a crow-haunted, granite fastness in a windswept part of Northumberland where you had to be hardy to survive. Her father had been a distant and rather frightening figure. Her mother she remembered as always either pregnant or in childbed, a faded creature who had given up the struggle and died as soon as, after three daughters and several miscarriages, she had presented the earl with a live son. Maud, then aged eleven, had been forced into the position of mistress of the house and mother to her siblings. Responsibility had forged the iron at the centre of her character. There had been no room for softness.

Her father had never hidden his disgust at having three daughters before the required son, and Maud understood early that they could only redeem themselves by making good marriages. Victoria, the youngest and prettiest, had secured the Prince of Wittenstein-Glucksberg. Caroline, the sweetest-tempered, attracted Sir James Manningtree who,

1

though only a knight, was one of the richest men in London. Maud was the plain one of the three, but a Forrest girl might look as high as she wished. She hoped for a duke; but when the time came there weren't any dukes or marquesses of the right age.

Still, William Fairburn Louis Tallant, 5th Earl of Stainton, had a good pedigree, a fine country seat – Ashmore Castle – and a large estate. She had married him, run his house, borne his children, and occupied the position in society that was her due. Willie Stainton was everything an earl should be in public. Maud knew nothing of his profligacy, his mistresses and his gambling, and only when he died, suddenly, on the hunting field, did she learn he had left the estate near to bankruptcy.

Her elder son, Giles, had inherited the debts along with the title, and to recoup the fortunes of the estate he had married an heiress. Now that heiress was Countess of Stainton. Maud didn't like it. There couldn't be two Lady Staintons – but there were, and she was not the important one.

It was over the Christmas season, during two weeks with all the family gathered, that the discontent had crystallised. She had lost her place in the world. Willie Stainton, damn his eyes, had made her a dowager. She didn't know what to do with herself.

This morning, just after New Year, she examined the faces around the breakfast table. Her eldest daughter Linda had come for the season with her husband and two children. Linda was tall and plain like her mother, and growing scrawny: she was shovelling away a second plate of kedgeree as if she hadn't eaten for a week. Linda's marriage to Viscount Cordwell had been arranged by her father, who had not asked enough questions: the extent of the Cordwell estate's indebtedness had not come to light until it was too late. Gerald Cordwell was a pleasant, likeable man, but niceness buttered no parsnips. He had proved ineffectual in rescuing his fortunes, and

Linda spent every waking moment scheming how to be anywhere but at Holme Manor, his dilapidated seat.

Maud despised them both.

At the far end of the table her second son, Richard, home from soldiering in South Africa, was chatting to his younger sisters, Rachel and Alice, and making them laugh. Everyone liked Richard. Even Maud had been known to smile at him. He had inherited his father's good looks and easy charm.

Alice was not out yet, and therefore of no interest to Maud, but Rachel had turned seventeen last summer, and Maud had been intending to bring her out this season. But now her plan was threatened. She turned her eyes back to the other end of the table where Giles was reading the newspaper and Kitty was toying with a piece of toast and staring at nothing. Kitty was pregnant, and expecting the child in May. If she had wanted to annoy her mother-in-law she could not have timed it better. She looked like the sort of girl who would make hard work of carrying, and Maud had intended a lavish come-out for Rachel, to be followed in short order by a dazzling marriage; but now there was Kitty's condition hanging over everything. She would be sure to go into labour at the very peak of Rachel's debut. She would probably make such a piece of work of it that Rachel's triumph would pale into insignificance beside Kitty's drama, and all Maud's hard work would be for nothing.

Maud seethed. After a lifetime of stoicism and doing her duty, it had come to this, that she was a mere dowager, tolerated in the house that had been hers; taking second place to a nobody, having her plans disrupted; and there was nothing she could do about it. Giles – *Giles!* – had taken her husband's place, and was as indifferent to her wishes as she had always been to his. Damn Stainton for dying! Damn him!

Rachel had felt the eyes upon her. More timid than Alice, she was always afraid of being scolded, and as she looked apprehensively at her mother, a blush of automatic guilt

3

coloured her cheeks. It was a pretty face, framed by long, fair ringlets, but Rachel had seemed out of sorts lately. Maud had noticed it, though it would not have occurred to her to ask the reason. But it gave her an idea. Suddenly the blood started rushing through her head as a plan came to her, with all its details slotting into place in a most satisfactory way.

Out of the corner of her eye she saw Linda put down her fork, her plate temporarily empty, and Giles begin the awkward, elbow-flapping process of turning to the next page of the broadsheet. She must catch the tide of the moment.

'I have decided,' she said – and everyone immediately stopped what they were doing and looked at her: she still commanded to that extent – 'that I shall go to Darmstadt next week, and Rachel shall come with me.'

The servants were assembled round their own breakfast table, waiting for Mr Moss, the butler, and William, the first footman, to come down from the dining-room. Ellen, one of the house-maids, who had been helping upstairs, scuttled to her seat, saying, 'That's put the cat among the pigeons! Guess what I heard?'

But she had sat down only in time to stand up again as Mr Moss entered and beat her to the news. 'Well, quite a significant change of plans has been announced. I wonder you didn't mention it, Miss Taylor.'

Miss Taylor, the dowager's personal maid, didn't know what he was talking about, and concealed the fact with a haughty look. 'Grace, if you please, Mr Moss. We may at least begin the day in godliness, even if we can't sustain it until evening.'

'Oh – ah – hm!' Moss looked annoyed at being caught out. In some great houses, religion featured strongly, with morning and evening prayers every day in the servants' hall and a strict discipline kept over language and morals. The devotional temperature below stairs depended more on the leanings of the butler than the dictates of the mistress, and Moss regarded himself as a rationalist, so the Almighty didn't feature strongly in his rule; but on the other hand, he was a great believer in tradition, and disliked having Miss Taylor trip him up. He glared sternly round the table until every head was bowed, and then pronounced the grace in suitably cathedral tones.

'Amen.'

Chairs scraped, everyone sat, the bread plate went rapidly round. The kitchen-maids Aggie and Brigid came in and planked down the big teapot in front of Mrs Webster and the hot dishes by Mr Moss, then hurried off to their own breakfast in the kitchen.

'Go on then, Ellen,' said Tilda. 'What did you hear?'

The family served themselves at breakfast, but the old earl had liked butler and first footman to be in attendance at the sideboard, and the new earl had not thought to rescind the order. Females didn't wait at table, but Ellen had been in the serving-closet just off the dining-room, stacking dirties onto a tray to take down.

'Well,' she said, 'you know her ladyship goes to Germany every year in January?'

'Whyever does she do that?' wondered Tilda, who was new since last summer.

'Because her sister married a German prince,' Ellen explained. 'He's got a palace, some funny name it's got, like the Washtub—'

'The Wachturm,' Mrs Webster, the housekeeper, corrected. 'Near Darmstadt.'

'A palace!' said pale, pretty Milly, who was also new. 'Fancy!'

William gazed at her adoringly, as though she'd said something deeply significant. His loves burned bright and brief, and rarely got further than adoring glances.

'Her ladyship is accustomed to visit there every year, for six weeks or so,' Moss said. 'Can I assist you to some kedgeree, Miss Taylor?'

'No, thank you,' said Miss Taylor firmly. 'That haddock was

definitely off. I smelt it when I came past the kitchen this morning.'

'But it's the same as they're having upstairs,' Moss said, shocked. 'Nobody complained in the dining-room.'

'Did anyone *try* it in the dining-room?'

'Her ladyship had some. And Lady Cordwell had two servings.'

Speen, Mr Richard's valet, laughed. 'That's no guarantee. They'd eat dung if you put it on a plate in front of them.'

Miss Taylor said, 'I would not express myself with such vulgarity, Mr Speen, but in essence you're right. The quality of food is a matter of indifference to my lady and Lady Cordwell. It has always been a matter of regret to me. But it doesn't alter the fact that the haddock is off and no amount of curry powder will disguise it. What's in the other dish?'

Moss lifted the lid. 'Fried ham,' he said.

Miss Taylor recoiled. 'Fried in the fish pan, by the smell of it. I'll just have to make do with bread this morning. That drunken fool in the kitchen gets no better, Mrs Webster.'

'Nothing I can do about it,' Mrs Webster said shortly. 'You'll have to speak to your mistress about replacing her.'

'I shall do no such thing,' Miss Taylor said indignantly. 'That is not my job. If you would have the kindness to pass me the marmalade . . .'

'Gooseberry jam,' Mrs Webster corrected. 'Marmalade's all finished, bar what I've kept back for upstairs.'

'*Well!* This house goes from bad to worse—'

Rose had tired of the conversation. 'What *is* this wonderful news you've heard?' she asked Ellen impatiently.

Ellen hastily swallowed the wad of bread with which she was subduing the first agonies of hunger, and said importantly, 'Her ladyship's going to Germany next week and she's taking Lady Rachel with her!'

Daisy, the housemaid who looked after the young ladies, said, 'First I've heard about it. Did you know, Miss Taylor?'

6

Miss Taylor was saved from answering by Rose, who said, 'That can't be right. I thought her ladyship wasn't going at all this year. It's supposed to be Lady Rachel's come-out this season. If they go to Germany, it won't leave time to arrange everything.'

'They won't be bringing her out this year,' said Ellen. 'Her ladyship said Lady Rachel's very young for her age, and it won't hurt to wait a year. She'll meet lots of people in Germany and get more confidence and show up all the better next year.'

Miss Hatto, Kitty's maid, who listened to everything but rarely spoke, said, 'Perhaps she's noticed that Lady Rachel's been out of spirits lately.'

'What do you mean?' said Daisy. 'She's all right. She's always been the quiet one of the two, but she's not ill.'

'I don't say ill – just not her usual self,' said Miss Hatto.

'Maybe she's in love,' Speen suggested in a ribald tone. He could make *pass the sugar* sound like an indecent proposition.

'But whoever could she be in love *with*?' Daisy said. 'They never go anywhere. Anyway, I'd know if that was it. She'd tell me.'

Rose gave her a scornful look. She didn't think either of the girls would open their hearts to Daisy, who was an inveterate gossip. And not a good maid, either – lazy and self-centred. 'What I don't understand,' she said, 'is why we didn't know about this. Lady Linda would've said something to me if she'd known. She was saying only yesterday that it looked as though she'd have to go home next week, but if her ladyship was going to Germany, she'd be expecting to stay and be hostess.'

'But his lordship's *got* a wife,' said Tilda 'She's the hostess, surely.'

'That wouldn't stop Lady Linda,' said Rose. 'She'd say her young ladyship's condition means she shouldn't exert herself. Did her ladyship really say nothing to you, Miss Taylor?'

'My observation,' said Moss, feeling a little authority was needed, 'was that the announcement took everyone by surprise. Lady Cordwell, indeed, looked quite put out.'

7

'She would do. It's never occurred to her all these years to ask to go to Germany,' said Rose. 'She'll be wondering what she's missed.'

'But if Lady Rachel isn't out, how can she meet people over there?' Miss Hatto asked.

'His lordship asked the same question. Her ladyship said it wouldn't signify in German society,' said Moss. 'She also mentioned that the Grand Duke of Hesse would be at Dramstadt with a large party, and that everyone from the Wachturm would naturally be invited to their entertainments. That would be a great thing for Lady Rachel.'

'Still, it's not like her ladyship to decide things on impulse, like that,' said Rose.

'Just because none of *you* knew doesn't mean it was an impulse,' said Hook, his lordship's man. 'I knew all about it.'

The maids looked at him with interest, but Rose was scornful. 'Oh, you did not! You're just trying to make yourself important. As if her ladyship'd tell *you* stuff!'

'But she'd tell his lordship, and his lordship has no secrets from me.'

Crooks looked shocked, and mortified. He used to be Giles's valet, and had been ousted by James Hook to the lower position of valet to Mr Sebastian, who barely needed the services of a highly trained gentleman's gentleman. 'His lordship *confides* in you?' he said, in a cracked voice.

Miss Taylor disliked Crooks, but she loathed Hook. 'Pay no attention, Mr Crooks. Rose is quite right – James is just puffing himself up.'

'It's Mr Hook to you, Miss Taylor,' he said angrily. 'I'm not a footman any more. And a gentleman can choose who he wants to confide in without asking *your* permission.'

'His lordship certainly seemed as surprised as anyone,' Moss said doubtfully.

Miss Taylor hadn't finished with Hook. 'The day Lord Stainton confides in a counter-jumper like you, *Mister* Hook, the Four Horsemen of the Apocalypse will come riding up the drive from Canons Ashmore and hold a lawn meet.'

Moss was distracted. 'There is some doubt about whether the Four Horsemen are a truly Christian idea, Miss Taylor. The Book of Revelation has its critics—'

Mrs Webster intervened. Mr Moss owned an encyclopaedia called *The A-Z of Universal Knowledge*, and his love of imparting nuggets from it was not matched by anyone's love of receiving them. 'Well, I'm sure we'll hear all about it soon. There'll be preparations and packing to do. You always look forward to Germany, don't you, Miss Taylor?'

'The household at the Wachturm is well run,' she allowed. 'But it can be bitterly cold there in winter. I wonder what my lady will do about a fur for Lady Rachel. She'll certainly need one. I'd better have a look through the fur closet after breakfast, to see if there's anything she might borrow.'

There was a frenzy of preparation and packing. Rachel had no suitable clothes, and every woman in the house who could use a needle was recruited to create enough to last her until German mantua-makers could be called in. Housemaids cursed and pricked their unaccustomed fingers as they sewed ribbon and lace onto plain underwear and nightclothes. A dressmaker from the village came in with bolts of cloth, and two warm travelling-dresses were cut out and made up. Lady Stainton lent a three-quarter-length sable – which was full length on the smaller Rachel – along with a matching hat and muff.

'Are you scared?' Alice asked her sister, as Daisy laid a pile of linen on the bed for Rose to pack. 'All those new people to meet, royals and everything.'

'A bit,' Rachel admitted. 'But excited mostly. And Aunt Vicky and Uncle Bobo are so nice, I'm sure it will all be lovely.'

'There'll be the Grand Duke of Hesse to meet,' Alice reminded her. 'He's Queen Victoria's grandson, you know.'

'But Mama says Ernie Hesse is very approachable and jolly.'
She enjoyed the sound of herself saying 'Ernie Hesse' as if
she knew him. 'Though she disapproves of him a bit because
he's divorced. But Queen Victoria gave her permission for it,
so nobody can say anything.'

'If he's divorced, how can he entertain? He'd have to have
a hostess.'

'Aunt Vicky said in her letter that his sister Irene will be
hostess. She's Princess Henry of Prussia. One of his other
sisters is Queen of Romania and another one is a Russian
grand duchess. I wonder if they'll be there?'

Alice laughed. 'Goodness! You'll be scared rigid!'

'She won't,' Rose intervened. She had known the girls since
babyhood and could take certain liberties. 'She'll behave just
as she ought and be much admired. She'll have a lovely time.
Don't upset her, Lady Alice.'

'I'm not, I won't. But grand dukes and princes – it's a bit
different from—'

She didn't complete the sentence, but Rachel knew what
she meant. *Victor Lattery*. Rachel had fallen in love with him
the year before – her first love, her first secret kisses. And he
had gone off to America with a cheerful wave and without, it
seemed, the slightest regret at parting from her. She had been
in mourning all winter, until now. She shook her head at Alice,
and said, 'I want it to be different.'

Alice thought, *She's got over him*. She was glad. She'd never
thought Victor was such a much.

'Your turn will come, Lady Alice,' Rose said, thinking Alice's
silence was envy.

'It needn't bother,' Alice said. 'I like being at home. And I
wouldn't miss the rest of the hunting season for anything.'

The recent snow that had suspended hunting had mostly worn
away, lingering only in the shadows of walls. Last night's frost
had been sharp: it glittered in a crust along the branches, and

there was a skim of ice in the ruts that cracked like small-arms fire under the impact of twelve striking hoofs. The swollen ball of the sun had just managed to haul itself clear of the net of bare treetops, and its scalding orange light turned the frost diamond to fire, and left cobalt shadows in the hollows, as if winter had been distilled to a cold blue liquid.

It was an act of heroism on Alice's part to take Linda's children to the meet. Arabella at eight was not a bad little rider, but Arthur at six was still on the leading-rein, and on the two trap ponies, Biscuit and Goosebumps, they would hardly be more mobile than foot-followers, so it was a sacrifice to give up what promised to be a good day in the field to shepherd her niece and nephew about the lanes.

Still, Giles had shown some heroism of his own in allowing Linda to leave the children at Ashmore when she and her husband were packed off home. He had told her bluntly – there was never any point in hinting to Linda, who could ignore anything more subtle than a direct order – that she would have to go when Mama and Rachel left for Germany. Allowing her to leave the children had been for their sakes, not hers. He felt sorry for them.

Linda never brought their nursery-maid with her to Ashmore, expecting Daisy to look after them. 'She loves children,' Linda said. 'And with Rachel away, she'll have hardly anything to do. I'm sure Alice doesn't need much maiding.'

In fact, Daisy didn't much like the little Cordwells, and while she would attend to their washing, dressing and feeding, she didn't see why she should have to entertain them, and was inclined to leave them in the nursery with a book and a stern instruction not to move. In sheer pity, the girls sometimes felt they had to rescue them. On their last visit, they had started teaching them to ride. Now, on an impulse, Alice had offered to take them to a meet.

It was at Lord Shacklock's place, Ashridge Park, the next estate along. Here the Ash Valley widened out into lush meadows, so there was plenty of room for a proper lawn meet, unlike at Ashmore Castle, which hadn't much in the way of adjacent flat land. Pharaoh was fresh, despite having had a good gallop the day before, and Alice thought wistfully of the hunt she could have had, while absently telling Arthur to sit up straight and keep his knees in.

As soon as they turned in at the park gates, Pharaoh's head went up, his nostrils flared, and he let out a tremendous long whinny that shook his sides. He knew exactly what was up ahead.

Arabella said, 'What's wrong with him? Why is he making that noise?'

'He's excited, that's all. He can smell hounds.'

'Well, it sounds awfully silly,' Arabella said. 'I'm glad my pony's not doing it.'

'You attend to your reins,' Alice said. 'They're in loops! If Biscuit were to bolt, you'd have no control at all.'

'Biscuit would never do that,' Arabella said. At the same instant, Biscuit caught the exciting flavour on the air and, realising his rider wasn't paying attention, broke into a brisk trot and carted her up the drive.

It took a moment to bring the indignant Pharaoh under control, and by then Arabella had disappeared round the bend. Alice followed with Arthur at a sedate jog, dreading what she would find.

There was the gravelled forecourt of the handsome old house, glamorously peopled with horses and riders; there was the pack, sterns waving, being held together by the whips; there were servants carrying round trays of hot pasties and glasses of stirrup cup. And there was Axe Brandom helping Arabella to regain her lost stirrup while Biscuit nuzzled his pockets for titbits. Axe was the assistant blacksmith in the village, and knew every equine in the district.

'Now, Miss Arabella,' he was saying, 'hold your reins like this – see? Not too tight but not too loose. So he knows you're in charge.'

'I've been telling her that all the way here,' Alice said.

Axe let go of Biscuit, swept off his hat, and walked over to Alice. He laid a hand on Pharaoh's neck, and the liver-chestnut pushed his nose to Axe's ear and blew into it, then continued to stare goggle-eyed over his shoulder at the scene. Axe smiled up at Alice. 'I heard you coming, right from the gates.'

'You'd think he'd never seen hounds before. Thank you for catching Biscuit.'

'Warn't no catching to it,' Axe said. 'He come straight to me.' He glanced behind Alice. 'No Josh with you today?'

Josh, groom to Rachel and Alice, was Axe's brother.

'He's got Richard's second horse,' she explained. 'Richard's taken Rachel's Daystar, then he's changing on to Kitty's Apollo. It's lucky he's so light. But Josh will have to walk Daystar home – she'll never carry him after a run.'

'Can always leave her somewhere and fetch her later. That's what I'd do,' Axe said, fending off Pharaoh gently as the gelding mouthed in a friendly manner at his red-gold hair. 'So you'll not get much hunting today, then, taking care of the childer?'

'No,' Alice said, with a sigh. 'And Lord Shacklock's head man, Aigburth, told our Giddins that it was going to be a spiffing day, with two earths stopped up at High Spinney and Crown Woods.'

Axe nodded. 'If they run as far as High Spinney, likely they'll go on and draw Motte Woods. There's an old fox up there.' He paused. 'Have you heard about Aaron Cutmore? You know his cottage is up in Motte Woods?'

'What about him?' Alice had always thought he had the perfect name for a woodsman.

'Had a bit of an accident cutting poles and laid his foot open. He's thinking about giving up. Getting too old, he says.'

'I wonder who'll replace him,' said Alice.

'I've asked Mr Adeane for the job,' Axe told her. Adeane was the estate bailiff.

13

'Do you think you'll get it?'

'Mr Adeane knows what I can do.' He sounded quietly confident.

Alice was silent, wondering how this would affect her. She had known Axe as blacksmith ever since she could remember, but lately she had been visiting him at his cottage on his day off – she loved animals, and he always had an orphaned or injured animal or two in his care, as well as Dolly, his terrier.

Axe watched her face as if he could read her thoughts. ''f I get the job, I'll get Cutmore's cottage. Motte Woods is a bit far for a walk, but you could ride there easy enough. And I'd be there all the time, not just on my day off.' He saw her working through the implications, and added the clincher. 'Got a goshawk. Found him caught in a net just after Christmas. Hurt his wing.'

Her face lit. 'Oh, I'd love to see that.'

'And Dolly, she misses you. Asks about you all the time.' He smiled, to show it was a joke.

'Have you still got your jackdaw?' she asked.

'Captain? Yes. But he's getting old now. Won't be with us much longer.' Now he met her eyes, and she felt a heat run from her face all the way down her neck. He held her gaze for a moment, then glanced back at Arabella, sitting with such a loose rein that Biscuit had decided it was all right to graze. 'You don't want to miss the hunt, my lady. What say I look after the young 'uns? They'll only be walking as far as the first draw, I dare say?'

'That was the idea. It's very kind of you to offer,' Alice said wistfully, 'but—'

'I don't mind walking 'em back to Ashmore after. They'll be safe with me.'

'I know they will, but—'

'Wouldn't want Pharaoh to miss a good run.' He glanced back again. 'Looks as though they're about to move off. Shall I take the young 'uns for you?'

Bathed in the sort of kindness and attention she never got at home, Alice yielded to temptation. Linda would have a fit if she ever found out that Alice had abandoned her children to the blacksmith – but why should she ever know? And he was not any old blacksmith – he was Axe Brandom, Josh's brother, practically family. 'Thank you,' she said. 'And I hope you get the job.'

He took the leading-rein from her, put on his hat, clicked to Goosebumps and led him towards Arabella and Biscuit. Arabella took in the new situation with remarkable quickness. 'Oh, are you taking us? That's nice. I don't think Aunt Alice really wants us. Look at Biscuit, watching the hounds. Isn't he funny? Did you hear Aunt Alice's horse making that awful noise? Have you got a horse? I'm going to be nine this year. Do you think I'm old enough to have a pony of my own? I asked Daddy last birthday but he said I wasn't old enough. But Mummy told me once she had a pony when she was five. Janet our maid says Daddy only said no because he's got short arms and long pockets. What does that mean?'

She chattered happily to Axe as he took Biscuit's redundant rein and led him away, with Goosebumps on his other side, while grateful Alice rode the eager Pharaoh to join the field as it moved off.

# CHAPTER TWO

At the end of the most embarrassing hour of his life, Joseph Cowling seated himself, fully dressed again, in the chair across the desk from the doctor.

The chair was antique, Sheraton or one of those – Cowling was no expert, but he had visited enough rich men in their houses to know one when he saw it – and the desk was large and handsome; the carpet underfoot was Persian and must have cost a few bob. Most telling of all, the doctor chap – specialists, they called themselves these days, when they were expert in some particular field – was wearing a very fine pair of hand-made shoes: William Lobb, if he was any judge, ten guineas if they were a penny, not new but lovingly polished. Cowling could see them down there, below the desk, and they reassured him. A doctor who could not afford the best would not be one Joseph Cowling cared to consult; and a man who did not take care of his boots was not someone Cowling wanted to know. He had been in the shoe trade all his life, started off as a 'prentice cobbler in a village in Leicestershire, and now owned three factories and was rich enough to lend money to the King. He tended to judge men by their footwear – and it wasn't such a bad benchmark, either.

'Well, then, Sir Grenville,' Cowling said, because he'd sooner get down to business than wait about feeling nervous, which was not a natural state for him, 'what have you got to tell me?'

Sir Grenville Kennet folded his hands on the desk in front of him. 'I have no definitive answer for you,' he said. 'From my examination I cannot find anything functionally amiss. You seem, indeed, to be both in the prime of life and at the peak of health.'

Cowling was taken aback. 'What's going on, then?' Kennet had been recommended as the best. Was this all he was going to get?

Kennet did not exactly smile – that would not have been appropriate – but his handsomely-carved features softened just a fraction. 'Yours is not an uncommon problem,' he said. 'In fact, I should say that most men suffer from it at some point in their lives. To one extent or another. Sometimes it is a fleeting thing, at others, as in your case, it can persist for a while. It is something about which I am often consulted.'

He said it as though Cowling should take some comfort from the knowledge. Safety in numbers, was that it? But he was not paying top brass to a top man to be told he was just like everyone else. 'Aye, well, you should have an answer, then, shouldn't you, after all that practice?' he said roughly.

Kennet resumed, unflurried. 'You say that you had no difficulties with your first wife? Quite so. Well, where there is no illness or physical abnormality, one can only surmise that the problem lies in the mind.'

Cowling bristled. 'What are you saying now? That I'm touched? That I'm milky in the filbert?'

'The human mind is a complex and mysterious organ, Mr Cowling, about which we know almost nothing. But ultimately it controls everything we do. I take it that your present wife is, shall we say, receptive?'

'She's a jewel,' Cowling said shortly. 'She's everything a man could want.'

'Just so. Indeed. And a good deal younger than you?'

'She's eighteen.'

'Hm.' He steepled his fingers and stared judicially off

into the distance. 'It is possible, you know, for the mind to interfere with what should be a perfectly natural function. Imagine, if you will, a schoolboy called out to recite before the class. He knows his piece off by heart, but with all eyes upon him, he is struck dumb, he cannot bring forth a single word.'

'And gets a thrashing for it, like as not!'

'Indeed. But, my dear sir, he will grow out of his shyness. He knows his stuff all right; and in time his confidence will grow, his mind will allow his body to relax, and he will . . . rise to the occasion.'

If Kennet had smiled at that point, Cowling might have forgotten himself. But he remained perfectly grave. Cowling breathed out hard, considered, and said, 'What am I to do, then?' He hated to hear his own voice come out so pleading. He hated not to be in charge.

'Be patient. You are a perfectly well man, Mr Cowling. In time everything will come about. Nature will take over. Nature is a powerful force, you know, and will not be denied. Carry on with your life, approach your wife as usual and try not to fret. The less you think about it, the more likely it is that you will succeed. It will happen in its own good time.'

'Aye, well, I'd sooner it happened in *my* good time.'

Sir Grenville stood and offered his hand across the desk to indicate the séance was at an end.

Cowling stood too, but eyed the hand with disfavour. He didn't feel he'd got value for his money. 'I thought you'd give me something – some jallop or other.'

'I'm afraid there's nothing that would help.'

'Mebbe I'd have been better consulting a veterinarian,' Cowling said grumpily. 'At least they always give you a ball, or a drench.'

'There *are* quack remedies on the market, Mr Cowling, but I assure you they are worthless. I would not insult you by offering you some useless palliative. I respect you, and

18

myself, too much for that. Please be assured, the problem will right itself in time. The essential thing is not to worry.'

A little later Joseph Cowling emerged onto Harley Street in the pallid March sunshine, a poorer man by the specialist's reassuringly hefty fee, but not much the wiser. But Sir Grenville had said there was nothing wrong with him. He'd been definite about that. Don't think about it, he'd said. Cowling was not sure that was helpful advice. As well tell a man to walk three times round a donkey and not think of its tail. He stumped away to his business meetings, with humiliation like a lump of something unpleasant in his breast pocket.

Nina – Mrs Joseph Cowling – had jumped at the opportunity, when Mr Cowling suggested it, of accompanying him up to London. 'I've business to do, so I shan't be able to squire you about,' he'd said apologetically. 'But I thought you might visit your aunt and do some shopping and p'raps meet a friend.'

'I'd love that,' Nina said, her face lighting in a way that Mr Cowling noticed with a small pang. He'd been busy as a cat with ten kittens since Christmas, but he hadn't been too busy to notice that his bride didn't seem as happy as he'd hoped. He'd promised her a honeymoon trip when things quieted down, but they never had. She'd said she didn't mind, bless her, and she never complained, but when a man of forty-six marries a girl of eighteen, he'd better not take her for granted.

'Buy yourself some pretties,' he urged. 'You can have everything charged – everyone knows who I am. But just in case . . .' And he had thrust a handful of banknotes into her hand, which she had later counted and been slightly shocked by.

Nina had been trying hard not to let it show that she was restless and bored. But when she called on her Aunt Schofield in Draycott Place, and her aunt, who had brought her up since she was orphaned at the age of ten, asked with routine politeness how she was, she couldn't help letting it spill out.

'Northampton is so dull, Auntie! The married women I meet are much older than me, and all they talk about is their children and their servants and their ailments. The only time I have a proper conversation, it's with Decius. But he's so busy, it's hardly more than once a week that he has time to chat.' Decius Blake was Mr Cowling's secretary and factotum.

Aunt Schofield seem to recoil slightly. 'My dear Nina,' she protested. She was watching Nina's little dog Trump bustle round the room, sniffing all the new smells, and interrupted herself to say, 'If that dog makes a mess—'

'He won't. He's very good now. And I made sure he went outside before we came in.'

'I'd have thought you'd have left it at home. London is no place for a dog.'

'But Mrs Mitchell hates him so, I was afraid something might happen to him if I left him. That's the other thing,' Nina rushed on, suspecting she was about to be stopped. 'I thought I could do things about the house, but Mrs Mitchell simply *hates* any interference. I moved a little table the other day because it was in my way when I went to the window, and she came and quizzed me about it and said everything in the house was the way Mr Cowling liked it, as she should know having been his housekeeper for twenty years. I don't understand,' she went on, forestalling her aunt's indrawn breath, 'how she even knew I'd moved it. I think Nellie must have told her. I'm sure the servants spy on me. The *only* thing I've managed to change is that we have Gayetty's Medicated Squares instead of newspaper in the privy. And Mrs Mitchell only agreed to that because it frees Nellie from having to cut up the newspapers and gives her more time for spying.'

She paused for breath and Aunt Schofield seized the moment. 'My dear Nina, listen to yourself!' she said. 'I didn't expect this flood of complaint. You were fully aware when you accepted Mr Cowling that your life would change. You were not forced into the marriage. I took pains, indeed, to make you think hard about it. And now, because married life is not perfect in every respect—'

Nina broke in. 'I miss your parties, and your friends. We had such wonderful conversations. About everything in the world. But all Mr Cowling's friends discuss at dinner is business, and their wives! Mrs Amberley, for instance, talks endlessly about the trouble she has with her *teeth*.'

'Nina, stop,' Aunt Schofield said sternly. 'You are not a child any more. You are a grown woman, a married woman. I've taken care of you as I promised your father I would do, but you are not my responsibility any more. I have a life of my own to lead. Find something to do with yourself – and if you can't, you are not the Nina I brought up. Above all, do not come complaining to me about your lot. I have no more advice to give you – and these domestic frictions are as uninteresting to me as Mrs Amberley's teeth are to you.'

Nina felt as though she had been slapped. Tears came to her eyes, but she blinked them back, knowing they would only annoy her aunt, and shut her lips tight. Aunt Schofield immediately began talking about a lecture she had attended at Senate House, and Nina tried to listen and respond intelligently. She found it difficult, which made her fear that her mind was already deteriorating; and she was actually quite glad when her aunt cut the visit short, saying that she had a prior engagement to keep.

From Draycott Place Nina went to the Morrises' house, where the parents of her best friend Lepida hugged and petted her, Lepida took off her hat with her own hands and brought her sherry, and Trump was cooed over, then borne off by a maid to the kitchen to be spoiled. In the drawing-room the chat flowed freely, interspersed with laughter. Mawes Morris was a famous cartoonist, and had acquaintances in every field, from sportsmen to actors to financiers to the King himself, so he always had amusing stories to tell.

He talked about a small dinner he had attended two days earlier, given for the King by Sir Ernest Cassel. 'Hamilton at the Treasury deplores the King's dining with Cassel,' he said. 'He thinks the King should dine only with the upper classes. But the fact is that Tum knows his own interest. Cassel is some sort of genius when it comes to money. The King gave him twenty thousand to invest last November, and by January it was worth thirty thousand, despite the fact that the King had withdrawn ten thousand just before Christmas!'

'I wish he'd do as much for us,' said Isabel Morris. 'You should ask him, Mawes.'

'Next time I have twenty thousand to spare I certainly shall,' Mawes laughed.

'Does Mr Cowling invest with Cassel, Nina?' Isabel asked.

'I don't know,' said Nina. 'I know they're acquainted, but Mr Cowling doesn't talk to me about money.'

'Quite right,' said Mawes. 'There are better subjects to beguile the ladies. And talking finance makes men dull. Cassel is not the most sparkling of company, it must be said, but he's so important to the King they call him Windsor Cassel! I'm thinking of doing a cartoon on the subject, by the by, if the right moment comes. I'd need a story to attach it to. And if Cassel can't talk, he knows how to surround himself with those who can. The Keppels were at the dinner, and they're both amusing and witty. Mrs George Keppel in particular – she always has something interesting to say, and says it in such an engaging way. She has great charm – though she's not really a beauty.'

Nina asked a question she had often wanted to voice, but could not have done when she was an unmarried girl. 'Is it true that Mrs Keppel is the King's mistress?'

'It's hard to say,' Mawes answered. 'She's certainly the King's favourite, and he admires her intensely. Can't take his eyes off her when she's present. But I get the impression it's more a matter of companionship than passion. It must be a lonely business, being king.'

'Yes, poor king, surrounded by adoring people hanging on his every word,' Lepida agreed.

'Toadies and flatterers, looking for preferment,' said Isabel. 'Not true friends.'

'But I'm sure Mrs George genuinely likes him,' said Mawes. 'Though the Keppels certainly do all right out of the relationship. You may get to meet her one of these days, Nina. And the King.'

'Me?' Nina stared in surprise.

'Why not? As Hamilton said, most disobligingly, if the King can dine with Cassel he can dine anywhere. Why not with the Cowlings? You may become a woman of influence, a great political hostess.'

'Mawes, don't tease the girl,' Isabel said.

Nina reflected that the first time she had met Mr Cowling, he had been in a party the King had brought to a country-house ball she was attending with Kitty. Mr Cowling knew the King, gave him advice, lent him money. It was not beyond the realms of possibility that he should entertain him one day. But then she thought about Beechcroft House in Northampton, with its Victorian clutter, and Mrs Mitchell, and the plain, serviceable meals that were served there, and imagination failed.

'Don't worry, Nina,' said Mawes solemnly. 'If you ever have to be hostess to royalty and the great names of the day, I'll come and give you advice. As long as you let me draw everyone. I'll conceal myself behind a curtain – they'll never know I'm there.'

'If I'm hostess to the great names of the day,' Nina promised him solemnly, 'you'll all be among the guests.'

It was balm to her feelings to be with people who so obviously liked her and enjoyed her company. Her aunt's rejection had hurt her more than she would admit.

And when Trump was brought back in, he was much rounder, and seemed very satisfied with life.

After leaving the Morrises, Nina took a cab to Piccadilly and wandered through the Burlington Arcade to look at the shops. She bought herself a pair of good nail scissors, and pondered a pretty silk scarf but could not raise enough enthusiasm to buy it. Mr Cowling had told her to buy herself things, but there didn't seem any point, for her life in Northampton. She didn't want to go back there – didn't belong there – but she didn't belong in London any more, either. Then she shook herself. No self-pity! Aunt was right, she was a grown woman and had made her decision with a cool head. Now she must make the best of things. And Mr Cowling was very kind to her. She decided to go across to Fortnum's and buy him a jar of the particular relish he was fond of, to show him she cared for him.

Leaving Fortnum's, she wandered westwards, drifting through the crowd, feeling like a leaf borne along by a stream. Trump began to drag at the lead, complaining that the pavements were hard, and that he was a very small dog in a world full of boots. At the corner of St James's Street she stopped and picked him up, wondering what to do next, and was almost run into by Richard Tallant as he came round the corner.

'Miss Sanderton! No, what am I thinking? It's Mrs Cowling now, isn't it? What are you doing here? Is this your dog? He looks a likely fellow.' He scratched the top of Trump's head, and the dog, knowing an expert when he met one, gave the hand a lick.

'It's nice to see you, Mr Tallant,' Nina said, meaning it more than the conventional words could express. In her mind he represented the metropolis, civilised company, the interest and freedom of her come-out year – everything that was not Northampton.

'You look lost,' Richard suggested. 'But no one can be lost on Piccadilly. Simply isn't possible.'

'I was just thinking how thirsty I am and wondering how to get a cup of tea.'

'Nothing could be simpler,' he declared. 'There's Rampling's, just a few steps away. Will you allow me the pleasure of escorting you?'

This was a new problem. Was it all right to go into a restaurant with a man, without a chaperone? She hesitated. 'Um . . .'

It was as if he could read her mind. 'You are a married woman, Mrs Cowling, in case you've forgotten. There is absolutely nothing improper in taking tea with me in a well-lit public place in the middle of the afternoon.' He offered his arm. 'After all, as the brother of the husband of your best friend, I'm practically family,' he added.

She wished he hadn't said that. She had been trying not to think about Giles, and there was just enough family resemblance in Richard to taunt her. She had made a rule for herself, when Kitty married Giles, that she would not think about him, ever, and on the whole she managed pretty well. She had two people now, Kitty and Mr Cowling, who would be dishonoured by it. But just for a moment, glancing at Richard's profile, everything flooded over her with such force that her legs felt weak, and she wanted to sink to the pavement and howl like a lost child. But she seized control again with a violent effort, and a few moments later she walked into Rampling's tea room on Richard's arm with calm dignity, thinking nothing more weighty than that she was glad she had put on her best hat that morning.

'So, Mr Tallant—' she began, when they were seated. Trump, tired out from the walk, lay down under her chair and put his nose on his paws.

'Richard, please,' he interrupted. 'Mr Tallant makes me feel old.'

'Richard, then. Are you living in London now?'

'No, still down at Ashmore. I came up to do some business for the estate with Vogel, our banker. And, more importantly, to get a haircut in Jermyn Street. Whence I was coming when I bumped into you so delightfully. Do you live in London?'

'No – Mr Cowling came up for business and thought I might enjoy a pleasure trip. Did your business go well?'

'Not especially,' said Richard. 'Did your pleasure trip go well?'

'Not especially,' Nina said. They looked at each other, with similar expressions of discontent.

'You first,' said Richard. 'Please. Think of me as the safe hole in the ground into which you can whisper your secrets.'

'I don't think the hole turned out to be very safe, did it? Didn't King Midas kill the barber afterwards?'

'It's such a pleasure talking to someone who understands one's references,' Richard said. 'Tell me anyway – what's happened to vex you?'

Nina told him about her aunt's rejection. 'She didn't want to listen to me, was too busy with her own affairs. She's never been sentimental,' she concluded, 'but I thought she was fond of me. And she's the only family I have.'

'I'm sure she *is* fond of you,' Richard said. 'The best sort of fondness, the sort that does what's right for the other person. She's pushing you out of the nest and making you fly. After all, what did you expect her to do? She can't change anything in your life now, can she?'

'I suppose I didn't expect her to *do* anything,' Nina said, forced to think it out. 'I just thought she would . . . well, *sympathise* with me.'

'And what good would that have done? I expect it hurt her more than it hurt you – especially if you let it show on your face that you minded.'

'Oh dear,' Nina said. 'Now I feel guilty as well as sad.'

'Don't be sad. Tell me what's troubling you about your new life in – where is it you're living?'

'Northampton,' she said.

'I don't know the place at all. I may have passed through it on a train.'

He raised his eyebrows receptively, but she couldn't tell him, of course, about her relationship with Mr Cowling, and her puzzle over the bedroom business. She couldn't even tell him about Mrs Mitchell and the domestic stalemate – he wasn't *that* much of a brother. She fiddled with a piece of bread-and-butter for a moment, and then said, 'I *hate* Northampton. It's so dull!' And was aware that it sounded childish and petulant, not smartly metropolitan at all.

'Then why do you live there?' Richard asked, sipping tea.

'Mr Cowling has a factory there.'

'Is it necessary to live near the factory?'

'I don't know. I suppose so, since he does. Although he has factories in Leicester as well, and he doesn't seem to need to live *there*.'

'Well, it's all beyond me – I know nothing about manufacturing. But surely you could ask him. Then, if it's not necessary, you can move somewhere else. After all, I'm sure he wants you to be happy. And if it *is* necessary to live there, at least you'll know, and then you'll just have to make the best of it.'

It was so simple and obvious, Nina didn't know why she hadn't thought of it. 'You do give very wise advice,' she said, impressed.

He looked alarmed. 'Please don't say that – you'll ruin my reputation for frivolity. I'm famous for never having said a rational word since I was weaned.'

'As I remember, we've had many a sensible conversation in the past,' Nina said. 'Now it's your turn. Tell me why your day was unsatisfactory. Perhaps *I* can advise *you*.'

He hesitated. He had visited Mrs Sands that morning, and

she had obviously been glad to see him, but at the same time had not wanted him to stay. She had been nervous about his presence, metaphorically looking over her shoulder the whole time in case they were observed. There was no thrill for him in the atmosphere of subterfuge. He wanted to be her acknowledged love. He wanted – dear God, it was true! – to marry her. But even if she would have accepted him, he couldn't ask: he had no money, no establishment to invite her to. She lived in lodgings paid for by the estate. And he lived on the estate, and was paid a small salary to act as apprentice land agent. Her lodgings were not even private enough for him to conduct an affair with her – not that she would have done such a thing, even if, as he suspected with more hope than conviction, she was beginning to care for him.

The big, the insuperable barrier between them was that she had been his father's mistress. In her eyes, that made intimacy between them tantamount to incest. He didn't see it that way. She had slept with his father. He accepted the fact with a shrug. It was long ago, and his father was dead. But he supposed women saw things differently. He had kissed her once, and felt the passion just below the surface. But she was determined he should never kiss her again.

He couldn't tell Nina any of that. In the end, all he could say was, 'I am in love with the wrong person.'

'Oh,' said Nina, and felt a rush of sympathy. She almost said, *I know what that feels like,* then realised what a betrayal it would be. She blushed. 'I'm afraid I haven't any wise advice for that situation.'

He had observed the blush, and wondered, but did not probe. 'I expect it's a fairly common condition,' was all he said.

She changed the subject hastily. 'How is everyone at Ashmore Castle? How is Kitty?'

'Flourishing,' he said. 'Especially now my mama has gone away and left her in peace.' He explained about Darmstadt.

'And we've had a telegram to say they're moving with my aunt and uncle to the summer palace, and won't be back before Easter, so presumably things are going well. Christmas was perfectly grisly, you know. Well, it always is, but I'm used to it, and Kitty's not. I did my best to liven things up but it's a thankless task. And Giles doesn't help. Frightfully serious fellow, Giles, not the life and soul of the party.' He saw her blush deepen, saw her fix her eyes on her teacup, and made some intriguing deductions.

'How – how is Giles?' She managed to sound fairly neutral about the question.

'Busy trying to find out everything that's wrong with the estate so that he can fix it. He's out all day long, week in and week out. Perhaps you could come and pay us a visit, cheer us all up. I'm sure Kitty would love to see you. Poor Pusscat leads a very confined life, now she can't ride.'

*He calls her Pusscat?* Nina thought. It was a very affectionate pet-name. Could it be, she wondered guiltily, that the 'wrong person' he was in love with was Kitty? That would be dreadful. She knew just how dreadful.

'I'd love to visit,' she said, 'but my time is not my own. I'm a married woman, you know.'

'I do know. But if, say, Lord and Lady Stainton were to invite Mr and Mrs Cowling for a Saturday-to-Monday, would they really refuse?'

Mr Cowling would be delighted, Nina thought, and would certainly accept. But would *she* want to go? To see Kitty again would be lovely – but painful. And to be under the same roof as Giles? She didn't think she was ready for that.

She smiled lightly and said, 'I can't answer hypothetical questions. No such invitation has been issued. May I pour you some more tea?'

Nina was to meet Mr Cowling at the railway station for the journey home. Richard insisted on accompanying her there in a cab. She felt much better and more positive about life after a long and amusing chat with Richard, who seemed to know exactly how to combine serious matters with fun in the perfect proportions.

Mr Cowling's eyebrows went up when he saw them approaching, and he hurried to meet them with a hearty handshake for Richard. 'Well, well, this is a nice surprise! How did you happen upon my lady wife, Mr Tallant? I call it very civil of you to bring her safe back to me.'

'The pleasure has been entirely mine,' Richard said. 'We bumped into each other on Piccadilly, and Mrs Cowling did me the honour of taking tea with me at Rampling's.'

'Oh, Rampling's – very respectable! Well, my love, have you had an agreeable day?' He surveyed her for parcels. 'You don't seem to have bought very much.'

'Very agreeable, thank you. But there wasn't anything I wanted to buy. And Trump got awfully tired. I think the pavements were too hard for his feet.'

'Aye, small dogs and London don't mix. Well, we had better be finding our carriage. Mr Tallant, thank you from my heart for taking care of my precious jewel.'

Nina winced inwardly at the language, but Richard took it in his stride. 'The pleasure was mine, as I said. And I hope we shall see you soon at Ashmore Castle. I was telling Mrs Cowling that I understand an invitation is in contemplation, and she assured me that it would not be disagreeable to you?'

Mr Cowling's face reddened. 'Disagreeable? Oh, my goodness, no, quite the contrary! We should be most obliged, quite delighted. Mrs Cowling misses her friend, I do know. And I've visited many fine country seats in my time, but never happened to be at Ashmore Castle. Pray tell your brother and sister-in-law nothing could be more welcome than an invitation.'

The train gave a warning *foop!* at that moment and Nina tugged her husband's arm and said, 'We must hurry. Mr Tallant, goodbye, and thank you so much.'

Richard touched his hat in response – and did he, as he was turning away, drop her the ghost of a wink? She wondered about that quite a lot of the way home.

Mr Cowling spent the journey reading the newspaper, while Nina sat with the sleeping Trump on her lap and tried not to feel depressed about going back. When they were not far out from Northampton station, Mr Cowling folded the paper, cleared his throat, and said, 'You enjoyed your visit to London, I hope?'

'Yes, very much,' Nina roused herself to say.

'Aye, I thought you did. You were sparkling when I first caught sight of you across the station. Chatting to that young man and sparkling.'

Nina was instantly wary. Did he mind her talking to Richard, being accompanied by Richard? Was it not proper? 'I thought,' she began falteringly, 'that as the brother of Kitty's husband, and Kitty being my oldest friend, he counted as, well, not exactly family, I suppose, but something very like.'

'He's a very nice, civil young man,' Mr Cowling interrupted, with a warm little feeling, where he hadn't even known he needed one, that she looked on Richard in a brotherly light. 'But, my dear, I was thinking you've had a dull time of it since Christmas, stuck away alone in the house while I've been working so much. And I did promise you a wedding trip.'

Nina's face cleared. 'Oh, I don't mind,' she said quickly. 'I know you've been busy.'

'So I have, but it doesn't change the fact that I've been neglecting you. So how would you like to go away for Easter?'

'Away? Oh, that would be lovely!' Nina cried.

'The fact of the matter is that I have to spend some time in Market Harborough. There's a stocking factory there that I'm thinking of buying, and I need to look over it, inspect the books, see what I could do with it. You've never seen my house there, have you?'

Not Paris, or Vienna, or Florence, then. But anywhere was a change. 'What's it like?' she asked.

'Market Harborough? Oh, a nice little old town, with a market place. Handsome church. Pretty country all around. And the hunt – though they won't still be hunting by then, I don't suppose. But we could hire horses and have a bit of a ride around, if you'd like that. Not that I'm anything of a horseman, but I might stick in the saddle for an hour to please you. It's not far from Wigston, where I was born, you know – fifteen, seventeen miles maybe.'

'I should like to see where you were born.'

'It's just a village, nothing grand, but Decius is from there, too, and his family is still there.'

'And what's your house like?'

'That's the slug in the cabbage. It's a very old house, nothing like Beechcroft, a bit grim to my way of thinking, and I'm afraid you wouldn't be very comfortable there. But for a short visit we might manage, perhaps?'

'I'm sure we could,' Nina said.

'I've an old couple looks after it, the Deerings. He minds the gardens and does odd jobs. She used to be cook for the Ampleforths, who owned the house before me. Old family, lived there for centuries, till they lost their fortune. I bought the house cheap, to do them a favour: Sidney Ampleforth was a good customer of mine. But I've never done anything to it. Most in general I take Moxton with me when I visit, and manage pretty well all round. But I'm useder to roughing it than you. We might take Mrs Mitchell—'

'Oh, no,' Nina said quickly. 'No need to trouble her. I'm sure we can manage beautifully with the Deerings.'

He looked pleased at her willingness to adapt. 'I can send Mrs Deering a note, ask her to take on a couple of maids. Deering and Moxton between them'll manage the other stuff. And one thing, you can be sure of good victuals. Mrs Deering's a fine cook. I've always done with plain grub, but it doesn't mean I don't enjoy a bit of fancy stuff now and then.'

'That reminds me,' Nina said, and produced the small package from Fortnum's. 'I bought this for you.'

He opened it, and looked as struck as if she had given him all the treasures of the Orient. His eyes, when he lifted them to her, were definitely moist. 'You remembered I like it,' he said reverently. 'You bought me a present – all those shops in London and this is all you bought? Oh, my dear . . .'

Nina blushed and looked away. It was too much thanks for something so small, and too much love for him to be feeling for her. She did not deserve it. Now she felt guilty that she had been surly and discontented all day. The burden and responsibility of someone loving you more than you loved them came home to her. Until now, she would have thought that the opposite situation was the more uncomfortable.

# CHAPTER THREE

The blue of the sky was April-pale, the sunshine was April-thin, but it was still glorious to be outside. The sharp wind was chilly, blowing small clouds like sheep before it; their shadows ran over the grass below, like the ghost of the flock. Kitty was warmly bundled up, but relishing the cold tang of fresh air after so long shut indoors. New leaves were beginning to show their green tips on the trees, and in unclaimed corners wild daffodils bent and jerked in the breeze, catching the eye and inviting a smile.

The winds of the past week had dried out the ground enough for work to begin on the new walled garden. The men had dug the foundations and stacks of bricks had been delivered. There wasn't much to see yet, but she liked to go and inspect progress every day if she could. When it was done, it would be one thing she could point to that she had achieved, one change for the better than she had made to Ashmore Castle. Her mother-in-law had no interest in gardens, and had raised no objection – indeed, she had barely listened when the plan was mooted.

Inside the house, Kitty had no authority. She was mistress only nominally. Her mother-in-law hung on to power with a fierce grip and Kitty was too timid to fight. She reflected, as she walked along the path through the old walled garden, past orderly ranks of cabbages and Brussels sprouts, that as girls in school they had all dreamed of marriage, the magic gateway out of the confines of childhood into the freedom of Real Life. In retrospect, she saw that her debut Season had been the most freedom she had ever known – parties and outings and dances and new clothes and new acquaintances. Marriage had shut it all down. There had been a few months of adjustment, of creeping around in terror of her mother-in-law, constantly afraid of doing the wrong thing, and then pregnancy: confinement to the house, needlework, and inaction.

And though Lady Stainton was now absent, which allowed Kitty to breathe more easily, she did not dare do any of the things she wanted to improve the house, because the dragon would return, and there would be retribution. And the fairy tale of marrying her adored and handsome prince had also faded: now she was pregnant, Giles never visited her bedroom, and he was so busy she hardly saw him. He breakfasted early, before the rest of the house was up, rarely appeared at luncheon, and often escaped to his business-room or the library after dinner. Even when they were together, he treated her with polite distance, as if she were . . . well, not a servant, certainly, but perhaps as he might treat an expert brought in to perform a particular job. She was engaged in making an heir for the estate – a skilled task, of course, deserving respect, but not one that required warmth from the master.

Still, he had told her he would be in to luncheon today, and that was something to look forward to. He was always more talkative during the day than in the evening. Her heart lifted in anticipation of seeing him, conversing with him, having him look at her, listen to her. She had been mentally compiling a list of things to say, so that there should be no awkward silences that might prompt him to leave. A flow of interesting talk would keep him at the table as long as possible.

She passed through the gate into the area that would be the new garden, and was immediately met by Peason, the head gardener, who took off his hat, and made a hovering sort of gesture with his hand as though he wanted to take her elbow. 'Mind your step, my lady. There's all sorts lying about. Can't have you tripping. Just step along this way, my lady – that's right. We should have a bench brought through for you,' he added in self-reproach, his pale blue eyes in his weatherbeaten face concerned.

'I'm quite all right, thank you,' she said. In fact, she was so large with child, she must look as though she might tip over at any moment. In addition she was uncomfortable in almost any position. Her ankles were swollen, none of her shoes fitted, and she frequently suffered from indigestion – though that might be because the food at the Castle was so terrible. But she always felt better out here; and Peason's attentiveness soothed her. He had liked her from the moment she had first shown an interest in the grounds, and the more plans she came up with, the more he approved of her. It was refreshing to be so right in someone's eyes.

'Not much progress to show you, my lady,' Peason said, lurking within grabbing distance as she picked her way along. 'Just a few rows of bricks. But we'll get on faster now, as long as the weather holds.'

'And will it?'

Peason looked up at the sky. His grey hair was cut short all over, which left his ears very exposed. They were slightly pointed, which somehow made him look much younger than what she supposed to be his years. 'Seems that way, my lady – though April likes to spring surprises.'

The fitful wind rattled at them, and Kitty said, 'Please do put your hat on. I should hate you to catch a cold.'

He smiled at her, and said, 'Thank you, my lady. But I never get colds. Working outside all the time chases 'em away.' Still, he did put the hat back on, and they fell into a familiar symposium of what would be planted and where, when the walls were finished.

'I thought of having the asparagus bed *here*, my lady,'

36

Peason said, sketching an oblong across the landscape with a finger. 'See, where I've lifted the turf.'

'Asparagus!' she exclaimed eagerly.

'Won't give a crop this year or next,' he warned, 'but it's worth doing. Once it gets going, you'll have all the grass you want. I thought I might as well make a start on it now, get it dug and dunged and the crowns in. There, where the bed'll go, is far enough from the walls that it won't get trampled by the workmen.'

'What a good idea. Is there anything else you can get in? It seems a shame to waste a whole year while waiting for the walls and paths to be finished.'

His eyes gleamed with enthusiasm. 'Well, my lady, I was thinking of getting in some peas – it's not too late for 'em. And spinach grows quick. We can dig out a few more beds in the middle here while we're at it. They won't need a permanent spot, like the 'sparagus, so it doesn't matter where we put 'em this year. Now, I was thinking, regarding the permanent shape, my lady, if you'll indulge me . . .'

He dragged from his pocket a grubby and much-folded piece of paper, on which he had drawn various squares and oblongs, and over which he and Kitty had pored long and often, with equal enjoyment. They walked about the field that would be a kitchen garden in satisfying discussion. In the background the quiet sounds of industry witnessed the wall inching higher, and above them rooks circled noisily, like fragments of burned paper blown on the breeze.

Indoors, Kitty had made the Peacock Room her preferred sitting-room. It was not as large or as grand as some, but it was a pretty shape, and it got the sun in the mornings. It was called Peacock not for the colour but because the plasterwork of the ceiling featured a large peacock in an oval cartouche. It was beautifully done, but the plaster was stained from years of smoke, and the decorative cornice was chipped.

The wallpaper – once green, now mostly brown – was rubbed all around at hip height, and worn right through in places. The curtains at the window had rotted in the sunshine and were threadbare on the south-facing side. And the Turkish carpet – red and brown with blue lozenges – was so worn and, she feared, dirty, you could hardly see the pattern.

Everywhere in the house was shabby in the same way, to a greater or lesser degree. When she first married, Kitty had thought her money would be used to make it all fine, but Lady Stainton had made it clear that even to notice shabbiness marked one out as a *parvenue*. As to 'making a home' for Giles, she had once mistakenly suggested it, and Lady Stainton had said coldly that in their stratum of society, it was for the earl to make a home for his wife, not vice versa. Later Kitty had overheard Linda, to whom Lady Stainton must have repeated the story, referring to her witheringly as 'the jam heiress'.

On her return from her walk, she settled herself beside the fire to warm her feet, and picked up some sewing. Faintly in the background she could hear Uncle Sebastian playing the piano in the small drawing-room just along the corridor. She was smocking a baby dress for her coming infant, white with blue forget-me-nots and pink rosebuds – an ambitious project, so she had to concentrate. The gentle music, the warmth of the fire, and the weariness of pregnancy all worked on her and her needle moved more and more slowly and finally stopped.

Something cold jabbing her hand jerked her awake. The lurchers, Tiger and Isaac, with their strange yellow wolf-eyes, were smiling and swinging their tails in greeting. She looked up gladly, knowing that if they were here, Giles would appear at any moment.

And there he was, in the doorway. Her heart swelled at the sight of him – to her, the most handsome man in the world, the person she loved most intensely and painfully. Just to see him was heaven. And to have time with him, to have his attention . . . *Luncheon with Giles!* She could ask no greater treat.

'Is your meeting finished?' she said. He had been in the library all morning with Adeane, the bailiff, and Markham, his agent.

'Yes, just this minute. You look cosy. Have you been out?'

'I went to look at the new kitchen garden. Peason wants to start some things off – he says we might have green peas this year.'

'Excellent news,' Giles said, but she could see his mind was elsewhere, and she felt a foreboding. 'I just came to tell you I shan't be in to luncheon after all. I'm going to ride out to one of the farms – Hundon's. Adeane thinks I should see conditions there for myself.'

Kitty was careful to show no disappointment. He grew irritated if he thought she was 'clinging' to him. She said evenly, 'I suppose Richard can look after me.'

'Richard's coming with me. We probably shan't be back before the dressing-bell.'

'Oh,' said Kitty. Then, with an effort, 'We needn't dress tonight, if you don't want. As there's no company.'

Giles nodded. 'Good. Then I shall see you at the dinner table.'

He was obviously about to leave, and she asked, almost at random, just to keep him a moment longer, 'Did Adeane say anything about Aaron Cutmore?'

'Cutmore? The woodsman?' She nodded. 'How do you come to know about him?'

'Alice said something about him retiring. I don't know how *she* heard. He had an accident, I think she said.'

'Cut his foot badly, and it's not healing properly, and he's feeling his age all of a sudden. So he wants to retire. Going to live with his sister and brother-in-law in the village, I understand.'

'Have you found someone else for the job?'

'Adeane's got someone lined up. Why the sudden interest?'

'Just because Alice was talking about it, that's all.'

'You can tell her we're going to offer it to the assistant blacksmith, Josh Brandom's brother,' Giles said. 'She'll know who that is – she was always hanging about the forge when she was younger.'

'The blacksmith?' Kitty queried. 'Is that an odd choice?'

'I don't know much about him, but Adeane thinks he has all the woodcraft skills he needs. And he's young and strong, which is an advantage. Well, I must be off. They're waiting for me.'

And, with a nod, he was gone, the dogs pattering after him.

Kitty sighed, and picked up her needle again. At least she would have something to tell Alice at luncheon – though there was never any difficulty in getting Alice to talk.

She had hardly done a dozen stitches when she became aware that she needed the closet, and heaved herself carefully to her feet. They'd had washdown water-closets at home: here there were chamber pots at night, and the two closets – one on this floor and one on the floor below – had to be emptied at night by the close-man. She had never dared to voice distaste for the system. She could imagine the reproach it would provoke: *middle-class squeamishness.* What else could you expect of a jam heiress?

As she reached the door, her foot caught in a hole in the carpet. Ungainly and heavy, she was unable to recover herself, and went sprawling, face down, half through the doorway into the corridor.

She lay breathless, shocked. *The baby!* her mind cried. *Have I hurt the baby?* She couldn't move or make a sound for sheer fright.

Someone was coming – one of the maids. It was the sewing-maid, Dory, with a basket of mending. 'Are you all right, my lady? Did you faint?'

'Tripped,' Kitty was able to say. 'Carpet.'

Dory knelt beside her. 'Let me turn you over.' She got Kitty on her back, propped against her knee, and said, 'By your leave, my lady . . .' She laid a firm but gentle hand on Kitty's bulge. 'Have you got a pain anywhere?'

'I – I don't think so,' Kitty said. 'But I fell. The baby! Have I hurt it?'

'You've had a shock,' said Dory, 'but if you've no pain, that's a good sign. We'll get you to your room, and you can rest. Try not to worry. Babies are very tough, you know.'

Kitty looked up into the kindly face. 'Are you sure?'

'I came from a big family, my lady. And I had one of my own. So I do know a bit about babies.'

Here now was Uncle Sebastian, hurrying towards them. 'I'll ring for help,' he said at once.

'No, please, I think I can get up,' Kitty said. Between them they got her to her feet, and helped her back to the sofa in the Peacock Room.

'You should be carried to your room,' Uncle Sebastian said. 'I'll ring for a couple of footmen. And the doctor must be sent for. I suppose Giles is out somewhere. Do you want your maid?'

'I'm all right, I think,' Kitty said. 'Just a little shaken.'

'Don't fuss her,' Dory said in a low voice. 'Let her be.'

Even in her shaken state, Kitty thought it was an odd way for the maid to address him – as though they were equals, or old friends. 'I'll just rest here for a bit,' she said. 'Then I can walk back to my room.'

'I'll sit with you, my lady,' Dory said. She looked at Uncle Sebastian. 'Mrs Webster did ought to be told, though, just in case.'

'I'll do that,' he said, 'And we'll have the doctor. Better safe than sorry.' With one more concerned look at Kitty, he went out.

Dory smiled at Kitty. 'There, he's gone. Men always get

in a fuss when it's anything to do with babies. Now, you're sure you've no pain? Good, then a little rest, and I expect you'll be fine again. What was it tripped you, my lady? Oh, yes, I see it. That's a bad place to have a hole, right by the door. I'll get that mended right away.'

'I don't know if Lady Stainton would want it mended,' Kitty said dolefully. 'She doesn't like anything to be changed.'

Dory gave her a sympathetic look. 'She won't even notice, I promise you. New things perhaps, but not old things that are just a bit less worn and torn.'

That made Kitty think, which was a good thing as it stopped her worrying about the baby. And as she rested and watched Dory working on her mending, she started to devise a plan.

The fresh and breezy day was perfect for riding. Giles was on Vipsania, his new road horse; Richard was riding one-handed on steady old Trooper, his other hand tucked in between his buttons to rest his damaged shoulder. The London sawbones had said it would probably never be quite right after he broke it in a motor-car smash. Adeane, the bailiff, was in the pony trap, pulled by dun Biscuit, and Tiger and Isaac ranged about to either side of the track.

They passed Gale's Cottage, the garden trim with growing shoots of vegetables, and Richard waved to Mrs Gale, taking advantage of the breeze to hang out washing. Beyond Gale's the verge and ditch that should have bordered the road gradually disappeared under a tangle of blackberry and hemlock, and some thrusting, upright pale green plants Richard did not recognise. Beyond, the gentle slope of the field was covered with bracken, into which the lurchers plunged excitedly and disappeared.

Richard thought the bracken looked rather handsome, bending like a green sea in the breeze, and it was fun to see the movement the dogs made through it – it made him think of sinister sea creatures waiting to break the surface.

But Adeane turned his head back to say, 'This is Bunce's Six Acre. Ought by rights to be cleared, my lord. Bracken is poisonous to cattle, as you know.'

'Does Bunce put his cattle in here?' Richard said. 'Surely not.'

'No, sir, but his hedges are in such poor heart, they could break out and find their way here easy enough. And he's let the rest of his fields tumble down into rough pasture.'

'The more I learn about farming, the more I wonder why anybody tries it,' Richard said. 'I always thought you just pushed an animal into a nice green space and waited for it to make milk or bacon or mutton cutlets. Now I learn all this lovely greenery is useless.'

'Not just useless, but dangerous,' Giles said. 'And thistle and ragwort and yew—'

'And buttercups, for goodness' sake!' Richard interrupted. 'Pretty little buttercups that I used to tease the girls with. Who could suspect *them* of villainy?'

'What we need,' Adeane said stolidly, 'is a programme of draining, harrowing and reseeding to get the pastures up to scratch.' He looked at Giles. 'Improve the grazing and you improve the stock.'

The dogs rejoined them, bursting out of a low gap in the hedge.

'We are what we eat,' Giles said.

'Was Hippocrates a farmer?' Richard asked.

'Virgil was,' Giles replied.

Adeane looked puzzled. 'Is that Virgil Smithson you're referring to, my lord? He's got a smallholding over Asham Bois way, but I wouldn't call him a farmer. Two pigs, four cows and a dozen chickens, last time I heard.'

'Different Virgil,' Richard said, suppressing laughter. 'Don't worry about it. Ah, is this the man himself, by any chance? I've never met the chap, but if anyone ever looked like a Bunce, this is he.'

A bone-thin man, trousers held up by baling-string, thread-bare jacket, cap pulled down hard over his head, and an unshaven, weatherbeaten face, was standing hunched, hands in pockets, staring moodily over a gate at the cows in the field beyond. He turned his head at their approach. A long-legged brown dog appeared from somewhere near his feet and ran towards Tiger and Isaac, and there was a tense, erect-tailed meeting in the middle of the track.

'Gerroff, dog!' the man growled, and the brown cur ran back to circle him, followed by the lurchers, who inspected the farmer's boots and trousers with unembarrassed interest.

'Now then, Bunce,' said Adeane, checking the pony. 'Here's his lordship come to see how you're getting on.'

Bunce removed his hands from his pockets and, after a moment's thought, his cap from his head, but he looked at Giles without welcome. 'Badly, how else d'ye think?' he muttered. The lurchers were inviting the brown dog to a lovely game, but Bunce growled at it again, and it slunk back to his side.

The men gathered at the gate and surveyed the cattle. They were ordinary, undistinguished brown cows, but on the bony side, a couple so elderly their udders were pendulous and brushing the grass. 'Don't you have twelve head?' Adeane asked, having counted.

'Clover's in the cowshed, with garget,' Bunce said resent-fully.

'I know that one,' said Richard. 'Inflammation of the udder, isn't it? Lord, the names you country people have for ailments!' he added aside.

'Thass right,' Bunce grunted. 'She's allus been susceptible to it.'

'We'll come back with you, if you don't mind, and have a look at the farm buildings,' Giles said. 'Adeane thinks there might be some repairs that need doing.'

Bunce wasn't ready to be pleased. 'And stick the cost onto my rent, I don't doubt.'

44

Richard sought to distract him. 'That field back there, all the bracken. Shouldn't it be cleared?'

'The Six Acre? I don't graze it,' said Bunce. ''S a cornfield by rights. Grew wheat there until ninety-five. When you could get thirty-five shillun a quarter. Now you'd be lucky to get twenty. I don't know what the world's coming to. Can't afford to grow wheat for twenty shillun a quarter. Might as well give it away – it'd come cheaper'n paying labour to plough and sow and harvest it.'

'Why not turn the field into proper pasture, then?' Richard suggested, addressing himself to Adeane.

It was Bunce who answered. '*I* can't afford to clear and seed it!' he said indignantly. 'Price o' seed what it is – and I haven't got the labour, anyhow. Had to let our cowman go last Michaelmas. There's only me and the missus and our John now. And he's talking about leaving. Get a job in town, he says. Send money home. Bah!' He spat sideways to show what he thought of that.

'Let's move on, Giles,' Richard murmured to his brother, 'before this fellow has me so depressed I cut my throat.'

Hundon's, Bunce's farmhouse, had once been a small manor-house, dating from the fourteenth century, but half of it had fallen or been taken down over the years and the wood used to make outbuildings. What remained made a tall, narrow, crooked and infinitely shabby dwelling for the farmer and his family. Mrs Bunce was as thin as her husband, depressed and depressing in a sacking apron, hair coming down, and a drip at the end of her long, red nose. But she knew her manners, curtsied to Giles and asked the gentlemen in. 'We gotter dropper parsnip wine somewheres,' she suggested vaguely.

'Thank you, Mrs Bunce, you're most kind, but we really haven't time,' Giles said, with manners of his own. 'And we mustn't take you away from your work.' A small grubby child

45

of indeterminate sex had appeared behind her, and the lurchers rushed to greet it, making it laugh in astonished pleasure as it patted various bits of them and had its face washed in reciprocation.

The men carried on with their inspection. The farmyard had once been cobbled but now was mostly mud, with large inconvenient holes filled with yellow water. It was flanked on two sides with outhouses that seemed to have been patched and repaired by a vigorous but inexpert hand, and on the third with a small alp of a midden. The hay barn was virtually empty; the mangold clamp entirely so. The cowshed had the same kind of floor as the yard – full of holes where urine and faeces pooled. It was windowless, but there were holes in the roof that let in some light, and illuminated the suffering cow, which stood on a the bare dirty earth floor and held one foot off the ground – lame as well as sick.

'You know,' said Adeane to Bunce, whose hands were back in his pockets, 'you wouldn't get so much garget – or lameness – if you kept the place cleaner. Look at the muck on the floor and in those holes. It's a wonder they're not all down with it.'

'Ar, all very well for you to talk, mister,' Bunce said. 'Got no money for repairs, and no time to do it neether. Had no labour for haymaking last summer. John and me done what we could, but we couldn't get it all in before the rain come and spoiled it. Now hay's near gone, and the grass ain't good enough yet without extra feed, but what can a man do? Hedges need laying, got no labour for that, neether.'

'I see your bull box is empty, and he wasn't out with the cows,' Adeane said.

'What, Sampson? Owd bugger up and died last back-end. Left me in a fix. Winscott up at Topheath wants *payin'* for a loan of his bull.'

Richard caught Giles's eye and made a throat-cutting

gesture, which Giles rightly ignored. 'Now, Mr Bunce,' Giles said, 'I want to help you get this farm back on its feet.'

'Ar, then up goes my rent, I don't doubt,' Bunce said savagely.

'Not until you can afford it,' Giles said. 'What's good for the land is good for both of us. Things have been allowed to slip in the last few years, but this is good farming country at heart, and if we put our minds to it, we can get it back in shape. I want my tenants to work with me, not just for my benefit but for their own. I'm ready to invest in the estate, to get it to the point when it's able to pay me back.'

'What's "invest" mean when it's at home?' Bunce asked suspiciously, but, affected by Giles's obvious good will, he added grudgingly, 'My lord. What d'you mean to do?'

They would have to have time to work out a plan, so now was not the moment to make specific commitments. Adeane cast Giles a warning look, but Giles only said, 'We will have to work that out, Bunce. But for the moment you can tell your wife that I shall repair that hole in the farmhouse roof as soon as possible.'

'Oh, you noticed that? Well – my lord – I don't deny she'll be pleased about that. I could've got up there with a bit o' tar paper, if I'd had the time. But there's not enough hours in a day as it is, and that's a fact.'

As they rode away, Richard said, 'What's a fact is that the more a man complains about having too much to do, the less he does of it.'

'That's true, sir,' Adeane said approvingly. 'There's an old saying: if you want something done, ask a busy man.'

Giles felt unaccountably sorry for Bunce. 'When a person gets thoroughly miserable, a sort of inertia sets in. I can understand it.'

'Well, he's got to buck up,' Adeane said from behind them, 'or we'll have to look for another tenant.'

47

'Is he a good farmer?' Giles asked.

'He *was*,' Adeane said cautiously. 'It's a shame to see that place go down. But you know how it is, my lord, improvement costs money, and without improvement, less money comes in. It's a vicious circle.'

'Then we shall have to make it virtuous again,' said Giles.

They continued in silence, and Giles, riding in front, looking round him, was aware of an unexpected feeling of contentment. He was as little given to introspection as his mother, but for different reasons: she believed so completely in her own rightness that self-examination was unnecessary; he merely found it boring. But on this fine spring day, with the cloud-shadows bowling across the newly green land – *his* land – he noticed his contentment enough to analyse it.

He couldn't deny he had enjoyed the various hunting parties they had hosted since Christmas, but now the season was over he was glad to get back to work. The emotional turbulence of the previous year was behind him. He had been resentful of being forced to take up this life at all. Then he had been forced to seek a rich wife and had hated the necessity. And while trying to do his duty he had fallen in love with someone he couldn't have, and that had been the worst of all.

But now the complexities of managing something as intangible and irrational as 'feelings' – his own and other people's – were done with, and the problems he had to grapple with were solid and practical. The land needed to be improved, and now he had the money to do it – Kitty's money. And with Adeane's advice and his own ability to absorb and learn, he was going to make the Ashmore Estate into a model. He was going to create something – and to create was man's most basic instinct.

Yes, and speaking of creating, he had a child on the way: a son – he hoped – who would inherit whatever he succeeded in making. There was a little corner of his satisfaction that was generated by the expected child, but in his absorbing days he rarely thought about his wife. Last year there had been a period when he had discovered, for the first time, the pleasure of sexual intercourse, and could hardly get enough of it. He had been grateful to Kitty for her part in it, but now she was pregnant and it was *verboten*, he had almost entirely forgotten about it. Sex had been nice, but it wasn't important in the scheme of things.

And 'love' was a delusion and a trap. He never allowed himself to think about Nina. His was a man's world, and he had his job to do. He trusted Kitty to do hers – to bring forth a child – but for the rest, she belonged to that messy last-year world of emotions. He lived somewhere else now.

# CHAPTER FOUR

Dory poked her head cautiously round the door of the small drawing-room. Mr Sebastian was seated at the piano, a cigar clenched in his teeth, his head tilted back to avoid the smoke. His hands were rippling across the keys. When he saw her he continued to ripple with his right hand, while with his left he removed the cigar and placed it in the ashtray on the piano-top, and said, 'Yes, that's right, come in! I'm ready for some conversation.'

'I don't want to disturb you, sir.'

'I was just doing scales and arpeggios. Trying to keep the old hands flexible.'

Dory looked innocent. 'I thought p'raps it was one of those modern composers that don't hold with tunes.'

Sebastian gave her a mock scowl. 'Don't be naughty, miss. Sit down there and talk to me – and do some mending, in case anyone comes. Here, is this enough of a tune for you?'

'That's nice,' Dory said, settling in the chair he had previously placed where he could both see and hear her. 'I could nearly sing to that. What is it?'

'Schubert, "The Trout".'

'It's pretty.'

'Tell me what's going on in the house. Is Lady Kitty really all right after her fall?' He referred to her that way in their conversations to distinguish her from the dowager countess.

'Oh, quite,' said Dory. 'Young things like her carry easily

– their insides are like elastic bands. It's older ladies who have to be careful.'

'I'm glad to hear it. She seemed all right at breakfast, but of course she wouldn't tell me anything. What's happening below stairs? Who is William in love with these days?'

'Still Milly.'

'Amazing. That's lasted a long time.'

'Longer than I did. He was over me in weeks. I should feel insulted, shouldn't I?'

'Do you crave the admiration of such as William?'

'No, sir. But a woman has her pride.'

His left hand stumbled a note. He vamped a little while he retrieved his cigar, waved it and said, 'Do you mind?'

'No, sir,' said Dory. Seeing that it had gone out, she stood, picked up the matchbox and struck a match for him so that he could keep playing. With the lightest touch he guided her hand. When the cigar had caught, he looked up at her from under his shaggy brows, and for a moment their eyes met. Then she drew back, blew out the match and sat again.

'I think Milly's getting tired of being mooned over, though,' she resumed, as if there had been no interruption. 'She was too shy when she first came to say anything, but I happen to know there's a nice boy in the village who's interested in her, and she's afraid he'll find out about William and get the wrong idea.'

'Age-old problem.' Sebastian nodded. 'The Two Suitors. Sounds like a Sherlock Holmes story, doesn't it? But life is hard for the acknowledged beauty. Though she's a little too much "white mouse" for my taste.' Dory smiled at that and shook her head. 'What else?'

'There was a big fuss yesterday over some wine. There was a delivery from the merchant, and Mr Moss had James – Hook, I mean – help him put it away in the cellar and record it in the cellar book. Then Hook starts checking the book against the bins, and says there's bottles missing. Mr Moss was terribly upset. The cellar key never leaves him, he says, so nobody could have taken it. Hook said he must just have forgotten to record some bottles when he brought them up for the table.' She glanced up at Sebastian. 'Mr Moss doesn't like that suggestion either, because it would mean he was careless or forgetful or—'

'Yes?'

'Hook says he's getting too old for the job.' Dory made a face.

Sebastian looked thoughtful. 'He's an ambitious man, James Hook. I was aware of it when he used to valet me. He'd like to be butler himself.'

'He's not the right sort for a butler, though. Hasn't got—'

'The gravitas?' Sebastian suggested.

Dory didn't know the word, but it sounded right. She nodded. 'Course, it seems most likely that Mr Moss did forget to mark out a bottle. Or else wrote the wrong figure down by mistake, or read it wrong in the first place. A three can look like an eight. It's easily done. Doesn't mean a person isn't fit for their job.'

There was such a thing as loyalty among servants, and she didn't mention that Mr Moss had once or twice fallen heavily asleep in his chair in the butler's room in the evening and had had to be roused to go to bed. It would be possible for an unscrupulous person to lift the key from his chain while he was comatose and gain access to the cellar. She didn't want to suggest that, either. It wasn't right to throw suspicion without proof.

After a pause she changed the subject. 'Oh, I don't know if you heard: Josh Brandom – Lady Alice's groom – has broken his foot or his ankle or something. He was exercising one of the horses and it slipped on the hill and fell, and his foot was caught under it. Dr Welkes plastered it up and says he can't ride for three weeks at least. Josh never was the sweetest-tempered man, and now he's worse than ever. Won't sit quiet with it up, like anybody would, but hobbles about the stable-yard on a crutch telling everybody what to do. I hear Mr Giddins is close to lamping him one, bad foot or no bad foot.'

That made Sebastian smile. 'I can just imagine—' he began, but broke off as a maid appeared in the doorway, looking nervous. It was Ellen. She bobbed a curtsy to Sebastian and said, 'Beg pardon, sir,' then hissed at Dory, 'Mrs Webster's looking for you.' A roll of her eyes suggested the unspoken words, *and you'd better not let her find you here.*

Dory stood, unflurried. 'If you'll excuse me, sir, I'd better go.' She hoisted her sewing-basket under her arm, and bobbed to him for Ellen's benefit. As she turned away, he plunged into a thunderous rendition of the funeral march, and she had to conceal a smile.

'You can't go out on your own, my lady,' Josh said, with his most mulish look. 'Her ladyship made it quite clear before she went away.'

Alice knew he meant her mother: Kitty didn't really exist for him. 'I'm only going to ride on our own land,' she said impatiently.

'You and Lady Rachel riding out alone together when you was little girls was one thing. But she's not here. And you're older now. It's not fitting. Her ladyship said specifically, she said, "Lady Alice is not to go careering about on her own like a hoyden. She's to be attended all the time." That's what she said. "I look to *you*, Brandom, to see to it," she said.'

'Her ladyship isn't here,' said Alice.

Josh scowled. 'It's taking advantage, my lady, that's what it is. And I shall feel obliged to tell her ladyship when she comes back. It will be my duty to let her know what goes on when her back is turned.'

Alice drew an irritated breath. *What a tattle-tale!* she thought. But he would do it – she knew he would. He never forgot a grudge. And his loyalty to her mother was unshake-able. 'All right,' she said, 'I'll take one of the boys. I'll take Timmy.'

'Timmy's not here today, my lady. His day off.' He said it with a hint of triumph that riled her more.

'The little one, then – the one with the ears. What's his name?'

'Oscar, my lady? He's too young.' Oscar was timid, and would do what Lady Alice told him, which Josh knew as well as she did. Oscar would be no replacement for a grim, watchful groom with a lifetime's training in strict propriety. 'He's not been here long, so he doesn't know the tracks.'

'But I do.' Alice smiled serenely. She knew she'd got him. 'You want me to take someone, and I shall. I choose Oscar.' She turned and beckoned to a passing groom. 'Have Pharaoh saddled for me, and tell Oscar he's to accompany me. I shall be ready in ten minutes.'

'Yes, my lady.'

She turned and walked briskly away. Josh tried to follow her, but his crutch had sunk in and the jerk almost toppled him. By the time he had worked it free she was gone.

Oscar looked very young and rather small on board Dickie, one of the grooms' horses, and it was obvious that Josh had managed to get at him before Alice came back because he was plainly nervous. Pharaoh had a long, free stride and was glad to be out, while Dickie was rather a plod, and the poor child had to keep chivvying him along to keep up. The clicks and giddups from behind her were an unrestful accompani-ment to her ride.

When they reached the brow of the hill and were out of sight of the house, Alice checked and beckoned the boy alongside. 'Now, Oscar,' she said, 'I'm going to gallop, and Dickie won't be able to keep up. And I don't need you with me anyway.'

'Oh, my lady, Josh said—'

'I know what he said. That he'd skin you alive if you let me out of your sight. Am I right?'

'Yes, miss – my lady,' he admitted, with a worried gulp. 'Sort of.'

'Well, Josh is not your boss, I am. And it's not your fault if Dickie is too slow. Just stay on this track, and walk Dickie along till you get to the other end of the spinney. There's a gate there and a stile, and you can tie him up and sit on the stile and wait for me. I'll come back that way and collect you before we go home.'

'Yes, my lady,' Oscar said, close to tears.

'You're not to worry,' Alice said impatiently. 'Josh will never know. *I* shan't tell him – and you won't either, will you?'

'What if he asks me?' Oscar whispered. It was a sin to tell a lie, wasn't it?

'Here . . .' She fished a sixpence out of her pocket and gave it to him. 'Buy something for your mother next time you go home.'

'Thank you, my lady.' Contemplating the sixpenny bit, he looked a lot more confident. Rows and shouting were unpleasant, but they didn't kill you, and coin of the realm was coin of the realm. A penny would have been acceptable, but a *sixpence* now! That bought a lot of loyalty. He raised his eyes hopefully to her ladyship. Perhaps she would protect him.

Alice read the look. 'I promise I won't let you get into trouble,' she said, put her heel to Pharaoh, and was gone.

The woodsman's cottage was in Motte Woods, at the edge of the land covered by Hillbrow Farm. It was solidly built, and had several large outbuildings – a tool shed, a log store, a vast work-shed with a saw pit big enough to cut tree trunks, a barn, and a stable with an open-sided cart-shed to one side and saddle-room to the other. Compared with the little cottage

Axe had lived in before, it was palatial. He had had to rent the former himself, and it had been all he could afford, but this house came with the job.

Axe was in the yard when Alice rode in, and his face warmed with that long, slow smile of his that she forgot when she hadn't seen him for a while. Pharaoh whinnied when he saw his old friend, and Axe came forward to catch the bridle and let the horse thump him in the chest with his muzzle in greeting. 'He's getting chatty these days, isn't he?' Axe said, squinting up at Alice against the light.

'More chatty all the time. He embarrasses me sometimes,' Alice said.

'Passing through, my lady, or would you like to get down?'

'Of course I want to get down. I came to see how you're getting on. I want to see everything.'

He came round to the near side, she freed her leg, and let him jump her down. Normally she resented anyone trying to help her dismount – as if she couldn't manage it by herself! – but she loved the feeling of his big hands on her waist. In the moment that he was close to her, she smelt the familiar smell of him, leather and saddle soap and warm skin and a clean hint of horse. And something new now – just a little scent of sawn wood.

'Axe Brandom, woodsman to Lord Stainton,' she said.

'That's a fact,' he said genially.

'It's quiet here.' There was no sound but birdsong, and a little rustling of leaves. 'Very different from the forge.' She had always thought of him as the blacksmith. He had been inseparable from his calling in her mind. 'Will you miss your old job?'

'I'll miss the horses,' he said. 'Won't miss the heat, or the dirt, or the noise. Coming home black from head to foot every night. Smell of coal and hot iron in your nose all the time so you can't smell the grass and the earth and the rain.'

'I never thought of rain having a smell,' she said.

He didn't answer, but took hold of the reins. 'We'll put him over there, in the shade. It's hot for April.'

When he had tied Pharaoh up and loosened the girth, she said, 'Can I see inside your house?'

'You can, and welcome, but there's not much to see yet. It's a bit empty.'

'Didn't you bring your furniture with you?'

He gave her a patient look. ''Twadn't mine, was it? I only rented that place.'

'Oh,' said Alice. She hadn't realised that when you rented a house, you rented the furniture too. Her own home was full of solid pieces accumulated over centuries. She hadn't realised it was possible not to own your bed and chairs.

'Now, Cutmore, see, he'd been here a long time,' Axe went on, leading her to the door, 'so some of the stuff here *was* his own. But he left other bits, enough for a start.'

The door led straight into the kitchen-living-room, as was customary, but it was larger than in his old place, and seemed larger still because there was no bed in it. 'Bedroom through there,' he said. 'Shan't know myself for posh, having a separate bedroom!'

One whole wall was covered with an enormous dresser of shelves, with cupboards and drawers below, and a few plates and mugs only made it look more bare. The centre of the room was occupied with a solid, scrubbed deal table with a wooden bench down either side. The wide chimney place was occupied by a range and an open fire, with the usual high mantel-shelf above it, and the sitting end of the room had a high-backed wooden settle, like a church pew, against the wall, and a rectangular rag rug on the floor in front of it.

It certainly was 'a bit empty'. Alice sought for something nice to say. 'It's a lot bigger,' she said. 'And it smells nice – like wood shavings.'

'I been doing a bit of work out in the barn,' Axe explained. 'Brought it in last night for the light, to finish off.'

'I expect a woodsman's house ought to smell of wood, anyway,' Alice said. 'The dresser's very handsome.'

'Cutmore had to leave that, and the settle, being as they're fixed into the walls. And he left the table and benches and his big bed, because they wouldn't've fit into his sister's house. My sister Ruth, she was worried about me, starting up here on my own. She's the eldest and she always fusses about us. Anyroad, she's gone round everybody and scrounged me a bit here and a bit there. So I got pots and pans and cups and plates enough. Got a stool and two chairs – one's got a broken leg, but I'll soon mend that. A chest of drawers she got me – wants knobs, and a foot's missing, and the back's split, but I can fix it. Esther, my other sister, she give me the rug. And Mary, our Seth's wife, she give me a little looking-glass for the scullery so I can shave meself decent.' He looked at her slightly anxiously. 'I mean to make it nice here, once I've saved up a bit. No rent to pay *and* the wages are higher, so I shall be well set. I'll get some material and make curtains, and cushions for the settle. I'm handy with a needle.'

'How clever you are,' Alice said. 'I'm no good at sewing.'

'I don't suppose you need to be,' he said politely.

'And I see you've got your tea caddy and your shepherdess,' she said, gesturing to the mantel-shelf. 'And another tin – that's new, isn't it?'

'Biscuit tin,' he said. 'Our Seth's Mary give me that as well. Nothing in it yet – I wasn't expecting visitors,' he apologised.

'You're a long way out, here, for visitors,' she said. 'Won't you mind being so far from everyone?'

'I've always liked it quiet,' he said. 'Family thinks I'm a bit strange that way. Our Ruth, she didn't even like it when I moved into the old cottage at the Carr, 'stead of living in the village.'

'And you're even further out now. How will you get to church? It'll be a long walk.' A delightful idea had popped into her mind, that she could offer to call for him in the pony-trap on a Sunday. It would be hard to get that plan past everyone at home, of course – her mother would flatly forbid it, Josh would be outraged, and probably even Giles would think it 'unsuitable', but—

'Don't you worry,' Axe said, and smiled, his blue eyes crinkling. 'I've got a secret. Want to see?'

'Of course,' she said.

He led her outside, where she was accosted by his little dog, Dolly. 'I wondered where you'd got to,' Alice said, squatting to make a fuss of her.

'She's been in the woods. Sniffs about in there all day long,' said Axe. He watched indulgently. Dolly's stump of a tail was a blur of ecstasy as Alice scratched behind her ears.

'So she likes it here,' Alice said.

'She likes *you*. She says she's not seen you for a long while. Thought you'd forgotten her.'

'Never! Not for a *moment*,' Alice said emphatically, looking up at him. 'What's this secret of yours?'

'I'll show you,' he said.

He led her to the stable. Inside there were two stalls, one of which was occupied by an enormous, glossy chestnut rump. 'You've got a horse!' Alice exclaimed in delight.

'Comes with the job,' Axe said. 'Name's Della.'

The mare turned her head at the sound of his voice, showing a neat, fine face with a kind dark eye and a long mane and forelock that were almost blonde. 'She's lovely!' Alice said. 'What sort is she?'

'Suffolk Punch. Best horses for working in woods.' He laid a friendly hand on her rich gold-brown buttock. 'Dragging logs in the chain harness. She pulls the big wagon and the pole tug too. But I've got an old pair of wheels I bought from Mr Rowse, and I'm going to knock up a little trap for myself for when I want to drive down to the village. Mr Rowse, he said he'd do the ironwork for me. So you see,' he smiled down at Alice, the thin sunlight slanting in through the doorway illuminating his red-gold hair and the fine floating dust in the air, 'I shan't be stuck far away from civilisation, like my sister thinks.'

'I'm glad to hear it,' Alice said. 'But I don't think you're far away from civilisation. This *is* civilisation to me. A place all your own, a horse and a dog – what more could anyone want?'

'Quite a lot, I should say, if you're born Lady Alice in a castle.'

'As if that matters. It's not really a castle, anyway, and it isn't mine. I can't help where I was born.'

He heard the discontent in her voice, and felt a stab of pity. She envied him his freedom – and, just then, he saw how very good it was, and how little of it she had, probably would ever have. She'd be watched and told what to do all the time, and then be married off to some old lord she didn't even like. (He had absorbed vague ideas about how the nobs went on from Ruthie's eldest, Polly, who read penny novels.)

Alice's cage might be golden, but it was a cage all the same. He looked down at her seriously. 'You can come here any time you like,' he said. 'You're always welcome. And anything I've got is yours.'

'Thank you,' she said, from the heart. Then, 'Can I see the rest of your animals? Have you still got the goshawk?'

'He's long gone. But I got three baby hedgehogs. You can help me feed 'em.'

Crooks hurried from the church and round to the side door to catch the choir as it left. The tall figure and sunburst hair of Axe Brandom stood out above the lesser heads like a beacon, but he was striding away, and Crooks, panting, 'So sorry . . . ! Excuse me . . . ! May I come through?' had to thrust his way past impeding bodies to try to get to him before he was out of sight. Bursting free of the press like a cork surfacing, Crooks saw his quarry turning down Back Lane, the narrow road that ran alongside the graveyard to the sexton's yard at the back. He didn't like raising his voice in a public street, but decided running was even more undignified at his age, and called Brandom's name.

Axe stopped, turned, and waited for him, looking a trifle put out. 'Morning, Mr Crooks.'

'There you are,' Crooks said, coming to a halt and catching his breath. 'Are you quite well? I was worried about you.'

'I'm very well, thank you, sir,' Axe said stolidly. 'Hoping you're the same.'

'But you weren't at church last Sunday, and you never miss. And then I – I went to your cottage, and you weren't there. It was all shut up, as if you'd gone away. So I was afraid you might have been taken to the hospital, or some terrible accident had occurred.' He hadn't liked to go enquiring of Mr Rowse at the forge, but that would have been his next recourse, had Axe not appeared this morning.

Axe didn't speak, seeming to be unsure what to say. He looked away, over Crooks's head, and his Adam's apple bobbed awkwardly.

Crooks prompted him. '*Have* you been ill?'

Axe cleared his throat, and though he addressed Crooks, his eyes were fixed on a spot over his shoulder. 'Truth is, Mr Crooks, I gotter new job, and I don't live at the cottage any more. Last Sunday, 'twas the only day I could manage with moving my things to my new place, and Rector and Mr Arden said I could be excused church for the once. My brother-in-law helped me move.'

'A new job? And a new house? You didn't tell me.'

The reproach was in the words, not the tone. Axe felt guilty, but the fact was he hadn't known how to tell the old gentleman, who had been helping him with his reading, that their lessons must end. He knew that, for some reason, Mr Crooks valued them as much as Axe had – if not more. 'It's

61

quite a step away, the new place, up at Motte Woods,' he said apologetically.

'Motte Woods? That *is* a distance,' Crooks said, dismayed. It was too far for him to walk there, as he had walked to the cottage at Ashmore Carr.

'I was meaning to write you a letter to say thank you when I'd got settled. And to send you back the book you kindly lent me, about the time machine.'

'Oh, but I didn't lend it, that was a gift,' Crooks said.

Axe reddened. 'That's a deal too good of you, sir. You shouldn't've spent money on me.'

'It was my pleasure, my dear boy. But surely there's some way we can continue with our little sessions?'

'My new job will keep me much busier, sir,' Axe said firmly, 'aside from it's too far away. But I'm reading much better now, thanks to you, and I don't think I shall slip back. I've the Good Book at home, and the time machine one, thanks to you, and I reckon they'll keep me going. I shall never forget what you've done for me, Mr Crooks, and I do thank you, from my heart.'

He offered his hand and Crooks shook it, bemused, then had his own hand given back in what was plainly a terminal manner. Before he could summon up any further argument, Axe had resumed his hat and was striding away down the lane towards the yard.

Crooks started disconsolately towards home. The brake that brought the servants to church would have gone by now: it didn't wait for laggards. He walked along to the stile a little way down past the church, which gave access to the footpath that cut off a corner and joined up with Cherry Lane – a pleasanter walk back to the Castle than the main carriage drive, and a less steep hill.

At the stile he paused before mounting, looked back, and saw Axe come out of Back Lane driving a heavy wagon drawn by a chestnut carthorse. For a moment his imagination leaped to the offer of a lift, a pleasant, slow drive up the hill, and perhaps during the conversation some way discovered that the lessons could continue. But Axe turned the other way, and did not look in Crooks's direction.

He was sure Axe hadn't meant it, but he felt snubbed. And sad. A brightness had gone out of his life.

Early April was all that April should be: sunny, breezy days, refreshed by short showers; blue skies and dazzling white clouds; dancing catkins, stotting lambs, and heartbreakingly tender new greenness everywhere.

It was indeed pretty country, Nina agreed, gazing from the train window on the journey from Northampton to Market Harborough. It was quintessentially English, she thought: gentle rolling hills – as if a counterpane had been shaken and halted in mid-billow; a patchwork of fields, divided by trim hedges; neat small woods, little villages and farms tucked snugly into the folds. A grey church spire; white sheep and brown cows; black rooks circling a distant coppice. Here and there a man with a dog, or a horse and cart, or a woman hanging out washing caught her eye briefly as she was borne past, reassuring her that life was carrying on and the world was in good order.

Trump stood on her lap, forefeet on the narrow sill, and stared in fascination out of the window, making the occasional muted wuff of surprise. Mr Cowling had the newspaper open, but Nina suspected he was only pretending to read, while actually watching her for her reaction. He was still nervous about the visit, fearing she would find the house too uncomfortable – despite the message he had despatched to Mrs Deering to spare no expense. Mrs Mitchell had been very much put out by the whole plan, especially, Nina imagined, as Mr Cowling had made it clear from the beginning that she wasn't required to come, which denied her the pleasure of refusing to do so.

They took a cab from Market Harborough station ('Though it's no distance at all – you could walk it,' said Mr Cowling), and there were a couple of streets of nice old houses before they drove right through the market square, with shops and stalls set out, a glimpse of interesting backstreets, a strange old Tudor building up on wooden arches in the middle, and a pretty church. Leaving the square at the further end they came at once to a high red-brick wall on the right, and Mr Cowling said, 'This is it. This is the house.'

'But it's right in the town,' Nina exclaimed.

Mr Cowling looked anxious. 'Aye, I know. There's no rolling acres and long drive like at Dene Park.' This was the country estate where they had first met.

'Oh, but I like it,' Nina said. 'It's lovely to be close to the centre. I could just walk to the shops any time I wanted.'

'Is that the way you see it?' he said, sounding a little reassured. 'Well, here we are, here's the gates.'

They were tall and wrought iron, set in the red wall, with a carved stone plaque beside them which said Wriothesby House. Nina tried to read it. 'However do you pronounce it?'

He looked pleased. 'Aye, I had a job getting my lips round it at first. But it's just pronounced Robey. It's a joker! Something to do with some family that lived here long ago, but I don't know why they had to put in all those extra letters, except to flummox folk. Ah, here's Deering.'

A spry old man was opening the gates for them. He must have been on the look-out, Nina thought, told by Decius which train they would take and warned to be on hand. He was thin and old and weatherbeaten, but upright, and he took off his cap as the cab passed, then hurried after them.

There was no drive – the gates gave straight onto the wide gravelled area before the house – and as they pulled up, Decius was there to open the door and help Nina down.

64

Behind him was the long façade of the house, three storeys high, in warm red brick, with a very simple white stone porch on Ionic pillars in the centre, and a white stone parapet hiding the pitch of the roof. The windows were tall twelve-paned sashes. It was all quite plain but, because of the proportions, elegant and satisfying.

'Well, what d'you think, love?' Mr Cowling asked, hurrying round from his side to read Nina's face. 'It's not much of a place, I'm afraid.'

'It's *beautiful*,' she said, with feeling.

He looked as though he couldn't believe her. 'But it's plain as bread, with a face as flat as a pancake! Never a bit of decoration – not a turret or curlicue or bit of fancy stone work about it! Not even a bay window!'

'I think it's lovely,' she said again. 'Is it Georgian?'

'A bit earlier,' Decius supplied. 'Queen Anne, though there's a part at the back that you can see is even older. There was probably a house here as far back in history as you like to go. The stables are more modern – about thirty years old. They're round the side.'

He gestured in the direction they had been travelling, where the gravel courtyard became a carriage path and turned the corner of the house.

'And the grounds are on the opposite side to this, running along beside the road behind the wall. There's a walled kitchen garden, a pleasure garden – small, but rather nice – and some lawns and shrubberies, all leading down to a lake with a Greek temple by way of a gazebo.'

'A lake and a temple – not really? It sounds as if it has everything!'

'A rather weedy lake, and the temple needs repair, but still,' Decius qualified, enjoying her pleasure.

'Can you really like it?' Cowling said wonderingly. He shook his head. 'Ah, but wait till you see the inside. You'll be begging me to take you straight back to Beechcroft.'

Nina laughed, and put down Trump, who was wriggling, and watched him scurry round in happy circles, nose down. 'I bet I don't,' she said stoutly, and that made Mr Cowling laugh.

# CHAPTER FIVE

Mrs Deering was a wisp of a woman, as thin as her husband, with grey hair pulled back into an uncompromising bun. But her handshake was firm and her voice strong as she returned Nina's greeting, and when Nina smiled, she did too, shyly.

'Welcome to Wriothesby House. I hope we can make you comfortable here, madam,' she said.

'Aye, I hope you can as well,' Mr Cowling said sternly. 'Nothing but the best is good enough for Mrs Cowling,'

Trump came bouncing in. 'Oh, is this your little dog, madam? He's a treasure, isn't he?' said Mrs Deering, stooping to pat him (and winning Nina's heart. Mrs Mitchell loathed him). She straightened and addressed Mr Cowling's question. 'I've had two cleaning women in, sir, and gone over everything from top to bottom, so it's all clean and polished, and everything's been aired. And I've engaged two house-parlourmaids, in accordance with your instructions, and the girl who helps me in the kitchen is coming full-time. But if anything is found wanting, I shall see to it right away.'

The front door had led straight into a large panelled hall, with oak floorboards and a massive oak staircase straight ahead. All the wood was gleaming with lavender wax, and on a stand at the foot of the stairs was a large blue-and-white vase with an arrangement of white narcissi, yellow ranunculus, purple-blue hyacinth, and a few stems of catkins.

Nina, wanting to give something back for Mrs Deering's

kindness to Trump, said, 'What lovely flowers! Did you arrange them yourself?'

Mrs Deering looked pleased. 'I did, madam. There's not so much available this time of year. But spring flowers are always welcome, I think.'

'Purple, white and gold,' said Decius. 'The colours of Easter. Liturgically correct, Mrs Deering.'

'If you say so, sir,' she replied, smiling in a way that told Nina she liked him and didn't mind his nonsense. Nina felt something loosen in her: she would be happy here. She would understand, and be understood. She would not be the alien invader that she was at Beechcroft.

'Flowers are all very well,' Mr Cowling said impatiently, 'but you'd better see the rest of the house, my love, before you get too cheerful. It's very bare, to my mind. Not much comfortable about it.'

Moxton and Deering disappeared upstairs with the luggage, and Mrs Deering conducted Nina around her domain, with Mr Cowling and Decius following, one anxious and one amused. There was a small parlour to the right of the hall, with a round mahogany table in the window, a couple of French armchairs by the fireplace, and a faded blue-and-yellow Turkish carpet on the floor. On the mantelpiece was a little gold-and-white china clock and two matching candle-sticks.

'This room gets the sun in the morning, madam,' said Mrs Deering. 'I thought you might like to take your breakfast here.'

'I think I should,' Nina said. There were flowers here, too – a simple white vase of daffodils in the centre of the table.

Back across the hall and to the left was the door to the dining-room, which was huge and occupied most of that side of the house. It, too, was panelled, the floor was bare polished oak, a long mahogany table occupied the centre, and there were a couple of side tables against the wall. The wine-coloured curtains were faded, but everything, again, was rubbed to a shine.

There was an enormous, elaborately carved marble fireplace: scrolled, fluted and embellished with ribbons, acanthus and grapes, with what looked like Greek goddesses forming the jambs and holding up endblocks in the shape of urns full of fruit and flowers. Mr Cowling's worried frown dissipated a little as he drew Nina's attention to it. 'Now, this is something like – eh, my love? This is fancy enough for the King! You wonder why they didn't do a bit more of this sort of thing while they were about it. Everything's so plain, you'd think they hadn't two pennies to rub together.'

'The Queen Anne style *is* plain, sir,' Decius said, with the air of one who had explained this before. 'The fireplace isn't original, of course – a later addition.'

'Aye, well, they should have gone on adding,' Mr Cowling said ungraciously.

Beyond the dining-room was the drawing-room, which ran along the back of the house, with French windows onto a terrace and the garden beyond. This room had a square of carpet in the centre, which Mr Cowling allowed grudgingly was better than all those bare floors, though it left enough wood on view all the same. There were two settees, each with a pair of Bergère armchairs, and a couple of console tables. The fireplace was Queen Anne – 'Plain as the sole of my boot,' Mr Cowling mourned – and on the mantelpiece there was, shockingly, nothing. Nothing at all!

'We should have brought a few ornaments with us from Beechcroft House,' Mr Cowling said. 'Just to make it more home-like.'

Nina crossed to him and laid a hand on his arm. 'But I like it like this, truly I do!'

'Now you're just trying to butter me,' he said gruffly. 'Nobody could like bare empty spaces. But this was just how it was when I bought the place, and I've never been here much so I never did anything about it. My Mary didn't like it here, so we lived at Beechcroft. We did that out in top style, as you've seen.' A thought seemed to strike him. 'Of course, that's all her liking. You p'raps don't care to be taking over her shoes. I should have thought.' Nina began to protest, but he overrode her, kind but implacable. 'You must do it up your own way – furniture, curtains, all the bits and bobs. Make it your own. Spend what you like. And never ask me – I'm not educated like you, and young Decius.'

Decius coughed and turned his head away. Nina squeezed her husband's arm, trying not to feel sad. 'You are the kindest man in the world,' she said.

He looked pleased. 'Who should I be kind to, if not my own wife? Now, then, Mrs Deering, Mrs Cowling can wander round later and see the rest in her own time. Let's just have a quick look at the bedroom before luncheon. I'm sharp-set for it, so I hope you've something good for us. Decius, you will stay?'

'With your leave, sir, I'm expected in Wigston.'

'Aye, aye, it's Easter, of course, I'd forgotten that for the minute. There'll be the big gathering of Blakeses at home! You'd better get off, then. Thanks for all you've done, and I'll see you bright and early Tuesday morning to have a look at that factory.'

Nina saw him go with a little disappointment. Conversation always flowed more easily when Decius was at the table. She followed Mr Cowling up the stairs, with Trump dashing on ahead, his nails skidding a little on the broad oak boards.

'Noisy these passage floors,' Mr Cowling complained. 'They want carpeting.'

A plump maid was just coming out of the bedroom, and dropped Nina a curtsy. 'This is Tina, madam,' Mrs Deering introduced. 'One of the new maids I've engaged. I thought she could attend to you – she's looked after a lady before.'

'Thank you,' Nina said, and was about to say she didn't

70

need looking after; but Mr Cowling was nodding approvingly, and Tina was giving her a ready smile that was almost a grin, so she left it at that. It would be nice to have someone friendly to help her with her buttons.

The bedroom was very large, with a high ceiling, and the bed had enormously tall posts carrying a tester, but the posts were slim and unadorned, and there were no side curtains, so it was not oppressive. There was a dressing-table with a mirror above it and an enormous wardrobe. An armchair by the window – which gave over the gardens – looked as if it had been placed there for taking one's ease and contemplating nature. On a small table beside it was a vase of tulips, white and red.

'Beautiful,' Nina said. 'It's early for tulips.'

'Deering brings them on in the greenhouse, madam,' Mrs Deering said. 'We always did have tulips at Wriothesby House. The previous mistress liked them.'

'I like them too,' Nina said, and earned herself a smile.

'Your dressing-room's through here,' Mr Cowling said, opening a door on one side, 'and I've got my usual room, which is the next one along. I'll leave you to get ready for luncheon, my love. Don't be long.'

In the dressing-room, Nina discovered, there was a wash-stand, with a ewer of hot water, which, presumably, Tina had just brought. There was also a cheval mirror, a towel horse, a rattan chair – and a commode. Oh, well. You couldn't expect modern plumbing in a house of this age. But she didn't mind it so much here, where everything was so beautiful and serene. Left alone, she washed her face and hands, tidied her hair, and went down to luncheon.

Another cable announced that the dowager and Rachel were staying with Vicky and Bobo at the summer palace for Easter. Kitty felt only relief. She was very large, and felt good for nothing but lying on the sofa or taking gentle walks in the garden. She did not feel equal to company.

'Though I suppose Linda will be coming,' she said to Giles at dinner one evening, trying not to sound unwelcoming.

'No,' said Giles, managing to be equally neutral. 'They've had an invitation to go and stay at Croombe Park – the Willoughbys' place.'

'Hard luck on the Willoughbys,' Richard said. 'I suppose it was their turn.' Giles gave him a stern look. Richard returned it with a cynical grin. 'Oh, what? Don't pretend you haven't thought about getting up a rota to spread them more thinly.' He turned to Kitty. 'They'll love it at Croombe Park – interesting old Tudor place, hardly touched since Queen Elizabeth last slept there. All the medieval comforts. So we'll be all alone here, will we?' he asked Giles.

Giles hesitated. 'I did think – if it won't be too much for you,' he said to Kitty, 'of having a couple of my old friends to stay. London people.'

Richard perked up at that, but cautiously. 'When you say "London people", are we talking about people of fashion – amusing, debonair, sophisticated? *Les gens du monde*?'

Only Alice saw Kitty shrink at the idea.

'I was talking about my archaeology friends,' Giles said.

'Oh,' said Richard, blankly. 'What fun.'

Alice stifled a giggle.

Giles addressed Kitty. 'Not a huge crowd,' he said. 'I was thinking just Archie Baxter and John and Mabel Portwine. Should you mind it? I've been concentrating on the estate so much, I haven't had any intelligent conversation for – I don't know how long.'

Uncle Sebastian looked up from the 'cutlet' with which he was wrestling – it seemed to have come from some animal with more sinews than the average sheep. 'I observe they didn't teach tact at University College. Perhaps you should have gone to Oxford after all.'

'You know very well what I mean,' Giles said crossly.

Alice lost control of her giggles. 'Oh, Giles!' She snorted. 'Your face!'

'Behave yourself,' Giles snapped at her, 'or you can go back to eating in the nursery. I'm only concerned with Kitty's feelings. Would you be equal to some company here from Saturday to Tuesday? Would it be too much for you?'

Kitty was so touched that he was asking her that she said at once, 'Oh, no! I mean, yes, of course invite them. I should like you to see your friends. You work so hard.'

'You needn't worry about having to entertain them,' Richard told her gravely. 'They'll disappear into the library straight after breakfast, and talk about old bones until they turn into fossils themselves. And for a little light diversion on Easter Monday, Giles will take them to stare at a bit of broken wall.'

Nina explored the rest of Wriothesby House alone, while Mr Cowling was occupied with a note that had arrived by hand on Saturday morning.

It was a grand house, and had once been attached to considerable land, which the previous owners had sold off parcel by parcel until there was nothing left to sell but the house. But she could see it would have been fit for a lord, and that they must have entertained in grand style at one time. As well as the huge dining-room and drawing-room on the ground floor, there was a long gallery on the first floor, running along one whole side above the dining-room, where one could have held balls.

All the rooms were panelled, which she thought gave a cosiness to the grandeur: it was not an overpowering house like Dene Park, where she and Kitty had once attended a ball. There were two more small parlours on the ground floor, one of which Mr Cowling was obviously using as a business-room. On the first floor, apart from the bedrooms occupied by her and Mr Cowling, there were three more, one of them a state bedroom, whose even more massive four-poster bed had blue velvet hangings and ostrich feathers sprouting from a gold-painted crown at the apex of the tester.

There were a further six bedrooms on the second floor, none of them now furnished. And there was actually a bathroom, though it was only a little slip of a room, and contained nothing but a high-sided bath on claw-footed legs. Water would have to be brought up in cans from the kitchen. Getting down on her knees, Nina saw that the plug hole sat over a zinc cistern which could be dragged out and emptied – presumably into the same cans, for disposal downstairs. It accounted for why the bath sat on such tall legs.

'And it's up here because these are the bachelor rooms,' she instructed Trump, who was under the bath searching for rabbits, 'and only gentlemen would be expected to use a bathroom. Ladies bathed in their bedrooms beside the fire. Still, it is a beginning. If there's one bathroom, there can be others. And there's certainly enough room. We don't need eleven bedrooms, do we?'

Trump emerged, a little dusty about the ears, and looked at her enquiringly. She looked back, and he gave a yap.

'Yes,' she said. 'I suppose I am thinking about it. But it's no good, is it? He doesn't like the place.'

Trump made a short whine.

'All right for you,' she said. 'You wouldn't be the one to get into trouble. Shall we go and look outside?'

There was a pleasant terrace of broad flags outside the French windows, with a balustrade punctuated by large urns dividing it from a lawn. Formal flowerbeds were cut into it, in which Nina saw the pointed green noses of bulbs beginning to come through. At the end of the lawn was a pergola stretching right across, occupied by tightly clipped roses, dividing it from the rest of the pleasure grounds. Evidently Deering wasn't able, alone, to keep up all the grounds, for beyond the pergola everything was overgrown and neglected, specimen trees and shrubs with winding paths among them leading down to the small lake and the stone temple. This was placed, Nina realised, so that the sun would slant into it and warm the person sitting on the stone bench inside. A perfect place for solitude and thought. The lake was overgrown and silted up, but she imagined it cleared and planted, with water-lilies, clumps of iris and bulrushes, and bright ducks paddling about.

Trump, burrowing about at the lake's edge, had dislodged a frog, whose enormous leap made him scuttle backwards in fright. Nina laughed, then pressed her hands tightly against her breastbone to stop her excitement rising. *We won't be living here*, she told herself, *he doesn't like it*. But the damage had already been done. The thought of Beechcroft was more prison-like than ever.

On Saturday afternoon Mr Cowling took her for a walk around the little town, which was charmingly compact, centred on the marketplace. All the people they passed smiled and greeted them pleasantly, as if they were happy to be living there.

He had something in particular to show her. Just around the corner from the church, and coming as a surprise in that location, was a massive factory, the front stretching right along the street. It was four storeys high, built in the same handsome red brick as Wriothesby House, with a multitude of big windows as if it were a great mansion rather than a workshop.

'It's right in the centre of the town!' Nina marvelled.

'Why not?' Mr Cowling said. 'Work is the heart of a place, just as much as church. A man with no work's got nothing in his belly and no stomach for sermons.' He looked up at the façade with interest and pleasure. 'Aye, there can't be many folk in the town that haven't depended on this place for their bread and butter, one way or another.'

'This is the one you're thinking of buying?' Nina asked.

'That's right. Crawford's stockings. It'd go well with Cowling's boots and shoes, don't you think?'

*And you could walk here from Wriothesby House*, Nina thought longingly.

Easter Sunday was a bright, breezy day of sudden sunshine and racing shadows, with a taste of fresh dampness on the air. There was a bowl of primroses on the breakfast table. Nina thanked Mrs Deering with a heartfelt look as she brought in the coffee. And when she came downstairs dressed for church, the housekeeper brought her a little bound bunch of violets to pin to her coat, their purple faces still damp, and smelling of spring. Nina was so touched she had no words, but Mrs Deering looked content, as though she had read her mind.

Trump came bouncing up, ready for a walk. 'No, you can't come,' Nina said. Trump, reading her tone of voice, lowered his tail and his ears. 'Oh dear, poor dog, you do hate being left behind,' she said.

'I'll look after him, madam,' said Mrs Deering. 'Come along, you come with me to the kitchen. I've a bit of old rug I can put down for him by the stove,' she added to Nina.

Nina remembered Mrs Mitchell, and was almost tearful with thanks.

They walked to church. It was handsome, in the perpendicular style, full of light, simple and elegant – quintessentially English. She liked it as much as she liked Wriothesby House, and felt a twinge of guilt, suspecting Mr Cowling would prefer something flamboyantly Gothic. Oh dear. She hadn't known she had any taste, and now she was discovering that what she liked was the opposite of what her husband admired.

As they entered, many heads turned, and Nina knew herself subjected to inspection. Mr Cowling seemed to like it, and pulled himself up taller, pressing her captive hand against his ribs and strutting a little, proud of her. A sidesman scurried up to them and whispered, 'Allow me to show you the Wriothesby House pew, madam, sir,' which proved he, at least, knew who they were. In a small place, news gets about quickly. Nina would have liked to look about her but, as the stared-at person, had to keep her eyes forward and pretend serene indifference.

At the end of the service there was the usual press of people around the door waiting to talk to the vicar. Nina was resigned to joining the queue, but Mr Cowling spotted someone outside and drew her along with him, bypassing the pastoral blockage.

'Crawford!' he called. 'Over here, sir!'

It was a thin man with an anxious expression in slightly dusty-looking Sunday blacks. The woman on his arm was thin and mousy in a wide hat that looked too big for her, as if it were bent on squashing her into the ground. They turned and waited for Mr Cowling, who, though no taller than Crawford, seemed in his breezy confidence to tower over him.

'Nina, my dear, may I present Mr Arnold Crawford and Mrs Crawford – my wife. I'm glad to see you, Crawford. You hinted you had a plan to tell me about. Not changing your mind about selling?'

Mr Crawford removed his hat and bowed to Nina; Mrs Crawford gave her a nervous smile, and clung harder than ever to her husband's arm. 'Now, Mr Cowling, you know it was never an outright sale we mentioned,' Crawford said. 'My grandfather built that factory, and it's been at the heart of Market Harborough for three generations. It's my sadness that I haven't a son to leave it to. But to sell it outright would be like parting with one of the family.'

'Then, what's this plan of yours?' Mr Cowling asked impatiently.

'By your leave, sir, not here, not now.' For all his mild appearance, he could speak firmly when he wanted to. 'I'd like to put it to you when we both have time to consider it carefully. I have figures and drawings to show you. From what I know about you, I think it is something you will find interesting.'

'Ah, looked me up in my glory, have you?' Even Mr Cowling's jokes sounded too robust for this sad man. She imagined Mr Crawford giving away a beloved old dog because he couldn't afford to keep it – hoping it was going to a good home, but unable, of course, to be absolutely sure.

She spoke before she had realised she was going to. 'Would you and Mrs Crawford do us the honour of dining with us tomorrow? Then you and Mr Cowling can talk business after dinner, while Mrs Crawford and I have a comfortable coze by the fire.'

None of the other three looked at her with the surprise she felt in herself. But Mr Cowling said, 'Capital idea, my love! Yes, do come and dine, if you've no other engagement. There's no party, I'm afraid – it will be just us. But we'd be delighted.'

The Crawfords exchanged a glance, and Mr Crawford smiled and said, 'That's very civil of you, Mrs Cowling. We'd be delighted.'

'We'll dine early, if that suits you,' Cowling said. 'Then we'll have time to discuss this mysterious plan of yours. Six o'clock?'

Kindnesses were murmured, hats were touched, and Mr Cowling led Nina away. She felt anxious, and was assembling excuses for her strange outburst, when he said, 'A good notion of yours, my love, to get him onto my ground where I'll have the upper hand. I can see you'll be an asset to my business.' This was only partly a joke. 'As long as you won't be too bored. Mrs C doesn't look like sparky company. Pity we can't get young Decius over to entertain you while I dissect friend Crawford. You'll speak to Mrs Deering about putting on a slap-up dinner? From the look of them, they don't get many.'

Nina took a bracing breath. 'Speaking' to Mrs Mitchell had always meant listening while she told Nina how things would be. But Mrs Deering wasn't like that. And speaking to the housekeeper was something a real lady of the house did, a proper, grown-up married woman. She didn't feel particularly grown-up, but she thought that Mrs Deering would help her through. It would be her first dinner party as hostess – a milestone.

It might even be fun.

For all his greater age and experience, Mr Cowling proved more nervous about the engagement than Nina. He fussed about the menu Mrs Deering had chosen. He fussed about the bareness of the dining-room. He fussed about the laying of the table. He fussed about what Nina should wear.

'Is that all the jewellery you've got? You should have more. Why didn't I buy you more stuff before now?' he mourned.

Nina had worried that the diamond necklace he had given her for a wedding-present was too fine for the occasion. 'I don't think the Crawfords will be very dressy,' she ventured diffidently. 'I didn't want to look too—'

He wasn't listening. 'That's real silk, anyway, your dress. And they won't have seen it, which is a blessing. But we must get you up to London and buy you more things. You ought to have a dozen evening frocks. You ought to have a tiara.'

'A tiara? Surely that would be too much,' she protested, but uneasily – perhaps she was wrong and a tiara would be expected.

But Mr Cowling said, 'No, of course not for this dinner, but for when we're invited somewhere grand. I don't want you to be caught out. I don't want people thinking we don't know what's what, or I can't afford to buy you the best. I don't want anyone looking at you sideways.'

'I don't want to let you down,' Nina began.

He clutched her hand. 'You couldn't let me down if you tried! Never think it! I'm the awkward one. I'm just a plain village cobbler got rich.'

Nina was glad, on the whole, that her first dinner party was such a small occasion, so that she got to practise without too much anxiety. The guests had obviously taken the occasion seriously, for Mr Crawford's hair was freshly cut and his white tie looked new – bought that day, she wondered, after invitation? Mrs Crawford's evening dress did not look new, but was covered all over with bugle beads, and in a fashionable shade of mauve. Her figure was corseted into the correct serpentine shape, her hair was piled up into the fashionable style, and decorated with small feathers and a spray of crystal beads that glittered distractingly every time she moved her head.

Conversation in the drawing-room over sherry was stilted at first, but the men soon got onto current events and business news so the women were able just to listen. Then when Moxton, in his guise of butler, escorted them into the dining-room, Mrs Crawford exclaimed spontaneously, 'Oh, it does look nice! Such a beautiful room, this, I always think. We dined here a few times, when old Mrs Ampleforth was alive. The flowers are quite lovely. Did you do them yourself, Mrs Cowling?'

For her liking of the dining-room, Nina was prepared to forgive her for making her admit she hadn't arranged the flowers herself. And it gave her a conversational opening, in asking Mrs Crawford about the previous owners – a topic Mrs Crawford found comfortable, so the chat went on mildly though the dinner. Nina had accepted Mrs Deering's suggestions for the menu wholesale, not knowing any better, and thought it all good: artichoke soup, fillets of salmon, roast lamb with broccoli and new potatoes, coffee blancmange, a savoury of soft roes of herring, and dessert. She caught Mr Cowling looking at her down the table at one point, but didn't know what the look meant. Both the Crawfords seemed to have good appetites, despite their thinness – or perhaps they were thin because they didn't eat very much at home. In sudden anxiety, Nina pressed her guests to second helpings.

When dessert was finished, Nina rose and led Mrs Crawford

into the drawing-room, as she had seen done, leaving the men to talk business. Mrs Crawford made the rest of the evening easy for her by talking about Market Harborough and local families, a topic that interested Nina and about which Mrs Crawford had plenty of information. The men were so long that when they finally returned, the party reunited only to divide again almost immediately as the Crawfords departed.

'Well?' Nina asked Mr Cowling when they were alone.

'Pretty well,' said Mr Cowling. 'The dinner was nice enough, though it could have been more fancy – only one soup, no duck or fowl, no choice of sweets.'

'But I think for just four people . . .' Nina said uncertainly. 'More dishes might have been overpowering. Or don't you think so?'

'Aye, well, you could be right. But one of these days we'll give a right grand slap-up banquet and invite everyone. That table'd take thirty round it, easy – and I've a notion there's more leaves somewhere in one of the attics. *Then* you can wear your tiara,' he added, in what might have been a joke.

'Did your business talk go well?' Nina asked, to distract him from that train of ideas.

'Very well. He's got an interesting plan, all right.'

Nina waited, but he didn't elaborate, his brow buckled in thought. 'What is it?' she asked at last.

He came back from contemplation. 'Eh? The plan? Oh, I won't bother you with it tonight. You must be tired. And I want to look over the papers he's left me again. There's a lot to digest. You run on up, my love. I shall be a while.'

It was showery on Tuesday morning, rain and sunshine chasing each other like frowns and smiles across the same face, but after luncheon – which she took alone, Mr Cowling and Decius Blake having been out since early that morning – the sky cleared, the clouds grew high and white and innocent, and Nina went out into the garden with Trump for some much-needed exercise.

She was coming back through the wilderness from the lake when she met Decius coming the other way. 'You're back!' she exclaimed. 'Have you been at the factory all this time?'

'Yes, and Mr Cowling is still there, but he told me to come back and see that you're all right. He said I should take luncheon with you.' He smiled. 'I don't think he has any idea of the time. You must have lunched long ago.'

'I did. Are you hungry? I could ask Mrs Deering for something for you.'

'No, thank you,' he said. 'I'm rarely hungry at this time of day. The luncheon idea was for your benefit rather than mine. But I do need to stretch my legs and seize a few mouthfuls of fresh air.'

Nina made an expansive gesture. 'Take all you like,' she said. 'Shall I walk with you, or do you want to be alone?'

'Walk with me, please.' Nina turned with him and headed back down towards the lake. 'I'm charged with telling you about Mr Crawford's plan. You asked Mr Cowling last night, apparently, and he snubbed you. He's quite anxious about it. Were your feelings hurt? Do you actually want to know what the plan is?'

'No, and yes. I quite understood that he needed more time to digest it. And of course I'm interested. What goes on in that huge, handsome factory?'

Decius grinned. 'It is handsome, isn't it? And a nice place to work, I should think – lots of light. They make stockings and socks of all kinds and sizes. And corsets.'

'Corsets!' Nina laughed. 'I thought Mrs Crawford looked awfully well bound. So, tell me, what is this wonderful plan?'

He thought for a moment. 'I may have to go back a step or two. Do you know what cellulose is?'

'No. Though I think I've heard the word.'

'It's a material made from wood pulp – though it can be

made from anything like leaves or tree bark too – and it can be drawn into a thread, and then woven into cloth, which is hard-wearing and cheaper than cloth made from natural materials like cotton and wool.'

'Ye-es,' said Nina, doubtfully.

'About ten years ago, someone worked out a way to treat this fibre so that it resembles silk. Artificial silk looks so good, you can hardly tell it from the real thing. But as you can imagine, it would take thousands of mulberry silkworms a very long time to produce as much of the real thing as a vat of wood pulp can produce of—'

'Art silk!' Nina finished for him. 'Yes, of course, I've heard of that, though I didn't really know what it was. But what has this to do with Mr Crawford? And why is Mr Cowling interested?'

'Mr Crawford has a plan to utilise part of his factory to manufacture art silk and then weave it into socks and stockings. But he needs a capital investment. Mr Cowling has money to invest. And Mr Crawford has cleverly put it to him that, as the man who can't quite afford hand-made shoes buys a Cowling and Kempson factory-made pair instead, so he should have the opportunity to buy art-silk socks to go with them.'

Nina laughed. 'Yes, of course! It makes perfect sense.'

'Ladies too,' Decius said. 'Proper silk stockings cost the earth – so I'm told,' he added modestly.

They reached the temple, and sat down together.

'They are expensive,' Nina said. 'And one is always having to darn them, because they cost too much to throw away.'

'That's another thing,' he said. 'Art-silk stockings would be much harder wearing. And, I believe, they would fit better, the artificial fibre being more flexible than natural silk.'

Nina reflected on this for a moment. 'Do you think he's going to do it – Mr Cowling?'

'I think he will. It does make sense, and it looks like a

good business opportunity. Just as people always need shoes, they always need socks, too. And he does love innovation, and science, and modern thinking. They appeal to him as much as the commercial possibilities, I think. That's what I left them doing – looking at the earmarked section of the factory and working out where all the machinery would go.'

'Then,' she said, 'he would have to be spending more time here, in Market Harborough?'

'Certainly, at first,' Decius said cautiously, watching her face, not knowing what she was thinking, 'he would have to be here much of the time. But it isn't far from Northampton, you know, and there's the railway. I'm sure he won't neglect you. Or, if he's going to be gone for a week at a time, you could come with him and stay here. I know it isn't as comfortable as Beechcroft, but—'

'But I *love* it!' Nina cried passionately. 'I love this house – it's so much nicer than Beechcroft. And I love the Deerings, and I love Market Harborough. Oh, Decius, do you think he'd agree to come and live here permanently, instead of in Northampton? I *hate* Northampton.'

He smiled. 'I think he would do anything to make you happy.'

'But I want him to be happy too. And he does seem to dislike this place.'

'I don't think men mind half so much where they live as women do. And he'll always have to travel about anyway. You're the one who'll be at home, so it's more important that you're content. He'll see that, I'm sure. And there's one way you can find out.'

'Ask him,' said Nina, glumly. 'That's what Richard said. But I don't want to make him angry. If I ask and he says no, it will make things very difficult back at Beechcroft.'

Decius looked at her with some sympathy, thinking, *Thank God I'm not a woman.* He said, 'I'd ask for you, but I'm afraid it's something you must do for yourself. I couldn't interfere.

But if he asks my opinion, I shall tell him that I think you would much prefer to live here. And I can assure you that your happiness is paramount to him.'

They sat in silence for a while. Then Decius said, 'By Jove, look, old Trump has caught a frog.'

Nina jumped up, all other thoughts banished. 'Oh, no! He'll hurt it! We must get it away from him. Bad dog! Leave it!' Trump ran past with an idiot grin and the frog in his mouth, and it was an energetic chase before they could catch him and release the frog, which seemed unharmed.

Then Nina slid her arm through Decius's and said, 'You must be hungry by now, after all that running about. Come back to the house and have tea.'

He smiled. 'Now, tea is a meal I've always approved of.'

'I understand that, if you never have luncheon,' said Nina.

# CHAPTER SIX

The dowager Lady Stainton and her daughter returned to Ashmore at the end of April. 'For the Birth,' she said magnificently, making it clear that Birth had a capital letter. 'I was told the child was due in May.'

'The middle of May,' Giles said. He didn't much care whether his mother was present or not, since he had ways of avoiding her, but he had a vague idea that being upset wasn't good for pregnant women, and his mother's capacity to upset other people, especially meek women, and most especially Kitty, was unbounded.

Maud dismissed the objection. 'Tallant babies always come early,' she decreed. 'I shall go up and see Kitty when I've changed. And what have you done about an accoucheur?'

'A what?' Giles said, distracted.

She frowned at him. '*All* my births were attended by an accoucheur. A *London* accoucheur, of course. The best ones are booked months in advance. My grandson is the heir to the Stainton estate. His birth is a matter of the utmost importance.'

'It might not be a boy,' Giles objected feebly.

'It *will* be a boy,' she replied. 'And I gather, then, that you have done nothing to prepare for his arrival. Really, Giles, must I do everything? I go away for a few weeks and the house falls into wrack and ruin.' There seemed a hint of satisfaction in her voice about that.

'You've been away almost four months,' Giles said. 'And we're getting along very well.' But she had gone out of the room and didn't hear.

Hot on the dowager's heels came the Cordwells. 'Linda's amazing. She must have been lurking in the woods waiting to see Mama's carriage arrive,' Richard said wonderingly. 'How did she know, otherwise?'

'She knew Mama would come back for the birth, and Mama told her it would be in May, so she came at the first opportunity, that's all,' Giles said.

'How depressingly literal you are, dear brother', said Richard. 'Well, the Willoughbys have had a good long go of her. I suppose we can't really object to taking our turn.'

'I just hope she doesn't upset Kitty,' Giles said.

Richard looked thoughtful, and later that morning sent a telegram, the result of which was the arrival of Grandmère to swell the ranks – or, rather, to take control. She could out-general anyone, even Maud.

'So now it's all settled down again,' Dory said to Uncle Sebastian. 'As you will know, sir. Peace abounds.'

Her head was bent over a pale pink blouse, lace over silk, and she was repairing a tear in the lace with tiny stitches. Sebastian liked the way she pressed her lips together when she was doing something tricky.

'I did notice a certain increase in tranquillity,' he said, resting between pieces, hands unmoving on the keys.

'Although not so much below stairs,' Dory went on. 'Old Lady Stainton's maid, Simone, got into a big row with Miss Taylor over the booking of an accoucheur. When Miss Taylor found out old Lady Stainton had vetoed it, she was angry. Her ladyship always had Sir Desmond Wentworth, and Miss Taylor said it wasn't fitting that the heir to Ashmore Castle should be brought into the world by anything but a knight of the realm. She said old Lady Stainton shouldn't interfere, which made Simone mad. She said her ladyship was the one interfering, that she couldn't stand that she wasn't top dog any more, and that she ought to go to the Dower House and keep her mouth shut. So of course that set them at it like cat and dog, until Miss Hatto said that *her* lady – Lady Kitty – didn't want an accoucheur anyway, and that ought to be the end of it. And then, of course, Miss Taylor and Simone both turned on her and told her she'd only been a lady's maid five minutes and ought to respect her elders.' Dory tested a silk-covered button and decided that it was coming loose. She reached for her scissors. 'It doesn't help that Miss Hatto outranks them below stairs, her lady being the countess and theirs only dowagers. It just makes them madder when Mr Moss points it out. They think she's a flibbertigibbet upstart, and ought to sit at their feet and drink in their wisdom, until she's past forty and has a face like a pickled egg, just like them.'

Another thing Sebastian liked about the sewing-maid was her unexpected vocabulary. She didn't talk like any maid he'd ever known before. There was a mystery about her past that he'd like to uncover – one day. For now, he just said, 'So much conflict! It all sounds exhausting.'

She looked up. 'It is, sir. That's why I like to get away, up here. Except that I shouldn't be *in here* at all. I should be in the sewing-room.'

'You *should* obey orders,' said Sebastian, 'and my orders are that you stay while I play again. What do you say to a little Bach? How about a Goldberg Variation?'

'It's very good for sewing to, if you don't take it too fast, sir,' she said, with a hint of a gleam in her eyes.

Sebastian knew he couldn't play this most difficult of Bach's music fast – he wasn't good enough, and his hands were not so nimble these days. But did she know that? And was she saving his face? She disconcerted him – and he suspected she meant to.

★　★　★

Alice was pleased and excited to see Rachel again, but felt oddly shy at first. Her sister had changed so much. Her hems were down and her hair was up, she moved quite differently, and Alice wondered how her cheeks could be suddenly so pink. Could it be the new tightness of her corset pushing the blood up into her face?

When Alice persuaded her to go up to the old schoolroom for a private chat, Rachel wandered about the room at first, touching things idly, and said, in a voice unlike her own, 'Goodness, everything looks so different! Smaller, somehow. And how faded and shabby the Castle is compared with the Wachturm and Biebesheim.'

Alice said, 'Oh, Ray, don't be affected!'

Rachel blushed with annoyance. 'I'm not affected!'

'I've missed you so much,' Alice pleaded. 'Please be the same, so I can talk to you.'

Rachel looked serious. 'I can't be the same, because I'm not the same, but I've missed you too.' She sat down, and somehow seemed more like the old Rachel, which reassured Alice.

'You haven't changed,' Rachel said. 'What have you been doing since we went away?'

'Hunting, of course, and we had house parties for hunting weekends, which was nice. Otherwise, there's been no company. But I'm allowed to dine down all the time now. What else? Keeping Kitty company. Uncle Sebastian plays cards with me in the evening sometimes, but he always wins, because he remembers every single card that's been played. He says you have to, to be a proper card player. So I said I'd sooner just do it for fun and keep losing. Oh, and Kitty's maid Hatto taught me to knit. I'm not very good yet – I can only go in a straight line – but I knitted a scarf.'

Rachel seemed impressed. 'Can I see it?'

'I haven't got it now. I gave it to Richard for a present, but he laughed so much he cracked a chair leg. So I took it back and gave it to Josh, and he said it was very nice, which was something, coming from *him*.'

'How's my darling Daystar?'

'I kept him exercised for you, and hunted him a bit. But Josh has been *so* disagreeable, he insisted on turning him and Queen Bee out with the others after Easter, even though they'd hardly hunted at all, really. I was hoping to ride one of them while Pharaoh is out but he said no, they all had to rest. So if you want to ride this month it'll have to be one of the road horses, or the ponies.'

'That's all right, I don't need to ride,' Rachel said. 'We rode a lot in Germany.'

'Did you hunt?'

'Well, they called it hunting, but it was really just riding out into the forest and having a picnic.'

'Was it fun, over there?'

Rachel's face grew animated. '*So* much fun. Aunt Vicky and Uncle Bobo are so nice. And the cousins are lovely. We didn't see much of Freddie, because he's at cadet school, but he did come to one or two parties and looked *divine* in his uniform. He's nineteen this summer. Addie's fifteen and charming – she *so* admired me, it was almost embarrassing. She's longing to go to grown-up parties. Klaus and Giddy are just little boys, but much less annoying than little boys usually are. And the baby, Pauline, is simply *sweet*. She's going to be a great beauty. Nothing like Linda's Arabella.'

'But what did you do that was so much fun?' Alice pursued.

'Oh, parties – so many parties! And balls. I had to have dozens of gowns made – I'll show you some later, when I've been unpacked. And we went to a lot of military reviews. Goodness, German uniforms are smart! And there were the hunts, and picnics, and lots of things on the river. And when we moved to the summer palace, there was bathing as well.' Rachel blushed. 'I have a bathing dress,' she confided in a low voice, 'but I'd never dare to wear it in England.'

'I suppose you had lots of admirers.'

Rachel tried to look modest. 'Well, a few. But everyone danced with everyone else. It was very nice, really.'

'And I suppose you're madly in love with someone.'

'Of course not. I'm too young.' She said it as if it were a matter of course, but Alice wasn't convinced. Rachel coloured slightly. 'I don't mean to be in love at least until next year. I learned my lesson with you-know-who.'

'You mean there was no flirting?'

'Of course there was flirting. But don't tell Mama.'

'I won't tell. Who did you like best?'

'Well – Frittie Landau was nice. He dances divinely. He'll be the Margrave of Landau one day. And Vinnie Pazzalo was great fun. He's Italian, a viscount, such a joker! He has very dark skin – they say his mother was an Ethiopian princess. And Nicky Hohenloeuwe taught me archery one day at the Wachturm when they had a competition. I managed to hit the centre bull one time. He said I had a natural eye for it. But I think I liked Frittie Landau best. Oh – there was one horrid old man who was always hanging around us, the Prince of Usingen. He's old as Mama, very rich, and he kept trying to make friends with me. Frittie teased me that he was going to make me an offer. When I saw him coming I had to go and hide.'

'So did anyone make an offer?' Alice asked, feeling sad. She knew Rachel would marry one day and go away, but she had hoped it was a long way off.

'Of course not, I'm not old enough,' Rachel said, but with a conscious look that suggested the opposite. She seemed to change the subject. 'Oh, such an interesting thing – one of the guests at Biebesheim was the Landgravine Ortenberg, who's an American, and we got talking together at one of the parties and she said her sister went to school with Kitty. What d'you think about that? Her name before she married was Brevoorte. I must ask Kitty about her. She's not long been married, and she's expecting a child.' She remembered some-thing, hesitated, and lowered her voice. 'I had a maid assigned to me at the Wachturm, and she told me – about how you get a baby.' She looked at Alice, shiny-eyed, excited and appalled in about equal proportions. 'There's a Thing husbands do, and then you swell up and a baby pops out. I should like a little baby,' she added, 'but I don't like the idea of the Thing.'

'What is it?' Alice asked. 'The Thing?'

'I couldn't possibly tell you,' Rachel said, redder than ever. 'It's too awful.'

Alice giggled. 'Do you think Giles did it to Kitty? Must have, I suppose.'

'Oh, don't!' Rachel cried. 'It's too horrid to think about.'

'On the whole, a very satisfactory visit,' Maud said. She had tracked Giles down in the library, and Linda had followed her in, blocking his escape.

'I assumed it was,' he said, 'since you stayed away so long.'

'It was exactly what Rachel needed,' Maud went on. 'It has made a different girl of her. She's become poised, confi-dent – quite a young woman. And she was much admired. Everyone thought her a beautiful girl.'

'Well, she's pretty, I suppose,' Giles said vaguely, looking longingly at some milking records.

'Pretty? She's generally thought quite lovely,' Maud said.

'She's certainly had a great advantage bestowed on her,' Linda said sharply. 'Not every girl gets exposed to high German society like that – and before she's even out.'

'All the German boys were very correct,' Maud said. 'I had no fears. It's the military training, of course – they're taught how to behave themselves in the cadets. It's something we could do with more of in this country. And I must say, they all look very well in their uniforms. Very dashing.' She paused for a moment, suddenly remembering a certain young

92

cavalry officer with whom she had danced in her come-out year. He had been killed in the Kush. She suppressed a sigh.

'I suppose she's fallen in love with someone,' Giles said resignedly, since he seemed bound to hear it all.

'Never mind that,' Linda interrupted. 'Is anyone interested in her? Did you receive an offer for her, Mama?'

'I did not go there with that intention. I wished merely to show her a little, and harden her off for next Season. But, as it happens—'

'Ah, I knew it!' Linda exclaimed. She hoped it wasn't anyone too exalted. If she had only had Rachel's opportunities . . . She'd had to settle for a viscount, and a ruined one at that.

'As it happens,' Maud said, 'I did get the impression that Prince Paul of Usingen was taking a serious interest in her. He was at pains to get to know her – in a very quiet and proper way, needless to say. He is perfectly well-bred. And he was very attentive to me. He's somewhat older than her, but that is not necessarily a disadvantage. Vicky and Bobo have known him for years, and his estate is a good one. I made what discreet enquiries I could – one does not wish to be taken in—' she threw a cold look at Linda, whose carapace was not even dented by it, 'and it seems from what one can gather that he is *very* wealthy. He gave a party at his house in Darmstadt while we were there – a sister was hostess for him – and it seemed very handsome. Not only that, but he asked his sister to show me around it, as if he had some particular reason for impressing me.'

Giles sighed. 'So you want to marry poor little Rachel off to this rich elderly German?'

'He's not elderly, Stainton, he is about my age. And there's no question of marrying her yet. But I thought you would wish to know. You are legally her guardian.'

'Yes, I suppose I am. Thank you, Mama, for keeping me informed.'

Maud looked at him sharply. 'There is,' she said, 'the matter of her dowry.'

Linda snorted. 'No use asking him for money, Mama. He won't even pay me the allowance Papa gave me. Why should he put his hand in his pocket for Rachel when he won't for me – and *I* have two poor little children dependent on me,' she concluded pathetically.

'Because,' said Giles impatiently, 'I am responsible for Rachel, and I'm not responsible for you.'

'Linda, you had better leave,' Maud said. 'I have private matters to discuss with your brother.'

Giles made a shooing gesture that embraced them both. 'I would be glad if you would both leave. I have a great deal of work to do. And, with respect, Mother, I am not going to discuss dowries with you now. You've said yourself there's no question of Rachel marrying this year—'

'One needs to know what one is working with,' said Maud, her nostrils flaring in annoyance.

'At the moment, I have no idea what I shall be able to provide for the girls. You know very well I am in the process of sorting out the estate. By Christmas I might have some idea of what can be spared, but not now.'

'I told you so,' said Linda. 'Stingy, that's what he is. What is it, Giles? The Jam Kingdom not rich enough for you? Or are you saving it all for the Jam Prince?'

*There's no point in getting angry with Linda*, he told himself. *She's so steeped in envy that everything that comes out of her mouth is pickled.*

'Go, please. I have work to do. Go!'

They went. The dogs, who were lying beside his desk, had been roused by the forcefulness of his last command, and came to see if he was all right, or if a cold nose pressed into his palm might perhaps make him feel better. He caressed their rough coats and unexpectedly silky ears, and they beat their iron-bar tails in joy at his attention. How easy it was to please them, he thought. And he had a resurgence of the old longing, to be anywhere but here. The friends he had entertained at Easter had roused the sleeping urge to run with their talk of an expedition that was in planning, to the Valley of the Kings in December. Howard Carter was to work further on KV20, which had been thoroughly blocked by rubble carried in by floodwater, and never cleared beyond the first chamber. It was thought this time they would break through.

He pushed the thoughts from his head and the dogs from his knees and sat down at the desk to address himself again to the estate. His proper work.

'I'm going to be here for a while – a couple of weeks, perhaps,' said Mr Cowling at dinner. 'There's a lot to be looked into. But you needn't stay, dear – you can go back to Northampton if you like. You could take that little maid with you, as you seem to like her. It's time you had a lady's maid. Mrs Deering says she's a good girl, and she'd like to see her in a permanent job.'

'I do like her,' Nina said, 'and I don't mind having her as my maid, if you really think I need one. But, oh, please, couldn't I stay here? I don't want to go back to Northampton.'

He looked pleased, but said, 'You needn't worry about me. I'm used to being on my own.'

'I want to stay with you, of course,' Nina said, embarrassed at the misunderstanding, 'but I really like it here. I much prefer it to Beechcroft House.'

'I don't see how you can,' he said flatly.

'But I do. I think it's beautiful, and spacious, and elegant. And I love the town – so compact, and everyone's so friendly. I don't know anyone in Northampton, and it's too big to get to know people. Oh, please, *please* believe me – I love this house. I would like . . .' She hesitated. 'I would like it if we could live here all the time.'

He frowned, contemplating. 'Well, if that's the truth of

it . . . But it passes me. I always thought Beechcroft House was bang up to the mark, everything done in the best style, money no object.' He looked around vaguely. 'I suppose you could do something with this place, if you had the fancy for it. Board over all that panelling and wallpaper it, lower the ceilings maybe—'

'Oh, please not!' Nina pleaded. 'I like it the way it is.'

'You're not gammoning me? Well, there's no accounting for taste. And I saw such a pretty wallpaper the other day – white, with blue flower-de-looses all over it and little gold cross-things – thought it would be just the job for the drawing-room. No? Well, but it has to be said, it does look more like the nobs' houses I've been to than Beechcroft, though I've always thought that was because they couldn't afford to do them up. Impoverished gentry, you know. But maybe they like this sort of thing too?'

'I couldn't say,' Nina said, 'but I do. And Decius does too. He understands.'

Mr Cowling pouted. 'Ganging up on me now, the two of you?'

'Oh – no, really—'

'I'm just funning you. Well, my dear, all I want is for you to be happy, so if it's what you want . . . we'll stay here, and you shall make it your own. Buy what you like – carpets curtains, furniture, knick-knacks – you'll need a deal of stuff to fill the place, but I can stand the nonsense. You don't need to stint yourself. You've been thinking about it, I gather?'

'Ever since I got here,' Nina admitted. 'And I did wonder whether – if you would agree—'

'Out with it! What scheme have you dreamed up now in your pretty head to bankrupt me?'

'It won't bankrupt you,' she said, though aware that in a funny way he'd have rather liked her to want something extravagant, 'but I would like to put in a proper bathroom, if you wouldn't mind. I know it's rather modern, and it would involve building work – and Decius says you'd need an architect to make sure it didn't spoil the house.'

'Oh, you've talked to Decius about it, have you?'

'No, I wouldn't do that. I only asked him whether in theory it *could* be done, and how one would go about it if one *did* decide.'

'In theory, eh?' He chuckled. 'You won't have fooled him, my love. You have to be up early in the morning to get ahead of young Decius Blake. Well, have your bathroom. It'll put us out in front of the local nobs, that's for sure. The King has bathrooms, you know. And since I lend him money, I don't see why he should have anything I don't, bar the crown. Have two bathrooms, one on each floor – might as well, while you're chopping the place apart.'

'Oh, *thank* you!' Nina said.

'And I tell you what – I'll move Mrs Mitchell over here, permanent. Mrs Deering can stay as cook, but you'll need more maids, and a footman too, and Mrs Mitchell's the one to organise all that. She'll have your house running like clockwork.'

'Oh, but – you'll need Mrs Mitchell at Beechcroft, for when you have to stay there. She wouldn't like it here, and I wouldn't like to disrupt her life. I'm quite happy with Mrs Deering, and I think she manages beautifully. She *understands* the house.'

'And Mrs Mitchell wouldn't? Well, you might be right there. She'd take one look at all these bare floors and gloomy panelling and have a fit. All right, then, if you prefer Mrs Deering, I'll leave it like that. But if any time you find she can't manage—'

'She will. And I'll be so happy. Oh, *thank* you!'

He basked in her gratitude, and invited her to tell him all her plans, and shook his head in wonder at the style and extent of them. He did like the idea of clearing the lake, however, and proposed enlarging it while they were at it.

'Once it's big enough, you'll soon get ducks and moorhens and suchlike moving in. And you could have a nice little bridge going over it, so you can walk to the middle and look down at the water. Just like that French picture.'

'Which one?' she asked, but he couldn't tell her. She picked up from the air an image of a woman in white muslin with a parasol standing on an arched wooden bridge with water lilies below, and wondered if it was Monet he was thinking of.

The evening passed pleasantly, and she felt more at ease with him, and they had more to say to each other than at any time since they were married.

That night he came to her bedroom – something he had not done in weeks, not since before the trip to London. She welcomed him into her bed, with a warm, affectionate feeling towards him. There followed the usual fumbling and mildly embarrassing activity below the bedcovers, which ended with him sighing and rolling over, and then drawing her onto his shoulder to hold her for a while, before he got up and went away to his own room.

She was a little damp and sticky down there, but she still had no idea whether the act had been properly concluded or not. She wished with all her heart that her aunt had not shown her the drawings and tried to prepare her. If she had been completely ignorant, she would not now be left wondering if all was as it should be.

Grandmère took Kitty out to walk in the garden early, before it got hot. 'You have been sitting indoors too much,' she said. 'It is not good for you. Alone as well,' she added sternly.

'Alice sat with me sometimes. And Richard visited once or twice,' Kitty said.

'Does Giles not visit you?'

'He's very busy,' Kitty said loyally.

'Hmm,' said Grandmère, having learned all she needed

from that brief exchange. 'You have been left in solitude to brood and frighten yourself, *n'est-ce pas?*'

'I am afraid – a bit,' Kitty said.

'That is natural, but you are young and will make nothing of it. There is nothing to be afraid of.'

Kitty looked sidelong at her. 'Will it hurt?' she asked hesitantly, not entirely sure if she wanted to know the truth.

'There is pain,' Grandmère said unemphatically, 'only it is not the pain of injury but the pain of life and you will not mind it. It is impossible to explain to one who has not felt it. But it is nothing to be afraid of.' She changed the subject abruptly. 'Ashmore Castle has never had a good garden. One likes a pleasure ground to walk around in fine weather. What would you do, Kitty, to improve this one?'

Kitty's face lit, and she plunged at once into her ideas for the gardens. 'There was only time between getting back here and finding I was expecting a baby to make a start on the walled garden. But after the baby's born . . .' She distracted herself, and looked down at her feet for a moment. 'I do hope it's a boy,' she said in a low voice. 'Everyone will be so cross with me if it's not. Especially—'

'Especially Maud?' Grandmère supplied. 'But, *ma chère petite*, don't forget *she* had a girl first, so you need only point it out if she should say anything disagreeable to you.'

'Oh dear,' Kitty said, thinking of what it was like when her mother-in-law said disagreeable things.

'*Tiens*, Kitty, have some spirit! What can she do to you? *Rien du tout!*' She took Kitty's hand and tucked it through her arm. 'And I tell you a little secret. She has more to fear from you than you from her. *Vraiment!*' she added to Kitty's disbelieving look. 'You can banish her to the Dower House, and she knows it.'

'Oh, I never could,' Kitty faltered.

'Well, she knows that, too,' Grandmère said frankly, 'but the day will come . . . When I lived here, when Willie was a child, there was a bull at the home farm, called Duke, which had been raised from a calf and was as tame at a kitten. Willie used to go and feed it and pet it and it let him climb all over it, and would lick his face like a dog. Then one day when he was going to climb into its pen, a certain look came into its eye, and it scraped the ground with its foot, and the farmer stopped him. He said, "Duke has just worked out that he's the bull, and you're the boy. You can't play with him any more." And one day, *chère* Kitty, you will discover you are the countess and a certain look will come into your eye. Then playtime will be over. This also Maud knows.'

They strolled on in silence for a while, until Grandmère said, 'How pleasant England is in May. One forgets . . . You are very quiet, Kitty.'

'I think,' Kitty said, 'that I don't feel very well.'

Uncle Sebastian gave Giles a robust slap on the back that made him stagger. 'A boy! Congratulations! A boy first time out!'

Giles steadied himself and addressed the doctor. 'My wife – her ladyship? How is she?'

'Very well, my lord. There were no difficulties. Her ladyship came through with colours flying.'

Dr Arbogast faced Giles with a smile that contained a touch of relief. Ashmore Castle was new territory to him. He had a good relationship with most of the local gentry families, but the dowager countess had never used him. She would summon the lowlier Dr Welkes for the servants or the children, but she and his late lordship were never ill; and if they wished to consult a physician for any reason, it would be a grand one from London. To attend the birth of the heir to the earldom was an honour Arbogast knew he would enjoy more in retrospect, from a safe distance: the things that could have gone wrong – could still go wrong – put him in a cold sweat. His wife had said goodbye that morning with the sort of brave smile women reserve for soldiers going off to war who they fear might never return.

He had at least been spared the terrifying presence of the dowager. She had decided for herself that the baby would not come for several more days, and had taken Rachel over to Asham Bois to spend the day with the Massingberds, who had a house party. Kitty had taken everyone by surprise: the birth had begun unexpectedly and had been all over remarkably quickly.

'I told Kitty she would manage beautifully,' said Grandmère. 'She is young and healthy.'

'Can I see her?' Giles asked the doctor.

'Very soon, my lord. I shall return upstairs and make sure all is well, and let you know as soon as she is ready for visitors. Ah – your lordship's son!'

Alice came in with a bundle of white wool in her arms, and one of the maids – Doris – hovering behind with an air of thwarted professionalism. Alice proffered the bundle to Giles, saying, 'He's very sweet, but piglets are prettier, I think.'

'At this stage perhaps,' said Grandmère, 'but that will soon change.'

'We had better hope so,' said Richard, 'or he'll have trouble finding a wife in twenty years' time.'

Giles took the bundle nervously, pushing away the inquisitive attentions of the dogs with his knee. It seemed ridiculously small and light. Swathed in the folds of the shawl there appeared a tiny face, round, red, creased, with eyes screwed shut as if determined not to be woken. *Your lordship's son.* Giles had always known it was his duty one day to have an heir and secure the title, but his relationship with his own father had been cold and distant, even hostile. He had not known how he would feel at this moment, but he was not prepared for such a tremor in the gut, such a loosening in the loins. He looked up, shocked, and met Sebastian's eyes.

And Sebastian smiled understandingly and said, 'I've never

had one of my own, but even I feel something for very new babies. Don't worry, my dear boy, you won't break him.'

'But . . .' Giles began, not knowing how to put into words the feeling of terrible vulnerability that was weakening his knees. He was responsible for this boy. Suppose he made a mess of it? Suppose in thirty years' time this child felt as little for him as he had felt for his father?

Grandmère seemed to read his mind. 'The past is no template for the future.'

Richard slapped him on the shoulder. 'That I should see this day! Steady, unimaginative old Giles thrown all-of-a-heap by a little baby.'

'Let me take him, my lord,' Doris said, brought up on the principle that fathers could not notice their offspring for more than a few seconds at a time. 'I should get him back to the nurse.'

But Sebastian said, 'Let me have him for a moment.'

Doris handed him over reluctantly, but Sebastian had held a lot of babies in his time, and handled this one with confidence. He looked down at the small face, and touched a forefinger to the perfect velvet cheek. 'Lord Ayton,' he murmured. 'Such a big world waits for you out there. God bless you, child.' And the screwed-up eyes prised themselves open just a crack, just for an instant, as if in acknowledgement.

Doctor, maid and baby departed, and Giles said, 'I wish I had your touch.'

Sebastian said, 'It's the same as with horses. They know if you're nervous. Pretend a confidence whether you feel it or not. Now then, there are practicalities to address. A telegram to your mother first of all, I think.'

'Right,' Richard agreed. 'Mama will be furious enough that Pusscat dared to do it without her supervision. She mustn't wait until she gets back to hear of it.'

'I shall deal with Maud when she arrives,' Grandmère said firmly. 'She shall not upset Kitty.'

'I'll go up and sit with her now,' Alice said, hastening after Doris. And the baby. Her nephew! It really was rather sweet.

Sebastian continued. 'The parson should be sent for – there's a christening to think about. And the servants should be told – they'll know already, of course, but a formal announcement is always appreciated.' He thought of Dory, who had laundered the ancient christening gown and yesterday had been repairing the delicate silk and lace. 'And it's traditional to ring the house bell when an heir is born.'

The birth of a future earl was a public event. Giles gave a small, tight quirk of lips. 'I'm glad you're here to advise me,' he said.

Giles went upstairs a little nervously, having never seen a woman who had just given birth. Childbirth was such a closely guarded female secret, with its hints of almost religious ritual, suffering, blood and blame, that he feared he would have to witness some terrible aftermath and be racked with guilt.

But Kitty was sitting up in bed in a pretty, ribboned bed-jacket, with colour in her cheeks, looking more or less normal, and only as tired as she might be after a day's hunting.

He crept up to the bed, wondering if some devastating damage was being concealed from him. 'How are you?' he whispered.

'Oh, Giles, have you seen him?' Kitty cried. 'Is he all right?'

'He's perfect,' Giles said, and then, driven by honesty, 'As far as I can tell. I don't know much about babies. But Uncle Sebastian knows all about them, and he seems to think he's fine.' He took her hand, which to his relief was not cold and clammy with encroaching disaster, but dry and warm as usual. 'You are clever, having a boy straight off.'

'Is he beautiful?' Kitty asked.

'I think so. Don't you?' Giles noticed at last the tenor of her questions. 'Haven't you seen him?' She shook her head. 'Not at all?'

'The nurse won't let me. She took him away and won't bring him back. She says I have to rest. But I don't want to rest. I want to see my baby.'

Something practical for a man to do! Giles stood up, looking stern. 'We'll see about that. Don't fret, Kitty, you shall have him.'

Nurse Belton was tall and bony, like a horse. Giles had vaguely thought midwives would be round and cushiony and was taken aback. And though he was not a great one for formality, he was also surprised by the undeferential way she looked him straight in the eye and called him 'Lord Stainton', not 'my lord' or 'your lordship'.

'Baby has been taken to the nursery, as is customary,' she said. 'The mother needs to rest.'

'She wants to have him with her,' said Giles. 'As any mother would.'

Nurse Belton raised an eyebrow. 'I hardly think, Lord Stainton, that you are in a position to know what is best for mother and child. New fathers are always needlessly anxious. Baby is being looked after. It is not healthy for mothers to brood over their infants. It is not done,' she gave it as the clinching argument, 'in the best houses.'

'Confound the best houses!' Giles retorted. 'My wife wants to hold her baby. It's inhumane to separate them.'

She was maddeningly unmoved. 'My last confinement was Lady Stavesacre of Holm Abbey, and she did not even see Baby until three days after the birth. A very superior family, the Stavesacres. Everything done in the best style. The nursery at Holm Abbey is extremely well-appointed.'

He drew himself up, and managed, just, to overtop her. 'Nevertheless,' he said, 'if Lady Stainton wants to have the baby with her, she shall. Where is he now? I will carry him there myself.'

The gimlet eyes bored a moment longer, and then, with

no change of expression, Nurse Belton said, 'There is no need of that. I shall bring Baby, if that is your wish, Lord Stainton.'

'At once, if you please.'

She inclined her head stiffly and walked away.

Nothing in a great house goes unremarked. Nurse Belton had only been in situ a few hours and had already made herself unpopular below stairs: her criticisms of the nursery's appointments and the general standards of cleanliness had been faithfully reported. Rose, the head housemaid, brought the news of her besting gleefully to Mrs Webster, who felt a little balm to her soul.

'So now her ladyship's to have him with her whenever she likes,' Rose concluded.

'All the same, she's not wrong, that nurse,' said Miss Hatto, who had been with Mrs Webster when Rose came panting in with the story. 'In high-up houses they do keep the babies in the nursery, and the mothers aren't supposed to take much notice of them.'

'I don't think his lordship sets a lot of store by what other high-ups do,' said Mrs Webster.

'You're right,' said Rose. 'All that time he spent out in Egypt, mixing with dear-knows-who . . . Her ladyship will have something to say about it when she comes back.'

Miss Hatto said, 'It's not her that matters, it's my lady.'

'That's what you think,' said Rose.

'All the same,' said Miss Hatto, with something of a volte-face, 'it's the prettiest thing you ever saw, to see her with that baby.'

'What are they going to call it?' Rose wondered.

'Nothing's been said yet,' said Miss Hatto. 'Not when I've been listening. I'll let you know as soon as I hear. And now I must take up my lady's warm milk.' She got up to leave.

'Good job she likes it,' Rose called after her. 'That's a drink

I never could abide. Cold is all right, but warm milk tastes of cows.' Mrs Webster stared at her for a moment, and Rose shrugged. 'Well, I know what I mean.'

Moss noted the set of the dowager's lips as she re-entered the house from the carriage, and felt Rose had been closer to the mark than Mrs Webster. *Trouble brewing,* was his thought – a slightly muzzy thought, since one of the bottles of the '95 he had opened for dinner last night had proved to be past its best and not good enough to be sent upstairs, so he had been finishing it off in honour of the new heir. A sin to waste it. And useless to send it to the kitchen for cooking wine, as happened in some houses, since Mrs Oxlea wasn't that sort of cook.

'Wonderful news, my lady,' he said hopefully. 'The staff would wish me to extend their respectful congratulations . . .' The two long words nearly floored him.

Maud walked past him without response and headed for the stairs. She was not sure what she felt yet about the whole situation. It was typical, of course, that Kitty should have the baby while she was absent. It would have been much more proper of her to wait until the child's grandmother was present. But could you hope for better from a girl like that? She would do anything gain attention.

It was good, of course, that she had had a boy. Maud was glad that the succession was assured – or, at least, she would be when she had inspected the child and seen how likely it was to survive. And so many things could happen between birth and maturity that it was imperative there should be a second son as soon as possible. She hoped Kitty knew that. She must speak sharply to Giles about his duty – he was so vague and woolly in that area, there was no knowing if he had taken the realisation on board.

But, glad though she was about the birth of an heir, she couldn't help knowing that it was one more thing pushing her off her throne. Giles's wife was just that – nothing more than his wife – until she had consolidated her position with a child. Now Maud feared the power and prestige of the position would begin relentlessly to drift towards the younger woman, leaving her with nothing to look forward to but old age.

She was so deep in her resentful thoughts she almost bumped into her mother-in-law, who was coming along the passage in the other direction.

'I thought I heard you arrive,' Grandmère said. Maud tried to walk past, but the old lady blocked her passage. 'Now, Maud,' she said, with her most annoying smile, 'I hope you are not going to cause trouble?'

Maud raised her eyebrows. 'What on earth are you talking about?'

'Let the child enjoy her baby. Let the young parents have the joy of it.'

'Sentimental rubbish!' Maud exclaimed.

'Ah, yes, I know how you English are. You love your dogs, but your children— *pfui*! *Ils sont considérés comme un atout agricole.*'

'Please don't speak nonsense,' Maud snapped. 'I won't be lectured on your foolish French notions of "love".' And she walked past.

Grandmère smiled to herself and called after her teasingly. 'Little boys sent away to school to learn not to cry. Girls shut up at the top of the house until they can be married. *Tiens, la froideur des anglais est bien connue!*'

Nurse Belton hadn't known how to deal with the old lady. When she had tried to express outrage at the idea of the countess feeding the baby at her breast, the flood of rapid French, the bright fierce eyes and the fluttering fingers had driven her back like a flock of birds flying into her face. She felt relieved when she heard the dowager had arrived, knowing

107

a little of her reputation, but she missed her mark there, too. Her murmurings about 'the best houses', 'not done' and 'dear Lady Stavesacre' slid off like water from a duck's back. Maud had been born a Forrest, and so high above everyone else in the land, she could barely have seen Lady Stavesacre through a telescope. Snobbery did not apply to her. She was the yardstick by which everything was measured.

'I will see the baby,' she said, cutting through Nurse Belton's narrative as if she hadn't heard it – which she hadn't. She took up the child, handling it firmly as one accustomed, and assured herself that it looked healthy and whole, had all its limbs and digits, and a reasonable chance of beauty once the crushed redness of birth passed off. It tried to open its eyes, and its starfish fingers tried to close over one of hers as she inspected it, and she did feel a tug of something frighteningly visceral at that moment, but she resisted it. 'Satisfactory,' she said sharply, pushing the bundle back at the nurse.

Nurse Belton couldn't help being impressed by her ladyship's grandeur. Here was real power, she sensed. 'He is a fine baby in every respect,' she gushed. 'Would your ladyship like to see the mother?' *She'd* make the girl see sense, Nurse Belton thought. Lady Stainton was one of the old school. She much mistook if even Lord Stainton ever defied her.

But Maud turned away without answering. She had seen the baby. She didn't want to see the mother. Kitty would need rest and quiet, she explained to herself. But the fact was that she didn't want to see that – that *suburban miss* in her moment of triumph. She would rather think of the heir in isolation, as if he had been dropped into the nursery by a beneficent angel.

Giles entered Kitty's bedroom to find her sitting up in bed with the baby in her arms. 'Was that Dr Arbogast I saw leaving?' he asked. 'Is everything all right?'

'I was worried about the baby's rash,' Kitty said, not looking up from the adored face. 'Nanny said it was only a milk rash, but I wanted to be sure.'

Nurse Belton's three-day reign of terror was over. Nanny Pawley and nursery-maid Jessie had been installed and now had care of the baby, while Miss Hatto had said she could take care of my lady's needs. Being only eighteen, Kitty had bounced back so quickly she'd have been up and about if the general female consensus hadn't been appalled by the idea. Even Rose, who had never had a baby, popped in to warn her that her insides would slip if she got up too early.

Her mother-in-law had returned, but so far she had been blessedly free of visits from her. Instead, a message of congratulation had been sent via Miss Taylor, delivered to Miss Hatto and thence to Kitty. It would have been possible, Kitty thought, to find an insult in there somewhere, but since she didn't *want* to see the dowager she preferred to think it quite normal behaviour. Nanny Pawley – who was round and comfortable – had said she mustn't be upset or it would affect her milk.

'And what did the doctor say?' Giles was asking.

Now Kitty looked up. 'That it was just a milk rash,' she admitted.

Giles perched on the edge of the bed. 'He seems pretty strong to me, and everyone who knows says he's very healthy.' Kitty hesitated, clearly on the verge of a confidence. 'What's wrong? Tell me.'

'Nothing's wrong,' Kitty said. And then it came out in a rush. 'I had a brother once,' she said. 'I never told you. But he died, when he was only four. He was strong and healthy before that.' She paused, then added in a low voice, 'I loved him so much.'

Giles pressed her hand. There was nothing he could say to reassure her. People died, children died, babies died, and there was nothing you could do about it. But you couldn't live your life in fear. You could only proceed on the assumption that people would live. Yes, but though he felt a powerful and terrible connection to this scrap of flesh, he was not a mother, and he couldn't know what *that* felt like. 'I'm sorry,' he said.

Kitty thought how impossible it was to explain exactly what she felt. Yes, she had loved her brother, had mourned him dreadfully when he died. She had thought before the birth that she would feel the same about her own baby, but something had changed in her when she had begun to feed him at her breast. Now there was a love that was like a strong plant rooted deep in her stomach, so tough that if anything tried to pull it out, it would rip the insides out of her. Loving her brother had, in comparison, been like loving a pet dog. And with this love came a fierce determination to protect her baby at all costs from anything that might harm him. The determination gave her courage. There was a steel deep inside her, that had only emerged once before – in the early days of their marriage, when she had felt herself slighted for another woman. She thought of that almost wonderingly – that something so trivial could have moved her so much. Her baby was of a completely different order of importance. Her brother was a faded flower by comparison – even Giles seemed just then almost irrelevant.

Giles took the baby from her, and she let him go reluctantly, her arms greedy to have him back.

'What was his name – your brother?'

'Peter,' she said.

Giles settled the baby in the crook of his arm, getting more used to holding him now. 'Would you like to call our son Peter?' he asked. He didn't like it much as a name, and it was not a family name, and he was sure his mother would not approve, but he wanted to please her.

'No,' she said. 'But thank you.'

Giles hid his relief. His mother had been suggesting names at the dinner table for the past three days – making up for her absence at the crucial moment, he thought, by taking charge of everything else she could. Better to choose a name privately with Kitty and present Mama with a *fait accompli* and no room for argument.

'We ought to decide on something,' he said

'Whatever you think best,' Kitty said. For now, her baby was such an absolute to her, it seemed almost silly to think he needed a name. She and he lived inside a tight bubble that was the whole universe. But there were people outside who needed references.

'What do you think about Louis?' Giles said. 'It was one of my father's names – Grandmère's father was a Louis. I don't really see him as a William, and William, Henry and George are the family names.'

'How did you get to be Giles?' Kitty asked.

'My father chose it – to annoy my mother, I think. But my second name's William.'

'Yes, I remember hearing it at our wedding. Giles William Henry Tallant,' Kitty said. She remembered, wonderingly, the wedding and the days immediately afterwards, when she had learned about love. She had loved him so passionately. It all seemed so far away now.

'Yes,' he said. 'I never liked any of my names. Perhaps people never do.'

'I haven't thought about it. I've always been Catherine, so it's hard to imagine anything else.'

So their conversations always went, he thought. A philosophical idea set free by him, and nailed down to the here-and-now by her. If only . . . But he must not think disloyal thoughts, especially now.

Kitty was watching him, aware, as always, of so much going on inside his head that she would never be party to. And now she was the same, a universe of thought he could not access. 'I like the sound of Louis,' she said.

'Then it shall be Louis,' said Giles. 'And what do you say to Sebastian? Uncle Sebastian would be so tickled.'

'Oh yes. I love Uncle Sebastian,' said Kitty. She added, 'Actually, I quite like Henry.'

'Henry's not too bad,' Giles agreed. 'Well, then shall it be Louis Sebastian Henry Peter?' He looked down at the absurdly small face. 'He's rather small for such a large name,' he said.

'Let me have him,' Kitty demanded. Giles handed him back. 'Thank you,' she said profoundly.

He didn't know whether the thanks were for the return of the baby, or the 'Peter' in his name.

# CHAPTER SEVEN

Rose was just beginning her walk back from the village to the Castle when a small boy dashed up to her crying, 'Miss Rose! Miss Rose!'

She turned, and recognised little Billy Dawkins, son of one of the waiters at the Crown. He was generally to be found hanging around the inn or the high street, looking for jobs to do for pennies. 'You should be at school, Billy Dawkins,' she said. 'How will you learn your letters else?'

Billy, who could not see how letters would make him better at holding horses or carrying messages, shrugged it off. 'Ma made me take our stuff down the bag wash. And then Mr Persons saw me come out and wanted a message run.' The Ideal Laundry was next door to the station. 'So I done that and took the answer back from Mr Gilbert what's in bed with a belly-ache. And then—'

'Never mind,' Rose said, sorry she'd started it. 'What were you calling me for?'

'I was getting to that,' Billy said, wounded. 'Then I went to see if Pa wanted anything, and I got to clean knives in the Crown kitchen for a bit, then I went back for the bag wash an' took it home, and on the way Miss Eddowes called me over and said if I was to see you, to tell you she wanted to speak to you right away, urgent. Cos she knew it was your afternoon off and you'd likely be in the village. And I'd seen you go into Poining's before, so I took the bag to Ma, then

I runs back to Poining's and they said you'd gone home and I runs out and I sees you just going for to climb over the stile. And that's what I been doing.'

He stopped, breathless. Rose filtered out the important section. 'Miss Eddowes wants to see me?'

'Urgent,' he said, nodding importantly, and his grubby palm crept out an inch in a manner both hopeful and suggestive.

'Miss Eddowes gave you something for bringing the message, didn't she?' Rose said sternly. She knew how things were done.

'A ha'penny,' he said brazenly. 'And she said you'd give me the other.'

Rose was as sure as she could be that Miss Eddowes had given him the whole penny. But she reflected how much a ha'penny meant to the likes of Billy Dawkins and how much less to her, and felt for her purse. Annoyingly she didn't have a ha'penny, only pennies, and one lurking farthing. She couldn't quite bring herself to palm him off with the farthing, and had to part with a whole penny, in bad grace and feeling she'd been had.

But when Billy Dawkins looked at it, his face brightened and he said, 'Gosh, thanks, miss,' with such pleasure that it softened the blow for her. *Philanthropy*, she thought. *Maybe that's why Miss Eddowes does it.*

She walked down past the church to Weldon House, where any pleasure she had been feeling dissolved before the news Miss Eddowes had to give her.

The cook's room was at the far end of the passage that ran right through the lower floor, which the servants sometimes called Piccadilly. All the domestic offices lay on Piccadilly, or down short spur passages leading off it. It was a world of its own, a place of echoing footsteps, clashing sounds, voices, smells. Most of the servants left it at various times to carry out their duties in the house above, and they went right up to the roof at nights to their bedrooms. But the cook and the kitchen staff had their workplace on Piccadilly, and Mrs Oxlea had her bedroom there as well, which Rose sometimes thought was unhealthy: she never got away.

The room was not particularly lovely either, being a stone-walled, stone-floored cell, with one window high up – and even that window had bars. There was space for a narrow iron bedstead, a chest of drawers, and a wooden chair, and a corner was curtained off for clothes. But at least, Rose thought, trying to find the good, Mrs Oxlea had it to herself. And the door had a bolt on the inside. The maids in the attic all shared, and there was no privacy for them.

Mrs Oxlea was not in the kitchen when Rose returned, so she went and knocked on the door of her room. 'Are you there, Deena? It's me, Rose.' There was a shuffling, the bolt was drawn, and the door opened a crack. 'I'm alone,' Rose said. 'Are you sober? I got to talk to you. It's important.'

Mrs Oxlea sighed, and yielded the door.

Rose slipped in and shut it behind her. 'You ought to go outside sometimes,' she said. 'Get some fresh air. It's not healthy staying in all the time.'

The cook shuffled backwards and sat on the bed. She had been writing in a book, Rose saw, but shut it firmly as if Rose might be able to read it across the room – though her one glance had shown writing so tiny and crabbed she probably couldn't have read it close up with a magnifying glass. Her diary, Rose guessed.

Rose moved the chair across to face her and sat down.

'Don't stare at me like that,' Mrs Oxlea said irritably. 'I'm as sober as what you are. Anyway, I'd like to see you working all hours in that kitchen in the heat and not take a drink of ale now and then to cool you down.'

'It's not just the beer, though, is it?' Rose said. 'You got a black bottle under the mattress, there? Wouldn't be the first time.'

Mrs Oxlea didn't answer. Rose had always been irritated by the cook, though mostly she felt sorry for her, because it was none of it Mrs Oxlea's fault, when you thought about it. Rose had had her own little brushes with his lordship over the years, and she knew how insistent he could be. Still, there was no room in a person's life for self-pity, and Mrs Oxlea was her own worst enemy. Her drinking was a problem for everyone – and when she was in the bag, she was loose in the tongue. Rose had often told her she'd end up in Bedlam if she wasn't careful. There was an insane asylum out at Asham Bois, and they said once in, you never came out. You had to hope her ladyship wouldn't think of that one – it would solve all her problems, because nobody listened to the ravings of a certified loony, did they?

But what she had to tell Mrs Oxlea now changed things. She wasn't sure exactly how the future would be different, but there was no doubt it would be. And it was she who had to deal the blow. Miss Eddowes had said she'd do it if necessary, but she thought it would come better from Rose, and be more discreet, and that was true, but it didn't make it easier.

Well, no sense in dilly-dallying. 'I've got some news for you, Dee,' she said. 'I've heard something.'

Mrs Oxlea sniffed. 'Not surprising in this house. Never knew such a lot of servants for tattling. What is it this time?'

'It's not gossip. I had it from Miss Eddowes in the village this afternoon.'

Mrs Oxlea drew in a sharp breath, and looked at Rose with an appalling mixture of hope and apprehension. It was the hope that upset Rose most. 'About – him?'

'It's not good news,' Rose added quickly. 'I'm sorry, Deena. I wish it was anything but this. I wish it wasn't me having to tell you—'

'No,' said Mrs Oxlea in a flat voice. 'No.'

'It was diphtheria. There was an outbreak in the village.

116

Lot of kids got it. There was nothing anyone could have done. He died, Deena. He's dead. I'm sorry.'

'No,' said Mrs Oxlea again. But the truth was in her eyes, the truth that she had always known she would never see him again. Yet the heart lives on hope, its constant food and strongest drink. Rose understood, and her pity hurt her. You consume that hope, no matter how much you know it's false, no matter how much more it will make things hurt in the long run. Because without it, what is there?

'When?' Mrs Oxlea asked, in a dead voice.

'A week ago.'

'A week?' It was a cry of pain.

'Miss Eddowes only heard yesterday. She thought about sending you a note straight away, but she thought it was better told than written. She sends you her – her deepest condolences.' Rose stumbled slightly on the remembered words.

There was a long silence. Mrs Oxlea's head was down, so Rose couldn't see her face. Her shoulders were hunched, her hands, clasped in her lap, twisted together.

'I'm sorry, Dee,' Rose said again. 'I know you must be upset. But it's over now. You can make a new start for yourself. Maybe you should get away from this place—'

'I got a photo, did you know that?' Mrs Oxlea said, as if Rose hadn't spoken. 'Miss Eddowes, she always told the people that took the babies, one photo when it's five. She made it a rule. One photo, then that's it, you won't get bothered any more.' She picked up the book in which she had been writing, and drew out from inside the cover the photograph, which she offered to Rose.

A small boy, seated in a very large photographer's chair, velvet-upholstered like a throne, with potted palms behind him and a glimpse of a backcloth of parkland and trees. A small boy in nankeen knickers, short jacket and long stockings, his small boots dangling above the floor. His solemn face

117

stared expressionlessly at the camera – he had been told he mustn't move. The hair was straight and very dark, the round, fixed eyes seemed light – blue, probably. He did look – well, Rose was looking for the likeness – but he did look a bit like his late lordship. Poor little chap! Well, it was all over now. Lives blighted and a life lost, and the only one who hadn't paid was the one to blame for it all.

Rose sighed and handed back the photograph. 'Burn it, that's my advice to you. No sense in brooding over the past any more. Get rid of it, and start afresh.'

'You don't understand,' Mrs Oxlea said in a low, desperate voice.

'No, I don't,' Rose said. 'You had rotten luck, I don't deny it, but if it was me, I wouldn't've let it rule my whole life. I'd've made an effort. And I wouldn't have hid inside a bottle, that's for sure.'

'I loved him,' Mrs Oxlea said. It wasn't the child she was referring to.

'Well, he didn't love you,' Rose said briskly. 'And now it's finally over.'

'It'll never be over for me,' Mrs Oxlea said. 'Go away, please, Rose.' She said it not angrily, which Rose could have lived with, but with a complete lack of emphasis, which worried her.

She got up. 'I've things to do,' she said. 'And shouldn't you be in the kitchen by now? Time's getting on. Pull your-self together, Deena – and if you *have* got a bottle under the mattress, don't even think about getting it out now. No need to make bad worse.'

Mrs Oxlea gave her no response at all, and Rose left her, sitting on her bed, staring at the photograph.

Her ladyship, she learned, had gone riding. She had insisted on having her horse brought up from grass the day before, and Giddins, the head man, with whom alone she dealt, had naturally not made any objections, as Josh had to Alice. What her ladyship wanted, her ladyship had.

For riding, the dowager Lady Stainton dressed anonymously in a plain black habit and a small tricorn with a veil, which from a distance nicely disguised her. But, Rose thought, watching her approach at a canter up the hill, with Giddins following a length behind her, everybody in the area must know Queen Bee. Though she was bay, and bays were pretty common, she had that distinctive white ring round her coronet. And, besides, she was a fine-paced beauty, much coveted by local lady riders. Rose, however, just recognised her, as one recognises any person one knows well.

When she was sure her ladyship had seen her, Rose stepped back into the edge of the trees, and Lady Stainton pulled down to a walk, rode a little past, and halted. There was a brief exchange with Giddins, then he rode on, and her ladyship came back to where Rose was standing. Bee blew out percussively through her nostrils, arched her neck and pawed at the ground a moment in frustration at being stopped. Her ladyship's gloved hand checked her easily. The voice came from behind the veil with icy brevity.

'What do you want?'

Rose took a step closer. She had never ridden herself, but she wasn't afraid of horses. Bee eyed her, then decided she was good for an itchy nose, and tried to rub her muzzle up and down Rose's shoulder. Rose pushed her away with one hand. 'There's news. From Miss Eddowes,' she said to the veil.

Maud drew a breath of annoyance at the very sound of that name, but a listening silence ensued as she contemplated what news the woman would send to her. It could only be one thing – couldn't it?

'What news?' she asked at length.

'The child's dead,' Rose said. There was no response from behind the veil. 'Diphtheria,' she added, for the avoidance of doubt.

She thought Lady Stainton whispered, 'Thank God,' but the wind was stirring the trees and it was hard to tell. She waited.

'Very well,' was all her ladyship said at length. 'You may go.'

Rose stirred. 'You think it's all over,' she said, 'but what do you think will happen now? You had a hold over Mrs Oxlea, but now she's got nothing to lose.'

The veiled head came round sharply. 'You told her?'

'Miss Eddowes asked me to. She had the right to know.'

'She has no rights at all, except the right to be silent,' said her ladyship savagely. 'And the same goes for you.'

'I don't know why you even care. I don't see how it matters now he's dead. If you ask me, the more you make a thing of it—'

'I didn't ask you. You are impertinent.'

Rose shrugged. 'I've always been loyal.'

'And I pay you well for it.'

'It's not something money can buy. Taylor and me, we stick by you because we stick by you. That's all.'

'You would be nothing without me, either of you. You'd do well to remember that.'

Bee snorted as her head was sharply wrenched round, and a boot heel in her side sent her from a standstill into a canter.

Rose watched horse and rider diminish into the distance. 'Never mind a thank-you,' she called after her – not that she would have heard. 'I can manage without.' *But I'd sooner,* she thought, as she trudged back towards the house, *be me right now than her.*

Her ladyship sat before the dressing-table glass as Miss Taylor did her hair. 'You'll have to send her away,' Miss Taylor said quietly. The dowager didn't respond. 'There's already talk in the neighbourhood about why you keep her on. If she was any good, it'd be another matter, but now there's a new master and mistress—'

'There is no new mistress.'

'So you say – but how long will that last?'

'You talk too much,' the dowager said viciously.

Miss Taylor waited a moment, and went on, 'Pay her off, that's my advice. Pay her a good bit to go a long way away. Scotland, maybe.' She went with her ladyship to Kincraig, Lord Leake's Scottish place, most years, and the food there – well, she didn't think Mrs Oxlea could ruin that. 'Couldn't his lordship find a place for her up there?'

'My brother knows nothing about this.'

Miss Taylor pushed in another pin. 'You should never have got yourself into it in the first place. You should have turned her out straight away. No one would be interested in a kitchen maid that got herself pregnant.'

Now their eyes did meet in the glass. Miss Taylor tried to read her mistress's expression. What was it they called it in the sensational papers? Baffled rage, that was it.

'For God's sake,' her ladyship said between clenched teeth, *'do you think it was my idea?'*

'Oh,' said Miss Taylor. And then, more humbly than she had ever said anything to her mistress, 'I'm sorry. I didn't know.'

*'He* insisted. And then – I was always afraid that she would talk. I couldn't bear—' She stopped.

*The humiliation* were the words she didn't say. A kitchen maid! Mrs Oxlea had been pretty in those days, in the common way servants sometimes were. He had told her he would leave her if she didn't keep the girl. Would he have? It had been a bad time; there had been things going on in his life that she didn't know about, and he had taken it out on her, enjoying tormenting her, and the more she fought him, the harder he fought back. It was like living in a volcano of conflict and misery. But better that than the shame and public disgrace of separation and perhaps – unthinkably – divorce. To have her husband publicly choose a kitchen-maid

121

over her – to be laughed at, sneered at – to be *pitied* . . .
That was the worst of all. So she had given in. The child . . .
She had had two miscarriages between Richard and Rachel.
She was worn out. He had made a fuss of the child, as if to
point up her failures. She had made one last stipulation, and
he had agreed.

The Eddowes woman was known for general philanthropy, but in a discreet circle known better for helping
girls who found themselves in trouble. She had them looked
after until they gave birth, found a home for the child
afterwards and a job for the girl. She had a network of
friends and colleagues who placed fallen women with
'liberal' employers, who didn't mind a shady past in their
servants. But once the baby had gone, Stainton had insisted
on her keeping Mrs Oxlea at the Castle. The child would
go – but the mistress she must keep, to teach her her place.
To teach *her*, Maud Stainton, a Forrest by birth, humility
and obedience.

Rose and Miss Taylor stood close together at the end of a
corridor. 'What's she going to do?' Rose asked in an urgent
undertone.

'She hasn't said. I advised her to send her away somewhere,
as soon as possible.'

'Poor Deena,' Rose sighed, but not dissenting.

'I wonder – was it right to tell her? Her ladyship, I mean,'
Miss Taylor said, suddenly doubtful. 'Let sleeping dogs—'

'Miss Eddowes was going to tell her. She said she had the
right to know. And I suppose she did. She was going to give
me a note to bring to her, but I said I'd tell her myself, and
she agreed it was better not to have anything written down,
in case.'

Miss Taylor looked scornful. 'As if she'd show a letter like
that to anyone – after all these years! Or leave it anywhere
to be found. She'd have burned it straight off.'

Rose shrugged. 'Oh well, it's done now. And I'm glad it's over. I was sick of being a go-between. And Oxlea – she'll have to get a grip on herself now, won't she?' Miss Taylor looked doubtful. 'She's *got* to get rid of her, hasn't she? Now she can.'

'God, I hope so,' said Miss Taylor. She hesitated on the brink of a revelation. She had always been intensely loyal to her mistress, though disliking her in many ways. 'I've never known her uncertain on any subject except this one. I don't like to see it.'

James Hook stepped out from the shadows and accosted Rose on her way downstairs. 'What's going on?'

'I don't know what you're talking about,' Rose said automatically. 'Get out of my way.'

Hook continued to block her path. 'I seen you talking to Miss Taylor, heads together, telling secrets. You and her, chalk and cheese, you never could be best pals, so don't tell me something's not going on.'

Rose gave him a withering look. 'Women's talk. Not for little boys to know.'

'Don't believe it.'

'Don't care what you believe. And since when did I tell *you* my secrets, even if I had any, which I don't? Now move yourself, James, I'm late.'

'I'll find out. Trust me for that. And it's not James any more. I'm his lordship's valet, and don't you forget it. You're just a housemaid.'

'Ooh, pardon me for living, *Mister* Hook. Go on then, let me past and I'll tell you my secret.'

He looked uncertain, then pleased, then uncertain again. He stood back. 'What is it, then?'

She lowered her voice. 'We're both in love with you, Taylor and me. We was arguing over who's to get you.'

For a brief moment, she had her reward in his peacocky

look of pleasure, before it was replaced with a scowl. 'Think yourself so clever, don't you?' he shouted after her, as she clattered on down the stairs. 'But I'll find out!'

It was not long before they all found out. As Rose passed Mrs Webster's room, she saw Ida, the head kitchen-maid in there, looking anxious.

'Rose – a minute,' Mrs Webster called.

*Oh, Lord, Mrs Oxlea's drunk again*, Rose thought, stopping. *I warned her not to go to that bottle*. 'Yes, Mrs Webster?'

'You talked to Mrs Oxlea earlier, didn't you?'

'I don't think so,' Rose hedged.

'Brigid saw you coming away from her room,' Ida said. 'She was in the still-room for some soap when you come past.'

'Oh – yes, I might have had a word,' Rose said vaguely. 'What's wrong?'

'She's not come to start work, and it's well past time,' said Ida.

'Well, start without her,' Rose said impatiently. 'You've done it often enough before.'

'I was, we have, I put the girls on the vegetables, but I want to get Lady Stainton's posset started' – Kitty was still having invalid meals in her room – 'but the lemons are in the larder and Mrs Oxlea's took the key with her.'

'Why don't you ask her for it?' Rose said.

'I did. I knocked at her door and called out, but she didn't answer,' Ida said. 'I knocked for ages in case she was asleep, but nothing. I don't know if she's gone out somewhere.'

'Was she all right when you spoke to her?' Mrs Webster asked.

'Well, you know her,' Rose said.

'Was she drunk?' Webster asked bluntly.

'No,' Rose said, glad to be able to tell the truth. 'Maybe she went out for a walk.'

124

'She doesn't like walking,' Ida said. 'She doesn't like going out. She never goes further than the yard. I looked for her out there, and all round here. She must be in her room.'

'Did you *look*?'

Ida was shocked. 'I'd never go in her room, not without she asked me. You don't.' In a house with so little privacy, someone's own room was sacrosanct.

'You know her best, Rose,' said Webster. 'See if you can get her to answer.'

All three went along Piccadilly to the door, gathering a small trail of other servants, keeping a discreet distance, but agog with interest. Anything to vary the monotony of life. Mrs Oxlea had been a source of entertainment on occasion in the past, when in her cups. She had once thrown a sauce boat at a footman who was hurrying her for the gravy for upstairs dinner; another time she had tripped over something and stabbed herself in the foot – the knife had gone through her shoe and missed her actual toes, but the point had stuck in the floorboards and it had been pretty exciting all the same.

Rose knocked and called out. 'Deena? It's Rose. Are you there?' Silence. 'You're late starting dinner. Are you all right?' More silence.

Rose looked at Mrs Webster and shrugged.

'Try the door,' the housekeeper said. When Rose hesitated, she added, 'She might be ill.'

Rose knocked again, and called, 'Deena, if you don't answer me, I warn you, I'm coming in.' Another silence. 'All right, I told you!' She grasped the door handle, turned, and pushed. 'It's bolted,' she reported to Mrs Webster. 'She must be in there.' She put her ear to the door and listened, but could hear nothing – no sobbing, anyway, thank God. 'Maybe she's asleep.' But even in drunken sleep, she'd always woken when the door was thumped enough.

Mrs Webster turned the gawping crowd to the right-about, seized William from among them, and ushered him, Rose, and a wooden chair outside. 'Not you, Ida. Go and get as much done as you can. The posset will have to wait. I'll help you with it later if I have to.'

'What are you afraid of?' Rose whispered to the housekeeper as they made their way through the chain of small yards outside that flanked the lower floor of the house.

Mrs Webster shot her a brief glance, white in the gloom. 'I've seen a drunk who drowned in their own vomit,' she replied. 'If she's not answering . . .'

Rose blenched, but said, 'She's never sick when she's drunk.'

Webster didn't say, *There's always a first time.* She didn't need to.

Because the house was on a hill, the lower floor was below ground at the back, but at ground level, under the terrace, at the front. Along the sides, the rooms had small windows at graduated height, all barred. Only Rose was sure which one was the cook's. William placed the chair and climbed up on it.

'Well?' Rose said impatiently.

'I can't see,' William mumbled. 'There's something in the way. She's hung up some clothes or something by the window.'

'Don't talk rubbish,' Rose said. 'Here, get down, let me see.'

William climbed down with bad grace. 'You won't see any more'n me,' he muttered, giving her a hand up.

Rose looked, then after a moment got down, her hand over her mouth.

'What is it?' Mrs Webster prompted. 'Did you see her?'

Rose shook her head, then nodded, then at last removed her hand. 'You'll have to break the door down,' she said in a curiously toneless voice.

William belatedly revised what he had seen. 'Oh, my good gawd,' he said, his voice high, like a child's.

The cook's room had once been a still-room, so the door was solid. The bolt was a good, strong one, and in the end, the

126

carpenter had to be sent for, to chisel out around the hinges until they could be unscrewed and the door removed that way. By then, there was no one in the house who didn't know what was happening. His lordship, rather grave and pale, came down and took charge of the operation. Uncle Sebastian took charge upstairs. Mrs Webster corralled the staff in the servants' dining room with bread and cheese to keep them occupied. Moss made the footmen take up cold meat, biscuits and wine for an upstairs scratch meal that no one much wanted, then retired to his own room to finish off the bottles he had decanted. Miss Taylor went to see to the dowager, who had retired to her room, and had her head bitten off. Miss Hatto went to sit with Kitty under Giles's orders, but did not obey his order to tell her nothing. She'd find out in the long run, and in the meantime it would only fret her to be kept in the dark, when something was clearly up.

By the time Gale, the carpenter, got the door off, Dr Welkes had arrived in his pony trap, but there was nothing he could do. William was beyond being helpful, and Cyril, the other footman, was too small, but Speen surprisingly pushed his way in and said calmly, 'Here, let me. I seen this before. All right, Mr Gale, I'll take her weight, you hop on that chair and cut the rope.'

Gale, who had been silent since the door came open, blinked at the chair and said, 'Beggin' your pardon, sir, but I'm a big man, and that chair don't look—'

'Never mind,' said Speen quickly. 'I'm light, I'll get up. You take a holt on the body – like this.'

Gale cringed so much that Rose wanted to slap him, but he did as he was told, and in a moment the body was down and laid on the bed. Rose took the place beside her, to see the decencies preserved. Dr Welkes leaned over with his stethoscope, but it was, of course, only for show, Rose thought. You couldn't be in any doubt, if you had caught a glimpse of that face . . .

'Will it go down?' she whispered to the doctor.

He glanced at her, surprised, then his face softened as he realised it was not prurient curiosity. *Touch her not scornfully, think of her mournfully, gently and humanly*, he thought. 'I'm afraid not,' he said quietly. 'It's fixed in death. Were you her friend?'

Rose couldn't accept any credit. 'She didn't have any friends,' she said. 'But she talked to me.'

'There will have to be an inquest,'Welkes said, straightening and looking at Giles. 'I'm sorry, my lord, but it's required in these cases. With the door being bolted from the inside, though, there won't be any doubt . . .'

'Quite,' said Giles. He looked for a moment at Rose, as if he wanted to ask her the one question: *why*? But he didn't. Instead, he said to the housekeeper. 'Did she have any family?'

'No, my lord, not that anyone knew about,' said Mrs Webster.

Giles thought a moment. 'Then we had better see to it ourselves.' He looked around. 'It's cold in this room. She can stay here until the morning. Then someone will have to be sent for, to lay her out. And the undertaker—'

'I'll have a message sent to Mr Folsham first thing, my lord,' Mrs Webster said. 'He'll bring a woman to do what's necessary.'

Giles glanced at Rose again, then said to Gale, 'Can you put the door back in place for now?'

Gales pulled himself together, though his voice was wobbly. 'I can fix the hinges again, my lord, temporary.'

'Do it. And,' to Mrs Webster, 'have someone stand guard on the door. We don't want everyone coming to stare.'

'I'll see to it, my lord.'

Rose was about to offer to sit by the bed, hold vigil over the departed, but at the last moment she kept silent. For all her pity for the departed, she did not want to stay in the

128

room with that face. And the body wasn't really Deena. She had gone somewhere, to be with her dead son, presumably. What was left was no more her than were her discarded clothes.

# CHAPTER EIGHT

'I don't care what you say,' said Daisy, 'it's a sin, and that's all about it.'

'A black, deadly sin,' said Wilfrid, the houseboy, bouncing excitedly in his chair.

'It's the same as murder, that's what my mum says,' Milly agreed. 'She says only God can take away a life, so it's like murdering yourself.'

'That is what the law calls it,' said Moss, who had the advantage of having looked it up in his *Book of Universal Knowledge*, knowing that little else would be talked about for days. 'Murder of the self. Only, of course, being the law, it's said in Latin. *Fellow de sea*, it's called.'

'Fellow of the sea? What, like a sailor?' Speen said contemptuously. 'Sure of that, are you, Mr Moss?'

Moss gave him a distracted look, but continued. 'In the old days, up until the Act of 1823, they couldn't be buried in Church ground at all. They had to be buried at night at a crossroads, and their goods and chattels were forfeit to the Crown.'

'She didn't have any goods and chattels,' said Rose.

She had made sure to be on hand very early in the morning when the undertaker, Mr Folsham, had arrived with Mrs Cargill, the woman from the village who did the laying-out for poor people. She didn't watch the process, but when the body had been laid in the plain pine box, she had gone in to place the photograph under poor Deena's hands. The book she had abstracted earlier and burned on the back of the kitchen fire. It would do no good to anyone to read that. Otherwise, all Mrs Oxlea had owned was her clothes and shoes, brush and comb, hairgrips and pins. Her wages had all gone to the little boy, so how could she own anything more?

'I've never understood about the crossroads,' Miss Hatto said. 'Why there?'

Mrs Webster answered quickly while Moss was still drawing breath, fearing he might be about to mention stakes through the heart. There'd been enough fuss already with maids claiming to be having nightmares. 'It was where felons were buried,' she said.

'Yes, but why a crossroads?' Miss Hatto persisted.

'To stop them wandering,' Miss Taylor answered. 'Damned souls were thought to be restless. All the boots and wheels passing overhead were supposed to keep them down. Of course, we know better now,' she said ironically with a ripe stare at the younger members of staff.

'Wot, you mean like wandering like ghosts?' Wilfrid asked.

Ellen made round eyes. 'Ooh,' she said, 'I'm feared of ghosts.'

'I'm not!' he said stoutly. 'I 'ope she comes a-haunting of us. Wooo! Wooo!' He waved his hands about in what he hoped were ghostly gestures. 'They rattle chains and you feels their ghostly touch at midnight like an icy— ouch!'

Rose had taken the trouble to get up and walk round the table to give him a clout on the head. 'Have a bit of respect,' she snapped.

'But will she really come haunting us, Rose?' Ellen pleaded. 'We never done her no harm.'

'Never done her no good, either,' said Mabel, through a mouthful of bread. 'Nobody never liked her, so why pretend?'

'There's no such thing as ghosts,' Rose said impatiently. 'When people die, they're dead, that's all.'

'Now, Rose, that's not a Christian thought,' Moss rebuked her. 'We all go to our judgement at the Throne of God.'

'Then *you* can all stop judging her and leave it to Him,' Rose said.

'I don't believe in God,' Cyril announced, and looked round to see what effect he had made.

Moss glowered at him. 'That's enough of that. There'll be no not believing in God in *this* house.'

There was a section of the churchyard, a neglected patch at the back up against the wall of the sexton's yard, where suicides were buried. Rose knew from Miss Eddowes, who had it from the rector, that his lordship had asked him to conduct a Christian service – the earl didn't know anything of her history, but she was an employee of the house, after all. But her ladyship had got to the rector first, and he had refused his lordship's request, as was his right. So Deena Oxlea went into the ground without ceremony. His lordship hadn't attended – that would have been excessive – but he had sent flowers, white lilies, which Rose thought very kind. She and Miss Eddowes had been the only people there. Miss Eddowes had brought white irises. When the grave began to be filled in, they had turned and walked together to the gate, exchanged one look, and parted without a word. What was there to say, after all?

Her ladyship had also used her influence over the inquest. Reputation said that coroners were the least swayable people in the land, but Mr Fothergill, the solicitor who acted as *custos placitorum coronae* for the area, was a fervent supporter of the local landed families and believed no one, rich or poor, benefited from the undermining of their status and influence. Lady Stainton had asked for the matter to be dealt with quickly, and he saw no reason not to comply. He held the inquest two days after the death, and called only Gale, the carpenter, to testify that the door was bolted on the inside, and Rose, to testify to the deceased's state of mind, before giving the verdict of 'suicide due to temporary insanity'.

'Why did she go for to do it, though?' asked Mabel. 'I'd never have the courage.'

'If I was to do it, I'd drown meself,' said Tilda. 'They say it's just like going to sleep, drowning. I couldn't do it any way that would hurt.'

'I don't reckon hanging's so bad,' said Cyril.

'Shut your mouth,' Speen said sharply. 'You know nothing about it.'

Cyril was undeterred. 'I reckon it'd be about like holding your breath, sort of. I bet it doesn't hurt. What d'you say, William? You saw her.'

William, who had been staring at his untouched plate – he had always a grand appetite, even for Mrs Oxlea's indifferent cooking – suddenly shoved back his chair and stood up, muttered something that included the word 'excused' in Moss's direction, and almost ran from the room.

Rose watched him go thoughtfully. Of all the household, he was the one who seemed most affected. Him and her ladyship, who had shut herself away and spoke to no one unless she had to, and went for long rides to escape company.


'Poor William – he's really cut up about it,' Dory said to Sebastian as she sewed up a tear in a blouse of Lady Alice's. 'He didn't know her, any more than anyone, so it must just be seeing the body. Can't have been a nice sight.'

'I believe not,' Sebastian said mildly.

'One good thing, though – it seems to have made him forget all about Milly. He hasn't given her a glance since it happened, which is a relief to her.'

'Who is he in love with now?'

'No one at the moment. I don't think love is on his mind. He's been going down to the Dog and Gun at Ashmore Carr a lot. I think it's just to escape – he's not a drinker. I know the barman there, Roddy, and he says William has a half of ale and sits and looks at it all evening. Mr Corbie, the landlord, doesn't like it – says he's putting off the other customers. But he's a miserable old besom, Corbie, anyway.'

'I suppose he doesn't like people using up seats and not buying drinks. It's reasonable,' said Sebastian.

'What I've never understood,' Dory said carefully, eyes on her work, 'was why Mrs Oxlea was cook here in the first place, if she wasn't any good.'

Sebastian ran a few scales through his hands before replying. 'She was kitchen-maid here a long time ago, under the old cook, whose name was . . . wait, I'll have it in a minute . . . ah, yes, Mrs Duxbury. She drank, as I remember. I suppose all cooks do?'

'No use asking me, sir,' Dory said, with an impish look. 'I couldn't boil an egg.'

'Well, Mrs Duxbury was all right with plain food. But she drank more and more, and finally had a dreadful accident. Fell in the fire while in her cups and was so badly burned she died soon afterwards. Mrs Oxlea took over the cooking as an emergency measure. Her skills were limited, but his lordship and her ladyship never cared much about food so she was good enough for them, and they never troubled to replace her. But things have got worse over the years. I suppose she caught the drinking habit from her predecessor.'

'Well, I hope Ida doesn't go the same way.'

'Ida?'

'Head kitchen-maid. She's been doing some of the cooking recently anyway, and now she's taken over as cook until they find a replacement.'

'How history repeats itself,' Sebastian murmured.

'Oh, I hope not, sir,' Dory said, looking up. She wondered what he really knew about the whole Oxlea situation.

He looked back, wondering the same thing. 'It's astonishing what rumours fly about in a big house like this,' he said. 'Unfounded gossip . . .'

'Silly stories,' she agreed, 'that couldn't possibly be true . . .'

'The important thing is to give them no credence, and to sit on them firmly whenever they lift their ugly heads.'

'I do, sir,' Dory said, resuming her work. 'I've seen enough in my life of the damage gossip can do.'

'Yes,' said Sebastian, staring at her thoughtfully. Then he roused himself. 'Chopin, I think,' he said. 'To liven us up.' And he plunged into the Revolutionary Étude.

After a bit, Dory lifted her head to watch in admiration. 'I don't know how you manage to play all those notes at the same time,' she said.

'I don't,' he said. 'I miss a lot out. But there's only us here, and I'm sure you won't tell.'

Maud was in a state of white fury. She had put up with the hateful presence of Mrs Oxlea in her household in a lifelong determination to avoid talk; and now the creature had precipitated her into a filthy sump of gossip.

Suicides were not so uncommon among the unregulated portion of society, and in the last ten years Victorian attitudes had softened so that it was more often regarded as a misfortune than a crime. Even among churchmen it was hardly now condemned as a rebellion against God's will – she had heard Dr Bannister, the rector, argue that if we must all humbly accept the pains we are sent, then anaesthetics and vaccinations are equally sinful. He would have spoken the words of the funeral service over Mrs Oxlea when Giles asked him to, if Maud hadn't intervened.

And she was aware that her intervention had rather increased the gossip than suppressed it – people who wouldn't have thought twice about a servant's suicide now wondered what her ladyship had against the cook. She had done her best to keep the inquest as brief as possible, and Fothergill had done his part, and had acted so quickly there had been no audience or journalists there. But that wretched Eddowes woman was a loose cannon: her attending the burial could only provoke speculation, and who knew what she would say if asked the right question? It infuriated Maud to be still at the mercy of other people, the three who knew the secret – Eddowes, Rose and Taylor. Would she never be free of it? Anything she did to suppress talk would likely backfire: a cook's suicide would not normally get into the papers, but if she tried to ban discussion of it, outsiders might start taking an interest. She hated to be whispered about and stared at – and she hated, *hated* most of all, the feeling of helplessness.

So, once the inquest was over, she sought out Giles and said, 'This atmosphere is very bad for Rachel.'

'Atmosphere?' he said vaguely, looking up from the farming monthly he was reading. Drainage, it seemed, was crucial, especially on clay soils. But it was labour-intensive, and so very costly . . .

'A suicide in the house,' Maud said tersely. 'Are you listening to me, Stainton? It is unhealthy for her to remain here when the servants *constantly* talk about it.'

Giles tried to get a grip on the conversation. 'Kitty,' he said. 'You mean bad for Kitty.'

'What *are* you talking about?'

'In her delicate condition – just having given birth. You think she ought to go away somewhere?'

'Not Kitty – *Rachel*,' Maud said, exasperated. 'It is very depressing to a young girl's spirits. And above all, we must prevent her future chances being damaged by any connection with an act of – of—'

Giles frowned. 'I don't see how the cook's unfortunate end can reflect on Rachel – and she doesn't seem terribly upset when I see her at dinner.'

Maud took refuge in magnificence. 'Allow me to know what is best for my own daughter. You are so bound up with your – your *agricultural* journals' – she managed to make 'agricultural' sound like something mildly obscene – 'that you never see what is going on under your own nose. I am not asking your permission, Stainton. I am *informing* you that I shall be taking Rachel away as soon as we can make the arrangements. If not tomorrow, then the next day.'

Giles gave the vestige of a shrug. 'Whatever you say, Mama. Where this time?'

'The South of France,' she said. 'Vicky and Bobo take a house there at this time of year, on the Côte d'Azur. We shall stay there for several weeks – perhaps until it is time to go to Scotland.'

Giles was about to say something cutting about her lack of interest in Kitty's welfare – but realised that his mother going away for an extended period was the best thing for Kitty's peace of mind.

So he said mildly, 'It sounds like a good idea. I'm sure Rachel will enjoy it. And you won't be troubled there by domestic matters.'

Maud gave him a suspicious look – she didn't trust compliance so easily won – then nodded and went away.

'May I come in?'

'Oh, Alice! Yes, you're just the person I need.'

Alice stepped in and looked around. 'Are you still sticking to your room? I'd have thought that now Mama has gone away you could come out.'

'It isn't just your mother,' Kitty said. 'Everyone said I have to rest for six weeks. Even Hatto, and she's quite modern-minded. Some of them say I should have stayed in bed all that time, but I simply couldn't.'

'I should think not,' said Alice. 'It would drive one mad. But I don't see how staying in your room is supposed to help.'

'I'm meant to be lying on the sofa and resting when I'm not in bed. But that's all over now. It was six weeks yesterday and I'm quite well, and my parents are to visit tomorrow—'

'Oh yes, I heard.'

'So could you please help me choose what to wear?'

'Me?' Alice was surprised, but pleased. 'All I ever wear is riding habit.'

'But you have the eye of an artist,' Kitty said. 'Some of your paintings are *beautiful*. I think you're good enough to do it professionally.'

Alice laughed. 'Do you think Mama would ever allow me to work for a living? I only have this bit of freedom because I didn't turn seventeen until March. As soon as the Season starts next year I shall be trussed up like a Christmas goose and taken to market.'

Kitty couldn't help laughing. 'It isn't like that. It's fun – most of the time. I'm sure you'll enjoy it when your turn comes.'

'Well, never mind me, anyway. Why do you need help dressing? And shouldn't you be asking Hatto?'

'I didn't like her choice. The thing is, my mama is terribly fashionable and smart, and I don't want her to think I've become a dowdy. But I have to remember I'm a mother now, so I can't be too gaudy.'

'Well, let me see your things,' Alice said. 'Though, honestly, I wouldn't worry too much about clothes if I were you. Surely the best thing about being a countess is that you can do as you like? I'm sure Mama does.'

Kitty, who hadn't yet found there were any good things about being a countess, and indeed didn't really believe she was one as long as her mother-in-law ruled the roost, just nodded, and led Alice to her wardrobe.

Kitty had received a nice note from her step-mother in reply to the announcement of the birth, but it had said it would not be proper for them to visit until her confinement was over.

Now, here they were, and after a brief word with his daughter and an inspection of the baby, Sir John had gone off to talk about manly things with Giles, while Lady Bayfield sat with Kitty, chatting brightly, while looking about her critically and fiddling with the braid on the sofa arm, which was coming off.

'It is a pleasant thing that you have settled so close to London,' she had said earlier, and Kitty had felt a little rush of pleasure at the words, until Lady Bayfield added, 'It means we can visit you without having to stay the night.'

'Oh,' said Kitty, blighted.

'Though Sir John and I are so busy these days that it's hard to find time even for a visit of one day. I promise you, if I were to show you my diary, you would stare! There are engagements every day until the House rises – multiple engagements on most days – and then we begin a series of country-house visits right through the summer. *So* many people have been pressing for us to come and stay, and one hates to disappoint – though some, of course, will have to be put off.' She laughed gaily. 'One can't be in two places at once!'

'It was nice of you to find time to visit me,' Kitty said dully.

'I hope I know my duty, Kitty. And of course I wanted to see my grandson, though Lady Richborough – I think her son was one of your dancing partners last year, wasn't he? – Lady Richborough says I look far too young to be a grand-mother. One must say there's something *ageing* about the term. But little Lord Ayton is very sweet. I think he favours your father for looks. You are looking rather peaked, Kitty. You must not neglect your complexion, even though you are a mother. A wife owes it to her husband to look her best. Be sure to keep using Pond's night and morning – and, Kitty, it wouldn't hurt to apply a little lemon juice each day to clear your complexion.'

'Yes, Mama.'

'And you should wear diamonds – diamonds worn close

to the face give it a sparkle.' She patted her diamond earrings affectionately.

'Lady Stainton says, "No diamonds in the country",' Kitty said.

Lady Bayfield was not daunted. 'Of course, the *dowager* Lady Stainton is of another generation. Things are different now.' Kitty could only admire the effortless way her stepmother demolished the ogre in Kitty's life. Lady Bayfield changed tack. 'I wonder what Sir John has found to talk about all this time. I suppose we must stay to luncheon,' she concluded with a sigh.

'Our old cook . . . left,' Kitty said. 'We have a temporary girl, but she's quite good. She can manage a light meal perfectly well.'

'We'll see,' said Lady Bayfield. 'I never eat much at luncheon in any case. It dulls the complexion.'

But when the time came, and the light repast of *omelette aux fines herbes*, artichoke hearts, poached chicken with salads and new potatoes, and strawberries was served, Lady Bayfield forgot her complexion, tried everything, and except for saying that the chicken was tough and should have been accompanied by a sauce, pronounced it all surprisingly good. 'Your temporary cook seems a vast improvement on the old one. You may tell her so from me. But tell her these early strawberries are better set into a jelly or made into a mousse. They haven't much flavour.'

Giles and Sir John seemed to have been getting on well during their absence. 'I have had a most interesting conversation, Kitty, with your husband about Egyptian genealogy. A number of examples of marriage between brother and sister, and between uncle and niece – which one couldn't condone, of course, but they perceived a necessity, one supposes. And they had female pharaohs! Such advanced ideas for such an ancient people.'

'One can hardly call it advanced, Sir John,' Lady Bayfield

objected. 'I hope, Lord Stainton, that the results of your studies do not descend to the general public, and stir up those unregulated women who have been agitating for the vote.'

'I have never heard that Egyptology formed part of their argument, ma'am,' Giles said patiently.

Alice was biting her cheeks, trying not to giggle.

The Bayfields did not stay long after luncheon. The carriage was called, Lady Bayfield offered her scented cheek for Kitty's kiss, and they were drawn away in style by the dowager Lady Stainton's matched greys to catch their train. Giles immediately disappeared, with the speed of a man who had catching-up to do. And later in the afternoon, Alice came to find Kitty and present her with a drawing of two women in Egyptian costume carrying a placard that said VOTES FOR WOMEN. It was the only thing that day that made Kitty laugh.

'You sent for me, my lady?' said Mrs Webster. She stepped in, folding her hands across her front in housekeeper style, and stood still, watching Kitty walk back and forth. At last, aware of things to do downstairs, she prompted, 'Is something wrong, my lady?'

'Oh, no, I—' Kitty stopped, screwed her hands together, started up again, and ended by the fireplace – empty now, of course, but for a fan of paper. 'The luncheon yesterday—'

'I hope Sir John and Lady Bayfield were not unhappy with it?'

'No, it was all very nice – at least, I thought so,' Kitty said. 'Ida did it all, did she?'

'Well, of course the other kitchen-maids played their part, but Ida was largely responsible.'

'And do you think Ida could continue to cook for Ashmore Castle?'

Webster considered. 'I think she has coped surprisingly

well so far. Of course, she was already doing quite a lot of the cooking before – before the unfortunate event. But—'

Kitty broke in. 'You see, I noticed that his lordship ate more yesterday at luncheon than he normally eats even at dinner. I don't think the food here has agreed with him. But the dishes yesterday – lighter, more flavoursome. Do you think . . .?'

'I understand, my lady. Of course, it would mean a whole new kitchen regime.'

'Do you think Ida could manage?'

'It is a large responsibility – especially if there were to be entertaining. But I think she would like the opportunity to show what she can do, my lady. She enjoyed making luncheon yesterday, I do know. But she would definitely need more staff. They are one short in the kitchen as it is.'

Kitty nodded, biting her lips. Mrs Webster tried, like a good housekeeper, to anticipate her mistress's wishes – and in this case, if she was right, those wishes corresponded with her own. 'If you were thinking of any large-scale alterations, my lady' – she saw Kitty draw a breath – 'this would be the ideal time to undertake them, seeing as her dowager ladyship and Lady Rachel are away, so the household is reduced somewhat.'

The breath was let out, and Kitty said, in a rush of confidence, 'There are so many things I would like to change. Oh, Mrs Webster, the way my mother looked yesterday! But I've never – I couldn't – Lady Stainton—'

'It wasn't to be expected that you could do much, my lady, while you were carrying, and of course it was very proper of her dowager ladyship to save you the extra burden. But now you are out of confinement, it would be very good, if I may speak frankly, for you to take up the reins of the house a little more.'

'Oh, *thank* you!' Kitty cried. 'I've been thinking about it a lot – not just yesterday but all through this year – things

I'd like to see done. But do you think she will mind very much?' She would throw herself in front of a mad bull to save her baby, would even stand up to her mother-in-law if it was a case of his welfare, but she wasn't sure about facing her over any other matter.

Mrs Webster had to suppress a smile. Mind? Of course she'd mind! And was this child, barely out of the schoolroom, strong enough to stand up to the other Lady Stainton, who'd been in command all her life? Well, it would make for a lively situation, at any rate, when the dowager returned. And who knew – maybe if it was all bedded well in by the time she got back, she would feel she couldn't be bothered to change things again.

'Honestly, my lady?' said Mrs Webster. 'I think she probably wouldn't notice very much. She might take offence over one or two things, but if we're careful . . .'

Kitty picked up on the 'we'. 'You'll help me?'

Mrs Webster drew herself up a little. 'It is what I'm here for, my lady, to carry out your instructions and see that the house is run the way *you* want it.' She put a very delicate emphasis on the 'you'.

'You'll need more staff,' Kitty said.

'At least three more kitchen staff, I would say, my lady. And two more housemaids. And we are a footman short, since James became valet to his lordship.' In fact, the only part of the house that had been well staffed was the stables. The old lord had not stinted there. 'We could do with another boy, too. And in most houses of this size I would have a still-room maid.'

Kitty nodded. 'Make me a list, and I'll ask his lordship about it.'

'I wouldn't ask. Gentlemen don't usually want to know about the details of housekeeping. And such decisions are yours, anyway, not his lordship's. I would simply tell him what it is you are doing.'

Would he mind? Kitty wondered. But then thought, a touch sadly, he probably wouldn't even take it in. He had a way of blanking out anything that didn't interest him.

Decius Blake had chosen an architect, who was coming to advise. 'If Decius picked him, he'll be a good 'un,' Mr Cowling said approvingly. He was just back from a flying visit to London, summoned by Francis Knollys and Victor Cavendish over some crisis in the King's finances. He was off to the factory now. 'What time is he coming?'

'Eleven,' Nina said.

'Can't get out of bed in the mornings?'

'I believe Decius wanted to go over with me what we want before he comes.'

Philip Leathwaite turned out to be an unexpectedly young man, though Decius told her later he was not as young as he seemed, but had a very youthful face. All the same, he was only about thirty, and Nina had expected an architect to be a venerable grey-beard.

He won her heart by being very enthusiastic about the house. He proclaimed the west façade the most perfect example of Queen Anne architecture he had seen, admired the largely unaltered interiors, and stroked the panelling as one would a fine horse and pronounced it 'beautiful'. They had walked about the whole house before going outside to inspect the outer walls and immediate grounds for their suitability for plumbing. He agreed with Decius that the pipework had better be on the east façade out of sight, which meant having the bathrooms on that side.

They had gone back inside to look again at exactly where the bathrooms might be sited, when Mr Cowling arrived, catching up with them in the hall and advancing on the architect with a beaming smile and outstretched hand. 'Thought I'd pop back and just see what's what!' Decius hastened to introduce them. 'Leathwaite, eh? Any

144

relation to Walter Leathwaite, from Manchester? The mill owner?'

'My father, sir.'

'Is that right? I met him back in ninety-six – we had a common acquaintance in the clothing industry. So you're his son? Didn't want to go into the family business?'

'I'm the fourth son, sir. I have three brothers to follow my father, so he allowed me to take a different path.'

Mr Cowling nodded. 'Well, you look very young, but I don't hold that against a fellow. I started young myself and it never did me any harm. What do you think to this house then, eh?'

'It's very fine, sir,' Leathwaite said.

'You think so? Step in here, lad,' Mr Cowling said, and led the party into the dining-room. Nina saw Leathwaite cast Decius a faintly nervous look. Mr Cowling had a large way of speaking that took some getting used to.

The master of the house led the way to the fireplace and made an expansive gesture. 'What about that, then?'

'It's very fine of its sort,' Leathwaite said cautiously. 'Of course, not original to the house. Added at a later date.'

'But it's something like, you'd agree?' Mr Cowling pursued. Leathwaite nodded uncertainly. Mr Cowling bent a little to approach his head closer to the architect's and said confidentially but forcefully. 'I've one thing to say to you, Leathwaite. French baroque.'

'French baroque, sir?' Leathwaite looked puzzled, but behind him, Nina saw Decius close his eyes for a moment.

'Aye, that's what I said. I was in London yesterday and talked to some people, and they said it was all the go. I met this chap Arthur Davis, an architect like you, and he said it's all to do with what the French call Bows Arse, and he's involved in plans right at this minute for a grand new hotel, smack on the park in Piccadilly, that's going to be the finest in Europe. He studied in France, and this new place is going to be all French baroque and slap up to the mark in every detail. It'll knock the Savoy and Claridges into a pair of cocked hats, I can tell you!' He turned to Nina, 'I can see now that Beechcroft House is a bit old-fashioned, a bit stuffy, a bit – a bit *provincial*' – he brought the word out as if it was one only recently learned and not fully understood – 'so of course you wouldn't care for it, and being the kind person you are you didn't like to tell me so. But this house,' he turned back to Leathwaite, 'we could really do something with. It's just about big enough, and the size of this room and the drawing-room are more than good, so what do you say?'

'French baroque,' Leathwaite repeated thoughtfully.

'All pillars and friezes and gilding – as grand as you like. You could start in here – we could have a painted ceiling, cherubs and clouds and suchlike, and ladies in bits of gauze, you know the sort of thing. It'd go much better with the fireplace than all this dowdy panelling.'

Leathwaite was hesitating, seeing the prospect of a much larger and more lucrative job opening out before him, while simultaneously remembering his previous admiration of the house's purity.

While he was silent, Decius stepped in. 'They're very sweeping ideas, sir,' he said, 'but wouldn't they put this room at odds with the rest of the house?'

Mr Cowling waved away the rest of the house with a dismissive hand. 'We can do the whole lot up. Top to toe. And the outside as well, while we're at it. Face the whole thing with stone. Greek columns, and statues in nitches, and urns all along the roof. We could have one of them dome things, as well – what d'you call it? A kew-pola. We'd have the sort of house the whole county'd be talking about.'

'I doubt whether the house could stand the weight of a cupola, sir,' Leathwaite said, 'not having been built with one in mind. It would take considerable structural modifications, and even then—'

'Well, I tell you what, then,' Cowling said, on wings of expansiveness now, 'we should mebbe think about building a new house from scratch.' He turned to Nina. 'We could pull this down and build on the same plot. Or, better still, there's lots of land nearby – no need to leave the town, my dear, since you've taken a fancy to it. This house hasn't got what you'd call a park, now has it? We can build us a grand house in the French baroque style, in the middle of its own grounds – our very own palace. What d'you say?'

Nina was pale, feeling that she had been picked up by a whirlwind and dropped far away in a strange place. She couldn't find any words. She looked past Mr Cowling and found Decius's eyes, and he understood.

'I beg your pardon, sir,' he said gently, 'but I think Mrs Cowling likes this house just as it is.'

Mr Cowling whirled on him, scowling. 'What makes you think *you* know what she likes? She can speak for herself, can't she? No need to be sticking *your* beak in.' It was the first harsh thing he had ever said to his secretary.

Decius subsided into hurt silence, his face reddening. Nina was ashamed of her own cowardice in letting him take the blow. She braced herself, summoned up her spirit, and said, 'I have spoken to Decius several times about how much I like this house, sir. And I do. I love its quietness and spaciousness and grace.'

'But it's *old*!' he cried, frustrated. 'Old and plain with nothing grand about it.'

'But I like old things,' Nina said. 'And it's grand to me. I really do love it – Joseph.' She said his name a little awkwardly, since she hardly ever used it, and never thought of him by it, but she guessed it would soften him, and it did. She saw the skin round his eyes relax at the sound of it. 'I love it just as it is. Even this funny fireplace.'

'Funny, is it?' Mr Cowling said, puzzled. He thought it the only thing in the house that was up to scratch.

She nodded. 'Just as it is,' she repeated, and added, 'except that there's no bathroom. I only wanted a bathroom to be added for the house to be perfect.'

He was silent a long moment, breathing heavily through his nose. Then he said in a resigned voice, 'Well, my dear, if that's really true, if that's what you want, so be it. It's my comical way to want my wife treated like a queen – and with a house to match – but I suppose I'm just old-fashioned.'

She slipped a hand through his arm and squeezed it. 'You *do* treat me like a queen,' she said quietly. 'And it isn't comical. And I honestly couldn't want a more beautiful house than this.'

He squeezed back and said, 'Well, it'll have to do for now, I suppose.' And then he brightened, as the thought came to him. 'We've not been wed long, and you're still getting used to it. I dare say your ideas will change when you see what it means to be a rich man's wife. No, no,' he added, as she opened her mouth to protest, 'never mind me, I'm just a daft old man that loves you. Putting in these bathrooms,' he threw suddenly at Leathwaite, 'it's a complicated job, I expect? Cost a bob or two?'

'If you want to protect the integrity of the house, sir, yes. It must be done carefully and with sensitivity, and that means extra time, trouble and materials to conceal the fundamentals within the fabric of the house. I would like people in the future who come to admire your house to say, "It's amazing – they look as though they've always been there."' Leathwaite was beginning to grasp the essence of Mr Cowling, Decius noted.

Mr Cowling inspected him for a moment. 'People will admire, will they?' he asked, in the manner of one baiting a trap.

'People already do admire this house, sir – it's known throughout the county as a very fine old manor house – but they'd be greatly impressed with the way you have managed

148

to import modern comforts while respecting its ancient and noble beauty.'

'You talk a lot, Leathwaite,' Mr Cowling said at last, 'but if you like the house, and Decius does, and my lady wife does, I suppose it must have something, for they're not fools. Carry on. Nina, my dear,' he turned away from the two men, drawing Nina with him for a private word, 'have it how you want. And spend what you want. Don't skimp on anything, d'you hear?'

'I do. And thank you, Joseph,' Nina said warmly.

He went up to London again a few days later, and came back with an emerald and diamond necklace for her. She perceived that he urgently needed to spend money on her, though she didn't yet understand why he felt that way.

# CHAPTER NINE

Kitty was pleasantly surprised when Giles came into the nursery, where she was indulging herself with holding Louis before he was put down to sleep. She was even more pleased when he said, 'Let me have him for a moment.'

'He's looking well, don't you think?' she asked. At the sight of her husband cradling her child, she felt an upsurge of love for him.

'Very bonny,' Giles said. 'I just came to tell you I'm going up to Topheath Farm with Adeane, so I shall be out all day.' This was the furthest away of the farms, mostly given over to sheep. 'They've had an outbreak of swayback, and I want to see if we can get to the bottom of what's causing it. I might not be back before dressing-bell.'

'I can have dinner put back, if you like,' Kitty said. She saw so little of him, and if he did not get back in time to dress, sometimes he would order a tray brought up to the library and she didn't see him at all.

'No, don't do that. No need to put everybody out.' He was making no move to hand the baby back.

'It's no trouble—' she began.

But he spoke over her. 'Am I imagining it, or is he bigger already?'

'Of course he's bigger! Babies grow all the time.' He smiled privately at her newly acquired expertise. 'He's put on two pounds since he was born,' she went on proudly.

Giles had no idea where two pounds stood on the scale of achievement. 'Magnificent. He's clearly an exceptional child.' He stared down at the sleeping face, glad the heir was apparently healthy, but also curiously moved on a personal level. Human babies did not have the instant appeal of, say, calves or lambs or kittens. You had to be attached to them in some way to find them attractive. But his son (oh, the emotional thump in the belly of those words!) was surely one of the nicer-looking specimens.

Kitty, seeing he was in no hurry to leave, seized her chance. 'I did want to talk to you,' she said, and quickly began telling him her plans for refurbishment. But she was afraid she only had half his attention, and that he was agreeing with her more or less at random, his mind already drifting away to the fields, hedges, lanes, buildings, tracks and livestock of his inheritance, which he seemed to find so much more interesting than anything Kitty could provide – except his heir.

'So you see, it will be mostly repairing and cleaning, not actually new things,' she said anxiously. 'Except for the drawing-room curtains. They really are beyond saving – even Dory says so, and she's wonderful at repairing things so you can't see the mend.'

'Yes, dear. Wonderful.' He looked round vaguely, caught nursemaid Jessie's eye, and indicated that she should take the baby. She scuttled over eagerly. She was so in love with Louis she could hardly bear even his legitimate parents to share him.

Kitty was still talking. 'They'll have to be replaced. But we've unpicked the seam to see what the colour was originally and Mrs Webster's sure she can match it exactly, so they will be the same curtains, really, only what they used to look like, not all faded and rubbed. So I hope your mother won't mind too much.'

'My mother?' Giles said vaguely, catching the end of the sentence.

'She doesn't like me to change anything,' Kitty said bluntly.

'Oh, I'm sure she doesn't care really,' he said, turning away.

'But the point is, Giles,' Kitty said desperately, 'that it will cost money, even though I won't be buying much new, only the velvet for the curtains – the maids can make them up at home – but it's an expensive material, and as the windows are so big, there will be an awful lot of it.'

'I'm sure you'll do what's necessary.' He was almost at the door.

'And I really do feel we ought to have new mattresses. Ours are quite dreadful, and I hate to invite people to stay when I know they won't get a wink of sleep. I can order them from Whiteley's and Mrs Webster says they will give me a good rate for a large order, but it will still be a lot of money and, Giles, you *must* listen!'

He paused and half turned back to her. 'I am listening. You want a new mattress.'

'New mattresses for *all* the beds. And to carry out my plans for refurbishment we must take on more servants.'

He said impatiently, 'For heaven's sake, Kitty, you are mistress of the house. Do as you like and don't bother me with all the details.'

'But, Giles, it will be a lot of money. And I know you need my inheritance for the estate, so I can't just buy things without asking you. And what if, when your mother comes back, she objects to what I've done? You *have* to support me.'

He turned back fully, recognising the urgency in her tone. 'My mother won't even notice. She has very little interest in the house,' he said.

Kitty retorted, 'She had enough interest to stop me changing anything. Enough to say wanting things not to be shabby is middle-class.'

'Oh, Kitty,' he said sadly. 'You mustn't mind her. I know she has a sharp tongue – I've been on the end of it myself often enough – but she can't actually *do* anything to you.'

*Except make me unhappy*, Kitty thought. But she must stick to the point, before he escaped again. 'But, Giles, do I have your permission for all this?' she persisted. 'If I do, then she *can't* object – not really.'

He looked at her with sympathy. *Poor Kitty*, he thought, *so afraid of everyone*. Yet the thought was not without a hint of irritation. He hadn't time to be bothered with all this nonsense. Still, he hunted out a reassuring tone of voice for her. 'Of course I support you. You are mistress of the house. Order what you like. And hire more servants if you want,' he had remembered something else she had said.

'But the money, Giles. I'll have to spend some of my inheritance, and I know you wanted it all for bringing the estate back to health.'

'But your inheritance isn't a fixed sum,' he said, in surprise. He saw her blank look. 'It isn't a big bag of coins that we're gradually emptying.'

'Isn't it?'

'No, dear, it's an income as well. There was a large sum of money on deposit, and thank God for it, but the Harvey's company continues to trade and make money.' He sought for an easy way to explain it to her. 'Every time someone buys a jar of Harvey's jam and hands over fivepence to the shop-keeper, part of that fivepence comes to you.'

She frowned. 'Only part?'

'Well, the shop-keeper has to make a little profit, or he couldn't stay open. Then there's the cost of making the jam – the fruit, the sugar, the wages of the workers, the upkeep of the factory and so on. When all that's paid for, the rest is yours. It isn't much on one jar of jam, maybe only a penny, but of course the company sells thousands of jars every day, and when you add up all those pennies, it comes to a good amount of money refilling that bag of coins you brought me when . . .' he reached over and took her hand '. . . you did me the honour of marrying me.'

She flushed with the pleasure of his touch, and his words. 'So you *really* don't mind, then?'

'Mind if you spend your own money on making your own house more comfortable? Of course I don't, foolish!'

But the tender moment didn't last long. He gave her hand a valedictory squeeze and pushed it back to her, saying, 'Now I must be off. Adeane will be waiting downstairs.' And he walked smartly out before she could say anything more.

Kitty sighed and, having seen Louis put in his crib, made her way back towards the Peacock Room, her mind drifting off to the rosy land of soft furnishings. Her mother-in-law surely couldn't object if she changed things in the Peacock Room, as it was her own sitting-room. A new carpet, the chairs and sofas reupholstered, different curtains – those ochre ones really were disagreeable . . . It would be nice, she thought, to see it all in peacock colours to reflect the name. Deep blue, green and gold. Surely someone somewhere made curtains with a pattern of peacocks? It might be a William Morris design – Liberty's would be the place to look. It would mean going up to Town, and wouldn't that be nice, after all the months and months of being in the country, the last few of them confined to a sofa feeling like a stuffed goose?

Giles only got as far as the back hall before he was waylaid by Alice, jumping in front of him as he stepped out of the door. She plainly wanted to catch him before he got to the stableyard. She was dressed in riding habit, and he noticed she was growing, though upwards rather than outwards. She was tall for her age, but barely had a figure at all.

The dogs, who had been running ahead of him down the stairs, discovered her like a long-lost lover, and mobbed her with thrashing tails and yards of adoring tongue. He checked his initial exasperation at being held up again, and said, 'Well?'

She looked up, hands busy around thrusting heads and

154

offered ears. 'Josh is being *so* disagreeable, Giles! Can't you speak to him? He won't let me ride out on my own.'

'I thought he still wasn't riding.'

'No, he isn't, because just when his broken foot was better, that horse trod on it, so it's sore again.'

'That would make anyone bad-tempered.'

'I know. But he makes me take a groom out with me and, honestly, Giles, you can't imagine how tedious it is, always to be trailing someone behind you who doesn't want to be there.'

He smiled at her. 'I *can* imagine. I shouldn't like it a bit.' She brightened, and he hurried on, 'But I'm a man and you're a girl, and there's nothing to be done about that.'

Alice skipped over her mother's embargo. 'But it's only because Josh thinks I wouldn't be able to get back up if I came off, and of course I would – there are always gates and tree stumps and walls and things. I've done it before, loads of times.'

'But what if you came off and were hurt, and there was no one with you?'

'Well, what if *you* did?' she pointed out.

'*I* shan't come off.'

'Neither shall I!'

He sympathised, but was unmoved. 'Pharaoh is a lively ride, and you can't rule out accidents. If he was a steady old plug, it might be different, but even then—'

Alice regrouped. 'So then you can't object if I go out alone in the trap, with Biscuit. I can't fall out of that, and there never was such a safe, wise pony.'

Both dogs were now on their backs on the gravel, switching their bodies from side to side, legs waving ridiculously in the air. The June sunshine was hot on his head, and just for a moment, he relaxed. 'Where do you want to go?'

'Nowhere in particular. Just round and about. I want to do some sketching – and actually it's better to take the trap because it's awkward carrying a sketch-pad and pencils and everything on horseback. And,' she went on before he could speak, 'I might do some painting if I find a landscape I like, and obviously I'll need the trap if I take paints and easel and everything. And you can't, you simply *can't*, make me take a groom with me, because they'd hate being made to sit for hours while I worked and they'd complain and disturb me and a great masterpiece of art might be lost to posterity all because of Josh's silly worry about respectability.'

He was laughing now. 'Quite right, Miss Gentileschi! We can't have the world of art made poorer by the loss of your genius. And, actually, I don't think there's anything *un*-respectable about your going out alone around the estate in the pony-trap. This isn't the dark ages.'

'Oh, *thank* you, darling Giles! And will you tell Josh? Because he won't listen to me.'

'I will tell Josh,' he agreed solemnly.

'You are the best brother in the whole world!'

She was plainly about to fling her arms round him, then checked herself. He felt a little pang. Had he made himself so inaccessible? Since he came back he had been feeling rather fond of Alice. She was the one with the lively mind: he never knew what she might say next, which amused him. She reminded him a little of – of one he never allowed himself to think about.

'You were angling for that all along, weren't you?' he said 'You thought if I refused to allow you to ride alone, I wouldn't have the heart to refuse to let you drive alone. You manipulated me.'

She showed him wide, innocent eyes. '*Me?*'

He reached out and pinched her cheek. 'You'll run some poor helpless husband round in circles like a chicken one day.'

'Oh, I shall never marry,' she said airily.

'Of course not. You'll be the great artist of our time, and they'll name a whole school after you. "She was the first of the Tallantists," they'll say.'

She looked at him indulgently. 'If you come and sit with us one evening after dinner, instead of scurrying off to the library, I'll draw your portrait. I know Richard's meant to be the handsome one,' she added judiciously, 'but you are more satisfactory from an artist's point of view. Artists love imperfections, and you have an interesting profile.'

He gave a mock bow. 'Thank you, madam. You keep my vanity in good order.'

'Then will you?'

'As long as I can read while you do it – I can't sit and do nothing.'

'You can read all you like. And if it comes out well, you can get it framed and give it to Kitty. I bet she'd love it.'

Axe was in his yard when Alice drove in, and came across to catch the rein. The dun pony gave a deep whicker of welcome. 'Well, if it's not my old friend Biscuit!' Axe said. He looked up at Alice consideringly, but only nodded a greeting.

One of the things she liked about him was his lack of questions. No *Why are you here?* Or *Why aren't you riding?* She rewarded his reticence with information. 'Pharaoh is quite all right. I went for a long ride early this morning. But I can come out without a groom if I drive in the trap.'

He nodded again, though a fleeting frown touched his golden brows. But Dolly had raced out from behind the woodpile where she had been suspecting a rat, and was barking for attention at the rear of the trap, going up on her hind legs in the urgency of her need to be close to Alice. Alice jumped down and squatted to give the dog her dues. Axe watched her in silence, slowly rubbing the pony's forehead. Biscuit blew out contentedly and shifted his weight to be comfortable. When Alice finally stood up, brushing off her skirt, a little silence ensued – not precisely awkward, but perhaps questioning. Since Alice didn't seem to be finding any words, Axe made the first move.

'I was just going to have a bite before getting to my work. T'isn't much, but you're welcome to share.'

Alice blushed. 'Oh dear, I should have thought to bring something.'

'What I got you're welcome to, if you're staying. Like it says in the Bible, you never know when you might entertain an angel unawares.'

'Well, I'm not an angel,' Alice said.

He smiled, his eye-corners creasing up. She had noticed, with a strange sort of intense vision, that those creases were white in his brown face when his eyes were relaxed. 'That's as may be, but are you staying?'

'Yes, please,' she said. 'I don't have to be back until dressing-bell.'

Together they unharnessed Biscuit and put him in the spare stall next to Della, with an armful of hay in the rack to keep him busy, then went into the house. Inside, Alice saw changes since she had last been there. Now there was a long seat-cushion on the settle against the wall, covered with a garnet red material. There was a high-backed wooden chair by the fireside, which had a seat cushion of the same material, and another rag rug on the floor in front of it. Chintz curtains patterned with autumn leaves hung at the window. In the middle of the big table stood a green glass jug bearing tall blue delphiniums, spitting their petals everywhere, supported by sprays of bright, pale-green lime leaves.

'You have done a lot,' Alice cried. 'And the flowers – how pretty! Did you arrange them yourself?'

'No one else has been here,' he said, amused.

'So clever to think of using the leaves like that.'

'Got to go with what's to hand,' he said. 'I'm going to plant a little bit of garden out the back when I've got time – just a few marigolds, say, and wallflowers and moon daisies. And a rose bush, if I can get aholt of one. I like flowers in the house. My sister give me the delphies yesterday from her

158

garden to bring back. They don't last long, but you can't beat the colour.'

'I like the curtains. Did you make them?'

'Our Seth's Mary give me the material,' he said.

He answered obliquely, she thought, for fear he should seem to fish for compliments.

'Sit you down, I'll get the grub. 'Tis only bread and cheese, but it's a nice fresh loaf I brought back yesterday, an' only took the end off this morning for my breakfast.'

She sat, feeling suddenly at ease, and watched him move about fetching things to the table. It gave her a warm feeling to see how quietly and surely he moved, like a creature in its own element. She loved to watch Josh grooming a horse for the same reason, or Grandmère embroidering, or Uncle Sebastian playing the piano: doing something they did so easily they didn't have to think about it. *I must draw him*, she thought suddenly and urgently, but did not make the connection with her own 'element'.

Two plates, two knives, a loaf on a bread board, a wedge of cheese on a plate, a crock of butter. A jar of honey. 'From Batty's,' he said. Mr Batty in Cherry Lane kept bees. 'Honey's good with cheese.'

'I've never tried it,' Alice said, interested.

'Marmalade's good too, but that's for winter.' He went out to the scullery and came back with a jug. 'Only water to drink,' he apologised, 'but it's cold and good from the pump here. Unless you want beer.'

'No, thanks. I tried it once but I don't like the taste.'

He twinkled at her. 'See you keep it that way.' He surveyed his table. 'It's not what you're used to, I'm afraid.'

'That bread smells divine,' she said firmly.

He took up the bread knife and carved her a careful slice. She leaned forward to examine the wooden board. It had clearly been made from a slice of wood cut across a tree trunk, and shaped and planed and polished. 'Oh, the little carving on the rim!' she exclaimed. It was a mouse nibbling at an ear of wheat, every detail perfect. 'It's beautiful. Did you do it?'

He nodded shyly. 'When I cut the board, there was a big knot there. I was going to saw it off and plane down the edge, but then . . .' He hesitated. 'I sort of saw the mouse in there. Sounds daft when I say it, but I knew that's what it had to be. Can't explain really.'

'I know *exactly* what you mean!' she cried. 'Often when I start a drawing or painting I can see it on the blank paper, as if it's there already, just waiting for me to bring it out.' He was watching her with an arrested look, and she felt an intense connection that she didn't quite know what to do with. She gave an embarrassed little smile and continued, 'Mostly it doesn't end up the way I saw it, because I don't have the skill yet. But I always know how it *ought* to be.'

He seemed to shake himself back into the mundane present, passed the slice of bread to her and pushed the cheese plate closer. 'Help yourself,' he said.

'Thanks.' She cut herself a piece of cheese, and looked around. 'Where's Captain?'

'Gone,' he said.

'He died?' she faltered.

'No – leastways, he might be dead by now, but I wouldn't know. He left, that's all. When we got here, he seemed different. Restless. Warn't interested in me. Kept listening as if he could hear someone calling. Then one day he flew off into the wood and didn't come back.'

'Oh dear, I'm sorry.'

He shook his head, brushing off the sympathy. ''Twas always his choice, to stay or go. I reckon he heard his own kind out there in the wood and went to find 'em.' He met her eyes and smiled at her creased brow. 'No need to look so downcast. 'Tis no sorrow to me. You can't keep wild things – only make 'em want to stay.'

160

'But why *didn't* he want to?' she protested, childlike. 'I'd want to. I'd stay here for ever.'

'You wouldn't like it so much in the middle of winter, in the cold and wet. *Then* you'd be pining for your nice cosy castle.'

She laughed. 'You've never been inside it, or you wouldn't call it cosy! This is much cosier.' She took a mouthful of bread and cheese and honey, and adored the simple, true flavours. No luncheon at home had ever tasted so good. 'You weren't at church on Sunday,' she said.

'I was too. I was up in the gallery. Saw you come in. Blue coat, brown hat with daisies.'

'But not singing in the choir?'

'Well, see, I've had to give that up. Can't be sure of getting to choir practice Wednesdays. That's a long day for me – I have to take the wood to the lumber yard out past Priestwood, and by the time I've got back, had a wash and a bit o' supper, it's too late. And Della's tired too. Don't want to take her out again and make her wait down there and come back up the hill after sunset, when she wants to be in her own stall. Mr Arden was very nice about it. Said I'd be missed but he understood. Said if things changed I could come back.'

'Will they?'

'Change? Not f' the foreseeable.'

'You'll miss the singing.'

'I will. But I got all those big empty woods – I can sing out there. God'll still hear me.' He took a polite bite at his bread, chewed and swallowed, and said, 'You got a new generation up at the Castle.'

'Baby Louis? I suppose he is a new generation. I hadn't thought of it that way.'

'Lot of expectations sitting on that young lad's shoulders.' He shook his head. 'Wouldn't be him for worlds. Not for all his silk suits and golden spoons.'

Alice laughed. 'He's a baby! No golden spoons. And he's dressed in wool and cotton.'

161

'He won't always be a baby.'

'Perhaps he'll like being earl,' Alice said, and then frowned.

He read her mind. 'Does your brother like it?'

She pondered. 'I think – he accepts it. He always seems worried, and too busy, so I don't suppose one can say he's enjoying it.'

Axe nodded. 'There it is. We all got our work to do in this life. I'm glad mine's all to hand, and nothing to get worried over. I wake in the morning with a glad heart. Must be hard not to do that.'

She looked at him, pondering. 'Yes,' she said. 'You're lucky.'

'I am,' he said. Then, 'Want to come with me this afternoon? Going up the wood with Della to bring out a tree trunk. Trimmed it yesterday, now the stock's ready to haul. You can see how she works. Knows her job, that lass – it's canny to see her pick her way, never puts a foot wrong.'

'Oh, I'd love to!' Alice said. 'May I really? Does Dolly come too?'

'Rides on Della's back.'

'I'd love to see that! And maybe we'll spot Captain, too.'

'Miracles do happen,' he said, enjoying her innocent delight.

Nina had discovered a pleasant walk nearby along the river-bank to take with Trump. In a cupboard in Wriothesby House she had found a duck-headed walking-stick some past visitor had left behind, and took it with her for the pleasure of swiping at stinging-nettles as she walked – and, more practically, in case she met an irate swan or a doubtful bull on the way.

On this lovely June day she had gone a good distance, and was thinking of turning back, when another dog came into view, running fast towards them. When it saw Trump, it put on a burst of speed, and while Trump was still bristling, trying to assess the situation, it bowled him over, and the two disappeared in a whirling mass into the long grass beside the path. Nina wasn't sure if they were fighting or playing – it *looked* like playing, but the other dog was bigger than Trump, and she was dithering on the edge of the situation, trying to insert her stick in a useful manner, when someone else came running up and with strong hands and a few practiced movements hauled the two apart and stood, panting slightly, with a collar in each hand and the dogs, forelegs held clear of the ground, effectively neutralised.

'How did you do that?' Nina marvelled. 'And without getting bitten? I wish you would teach me.'

The newcomer was a woman she guessed to be about thirty, sensibly dressed for walking in a navy serge skirt just above the ankle bone, a grey flannel blouse and a round felt hat with a brim and a jaunty red feather. She had a wide-awake sort of face, grey eyes, fair curly hair, and a few freckles that suggested she liked to be out of doors a lot. Nina liked her immediately.

'You just have to be quick,' she said. 'But they weren't fighting – though of course it can turn nasty. Luckily your dog is a Jack Russell, and the hunt keeps terriers too.' She noted Nina's slightly questioning look and said, 'Viking's a hound puppy – I'm a puppy-walker for the Fernie. Do you hunt?'

'I never have in England, but I'd like to. What's a puppy-walker?'

'Oh, people who take the hound puppies into their own houses and keep them until they're ready to join the pack. I do it most years. I'm afraid Viking's rather more boisterous than most. He got away from me for a moment. I hope you weren't frightened. Cur-dog hunting's a dreadful fault in a hound, that's why they run the terriers with the pack, but I don't think he's that way inclined. I don't think he would have hurt your dog.' She let go of both collars and the dogs sat for a moment, one either side of her, in a docile way, before cautiously sniffing each other, then trotting off together peaceably. 'Look, they're friends already. I'm Bobby Wharfedale, by the way, from Welland Hall, and I've already introduced Viking.'

'I'm Nina – Cowling.' She stumbled only slightly over the name. 'From Wriothesby House. And my dog is Trump.'

'Oh, after Parson Russell's bitch? But it's a good name for a dog as well. And of course you've just moved in, haven't you? I was so pleased when I heard you were coming to live there. I go past Wriothesby often and always feel sorry that it's been left empty for so long. It's such a lovely house.'

'Do you think so? I love it too.'

'I'm so glad. I knew the Ampleforths, who used to live there, so I've often been inside it.' She paused, surveying Nina with a satisfied look that was balm to her soul. 'Are you going much further?'

'I was just going to turn back,' Nina said.

'Shall we walk together, then? Our dogs seem to have come to a *modus vivendi*.' They were coursing about together, noses down, in the rough grass. The path was only a beaten track along a mostly untamed riverbank.

'I'd love to,' Nina said, and added shyly, 'The trouble with being new to a place is one doesn't know anybody.'

'That will soon change. In a small town you soon know everybody – and rather wish you didn't! What did you mean when you said you hadn't hunted in England?'

So Nina told her about India, and the horses there. She was a wonderful listener. At the end, she said, 'I must persuade you to join the Fernie. We're always looking for new subscribers, and we don't have nearly enough women hunting. Hunting properly, I mean, not just turning up at meets, ambling to the first gate and then going home.'

'I'd love to. But I don't have a horse.'

'You have very nice stables at Wriothesby House – I've often been in them. It's a shame to see them empty.'

'I'm sure my husband would buy me a horse if I asked him,' Nina said.

'Oh, what fun! Oh, please, please let me help you find one! There's nothing I like more than buying horses! And until you get one, you must come up to the Hall and ride one of ours. I'd love to have someone to ride with. I can show you the country, so that when you start hunting you won't get lost.'

'You're very kind,' Nina began.

'Not at all. Selfish as the day is long,' said her companion cheerfully. 'I'm desperately short of a really good bosom friend. I've been married ten years, and I still miss my brothers and sisters. Isn't it silly?'

'Not at all. I never had any, but I still miss my mother and father – they were good friends as well as parents.'

'No brother or sisters? Oh dear, poor you! You must have been so lonely. Don't you think marriage is a very lonely thing, anyway? Aubrey, my husband, is the dearest creature, but he's always busy about his own concerns, and hasn't time for my nonsense and chatter. And he's quite a lot older than me, so he was brought up in a different sort of world and half the time doesn't understand what I'm talking about.'

'Mr Cowling – Joseph – is a lot older than me,' Nina said, and as her new friend nodded understandingly, she had the odd idea that she had known that already, and had been giving Nina an opportunity to talk about it. 'What did you hear about us?' she asked, a little stiffly.

'That he's a powerful businessman and a friend of the King's, and that his wife is a delicious young creature, *very* clever but rather shy.'

'Is that what people are saying?'

'That's just the first ounce of gossip.' She was laughing. 'There's pounds more of it! But don't give it a thought. No one has said a disobliging thing about either of you, I promise. And I've been longing to meet you, and wondering how to go about it, since you haven't left cards yet. What tremendous luck our dogs brought us together like this. We can be friends, can't we?'

'I would like that very much,' Nina said.

'Then,' She held out her hand, 'please call me Bobby. Absolutely everybody does.' They shook hands. Bobby grinned. 'My dear Nina – may I call you Nina? – you remind me of me when I was first married and didn't know anything. I was lucky and had a family to steer me right. Will you let me – in the nicest possible way – guide you a little? You don't think me presumptuous, I hope?'

'I should be very glad of help,' Nina said. 'I have an aunt who has washed her hands of me, and my only female friend lives in London and isn't married so I can't ask her anything.'

'Well, you can ask me anything you like,' Bobby said, slipping a companionable arm through Nina's. 'And you and your Joseph must come and dine at the Hall so you can meet my lovely Aubrey, and we'll have a proper dinner party and invite all the people you ought to meet. Then you'll feel more comfortable. And you must come up to the Hall and go riding with me.'

'I'd love to,' Nina said, 'but I haven't a riding habit. I shall have to get one made.'

'Garner's, in the Square, have some very good ready-made things that can be altered to fit. Mention my name – I've had an account there for years, they know me. I don't see any point in being *terribly* smart, just for day-to-day riding, when no one is watching one, do you?'

'I hadn't thought about it, but you're right.'

'Good. So that's all settled. Now, tell me some more about India. Did your father play polo? I've always wanted to try it.'

'I did too,' Nina said. 'The polo ponies were so lovely – gentle and clever and so beautiful.'

They walked on, talking. Nina felt already as if she had known Bobby for years.

# CHAPTER TEN

Mrs Deering met Nina in the hall when she got back. 'Just in time for tea, madam,' she said with a kind smile. 'Shall I bring it to you in the drawing-room? Did you have a pleasant walk?'

'Very pleasant, thank you,' said Nina. 'And I met such a nice lady – a Mrs Wharfedale – who was walking a hound from the hunt.'

'Oh, you must mean Lady Wharfedale, madam. From Welland Hall, just down the road?'

'*Lady* Wharfedale?'

'His lordship's from a very old local family, madam, very highly thought of. And Lady Wharfedale is a popular hostess and a hard rider to hounds, so they say.'

Nina was glad she hadn't known before that her new friend was a ladyship, or she might have felt shy. As it was, she could think of her only as Bobby. In the drawing-room the French windows were open onto the terrace, and the warm air was flooding in. Trump found an oblong of sunshine on the floor, flopped onto his side and went instantly to sleep, worn out by the long walk. Nina was halfway through her solitary tea, and wishing she had company, when she heard voices in the hall, and soon Mr Cowling and Decius came in, followed by Mrs Deering with fresh hot water.

'Afternoon, Nina my dear,' Mr Cowling said cheerfully. 'I hope you haven't eaten all the scones.'

167

'Not quite all,' Nina said.

'I'll bring you some fresh, sir,' Mrs Deering said. 'I know you like them warm.'

Mr Cowling drew up a chair and observed Trump, who hadn't stirred. 'That dog's spark out,' he said.

'We had a long walk,' said Nina. 'And we met someone—'

'Aye, aye, so I've heard. Lady Wharfedale. I'm very pleased, my dear. That's just the sort of friend I'd like you to make. I'm not acquainted with his lordship, but I hear they're a fine old family and important people hereabouts.'

Nina felt unreasonably peeved, as if the specialness of her new friendship were being diluted. 'I didn't know who she was,' she said, a touch crossly. 'Our dogs met, and I just thought she was nice.'

Decius, who had been fetching a chair for himself, said, 'I've met her once or twice about the lanes. There's no stiffness or formality about her – she has a pleasant openness of manner.'

Mr Cowling didn't seem to be listening. He was putting sugar in his tea, frowning to himself. 'Aye, that's the sort of society we must aim at if we're to be living here permanent. The Crawfords are good enough folk, but I'd like you to be moving in higher circles, my love. You deserve it. I hear they're pretty wealthy, too. I wonder where his money comes from? Is it all old money? I could put him in the way of one or two things, if he cares to invest. I must make some enquiries.'

'She's asked me to go riding with her,' Nina said, defiantly keeping to her own point. 'But I haven't a habit.'

'Get one, get one made,' said Cowling promptly. 'Get everything you need! Riding clothes are very becoming. I'd like to see you in one of them little top hats with a veil. Very classy.'

'She said to go to Garner's in the Square. And she says I can ride one of her horses – I suppose she has several.'

'You must have a horse of your own,' he declared at once.

'We've all those stables out there doing nothing. I'm glad you want to ride, dear – it's healthy exercise, and ladies look so elegant on horseback! You must join the hunt, as well. That's the way to meet fine folks. They have dinners and balls and all sorts, as well as the hunting. If you get a horse you'll need a groom as well, and he'll need a horse. Decius,' he turned to his secretary, 'I don't doubt you'll know what's wanted, and if you don't know where to find a nice horse for Mrs Cowling, you'll soon find out, that's for sure!'

Mrs Deering came in with a dish of warm scones, and Trump woke from his first deep sleep, stood up, shook himself, and looked at her hopefully. 'Shall I take him into the kitchen, madam? I dare say he could do with a drink of water after that hot walk.'

Mr Cowling was all good humour. 'Aye, take him away and spoil him, Mrs D. I dare say you'll slip him some little treat or other, the lucky dog. My, those scones smell good! Have you heard Mrs Cowling's been invited to go riding with Lady Wharfedale? Isn't that splendid?'

'Very suitable, sir,' said Mrs Deering.

'Suitable, aye, that's the word! But, of course, we shall have to buy a horse, and a groom's horse, and find us a decent groom. Maybe a stable-boy, as well. Might as well do it properly. If you know anyone that wants a job, Mrs D, you just sing out, will you?'

'I will make enquiries, sir, if you'd like me to.'

'Do so, do so. Someone honest and reliable for the groom – not too young, we don't want a dasher – and I'd sooner it was someone local that you know all about. I'd feel safer that way.'

Nina felt her pleasurable little encounter had been run over by a juggernaut, but the main thing, she told herself sternly, was that she was to have a horse, something she had only dreamed of since she was orphaned. She caught Decius's eye, and he gave her a small, reassuring smile. He would take over the business, and she knew she could trust him. But she would ask Bobby if she knew of a suitable horse for sale and, if so, make sure to get the two of them together. She imagined the meeting – she knew they'd like each other.

Yes, the main thing was that she was to have a horse.

Or – no, she corrected herself with a feeling of content – the *main* main thing was that she had a friend.


William had wrung a good deal out of his dreadful experience, in terms of attention and sympathy. For a couple of weeks everyone had wanted to hear every detail of the events up at the Castle. He could repeat the story as often as he wanted, and if he had been a drinker, he could have drunk himself into a stupor without paying a penny.

But that evening when he had stepped inside the Dog and Gun, he'd felt a different atmosphere. One or two people looked up, but then immediately down again. Conversations were not broken off. No one called him over. The delicate click of dominoes on a wooden table top did not change rhythm. The collie lying under Phil Buckey's chair did not even lift its muzzle from its paws.

His time in the spotlight was over. Everyone had heard about the terrible black and bloated face, and exactly what William had felt and done immediately and for days afterwards. But the topic had died, its light had gone out, and as William asked Mr Corbie for his usual half-pint of ale, no one so much as looked round, let alone offered to buy it for him.

Corbie gave him a cynical smile. 'Penny-ha'penny, Mr Sweeting, I'll trouble you for. Thank you. Have you heard, Lord Shacklock's bull Caesar got out, went on the rampage right through Ashridge village? Killed the postman on his rounds.'

'Did it?' William said, startled.

'Poor Walter Horner, with a wife and three children

170

dependent on him. Aye, he was on his bicycle. Old Caesar must've thought it was another bull. He charged it, sent Wally flying. Got the bicycle tangled on its horns, and it must've maddened him, for once he got clear, he went after Wally.'

Roddy, the barman, oozed up to snatch a bit of the story. ''Orrible, it was!' he said gloatingly. 'Stuck its horn right through him, I tell you no lie! Right through and out the back, like a bloomin' sword! And then what d'you think it did? Ran right into a tree and pinned poor old Wally to the trunk. Just like a butterfly on a pin. 'Cept he didn't look much like a butterfly with a gurt horn through him. Eyes stickin' out of his head, so I heard. And blood everywhere.'

The others sitting at the bar had all turned in their seats now, and were eager to add their own details to the gruesome story.

'Got 'isself stuck proper, that ole bull! Stuck in the tree trunk. Couldn't get isself free.'

'Mrs Greenway from Larch Cottage come along and found him. Gor! Wish I'd bin there!'

'She never fainted nor nothing. Just tiptoes past and runs to fetch the policeman. That's a tough old dame!'

'Course, old Wally was dead by then.'

'Dead as mutton!'

'Policeman wanted to shoot the bull – well, who was going to risk trying to get it free?'

'But Lord Shacklock's bailiff wouldn't have it – said that bull was worth hundreds. Prize animal. Argued about it, they did, right there in the road—'

'And all the while poor old Walter Horner's pinned to the tree with 'is eyes wide open, a-starin' over that bull's head like he was surprised. That's what I heard from Frankie Gilbert, who come along while the argufying was still goin' on. Like he was surprised, he said.'

'Well, you'd be surprised if a bull pinned you to a tree! Gor, what a sight it musta bin!'

William listened, sipping his beer, and realising no one was going to want to talk to him any more. But he still felt shaken and depressed by his experience. Talking about it had helped him. His shoulders slumped more and more, and as the level went down in his glass he felt, for the first time ever, that he might even have another. Might as well. What was the difference? Who cared about him?

A powerful smell of otto of roses mingled with sweat enveloped him, and raising his eyes, though not his head, he found himself gazing into the fleshy canyon between Tabby Mattock's considerable bosoms. 'Cheer up, Mr Sweeting!' she said kindly. 'It may never happen.'

'Already has,' William mumbled.

She leaned closer, and laid a warm, damp hand briefly over his. 'Ah, never mind that lot. Why don't you have another half? Go on, do, it'll make you feel better.'

'Reckon I will,' he said defiantly, threw back his head and emptied his glass. On its way down again, his head reached equilibrium and his eyes connected with the barmaid's, just about on the level with his and brimming with sympathy. It warmed him to think someone was interested in his well-being. It also excited him a little bit because she was wearing face-paint, and he had never before been this close to a woman who did. It wasn't allowed up at the Castle. Mrs Webster was mustard on that, came down like a ton of bricks on any maid who dared so much as to put on a bit of rouge. And his mother had always warned him against 'painted floozies'. She said they were a trap and a delusion. She disapproved of scent as well, and Mrs Webster forbade it at the Castle. He had never noticed Tabby before, particularly. She was just a figure in the background of the Dog. She was not particularly pretty, and he had always thought she was a bit older than the maids who usually occupied his affections. But she was looking into his eyes now as if he were the most important person in the world, and it was balm to his troubled soul.

And then there was that bosom. It heaved just below his sightline. And Tabby's full, red, painted lips seemed to be pushing out towards him. He felt a thrill in a region below his waist that he was not accustomed to thinking about. And the exciting notion came to him that if he dared ask her, she might not be completely averse to kissing him.

'Why don't you tell me all about it,' Tabby purred.

He looked into her eyes, and felt himself falling ever so gently into a soft, warm, and infinitely inviting trap, and his mother's warnings seemed silly, and very far away.

'Well!' said Mr Cowling. 'This is something like!'

Nina, too, was impressed with the carriage that was waiting for them outside the station – black and glossy and polished, with two lovely dapple greys to draw it, and a coachman and groom in livery coats. The groom opened the door and let down the step, but Nina had lingered to look at the horses, and stroke a soft muzzle with a gloved hand. 'My dear?' Mr Cowling called her. She looked up and caught the coachman's eye. He had a nice, fatherly face, and when she said, 'They're lovely!' he smiled kindly. 'Nina, my dear,' Mr Cowling called, with a hint of impatience, and she obeyed this time and was helped into a crimson velvet interior.

The letter that had come in Kitty's neat schoolgirl hand had been impossible not to smile at.

*I've wanted for such a long time to invite you, but really I couldn't, until the new mattresses were delivered, because the old ones were simply dreadful and you wouldn't have got a wink of sleep. And I know you will laugh at me for it, but it has taken all this time to pluck up courage to order them, and I only dared because Lady Stainton is away and does not seem to intend coming back until the autumn, by which time I hope the newness won't be noticed. So please, dearest Nina, please won't you come? I so long to see you, and to show you my dear little baby.*

Mr Cowling had been pleased with the invitation, and

immediately said he would rearrange his work so that he would be free. 'I know you miss your friend Kitty,' he said, 'and you never know who else you might meet there. I suppose there'll be a party staying?'

'She doesn't say,' said Nina.

'Well, I dare say there will be. Grand folks, probably. Dinner on Saturday evening will be formal. What's your best evening dress?'

'My cornflower silk.'

'No, that won't do, not with your emeralds. You'd better get something new made – there's time. What's that pale green colour that's all the go? Eau-de-Nile? That would suit you handsomely and go with the emeralds. And don't worry about shoes – I'll have a pair run off for you to match.' He had had a last made for her shortly after their wedding. His wife, he had said, of all people should always be perfectly shod. 'Your blue will do for the Sunday, with your wedding diamonds. Now, what about day dresses?'

She had found his excitement about the invitation, and his minute overseeing of her wardrobe for the occasion, a useful distraction from thoughts she was anxious to avoid. She wanted to see Kitty – of course she did – but it meant seeing Giles. Being under the same roof with Giles. Being in Giles's company *with* her husband. The opportunities for mental disloyalty would be everywhere. She did not want to be that sort of person. And yet – and yet – to see him again! Just to see him . . .

They drove up quite a steep hill on a badly kept track, but Mr Cowling, leaning forward clutching the strap and peering out of the window didn't seem to notice the jolts. His reward was the first view of the house, just as it was meant to be seen from the curve of the track, looking down on them, long and white, its crenellations sharp against the blue sky. 'By golly,' he breathed, 'it's a fine-looking place. This is something like!'

He said it again when they pulled up in front of the great

door and he saw a butler and two footmen waiting to greet them, as well as Lord and Lady Stainton. 'This is *something* like,' he breathed, only varying the emphasis.

Nina had a moment of fear that he would be too ingratiating towards Giles, and she would be embarrassed. But of course he had met plenty of grand folks before, right up to and including the King, so he behaved just as he ought – friendly and natural with Giles, just a little fatherly with Kitty – and she felt ashamed of herself for not trusting him.

For her, there were Kitty's arms and a fierce embrace, and a whisper in her ear, 'Dear Nina!' Then she was set back and Kitty looked up into her face (she had forgotten how little Kitty was) and said, 'You haven't changed. I'm so glad.'

Kitty, she saw, had changed. She was still shy, but not paralysed by it. There was now a little firmness behind it. She was able to look directly at Mr Cowling as she shook hands with him; and in her clothes and bearing she was definitely a matron, not a maiden.

And then Nina had to greet Giles. Her heart was pounding, her palms were damp, and she felt a pressure in her ears as though she might faint. She felt his hand take hers, heard his voice like a touch on her skin – 'Nina, welcome.' She thought he might kiss her cheek, but after a moment's hesitation he released her hand and said, 'Shall we go in?' And so it was over, the first meeting – which had to be the hardest to bear, didn't it?

'No, there's no party, just us. Were you expecting one? I'm sorry.'

'Not at all, it's of no consequence,' Mr Cowling said genially. 'I know these two young ladies will have too much to say to each other to put up with having other folk around.'

Giles smiled, and said, 'As a matter of fact, we haven't entertained much yet, since the baby was born. And a lot of people are still away. But we'll try to keep you amused.'

'No need to be in a fuss about me. I'm looking forward to a good jaw with you about the estate.'

'Indeed?' said Giles, startled. What could Cowling care about the estate? He was trying not to look directly at him. He didn't want anything to remember about him later. He didn't want anything he could imagine Nina lying in bed with.

'You must come and see my baby,' Kitty said to Nina, and dragged her away.

Their old ease of communication did not immediately return. Partly this was because they no longer shared their days, so had no common ground. Partly it was the house, Nina decided. Could this chatelaine of the vast and grand Ashmore Castle really be the same Kitty who had shared a bedroom with her, who could never spell 'apparent', or subtract one-and-nine from half a crown?

At the top of the stairs Kitty turned and looked at her anxiously, disturbed by the silence. Her lips parted, but she couldn't find the right question.

Nina filled in for her. 'I can't believe you're really mistress of all this!' She waved a hand to indicate the vastness of the house.

'Except that I hardly am,' Kitty said.

But in the nursery, Nanny and Jessie treated her with proper deference. Nina felt again the distance that had grown up between her and her friend. Chatelaine or not, she was now a mother. Kitty had passed through gates into a different land.

As for the baby – perhaps you had to have one yourself to find them fascinating. Nina thought Louis quite a nice baby, as they went. While Kitty pointed out his various beauties, Nina noted that he did not bear any resemblance to Giles as far as she could see. He didn't look like Kitty either, for that matter. To the eye of the amateur, he was just a baby.

Kitty, cradling him, seemed ready to gaze at the sleeping face all day. 'I worry about him all the time,' she said.

'He looks healthy enough,' Nina said.

'Oh, he is well,' Kitty said, 'but so many things can go wrong. So many diseases. And accidents. Sharp things, hot water, stairs . . . They're so helpless and fragile. How do they ever survive?'

'Well, mostly they do – don't they?' Nina said, out of her depth.

'My little brother Peter was strong and healthy, and then suddenly he was gone. If anything happened to Louis, I don't know how I could bear it. I love him so much it hurts.'

'I don't know what to say,' Nina said after a moment. 'What you're feeling, isn't it rather wonderful to love someone so much? And as he grows up, he will love *you* just as strongly. That must be worth the price, surely?'

Kitty looked up. 'You're right, of course. Oh, Nina, I wish you could have what I have. But you will one day, I'm sure.' It was meant as a statement, but it came out rather more as a question. Nina didn't answer, and Kitty went on falteringly, 'You are happy, aren't you – with Mr Cowling?'

'Of course I am,' Nina answered promptly. 'He's very kind to me. He spoils me.'

'But—' Kitty still looked troubled.

'It's a different kind of relationship from yours with – Giles.' Nina brought out the name with an effort. 'But it's what I chose. You mustn't worry about me. You know I never expected to fall in love, the way you did.'

Kitty said no more, but on the way downstairs, believing her friend still to be brooding on the subject, Nina said, to change the subject, 'Are things still difficult with your mother-in-law?'

Kitty sighed. 'I know I ought to be stronger and stand up to her. Grandmère – Giles's grandmother – says she's just a bully. But people who don't mind standing up to bullies never understand what it's like to be someone who can't.'

'I understand,' Nina said.

'You *know*,' Kitty said, 'but you don't understand. You're so bold and fearless. You'd have known just what to say to her. She only has to look at me, and I seem to shrink.'

'Like a salted snail. Poor Kitty!'

'It's been wonderful, her being away. I dread her coming back. But Alice is a great help. And Richard. And dear Uncle Sebastian. They all try to give me courage.'

Nina noticed that she didn't say Giles helped her.

Giles had suggested Mr Cowling might like a turn in the garden. That way, he reasoned to himself, he could walk beside him and not have to look at him. He didn't want to look at Cowling's face. A disembodied voice was easier to bear.

He found himself apologising for the garden. 'We haven't extensive pleasure-grounds. My father and grandfather had no interest in horticulture, and I'm too busy about the estate at the moment.'

'Run down, is it, the estate?' Cowling suggested. 'In poor heart and hardly making a return?'

Giles frowned. 'Who told you?'

'Bless you, it's the same everywhere,' Cowling said genially. 'I've a lot of acquaintances among the landowning sort. I know all about the depression. I don't suppose you'd have read the Royal Commission of 1893 – ten year ago your interests were quite different, I suppose?'

'You are right, sir. Ten years ago I was still at school.'

'Aye, well, ten year ago I got hold of a copy on behalf of Lord Rockport – d'you know him? No? He's a friend of a friend and he asked me to study it and give him the gist, not being a great one for reading himself. And sorry reading it did make! Value of produce halved over twenty year, while cost of production keeps going up. Thousands of acres passed out of cultivation. That's with all this cheap American corn being imported, which is good for us manufacturers, because

178

it makes for cheaper bread for our workers. But English farmers can't compete.'

'Yes, my tenants have complained about the price of corn,' Giles said, surprised at Cowling's knowledge – and a little put out. He didn't want to admire anything about this man.

'Just so,' Cowling said. 'And to adapt the land to other uses needs capital, which few landowners have any left of, after years of decline. Not that pasturing's doing much better, with meat and butter and such coming in from abroad and forcing prices down. It's no joke being a stock farmer these days.'

Giles nodded. 'And the animals seem to suffer from so many diseases. We've an outbreak of swayback in the sheep on one of our farms at the moment. Can't seem to get to the bottom of it.'

'Swayback, eh?' Cowling's attention seemed caught. 'What sort of grazing is it?'

'They've recently moved the flock to a new field up on the hill,' Giles said, puzzled by the question.

'Hill pasture – a lot of gorse and heather and the like?'

'Yes, I suppose so. Why do you ask?'

'That'll be it. The grass is lacking. It often is where you see those sort of plants. You need to give 'em salt licks to make it up.'

'My dear sir, how would you know that?' Giles said in astonishment.

'My father was a shepherd,' said Mr Cowling, chuckling. 'No need to look surprised. I wasn't born a cobbler, you know. It's grand sheep-country where I come from, Leicestershire. Aye, my dad knew a bit about sheep, and the ills they come in for. How come your tenant didn't know about salt licks, any road?'

'The tenant, Marbeck, died suddenly last year. His widow and his sixteen-year-old son are trying to run the place between them.'

Cowling stopped and turned, so Giles could not avoid facing him. He looked flinchingly at the face of an older man – not old, but of a different generation – not ugly but commonplace. He was not stupid, but what was there in his stolid mind to attract a vibrant young woman? It was the face of a stranger, which he'd have passed in the street without a glance, except that this stranger was licensed to hold Nina in those arms and kiss her with those lips—

No, that way madness lay.

Cowling was speaking. 'He'll learn, but he'd better learn fast,' he said, giving Giles a searching look. 'Now, if you'll forgive me giving you advice, my lord, you must have an experienced shepherd on one of your farms. You should send him over to these Marbecks for a few weeks, to set them straight. You might have to pay his wages for them, if they're hard up, which I suppose they must be, but it'll only be a few shillings a week, and it'll be worth it to you in the long run. It's a rule in my world, that you have to invest before you can profit, and from what I've heard it's the same in land.'

'I know that,' Giles said, annoyed. 'And I am investing. My father took no interest in the estate, and left it in poor heart, but I knew from the start that I had to plough money into it. That's why—' He stopped abruptly, teetering on the edge of saying that was why he had married an heiress, which would have been unforgivable.

Cowling gave him a canny look, as if he knew how the sentence would have ended. 'Sounds as if it's in good hands now, any road,' he said pacifically, and changed the subject.

Giles walked on beside him gloomily, not wanting to be grateful for such tact.

The visitors met the rest of the household at luncheon. Richard claimed old acquaintance with Nina, and garnered a suspicious look or two from Mr Cowling at his teasing, which spoke of too much intimacy. Uncle Sebastian was a rumblingly comfortable presence for buffering any tensions. And Alice, whom Nina had met only once before, at the wedding, was openly admiring and frankly interested, eager to know everything about her, wanting details about her life at school with Kitty, and what Kitty had been like then. She asked how Nina had first met Mr Cowling, and when Nina spoke about the ball at Dene Park, she exclaimed, 'Oh, but that's where you proposed to Kitty, isn't it, Giles?'

'Not quite,' Giles said tersely.

'The ball was on the Saturday, and he proposed on the Monday, didn't he, Kitty?' Nina said. She couldn't look at either of them.

'It must have been a very good ball, if it resulted in two marriages,' said Alice.

'That's what balls are for, infant,' Richard said. 'How else do you think young ladies meet eligible bachelors?'

'On the hunting field,' Alice suggested.

'Dishevelled and mud-splattered, in your case,' Richard said. 'Let's hope the eligible bachelor has a taste for hoydens.'

Uncle Sebastian intervened. 'Market Harborough – that's in the Fernie's country, isn't it? Do you hunt, Mr Cowling?'

After luncheon, Kitty suggested Nina might like to ride. She had brought her newly acquired habit in the hope that a mount would be offered. Richard and Alice elected to come with them, Richard on Vipsania. Nina was offered Queen Bee.

Uncle Sebastian suggested to Mr Cowling a game of billiards, allowing Giles to escape to a meeting with his agent.

On the ride, Alice and Richard soon wanted to race off. Nina, who hadn't ridden much since childhood, and was on a strange horse, didn't mind keeping down to Kitty's pace. It was hot, but up on the crest of the hill there was a pleasant breeze, and they walked the horses, enjoying the view and the comfort of a chat. 'I'm not supposed to dash about, in any case, for a few weeks more,' Kitty said. 'But I'm looking forward to hunting this winter.'

'Yes, me too,' said Nina. 'Mr Cowling's promised to buy me a horse.' She told Kitty about meeting Bobby Wharfedale, about riding with her on one of her spare horses, and went on to describe the dinner Bobby had invited the Cowlings to, where they had met some of their neighbours, and the return dinner Nina had held.

'I'm glad you have a new friend,' Kitty said.

Nina thought it sounded wistful. 'Haven't you made any?'

'I seem to have done nothing for a year but lie about, expecting,' said Kitty.

The new mattress turned out to be extremely comfortable, but Nina couldn't sleep.

It had been a good dinner – she had seen Mr Cowling inspecting everything as it was brought to the table and nodding to himself with approval. Two footmen and a butler did the waiting. There were flowers and candelabra on the table. The silver was old, but well-polished. And at night you couldn't see the shabbiness of the dining-room, which Kitty had referred to in an unguarded moment. Nina had been placed between Richard and Uncle Sebastian. Protocol – they had been taught all this sort of thing at Miss Thornton's school – suggested she should have been placed on Giles's right. Had Kitty thought she would be more comfortable with Richard, whom she knew, and Sebastian, whom anyone could get on with? The day had been so arranged that she had hardly seen Giles and not had to exchange a single word with him. She was both glad and sorry.

There had been champagne, hock and claret, and she had drunk enough to be a little hazy – enough to stop her sleeping, anyway. The evening, in her memory, was a blur of moving candle-flames and the sound of silver on china and the

182

murmur of voices like bees in a border. The glint of candle-light on crystal. The spark of it catching Kitty's sapphires as she leaned forward. She had roses in her hair – creamy-coloured with pink lips – fresh against her dark curls. The candles and the length of the table meant Nina couldn't really see Giles at all. Richard had flirted with her, so blatantly that Sebastian had looked at him reprovingly once or twice. But in Richard's eyes there was pity behind the levity. She remembered his saying he knew what it was like to love the wrong person. Had he guessed her secret? Horrible thought! She must be more careful.

She tossed and turned, but in the restless churn of thoughts, one conviction began to crystallise – that she was desperately thirsty. She sat up, reached for her water-carafe – and managed somehow to knock it over. The water poured over the edge of the bedside table, some falling on her bedclothes, the rest soaking the carpet. She got out of bed, and stumbled about in the gloom, by the meagre light coming from between the window curtains, until she found matches on the mantelpiece and could relight her candle. No water left in the carafe. None, of course, in the ewer by the wash-stand. She licked her lips with a dry tongue. It was too late to ring. She would have to go and find some.

She put on her dressing-gown, and with the carafe in one hand and the candle in the other, she opened the door, listened, and stepped out. The house was quiet. It was past midnight; the servants would have gone to bed. If she hadn't been still a little elevated from the wine, she would have wondered where exactly she was going. In a normal-sized house, one could find the kitchen with its water-tap easily enough, but in a castle?

She reached the head of the stairs, and was hesitating when silently, round the turn of them, Giles came up. He was fully dressed, except for his tie and collar, and looked tired to death. He stopped when he saw her, then continued up. He

183

didn't ask, but she answered anyway, 'I spilled my water, and I'm very thirsty.'

'You should have rung,' he said automatically.

'I didn't like to. It's so late – everyone will be in bed.'

He looked blank for a moment, as if her reply was past understanding. 'You can always ring,' he said, as if expounding a universal rule.

She only looked at him – now, at last, feasting her eyes, knowing it was poison food, but craving it anyway. 'Giles,' she began.

'Don't,' he said, turning his face away wearily. 'There's nothing to say.' After a moment of silence, he said, 'Give me the carafe – I'll fill it for you.'

She handed it over, but neither of them moved. She wanted to touch him. 'You look tired,' she said. 'Were you working? This late?'

'There's so much to do. Always so much to do.'

'The boulder?' she said. It was how he had once described the responsibility of the inheritance – a boulder he must push for ever uphill, like Sisyphus.

'The boulder,' he agreed. He seemed pleased she had remembered. A little warmth started up in the air between them. 'It doesn't get easier. But one gets used to it.'

'You can get used to anything,' she said. She didn't mean it to, but it sounded bleak.

Bleak enough to affect him. 'Oh, God,' he said, and his controlled expression seemed to break up like water hitting a rock. 'Nina!'

She quailed before his need. She read in his eyes all he wanted to do. It was late, the whole house was asleep, it would be so easy . . . The flame wavered as the candlestick shook in her hand. She put out her free hand and laid it on his. His was warm, with the strong warmth of a man, of life. Her fingers were cold from holding the damp glass.

He looked at her desperately. If he hadn't been hampered

by carafe and candle, he would have taken her in his arms. Providence alone had saved him. 'Are you happy?' he asked. He wanted to say, 'With that old man?' but just had the sense not to.

She thought about it a long time. What to tell him, in this fragile, hopeless moment?

'No,' she said at last. 'But not unhappy, not really. Life is . . .' She couldn't think how to end that sentence, and stopped.

'Life is full of disappointments,' he finished for her, at last.

She nodded. 'Yes.'

'I want to touch you,' he said.

'I know.'

'But I can't.'

'I know.'

He looked down at the carafe he was holding, as if he didn't understand how it had got there. With an effort, he said, 'I'll fill this for you. And leave it outside your door.'

She saw he was looking at her hand touching his, and removed it, releasing him. He turned and went downstairs. She went back to her room, got into her slightly damp bed. Hours later, it seemed, he tapped lightly on her door, to let her know he was leaving her carafe there. She didn't get up to fetch it for a long time. She felt a thousand years old.

# CHAPTER ELEVEN

Kitty had had a pleasant morning talking to Peason about espaliered fruit in the new garden, where the walls were three-quarters finished. Already they were thinking beyond its completion. Succession houses, he had proposed: Lord Shacklock had an acre of glass, much of it heated all winter. Kitty had fallen in eagerly with his talk of peaches and grapes. And further down the line, a proper flower garden, lawns, walks, shrubberies – one day she would like to see them too. It would require a lot of earth-moving, Peason warned, but with relish. Cutting back the hillside, creating terraces – but what an opportunity, then, to have a descending water-course! There was water up the hill, the little Shel brook could be diverted. Cascades, pools, rockeries. Standing in the sunshine, with Peason politely holding her parasol over her, Kitty felt entirely happy, and at peace. There was no conflict here. She and Peason were of one mind, and she had the power to achieve what she wanted, without referring to anyone else, for neither Giles not his mother cared about the gardens. Here was one place in which she ruled unchallenged. She would create something – and it would be *hers*!

Afterwards, she went up to see Louis and, later, was approaching the door of her sitting-room when Giles came out of it, with Alice behind him.

'Ah, there you are! Come in – I've something to give you.'

Kitty looked enquiringly at Alice, but she only grinned.

She went obediently into the Peacock Room with the dogs swirling eagerly around her, and Giles conducted her with an expansive gesture, like a circus ringmaster, towards the round table, where a flat package wrapped in brown paper was lying.

'I'm sorry it's late,' Giles said. 'It was meant to be a present for our wedding anniversary but I couldn't quite manage it in time.'

'Oh,' Kitty said, disconcerted. 'But . . .' She was going to say, 'I didn't get you anything.' Their anniversary, on the 28th of June, had not been mentioned or marked in any way, and she thought that was the way it was meant to be.

But Alice interrupted her excitedly. 'Open it! Open it!'

It was a picture in a fine black and gold frame: the head of Giles, three-quarter profile, staring pensively away to the left. The original pencil drawing had been enhanced with water-colour and ink. Kitty looked up at Alice. 'You did it?' Alice was nearly always sketching away in the drawing-room after dinner, so much that Kitty hardly noticed any more, or wondered what she was drawing.

'It's not my fault it's late. I did finish it in time, but Giles wanted it framed and the framer took ages. What d'you think? Is it a good likeness?'

'It's wonderful,' Kitty said. A critical eye might object that he was not quite as handsome as the picture made him, but to Kitty he *was*, every bit.

'I've never tried colouring a face before, but I think it's come out rather well. I had to do a lot of practice on a spare sheet to get the tone right. Funny how we think of skin as being white or pink, but it isn't anything like either.'

'It's absolutely lovely,' Kitty said. 'You're so clever!'

'I did about a dozen sketches of him before I had one I liked. He's got a very difficult mouth.'

Kitty looked at Giles, and thought, *No, he has a beautiful mouth, and I want to kiss it.*

He smiled at her. 'The brat thought you'd like to have it as a present, so I took it to Aylesbury to get it framed properly. Happy anniversary, dear.'

Alice gave him an impatient nudge. 'Kiss her, then. You're supposed to kiss her.'

'I was just going to. Mind your business, infant!'

He laid his lips gently on Kitty's, and for a moment she revelled in his touch, the smell of his skin, the warmth of his closeness.

It was over all too soon. He straightened up, and Alice said, 'Where will you hang it?'

Kitty knew exactly where. 'On the wall beside the window,' she said. Opposite the chair where she sat to work, so she could see it every time she looked up. 'Thank you both. It's a lovely present.'

'I'll send one of the men up on my way out, to hang it for you,' Giles said. 'I'm meeting Moresby in the village, then going on to Ashridge Park. I won't be back for luncheon, I'm afraid.'

He was gone, the dogs close at heel, and Alice, after staring at her work a moment longer, recollected something and ran after him, saying, 'Giles! There's something I want to ask you.'

The room seemed suddenly very empty. But Kitty picked up the picture, and thought how good it would be to be able to gaze at him whenever she wanted, through all the long hours when he was elsewhere.

Moss did not like change. What butler did? The butler's business was to create order and ensure continuity.

Moss had been with his old lordship for many, many years, and while he could not claim there had been friendship or affection between him and his master – that would not have been proper, even if possible – he had got used to him, and admired him as the template of all that an earl should be:

grand, commanding, remote and, in all public dealings, correct.

Moss liked routine, rules, customs. He liked people to know their place, and remain in it. He liked to know what to expect. But now things had changed too much, too suddenly. The very manner of his late lordship's death had been horrible: he should have died in his bed in the amplitude of years. Moss had had an image in his mind, culled from reports in the newspapers, of the old Queen's death, with her eldest son holding one hand and her eldest grandson the other, with the rest of the family gathered silently at the foot of the bed as she breathed her last in appropriate solemnity. That was how Lord Stainton should have gone – not carried in on a hurdle from the hunting field, dishevelled, muddied, broken.

Moss felt old these days. He had not so much as opened his precious stamp album for months, let alone corresponded with other collectors, as he used to. His duties seemed to take longer, and left him with no energy for other interests. And he felt shaky. He had not yet spilled a drop on the cloth as he poured the wine at table, but the possibility that he might haunted him.

His new lordship did not set enough store by formality. Her new ladyship was very young – almost a child – and, frankly, not from their rank in society. Who knew what she thought, or might do? And her ladyship – the dowager – seemed to be turning her back on Ashmore Castle, leaving a hole where her certainty should be.

Then there had been the shocking death of the cook. Suicide – a black, black sin and a scandal. The idea that other servants' halls around the county would be discussing their shame made him lie in his bed some nights, pale and sweating, unable to sleep. He had never had any opinion of Mrs Oxlea, and had not understood why her ladyship kept her on, but she had at least had the advantage of speaking rarely and never drawing attention to herself. The manner of her departing changed all that. It would never have occurred to him to enquire into the happiness or otherwise of any servant, but the fact remained he was responsible for them. In the final analysis, he was master below stairs. He couldn't have known – but he should have.

Now there were new servants, new faces to bother him as he passed them along Piccadilly. Two new kitchen-maids and an Irish scullery-maid whose names he had not bothered to learn yet – he had very little to do with the kitchen. Ida, the previous head kitchen-maid, had taken over the cooking, and so far seemed to be managing. Mrs Webster gave cautious praise – cautious because they had not had any large parties so far to test her. When they did, they would probably need yet more kitchen staff – four was barely enough as it was.

There was a new, very young, houseboy, Eddie, who lived out, and was so young and undeveloped he seemed to be all ears and elbows. He did at least give Wilfrid, previously at the bottom of the pile, someone to boss. The new footman, Sam, was also young, and had only had two years' experience, but he seemed modest and willing to learn, which Moss found refreshing after the cockiness of James and Cyril, and the self-composed menace of Speen. He only hoped the lad would not be corrupted

The other newcomers he noticed more because they sat at the table at mealtimes. The new maids were Mildred, Ada and Addy. Mildred was a very thin girl (Worms? he wondered in passing) and constantly sniffed. He had already mentioned to Mrs Webster that Mildred needed to be reminded of the difference between a sleeve and a handkerchief. Ada and Addy – such similar names, such dissimilar girls. Addy, strong and fat, cheerful and stupid, was the sort of housemaid one always imagined on her knees, scrubbing. Ada – ah, quite another story.

She was tiny, to begin with – not so much short as small

all over, as if she belonged to a different, more delicately built race of creatures. Too delicate for housework, he had thought, when he first saw her, but Mrs Webster, when he suggested this, had said she seemed strong enough. She had fair, fine hair, pale skin, blue eyes and a wistful mouth. You would not have called her pretty, but with her resemblance to a porcelain figurine, you might have thought she was beautiful, in a way.

And she had an air of gentleness that he did not associate with servant girls as a whole. She had looked at him from the beginning with awe, as was correct in a new housemaid; but there had been underneath – or so he thought – a spark of something else. As though she were interested in him: not in Mr Moss, the mighty butler and below-stairs potentate, but in *him*, Albert Moss, son of Sarah and Abel Moss. Mr Moss was a monument of composure – but Albert Moss had a secret.

There had been a girl once. Madeleine. He had sat behind her at church, and her three-quarter profile, which was all of her face that he could see, sank into the depths of his soul and haunted his dreams. He had been fourteen, had just started as junior footman at Priestwood Hall, under old Lady Dunsmore – she who had perished in that dreadful fire twenty years ago which had burned the hall to the ground (after his time, thank God).

Madeleine was a laundry-maid, and whenever he passed her he caught a whiff of soap and starch, which was more entrancing to him than all the perfumes of Araby. His adoration had not been reciprocated – had never been communicated. She was two or three years older than him, and never appeared to notice him at all, though he waited in the church doorway after service every Sunday to watch her walk by giggling with the other maids, while he lurked, red-faced and silent, stifled by love.

He had loved her for almost a year, and then one day she

was gone, moved on to another place, as maids did, and he never saw her again. He had wept into his pillow every night until the other footman with whom he shared the room gave him a clout on the head and told him to stow it. A few months later, he had got a fine new position, second footman at Ashmore Court, and his career had become everything to him.

But he had never forgotten Madeleine. She'd had fawn hair and fawn eyes and a long neck on which her head sat like a flower on a stem. Sitting behind her every Sunday, he had longed to kiss it. Ever since, he'd had a weakness for the necks of the female sex. Where some men yearned after a glimpse of ankle or perspired at the thought of a bosom, a slender neck filled him with an almost overpowering desire to nuzzle it.

Ada had a neck – as he had seen in the first moment of clapping eyes on her. And her hair, dragged into the tight bun demanded by Mrs Webster, left vagrant soft wisps to curl at the nape, inviting touch, inviting caresses. Of course he would never *dream* . . . But he found himself looking for her, found himself smiling at her when they passed in Piccadilly. Once or twice, he addressed remarks to her at mealtimes, to try to draw her out – but he couldn't do that too often, for fear of being suspected of favouritism, and he had to speak to the other maids now and then to cover his spoor.

He became seized with the desire to have her smile back at him, but so far she had been too shy. She looked at him with solemnity, but always met his eyes, which many servants didn't, with a kind of simple trustingness that made him want to strain her to his bosom. She was so sweet, so pure, so innocent. He wanted to protect her from the buffets of the world – and especially from the attentions of men. Footmen like William, and valets like Hook sprang to mind.

One sleepy Sunday afternoon he was sitting in his room with the door open onto Piccadilly, beginning to revive from the somnolence brought on by the servants' dinner of roast pork and treacle pudding. He was leafing through his book, *The A to Z of Universal Knowledge*, to find where he had got up to, when Ada went past. On an impulse he called out to her, and she reappeared in his doorway, standing politely, hands clasped before her.

'Yes, Mr Moss?'

He had to think of something to say. 'This is interesting,' he blurted. 'Come and look.' She came in, shy but trusting, and he looked down to see where his finger had alighted on the page. 'Indigo,' he said. 'Did you know that almost all indigo dye is now artificial? It's made from the same stuff as mothballs.'

'Mothballs,' she said doubtfully. 'Fancy!'

'Before, of course, it was made from a plant, like most dyes.'

'Was it, sir?'

He looked questioning. 'You know what colour indigo is?' She shook her head. 'Come, Ada, the colours of the rainbow? Surely you learned those at school. Red, orange, yellow . . .' he prompted her.

'Green, blue, indigo, violet,' she completed obediently. It was one of the things they had learned to chant, like the times tables. She took courage from his smile. 'I never knew what indigo was,' she confessed.

'It's a very dark blue colour, sometimes known as ultramarine. That's Latin for "under the sea".'

'Goodness!' she said, looking impressed. 'What a lot of things you know, sir.'

'Oh, this is a wonderful book,' he said, tapping the page, feeling warmth spreading through him like sunshine. 'Anything you care to ask, the answer is in here. Indigo plants, for instance, come from India.' He turned back a page or two, on surer ground here. He had been reading about India on and off for months. 'Wonderful country, India.'

She twisted her head a little to see the page under his finger. 'Ooh, it's got pictures too, sir!'

'Oh, yes. Come round here and see.' She hesitated, then glided round to stand beside him. He caught a whiff of carbolic soap: his nostrils flared and his heart lurched. 'See, there's an elephant,' he said. 'Magnificent beasts.'

'Are they really that big?' she asked, for the illustration showed a mahout standing beside it.

'Oh, indeed! Have you never seen one?'

'No, sir,'

'Never been to the zoo?' She shook her head. 'You should go some time,' he said, a delightful but dangerous seed alighting in his brain. Easy enough to arrange his day off to chime with hers. Then, walk to the station, the train to London, the Underground to Regent's Park . . . He saw a summer day, Ada in a light cotton dress and a straw hat with flowers on it, Ada looking at him admiringly as he named all the strange and wonderful animals to her. He would buy her an ice-cream, and she would smile at him . . .

He dragged himself back to the present, and to India. 'They use them for transport, you know. Like horses. To ride and to harness. Now, an Indian elephant is quite different from an African elephant.'

'Is it, sir? Fancy!' she said.

'Oh, yes.' He allowed himself a glance up at her tender, fair face. 'The African elephant is actually smaller, but it has larger ears. Look, I'll show you. Just let me find the bit on elephants . . .' Keeping one finger in India, he leafed back urgently to the Es. 'Now, here's a picture – just put your hand there and hold the page down . . .'

He grew happily expansive, and forgot to enquire where his meek and receptive audience had been going when he'd stopped her.

The work on the bathrooms was taking longer than Nina had expected. The architect, Leathwaite, explained that the house was very old, and had to be treated carefully. 'And once we looked under the panelling, we discovered that the back part of the house is much older than the rest – probably fifteenth century.'

'Is that good or bad?' Nina asked.

Leathwaite exchanged an amused look with Decius, who said, 'Depends on your attitude to history. It's interesting, at all events.'

'It's not unusual,' Leathwaite said, 'to find a later structure built over an earlier one. A family puts up a house according to the fashion of the time, and the next generation, or the one after, adds to it according to *their* fashion. The good thing is that the earlier structure was well built and is very sound. But I'm having to go carefully so as not to damage or spoil anything. But I have my best men on it,' he added reassuringly, 'and they're well used to dealing with ancient structures.'

'By ancient structures,' Decius added with a wicked grin, 'he does not mean old Mrs Cornwell-Yorke of Yorke Place, who drove him to distraction by questioning every last nail.'

'I would never speak disrespectfully of a client,' Leathwaite said with dignity, though a smile lurked at the corners of his lips.

There was to be a bathroom on each of the upper floors – one above the other, it was explained, so that the pipework went in straight lines – and a proper water-closet below on the ground floor. It involved not only work inside the house, but the digging of long trenches outside, down the side of the house and across the gravel approach. Mr Cowling didn't seem to mind the dust and noise and disruption, and often popped home from the factory during the day to see what the workmen were up to. There was building work going on at the factory, too, where one wing was being emptied of its machinery and adapted for the new operation to be set up. 'But we don't have to worry about old beams and Tudor bricks,' he said, 'so we can get on a bit quicker.'

For Nina, the disruption was the perfect excuse to go and

visit Bobby Wharfedale. The initial attraction between them had not faded – they liked each other more the more they met. With Kitty she had been the leader and the talker; now with Bobby she found herself a follower and listener, and enjoyed it just as much. She had been to Welland House several times to ride, and once or twice to tea. She had met Bobby's husband, Aubrey, a tall, slightly stooped man with a vague, kindly manner, whose mind seemed to be so much elsewhere that Nina half expected him not to remember her if they met again. His passions, Bobby told her, were shooting, fishing and the history of the area and its old families.

She had learned a lot about Bobby's family. Her father was Lord Kibworth ('my darling old pa', she called him), her mother bred pointers, and she had an older brother, Kipper, a younger brother Jolly and two younger sisters, Missy and Pip. 'I miss them so much! We had such fun together. I *never* wanted to grow up – did you?' Bobby loved to talk about them, and tell stories of the pranks and adventures they had got up to.

She talked much less about her children – it wasn't until the second visit to Welland Hall that Nina even discovered she had any. Elizabeth was three, Rupert was five. 'We named him after Prince Rupert of the Rhine, my absolutely favourite character from history. Who is yours?'

Nina confessed she had never thought about having a favourite. Bobby seemed to regard history like a family almanac, and took the deeds and characters of the protagonists quite personally. She seemed more absorbed by them than her own children, who lived an entirely separate life in the nursery. 'I'll show them to you one day,' she said indifferently, when Nina asked a tentative question, 'but they're a bit boring at the moment. They'll be more interesting in a year or two. I can't get excited about babies, can you?'

Nina remembered Kitty's obsession with baby Louis, and was relieved she would not be required to gush. She was much more interested in their riding expeditions. Bobby had provided her with a mount, a brown mare called Florence. Followed at a discreet distance by a groom, they rode out and explored the country. Bobby was determined Nina should know her way around before the hunting season started.

'You'll have your own horse by then,' Bobby said. 'I've put out enquiries all over the county.'

'Decius has too,' Nina said as they rode down through a wood towards the river. It was a hot July day, and the shade of the trees was delicious. 'He says as soon as people bring their horses up at the end of the month there'll be a wide choice.'

'Quite right. I must meet this Decius of yours. He sounds a very sensible fellow.'

'And divinely handsome,' Nina said, and laughed. 'Quite absurdly so. My friend Lepida in London was struck all of a heap when she met him.'

'Are you similarly afflicted?'

'No, I seem to be immune to him,' Nina said. 'But he's very nice, and I do enjoy talking to him.' She gave a sidelong glance, and asked, a little awkwardly, 'Isn't it wrong to say another man is handsome when one is married?'

'Not if it's just a statement of fact,' Bobby said. 'I'm devoted to my darling Zephyr,' she leaned forward and patted his neck, 'but I can still appreciate someone else's beautiful horse.'

'But husbands are different from horses,' Nina said.

'Well, I'm devoted to my darling Aubrey, too. But my dear Nina, we are not blind and deaf just because we are married. Though, of course, there are husbands who think their wives should be. Let's take this path down to the river. The horses will be glad of a drink – it's so hot today.'

The path grew steeper, and came down to a ford, where the water ran chuckling over the stones. Bobby rode Zephyr into the middle and halted to let him drink. 'Just keep an eye on Florence,' she called back to Nina. 'She likes to roll in water sometimes. Don't let her go down.'

Nina rode in beside her and Florence lowered her head to snuffle the water, but did not seem to be thirsty. Then suddenly Nina felt her mount begin to sag under her. It was an alarming sensation. 'She's going! Hit her!' Bobby shouted, and when Nina, too surprised to react quickly enough, didn't move, she leaned over and hit the mare sharply behind the saddle with her whip, making her start and straighten up.

They both rode out of the ford and Nina apologised.

'Have you never had a horse do that before?' Bobby asked. 'Never mind, it's not your fault. I'm sorry I barked at you, but if she'd gone down you might have been trapped underneath.'

The groom, Buckland, came splashing through to join them. 'Florence up to her old tricks again, m'lady?' he said.

'Yes. I wouldn't have stopped in the water except that it's so hot. I thought they needed a drink.' She grinned at Nina. 'But it's all useful experience.'

'It felt horrid,' Nina said. 'Like the world going soft under your feet.'

'You'll know next time,' Bobby said. 'Shall we canter up here?'

When they arrived back at Welland Hall, there was someone waiting in the stableyard – a tall, well-built man with sun-whitened fair hair, standing bareheaded in the sunshine, his hands in his pockets.

'Kipper!' Bobby cried with delight. She rode Zephyr up to him, and he lifted her down and embraced her. 'So lovely to see you!' she cried. 'What are you doing here?'

'I got back last night, so of course I took the first opportunity of riding over to see you.'

'How are Ma and Pa?'

'Flourishing. I heard you had a new protégée.'

'Silly! She's a friend. Come and meet her.'

Nina had been helped down by the groom, and having

buttoned her habit's skirt and straightened it, she was ready to be introduced.

'My brother Kipper,' Bobby said, as if bestowing the greatest treat.

Nina shook the proffered hand, and looked up with interest into a lazily smiling face and crinkled blue eyes. She could see a resemblance between them, though the brother's eyes were bluer, and he was more conventionally handsome.

'She never grows up,' he said. 'Still hasn't the first idea how to make an introduction. I'm Adam Denbigh, how do you do? Kipper, indeed!'

'That's how she always refers to you. Why are you called that?' Nina asked, feeling immediately at ease with him.

'Because,' Bobby jumped in, 'when we were little and our governess told him to draw a fish, he drew a breakfast kipper *after* eating – just the head and the bones.'

'I liked the pattern the bones made. Like a ladder. And it *was* a fish, you can't argue with that. Still,' he looked down fondly at his sister, 'you needn't *always* address me as Kipper, particularly in public places.'

'Very well, *Adam*,' she said, as if it were the silliest name she'd ever heard. 'You always call me Bobby, I may point out.'

'At least Bobby sounds like a real name,' he said.

'Isn't it your name?' Nina asked. 'You never said.'

'No, it's a nickname. We all have them,' said Adam. 'She and I are a little older than the others, so when we were little, we spent a lot of time together.'

'I adored him,' Bobby interpolated.

'And I was quite fond of you, shrimp. Well, we were down by the river with our governess one day, and I went in to swim. I was about five, I suppose, and you would have been two, or so?'

'That's right. Miss Cudstone was sitting with me on the bank. She took her eyes off me for a moment—'

'—and Bobby got up and toddled towards me, arms outstretched, straight over the edge and into the water.'

'Goodness!'

'Poor Cuddy shrieked – she thought her baby would drown,' Adam went on, 'but the little devil came up to the surface, spluttering a bit, and just bobbed up and down, completely unafraid. That's why we call her Bobby – whatever life throws at her, she never drowns, just bobs.'

Nina laughed. 'Did you get into trouble?'

'Me?' said Adam. 'Not a bit – wasn't *my* fault. I hauled her to the bank and shoved her out, and what did she do but turn straight round and try to get back in, saying, "More water!"'

'I always hated being separated from him,' Bobby explained. 'I had no idea what a river was. I must have been quite surprised when it gave way underneath me – like you this morning with Florence, Nina.'

'Oh – did you have trouble with her?' Adam asked.

'She started to go down, but I gave her a whack,' Bobby answered for her.

'I'll know next time,' Nina said.

'Hm,' said Adam. 'But it's dangerous, you know. Riding side-saddle it's all too easy to get trapped underneath. You should—'

Bobby interrupted. 'Next you'll be telling me to have her shot. As long as you're prepared, it's easy to stop her. And it's only crossing water.'

Brother and sister were exchanging some sort of unspoken message and, afraid she might have precipitated a quarrel, Nina tried to change the subject. 'But if your real name isn't Bobby, what is it?'

Bobby avoided her eyes. 'Deborah.'

Adam gave her an amused glance. 'For some reason she hates it. When we all lived at home, she would hit anyone who called her by it. I bear the bruises still.'

'He's talking nonsense,' said Bobby.

But Adam went on. 'The last time anybody heard it was at her wedding, and even then she begged the rector to marry her as Bobby, but he said it wasn't legal.'

'That's absolutely not true. Don't listen to him, Nina.'

'I think it's rather a pretty name,' Nina said.

'I've just never felt like a Deborah,' said Bobby dismissively. She turned to Adam. 'Are you staying for luncheon? Nina is.'

'Then wild horses couldn't drag me away,' he said. Bobby had her arm locked through one of his, and he smiled and offered the other to Nina, who took it without hesitation, and the three walked into the house that way, like old friends.

Crooks came out of the valets' room and saw the new footman, Sam, standing a little further down Piccadilly, frowning over a tin he held in his hand.

Crooks hadn't had much to do with him in the fortnight he had been here, and had noted only that he seemed quiet and respectful. Crooks, who reverenced beauty and symmetry, saw now that you would not call him beautiful. His head was a little too big for his body, his neck unnaturally long, his Adam's apple too prominent. At this distance you could see that the reason he was not taller was that his legs were too short for his body. These were not deformities by any means, just slight disproportions: close up, you probably wouldn't even notice them. His features were undistinguished, and his hair was the sort of impossible fuzzy-curly type that would never look tidy, no matter how much oil you applied. This, he concluded, as he walked towards him, was no Axe Brandom.

Sam looked up at his approach, and blushed with either guilt or embarrassment. 'I'm sorry – I don't . . .' he began. 'I'm a bit—'

Crooks stopped. 'What's the matter?' he asked kindly. It

201

was refreshing to have a footman who needed help, rather than one who taunted and teased.

Sam looked at him, head tilted a little down so that he was looking up under his brows – a rather endearing posture. And at the same moment Crooks noticed that he had extremely beautiful eyes: hazel in colour, almond-shaped, and with very dark, fine lashes. It was somehow moving that this very plain lad should have one little bit of loveliness about him.

'Come on, you can tell me,' Crooks said, when Sam didn't speak. 'What's the problem?'

'Mr Moss sent me to get the furniture wax for a scratch on his desk, but I don't know if this is the right sort,' Sam said at last.

Crooks looked. 'That's boot blacking. It says it on the tin. Wren's boot blacking. There's even a picture of a wren.'

'We never had Wren's where I was before,' Sam said, looking as though he might cry. 'We had Tricker's. The tin looked different.'

'But, my dear boy, it says right here . . .' He paused. 'You can't read?'

Sam didn't answer at once, then whispered, 'Please don't tell, sir. I'll get the sack.'

Crooks swelled with protectiveness. 'Nonsense! Of course you won't. This isn't the dark ages. But how did you manage before?'

'I learned what things looked like, tins and such,' Sam mumbled. 'But it was only a small place. Everything's – there so much of everything here. And everybody rushes about so, and – and I don't like to ask.'

'Did you not go to school?'

'Not much,' Sam said. 'My ma was sick a lot, and I had to look after the little 'uns. Then my dad told me I had to get a job, for to send money home. So I never went at all after I was ten.'

'And how old are you now?'

'Twenty, sir. I know I don't look it, cos I'm short. The others said, at my last place, I'd never get on as a footman because posh places want footmen tall, so I was ever so grateful to get this job. I'd die if I lost it.'

'We don't worry about height here, as long as a man can do his job.'

'Mr Wilkins, the butler at my last place, said in the letter, the ref-ref—'

'Reference.'

'Yes, sir – he said I'd been well trained. He told me what he'd said. And Mr Moss said I could come on a trile. So I *got* to do things right. I *got* to.' His face reddened again as tears threatened.

Crooks laid a hand on his arm. He flinched but then was still. 'You mustn't be ashamed. It's not your fault. And you mustn't be afraid to ask. You can always ask me. I will help you.'

'You're ever so good, sir,' Sam whispered.

'We must all help each other in this life. And, look here, would you like to learn to read?'

'I reckon it's too late for that, sir.'

'Nonsense! Lots of people learn to read late in life. And you're hardly more than a boy. I've helped people to read before, I'd be happy to help you. With a lesson each evening, and some practice when you have your time off, you'll be reading in no time.'

'I couldn't trouble you like that, sir.'

'It's no trouble. I'm happy to do it. And you're a fine young man with all your life before you. You could go far, really make something of yourself. I'll look out a suitable book, and we'll start tonight, after supper.'

He gave the arm another pat and walked on, moving more briskly than usual, his heart lighter than it had been for months. Here was something to fill the gap left by Axe

Brandom, something to fill the long hours when Mr Sebastian didn't need him. And having the lad at hand, under the same roof, would make it all so much easier. He seemed such a nice boy, too. Crooks felt very warm towards him, as he considered the books he owned, and pondered about what he might borrow from the library.

# CHAPTER TWELVE

July heat lay over the land. The far fields shimmered with it; the woods stood motionless. Sunlight glinted blindingly off anything that reflected – a fragment of quartz, a glimpse of river, a distant window. The last of winter's rut-ridges broke down under passing wheels and hoofs, and dust hung knee high, with no movement of air to disperse it. Sheep lay up under the strip of shade afforded by walls and hedges; horses and cattle gathered under trees, listlessly whisking their tails and flicking their ears. Even the birds hid in the hedges in the middle of the day. But for mankind it was hay time, and their measure was to toil in the sun, not rest in the shade.

Giles was heading out of the back door when he saw Kitty coming towards him. Her face lit at the sight of him. She was pushing the old perambulator in which he thought he himself had once been taken for air by nursery-maids. His mother, he could feel reasonably certain, would never have pushed it herself. The dogs surged briefly round Kitty, then ran on to investigate walls and gate posts for new smells.

'Is that really my old pram?' Giles exclaimed. It was like a miniature carriage, with a coach-built body, high, thin wheels like a phaeton, and a leather hood.

Kitty looked anxious. 'Isn't it all right to use it? John Manley got it out for me and cleaned it up.'

'Of course you can use it,' he said with faint impatience. 'I'm just surprised it has survived so long. Are you going in now?'

'Yes – I wanted him to have his airing early, before it gets too hot.'

Giles bent to look at his son, propped up on his pillows. Louis had recently learned to smile, and did so now, beaming gummily at his father. Giles gave him a finger to grasp, and felt the familiar pang that was a mixture of pleasure and pain. He did not want to feel so much for this small person – it made him vulnerable. But the baby's smile was impossible not to respond to, and when he smiled back, Louis chuckled and beat his hands and feet in the air as if overcome with delight. Giles could not imagine that he had ever exchanged such moments with his own father.

Kitty said, 'You've been busy this morning.' It wasn't a question. He hadn't even looked in at family breakfast.

He straightened up. 'A bundle of accounts from the bank. Among them a large number of bills from my esteemed mother. I'm at a loss to know how anyone can wear as many clothes as she seems to think Rachel needs.'

'I suppose, moving in those circles, they have to change several times a day,' Kitty said doubtfully.

'She's spending a fortune. Doubtless she would call it an investment, a necessary outlay to secure Rachel a rich husband,' he said drily. 'Do you hear from them?'

'I don't. Rachel writes to Alice now and then, but she doesn't show me the letters.'

'Ah yes, Alice. I suppose we'll have to go through all this again when she comes out.'

'Perhaps not. She says she doesn't want to get married.'

'She says that now, but she's still a child. And she'll have to marry – what else is there for her to do?'

Kitty didn't like to say, *She can stay here. There's plenty of room*. She knew Giles would not agree, and it was so lovely talking to him, she didn't want to argue with him and drive him away. So she said nothing.

Giles cocked his head at her. 'I don't know how you feel

about having your fortune squandered on your sisters-in-law. When you don't even have a new baby-carriage for your son.'

'It's *your* fortune now,' Kitty said robustly. 'And I'm glad Louis has your old perambulator. I like to think of you lying there years ago. It's – tradition.'

He leaned over and kissed her cheek. 'You're very sweet. Take the young master in, then. I'm off up to High Ashmore to see how the haysel is going.'

He strode away, thinking she was obviously happy in her own little world, so he didn't need to worry about her. He remembered briefly their time of passion, just after they were married, and it seemed like a story, something that had happened to someone else. He was glad Kitty had presented him with an heir, and he supposed at some point they ought to make a spare, but there was no hurry. He could put it off, and was happy to.

He had been sexually innocent when they married, and Kitty had unlocked the mystery for him, for which he had been grateful and moved. But a year on, he understood that his pleasure in the act had come from the act itself, and was not actually dependent on Kitty. And he was too busy now, and too tired at the end of the day, to miss it. With the fog of sexual pleasure cleared from his head, he knew, as he had known before, that he did not love her. He was fond of her, and grateful to her, and had both the wish and the intention of protecting her and making her happy. But he had no intellectual connection with her.

And the same went for the estate. The work and the worry and the responsibility were enormous, absorbed his waking hours and sent him weary to his bed, but he was aware that at some deep level he was bored. Activity was not the same as interest. To be constantly busy was not the same as to be satisfied. He cared for the estate, and had both the wish and the intention of protecting it and nursing it back to health. But he did not love it.

'Come, dogs,' he said, and Tiger and Isaac left off their sniffing to bound after him, as he headed for the stables and Vipsania, to ride up to High Ashmore Farm.

The nursery-maid, Jessie, was waiting for Kitty in the back hall to relieve her of the baby – God forfend she should carry him upstairs herself! Having parted grudgingly with her child, she left the perambulator for someone to put away, and went through to the main hall to go up to her room.

Kitty was indeed almost entirely happy. She adored Louis, and apart from the occasional tussle with Nanny and Jessie over whose baby he actually was, he filled most of her days. The garden plans were taking shape and promised to use up years of her life. And she was enjoying putting into action her scheme for refurbishing the house. Every morning, after Mrs Webster had pretended to consult her on the day's menus, they would check the list they had compiled between them and decide what item to tackle next. And during the day, they would make inspections of work carrying out, and decide on new areas that needed attention. Very slowly, very carefully, a lovelier house was being revealed as layers of neglect were rubbed away. Kitty had the feeling that Mrs Webster approved of the whole process. It gave her more courage to face the eventual return of the dowager, to know she had someone on her side.

When she reached the main staircase she was pleased to see the estate carpenter, Gale, at work on the section of the handrail that had been damaged. A noticeable piece had been chipped out of it, and it had evidently happened some time ago, for the inside of the wound was not raw but had absorbed polish over what she guessed had been many years.

Gale had cut a short section out of the handrail and had made a new piece to match, which he was now fitting in.

She stopped to talk to him. 'How beautifully you've done it,' she said. The curve and groove exactly matched those of the old rail.

He gave her a pleased look. 'Once I've rubbed it down and varnished it, m'lady, you won't be able to see the join.' He patted the rail like a favourite horse. 'Grand piece of work, this old staircase. Heart of the house. You got to take care of things like this, m'lady, in my opinion.'

'I agree. I was sorry to see this damage left so long.'

'Must be twenty-odd year, m'lady, near enough.'

'Do you know how it was caused, then?'

'I do, m'lady. It was his lordship and Mr Richard, playing at pirates. They were fighting with cutlasses, and Mr Richard was driving his lordship backwards up the stairs. He took a swish at him and missed, and chopped a bit out of the hand-rail, like what you saw. O' course, they were just lads, never meaning no harm. They'd be about eight or nine year old, m'lady, and proper little tearaways, like you'd never believe nowadays, now they're grown men.'

Kitty's look betrayed her astonishment. 'But were they allowed to play with real weapons when they were just children?'

'Not as you might say *allowed*, m'lady, but there used to be a whole collection of old swords and pikes and suchlike on the walls of the hall, hung up like a sort of decoration, and they'd took them down for their play without asking. Got a thrashing each for it when his old lordship found out. Course, they're all gone now, m'lady, the swords and such, as you'll know.'

'Taken away because they were dangerous?' Kitty hazarded.

'Sold,' Gales said shortly. 'I believe a museum took 'em.' He gave Kitty a look both significant and conspiratorial. So many things in the house had been sold. He ran his hand lovingly over the handrail and said, 'It's good to see the old house being looked after again. 'Twas my great-grandfather first carved that termination, m'lady, did you know?'

'No, I didn't,' she said politely.

'Gales've been carpenters here for generations, m'lady. This termination, see, it's what's called a ram's horn – see the way it curls over, m'lady, just like a ram's horn?'

'Yes, I see.'

'But this one's a little bit different, you see, because right in the middle of the centre curl – see here, m'lady?' A thick finger indicated and she bent to look. 'See, it's a clock, with the hands set at five minutes to midnight.'

Kitty looked. Gale was positively purring with pleasure at being the one to enlighten her. 'The family motto, m'lady – you can see it on the coat of arms over the fireplace in the hall. *Tempus omnia edax*. It means "time consumes all" – as I know I don't need to tell you, m'lady,' he added politely. 'So my great-grandfather, he carved a clock, see, right at the heart of the house, so to say. A great craftsman, my great gran'fer. You can see his work all over the place. A lot of the poppyheads on the pews in St Peter's were done by him. I'm just glad that pirate battle all them years ago didn't damage this termination, m'lady, because that would've been a much bigger job to replace.'

Kitty walked on up the stairs, thinking that it was a curiously depressing motto: Time consumes all. Almost an excuse for inertia; in that case, one might say, what was the point of trying? She wished she could talk to Giles about it. She tucked it away in the back of her mind as something to bring out when they were next together. At school, they had been taught to prepare suitable topics to stimulate conversation should it flag. It was the hostess's duty to make sure talk flowed. She could have asked Uncle Sebastian, of course – he'd be bound to know – but Giles was so often absent in thought, even when present in body, that it was good to have a question ready to ask, to bring him back

By the time he reached the farm, Giles was aware that the heat was taking on a different character. The hazy blue sky had developed a steeliness; to the south-west, sullen clouds lined the horizon. It had been a long hot spell: the hay harvest had been good and most of it was in. But all hot weather ends in rain. A storm was coming, and High Ashmore had been the last to cut. It all needed to be got in before the rain came, because wet hay was worthless.

The farmyard was a hive of activity. Haysel was a time for coming together, for community effort. Everyone helped everyone else, and with their own harvests secure, every local farmer, with his men, had come up to High Ashmore to bring in the final one. That done, it would be time for celebration. Giles had been meaning just to look in and see how things were going, but having seen those clouds, and smelling the threat in the air, he was seized by the desire to help. *Everyone* had to pitch in, so why not the master?

Without asking – and no one had yet spotted him – he swung down from the saddle and led Vipsania towards the stables, to see if there was an empty stall he could leave her in. The first thing he saw was a round dun pony-rump that looked familiar; and as Vipsania knuckered a greeting and the pony turned its head and replied, he saw it was indeed Biscuit. He led the mare into the next stall, slipped out the bit and loosened the girth, tied her up, and went outside. A cart was just coming in, laden with hay, heading for the barn, and driving the big skewbald between the shafts was Alice.

She flung him one look of consternation, then assumed an airy insouciance and said, 'Out of the way, Giles! No time to waste. Rain's coming.'

He stepped forward and caught the horse's cheekpiece, stopping it. 'What are you doing here?' he said grimly.

'Helping,' she said blandly. 'It's haysel – everybody has to help.'

'Not young ladies. Not Lady Alice Tallant from Ashmore Castle.'

She made an exasperated movement with her head. 'Oh, really, Giles, why ever not? If I drive a wagon, it frees one of the men for pitchforking. I can *help* – and why shouldn't I?' She looked at him suspiciously. 'Why are you here, anyway?'

He gave in. 'To help,' he said, with a shrug and an embarrassed smirk. 'All right, you can carry on. But never, *never* tell your mother about this.'

She laughed, clicked to the horse and drove on.

He was not surprised to see his woodsman, the former blacksmith Axe Brandom, among the pitchforkers. Stripped to the waist, his fine, smithy-toned muscles gleaming, he was forking the hay up from the row into a waiting cart with a strength and rhythm that was beautiful to watch. Giles knew he could not achieve such balletic grace, or keep up such strenuous effort for any length of time. His place was up on a cart, spreading the received hay.

Axe spotted him, stopped, and straightened. 'M'lord,' he greeted him, with a nod. He had a piece of rag tied round one wrist, and used it now to wipe the sweat from his brow before it could get into his eyes.

'They got you here as well,' Giles remarked pleasantly.

Axe glanced towards the horizon. 'Storm coming, m'lord. Every man that can has come to help. Mr Webley put out the word yestreen.'

'Quite right,' said Giles. 'I've come to give a hand myself.' Over on the next row, he saw young Hugh Marbeck from Topheath forking as though his life depended on it. He'll wear himself out, the silly ass, Giles thought. Even he knew there was a rhythm to this sort of work.

Axe followed the direction of his gaze and said, 'Got a lot on his mind, that young man.' He wiped his brow again and turned back to Giles. 'I hear Lord Shacklock's got a baling machine, over to Ashridge Park.'

'A baling machine?'

''Sright, m'lord. You loads the hay into a kind of hopper, and a big tamper comes and squashes it down, and pushes it into a sort of funnel, and out the other end comes a square bale, all pressed and tidy and tied up with string.' He grinned infectiously. 'Gor, what'll they think of next! But it'd see an end of all this tedious-hard pitchforking, my lord. And you can store a lot more bales in the same space as loose hay.'

'I suppose so,' Giles said. 'I suppose machinery is the future of farming.'

'The future, m'lord. But right now I'd better get back to work.' And he bent his magnificent back again to the task.

Giles moved on, found another cart, and called to the man up on the load. 'Shall I take over from you? I'd be no use at forking up.' Very shortly he had taken his place in process. The heat settled on him like a heavy hand, and he was soon sweating. The hay began its usual maddening game of inserting scratchy tendrils down his collar and up his sleeves and through his buttonholes. The lovely smell of hay was in his nostrils, its unpleasant dust coated his tongue; his unaccustomed hands grew hot with friction. The dogs had gone off to join the farmers' collies and terriers in a fine game of rat-and-mouse hunting. The hay flew up and he levelled it. The work took him over and he lost track of time until the man below said, 'That'll do,' and he climbed down to stretch his back and watch the cart trundle away.

A woman was coming up the row with a jug of water and a tin mug, which she offered to him before she looked up and saw who he was. A blush spread over her face, and she said, 'Oh, your lordship, I'm ever so sorry! I didn't see it was you. You can't use this after everyone's been at it.'

'I certainly can,' Giles said kindly, but when he took the mug from her he turned away so that he could wipe the rim on his shirt end before he drank.

When he handed it back, she said, 'Why don't you go over in the shade a bit, your lordship, till the cart comes back. There's victuals over there, for folk taking a breather.'

At intervals along the hedgerow there were trees, and it was good to get out of the sun and into their shade. The cloud bank had climbed halfway up the sky, but still there wasn't a breath of wind. He joined a group sitting on the grass, and they shifted over with silent comradeship to make room for him. A large pie cut into wedges was lying on a cloth in the middle of their circle, and one of them picked up a wedge and offered it to him, saying shyly, 'Scuse fingers! Mrs Webley's veal an' ham, m'lord.'

He took it with a smile of thanks, and his benefactor seemed delighted with the small attention. Everyone was chewing, no one was speaking, but he felt a brotherly acceptance, which was more pleasure than the ache of his muscles was pain. He wondered if other earls of Stainton before him had helped with the harvest. Not his father, of course, but perhaps in an earlier age, before earls got so grand . . . He found his mind drifting, and felt he could have slept right there and then in the blessed shade of this tree . . . He was almost gone when the dogs found him again and came tramping in to wash his face and try to climb on his lap, delighted to discover him down at their level for once. Isaac got the last morsel of pie out of his fingers before he knew what was happening.

And his cart had returned – *a* cart, anyway. He heaved himself to his feet, shoving the dogs away, and stepped out into the brazen sunshine again, noting only out of the side of his attention that Alice was there, standing under the shade of the next tree along, and talking animatedly to Axe Brandom. She had always liked hanging around the forge, so she knew him quite well. Always nutty on horses, little Alice – and it didn't look as if she'd grown out of it yet.

The sky was completely grey now, and a slight wind had got up, but gave no relief from the heat, or from the tiny black flies that stuck to the sweat on every exposed patch of skin and flew maddeningly into his mouth. Thunder flies, the local people called them. There was that oppressive feeling to the air that said not just rain was coming, but a proper storm.

Now everyone worked in intense silence, frantic to get the last of the harvest in. Giles's hands were sore, but he ignored the coming blisters in the common purpose. Now men hurried to a new row as soon as one was finished; no one rested in the shade. Not that there was shade any more. With the sun hidden, everything was the same depthless grey.

A false twilight crept up as the clouds darkened. The breeze grew stronger, but fitful; there was a metallic taste on the air. Only one row left. The men ran to it, started forking madly. Every cart, every man was on the last row. Giles saw Alice, driving a different cart now, drawn by a square-jawed black. Hay flew at him non-stop from two forkers, barely giving him time to level it. The sky was plum-coloured; some of the horses were growing nervous; the cart he was on jerked back and forth as the horse tried to start and was checked.

Cart full. He jumped down, landed badly and stumbled, was caught by a large hand as hard as horn and set back on his feet without a word. He ran down the line to another cart. Every man, having cleared a section, ran to the next. The air was prickling with electricity. The sky was so dark it was hard to see. Nearly done – nearly done! A sharp little wind whipped cold past his sweaty cheeks, sending loose strands of hay whirling. A horse flung its head up and whinnied.

'Here it comes!' someone shouted.

But it was lightning first, a great searing blue gash of it that cracked like a whip, lighting the scene for a second, leaving a smell of ozone behind. And then a huge boom of thunder, ridiculously overdone, as though the god's hand had slipped. One-grandfather-two-grandfather, he had counted. Two miles off. Carts were dashing for the farmyard, drivers urging the horses into a clumsy trot. Last little bit. There was no place or pitchfork for him, but he couldn't leave. Four men forking like devils, one man on the top, the driver holding the horse back with difficulty, ready to race.

And the last bit was up, the cart was on the move, the forkers jumped and caught hold of the sides, and the one on the tail grabbed Giles's arm and shouted, 'Come on!' He made a stupid, tired, clumsy leap, got his sore hands over the edge of the tail gate, scrabbled for a foothold, was yanked into place by an arm more muscled than his would ever be, and was carried away.

And the rain came: large round drops like pennies, warm, falling separate onto the shorn field, making dark circles in the dust on the cart's rim. The horse was cantering, ears back, as if demons were pulling its tail, and it was all Giles could do to hold on as the wheels hit uneven places and the cart leaped into the air like a startled cat. When they reached the farmyard, he almost fell off, watched it go on towards the big barn. There was nothing for him to do there. Every man who had a fork was waiting to get it in. The rain increased, not the big warm drops now, but the cold hard ones, and even as he watched the last cart being emptied, there was another crack of lighting, and the heavens opened.

Rain streamed into his eyes, and he stood stupidly, trying to wipe it away, like trying to divert a waterfall with a teaspoon. Suddenly Alice was beside him, grinning at him through the sheeting rain. 'Glorious, isn't it?' she shouted. She was soaking wet, tendrils of hair glued to her cheeks, conducting the rain to her chin and thence to her chest. Seeing the state of her jerked him out of his stupor. He grabbed her arm and ran for the stables where he had left Vipsania. Everyone was seeking shelter. Someone was unharnessing the last horse from the last cart and leading it away. The cart was empty. The hay was in.

In the shelter of the stable doorway, Alice turned. 'We did it!' she cried, elated.

'That last lot might be a bit damp, but they'll save most of it,' he said.

She looked at him, shaking her head at his prosaic response. 'Giles, we did it!' she repeated. 'It was a heroic battle, and we *won*!' She smiled hugely, and he found himself grinning back at her.

'What a day,' he said. 'I've never been so tired.'

'Worse than a day's hunting,' she agreed.

'I shan't be able to move tomorrow. You're soaked through,' he said, touching her cheek. It was icy cold. 'We need to get you home and into a hot bath.'

She made an economical gesture out of the door, beyond which nothing could be seen but the rain, a flickering impenetrable sheet, with little silvery spurts and coronets where the drops hit the ground like bullets. 'We can't take the horses out in that,' she said.

A hunch of wet clothes, a dripping hat, and a screwed-up face in between poked itself into the doorway for as long as it took to shout, 'Beer and hot taties at the house!' and disappear.

Alice and Giles looked at each other. 'Hot potatoes,' Alice said. 'I'm starving!'

'Let's go,' he said.

The storm strode and bellowed about the tops, lightning cracked, and the rain pounded, rushed, rivered. Mrs Webster and Rose were busy calming the maids who were afraid of thunder and lightning, those who had been set off by the ones who were afraid, and those who just relished an excuse to have a good fit of hysterics. Kitty was in the nursery, calming Nanny and Jessie, and keeping an eye on her boy, who slept unmoved through thunderclaps that made the women shriek. Moss and Sebastian mustered the men of the house to fasten shutters, place buckets under leaks, and stop up ill-fitting windows and cracks under doors. The stable staff were fully engaged in calming the unsettled horses and diverting the streams of water coming down the hill away from the stalls.

Nobody had time to wonder where Giles and Alice were, although Giddins, the head man, did wonder anxiously what had become of Vipsania and Biscuit, and to hope that they had been put safely under shelter before this lot started.

The storm rolled away over the hills; the thunder died, muttering intermittently like someone who, with the argument long over, returns to say, 'And another thing . . . !' And then it was gone too far to hear.

The intensity of the rain eased: it ceased to pound and merely drummed, then gradually stuttered to a stop, leaving an eerie silence behind it, punctuated by the sound of drips and of gurgling in gutters. A greenish gleam of light appeared to the south-west, and widened; the clouds thinned and the darkness became twilight, and then a watery evening revealed itself. And just at the point when everyone would finally have had the leisure to wonder where the missing were, they returned, Giles driving the pony-trap with Alice beside him and Vipsania tied behind. Giddins was so glad to see his two horses dry and sound, and exhibiting an entirely normal desire for their evening feed, he barely noticed that the two humans were distinctly damp.

Moss, with Mrs Webster hovering behind, met them in the hall, and said, 'I took the liberty of putting dinner back, my lord.'

'Good,' said Giles. 'I could eat a horse. But Lady Alice needs a hot bath before that.'

'Hot water for both of you, my lord,' said Mrs Webster. 'I'll see it's brought up immediately.'

And by the time Giles and Alice reached their rooms, Hook and Daisy, flying up the backstairs, were there to greet them and help them out of their wet clothes. No one, of course, asked them where they had been or why they had got wet. Such explanations waited for the family, at dinner, where talk

218

was so lively, Kitty had no need of her stored question, and no opportunity to ask it.

The woodsman's wagon, drawn by Della, trundled into the stableyard, and Giddins, who happened to be crossing it, walked over, laid a hand on Della's rump, and squinted up at Axe Brandom enquiringly.

'Load o' fence posts,' Axe said. 'Where d'you want 'em?'

'Round the backyard, o'course,' Giddins said. 'You don't suppose we wants 'em in the stables?'

Axe was unembarrassed. 'Just askin'.' He seemed in no hurry to redirect his load. 'That was a storm and a half t'other day. I heard a big beech over to Ashmore Court got struck and come down on the stable roof. You had any damage?'

'No damage,' Giddins said. 'Horses was a bit spooked, but that's to be expected.'

Axe nodded. 'And Lady Alice – she all right?' he asked casually.

Not casually enough. Giddins frowned. 'What've you got to do with Lady Alice?'

'I see her at the haysel up at High Ashmore. Heard she got soaked in the rain. Hope she didn't catch a cold, that's all.'

'She's lively as a cricket, far as I know. But it's not for you to go asking, Axe Brandom, just because your brother's her ladyship's groom. You don't go bandying our young lady's name about.'

Axe shrugged. 'Civil enquiry, that's all. Don't go bustin' your braces.' He clucked to Della and started to back her round.

Giddins watched him with his bristly jaw set. 'And mind that gate post!' he shouted. Seeing the wagon clear the gate, he turned away, muttering to himself. 'Askin' after members of the family, as if he was anybody! Don't know what the world's coming to. 'Twouldn't have happened in his lordship's

219

day. People used to know their place. His lordship and Lady Alice helping with the harvest – the very idea!' He reached the core of his indignation. 'Comin' in soaked to the skin, lookin' like gypsies, for all to see. What'll people think? His old lordship would've never . . .' He had reached the tack-room door, and stopped, puzzled, having forgotten what he was on the way to do when interrupted by Axe Brandom. Blessed if he could remember! Uppish estate workers, coming meddling with his day! All the world was going to rack, if you asked him. Nothing was the same since the old Queen died . . .

Nina was at Welland Hall again, walking with Bobby towards the stables. Bobby halted when they reached the gate of the yard, and turned to her with an appraising look. 'Have you ever ridden cross-saddle?' she asked abruptly.

'When I was a child,' Nina said. 'Not since.'

'Have you thought about it?'

'I can't say that I have. Why?'

'Kipper and I were talking about it the other day, after you'd left. He was quite concerned about the accident you nearly had with Florence.'

'*Nearly* had,' Nina said with a smile. 'Not the same as *actually* had.'

'I know. But, you see, riding side-saddle is much more dangerous than cross-saddle. For a man, if his horse comes down, his saddle's designed to throw him clear. For us, the horns are designed to hold us in place. The chances of falling clear are small – and because of the imbalance of having our weight all to one side, it's more likely the horse will fall that way and we'll be trapped underneath.'

Nina looked at her in surprise. 'Are you saying you don't want me to ride your horses? You think I'm not good enough?'

'No!' Bobby said impatiently. 'That's not it at all. This isn't about you, it's about all women. Why do you think we ride side-saddle?'

'I don't know. We just do.'

'It's because the men *make* us. They claim that riding astride looks immodest. Their idea, of course, is that women should ride purely to be seen, and not for any pleasure they might get out of it. Side-saddle is awkward and difficult and dangerous, and bad for the horses, too. It puts a strain on their backs and lungs.'

'But – do you ride cross-saddle?'

'Often, when I'm alone. It's wonderful, Nina! The ease and freedom! The feeling you have of complete control over your horse! You know that, riding side-saddle, you have to carry your hands high, too high to have proper contact with your horse's mouth. And you can't use your legs the way a man can. Riding across is like being one flesh with your horse, like a centaur. Everything is so smooth – jumping is so easy – you feel as if you could never come off!'

'Is it so very wonderful?' Nina wondered, smiling.

'More than I can express,' Bobby said eagerly. 'I'm trying to get up the courage to hunt cross-saddle next season, but I'd really like someone else to do it with me. There is one lady who hunts with the Fernie who rides across, but she's very rich and eccentric and quite old, so nobody thinks much of it. It would be more shocking if I did it.'

'Shocking,' Nina repeated doubtfully. 'What does your husband think about it?'

'He's used to it now. He didn't like the idea at first, but when I explained how dangerous side-saddle is, he was converted, because he does love me awfully. He doesn't mind just out on hacks. I haven't tackled him yet over the hunting. But, Nina, wouldn't you like to try it? Today, just riding out with me, I mean. I promise you, it will be a revelation. And then, with two of us, we could face the world together over the hunting question.'

'I'd love to try it,' Nina said, 'but I don't think Mr Cowling would like it. He's said to me more than once how elegant a lady looks riding side-saddle.'

'Well, that's it,' Bobby said. 'That's the whole issue. Why should a man dictate to us how we ride? No woman would ever be twisted up and packed into a side-saddle again if she could help it, risking her life and health and her horse's well-being, losing the natural pleasure she might have, if she wasn't forced to prostrate herself before the tyranny of silly fashion!'

'You are passionate,' Nina smiled. 'But men decide everything we do, don't they?'

'And that's why Mrs Anstruther can hunt across – because she's a widow, and wealthy, so there's no man to tell her what to do. She's been doing it for five years. It caused a scandal in the papers the first year, but nobody says anything now.'

'But you say she's wealthy – isn't that also the point? We're married, our husbands keep us, without them we'd have no means to support ourselves. So we have to do what they want. Don't we?'

Bobby looked at her for a moment, then said, 'Well, that's an argument for another day. One thing at a time. Would you like to try it today? No one will see us. We'll just go over the fields and through the woods. Oh, *do*, Nina! You can't imagine how glorious it feels.'

Nina needed no urging to *want* to do it. She remembered scrambling about on her pony as a child, and the freedom it had bestowed. 'What do I wear?'

'Just what you wear now. You have breeches and boots under your skirt. You can arrange the skirt, once you're mounted, to cover your legs.'

She looked at Nina with an expression of such pleading and hopefulness that Nina laughed, and said, 'I can't resist you. Yes, I'll try it.'

Bobby beamed. 'I knew you were the right sort! I've held off from mentioning it before, until I was sure about you, but Kipper said the same when he met you. He liked you straight away.'

'I liked him, too. Do I still ride Florence?'

'No, she's not very good for cross-saddle. You shall have Andante – he's perfect. Come on, let's get going! I can't wait to see how you feel. It's like being reborn.'

She pushed open the gate, and Nina followed, feeling excited and just a little bit nervous – not about the horses, but about the possible consequences. Aunt Schofield had always said a woman should make up her own mind about things, but she had been a widow a long time, and her husband had been no Mr Cowling.

# CHAPTER THIRTEEN

Giles sought out Kitty in the Peacock Room, where she was embroidering a bib while Alice drew her.

'Not outdoors?' he queried, looking at Alice.

'Too hot now,' she said. 'I rode earlier. I'm going to persuade Kitty to come out later, when it's cooled down a bit.'

'Did you want me for something?' Kitty asked hopefully.

He waved the sheet of paper in his hand. 'Letter from Mama,' he said. 'It seems she's had an invitation from the Levens to spend Cowes Week with them. They have a yacht, the *Tutamen*, and they're inviting a whole party. She's going straight there from the South of France.'

'How did she hear from the Levens?' Kitty asked. 'Did they know she was there?'

'*They* were there,' Giles said. 'They were in Cannes on their yacht, and met Mama and Rachel at a party. I think Lady Leven took rather a fancy to Rachel. Anyway, the invitation was issued, and Mama says that since France is intolerable in August – her own words – they have accepted, though she doubts living on a boat for five days will be comfortable – her words again. Anyway, the point is, do we go to Cowes too? Not to stay on a yacht, I hasten to add. But there are hotels, or one could take a house.'

Before Kitty could speak, Alice jumped in. 'Oh, Giles, do we have to? We had to go once with Papa and it was *dreadful*! Nothing to do, just walking up and down, and everyone talking about boats all through dinner. And you couldn't see anything of the races – the boats were just little white triangles far out at sea. Honestly, it was the most boring week of my life.'

Giles laughed. 'I can see you're a yachting enthusiast!'

'Well, I might be if I was on one and actually racing, but *watching* it is like – like . . .'

'Like watching corn ripen,' he supplied kindly.

'Why on earth does Mama want to go? She doesn't like boats.'

'The King and Queen and the Kaiser will be there,' Giles said. 'It will be a glittering affair. And the Levens are close friends of the King, and know everyone. It'll be a gem if you care about that sort of thing. I must say, I don't particularly want to go either, but Mama says I should think about your future, and start introducing you to the right people.'

'I don't *like* the right people,' Alice wailed.

'I don't suppose you know any of them,' Giles said. 'Kitty, what about you? Would you like to go?'

Actually, she would have. She had never been to the Isle of Wight, or seen a regatta, or been on a yacht, and she thought it would have been fun to see the grand people, but in the face of two determined Tallants, she couldn't give her real opinion. 'Oh – no – not really – not if you don't want to.'

Giles wasn't listening closely enough to hear the qualification, or the wistful tone. 'That's settled then. I'm glad – I have so much to do. August is a busy month.'

'That's what you say every month,' said Alice, voicing Kitty's thought.

He smiled at her. 'It's true every month. But at least there's the Canons Ashmore Fair to look forward to. The fifteenth of August. It can be rather fun – and there will be the horse and cattle sale on the Friday.'

'Goodie! I love those,' Alice said.

'And I have my refurbishments to get on with,' Kitty said. The bright side was that it meant another delay before her mother-in-law came back and saw what she'd been doing.

Nina was delighted that Lepida was at last paying her a visit. Her parents had gone to the Isle of Wight, for Cowes week, because Mawes hoped to sketch the King and the Kaiser together, and then for a holiday in a cottage in Sandown. 'I don't care for regattas and Sandown is rather elderly, so I would sooner come to you,' Lepida had written.

Nina and Mrs Deering went into a frenzy of preparing a guest room fit for 'a young lady from London', as Mrs Deering described the potential guest with some awe. After seven weeks, the building work was still going on, but one bathroom was ready, except for finishing touches, though hot water still had to be carried up. A whole new boiler would have to be installed, plus a very modern sort of pump, before hot water would be coming from a tap.

She was eager to show her friend the countryside, and since Lepida didn't ride, Bobby Wharfedale offered the loan of a pony-trap, complete with pony, whenever Nina wanted it.

'That's so kind of you!' Nina exclaimed.

'Ah, but there's a price,' said Bobby. 'I must meet this friend of yours. For one thing, you've spoken so much about her. And for another, I've loved Mawes Morris's cartoons for years. Aubrey laughs like a drain over them. You must all come to dinner while she's here.'

So, instead of in a cab, Nina was waiting at the station with a pony-trap when Lepida's train came in. Lepida looked taller, and Nina quickly realised it was because she was thinner.

'You really have been ill,' she said, holding both her hands and looking into her face. 'I didn't realise it was so serious.'

'Oh, that's all over now,' Lepida said. None of the Morrises cared for health talk. Then she smiled. 'You don't think anything trivial would have kept me from visiting you all this time?'

'To be fair, the house wasn't in a fit state to receive visitors,' Nina said.

'I'd have slept on the floor,' Lepida said. 'Or a tent in the garden.' She looked around. 'Where is the divine young man?'

'Decius? He's with Mr Cowling – they're visiting the factories in Leicester. But they'll be back tomorrow. Mr Cowling was worried it was rude not to be here to meet you, but Decius said you and I would want to be alone at first.'

'Nina! Do you still call him Mr Cowling?' Lepida laughed.

Nina looked away, embarrassed. 'I can't help it. It's what comes naturally.'

'Well, I'm glad I shall be seeing Adonis tomorrow, at any rate,' Lepida said. 'I hope you will ask him to stay to dinner. He isn't betrothed, or married, or anything, yet?'

'He's married to his work,' Nina said. 'But if anyone has a chance with him, it's you. He loves intellectual conversation.'

Trump was waiting impatiently in the trap, and gave Lepida a warm welcome, which reminded Nina of Bobby. She had told Lepida in her letters about how she had met Bobby, and now said, 'By the way, I hope you aren't too tired by the journey?'

'Goodness, it's no distance at all,' Lepida said briskly. 'How could I be tired?'

'Oh good, because I'd arranged for us to meet Bobby for tea at the Copper Kettle. We can walk down this afternoon and you can see a bit of the town, which is very pretty.'

The meeting at the café went well: Bobby and Lepida took to each other, though a little cautiously at first. Nina sat between them, plying them with tea and slices of sand cake – a local speciality. She praised each to the other, wanting them to be friends, unaware that the hint of reserve she sensed came from jealousy over her. Lepida had known her longer, Bobby had spent more time with her recently; but Nina's

227

own warmth, and the good sense of the other two, soon overcame any pettiness.

When the second pot arrived, the subject of horses came up, and it was natural for Nina to tell Lepida her great secret – that she had been riding cross-saddle with Bobby. They had been going out several times a week, and Bobby's brother Adam had joined them on three occasions.

'It's a complete revelation,' she said excitedly. 'The freedom! The sense of security! You feel as if your horse's four legs are your own. And as if you couldn't possibly fall off, even over the highest jump.'

Lepida frowned. 'But what do you wear?'

'Oh, the usual sort of habit,' Nina said. 'Though the skirt doesn't really lie properly – it's a little awkward.'

'But there's a lady here who hunts astride, a Mrs Anstruther,' Bobby added, 'and she has a riding skirt that's divided down the middle, fore and aft, so the two sides fall naturally and cover your legs. I mean to get one made, if I'm to hunt across this winter.'

'And are you?' Lepida asked.

'I think I might have the courage to do it, now,' she said, with a glance at Nina. Then she laughed. 'I don't know why I need courage, but there it is. Society works against us poor women. Why *should* men determine how we ride?'

'For the same reason that they deny us the vote,' Lepida said. 'Because they can.'

Bobby's face lit. 'Oh, are you a suffragist?'

'How could one not be?' Lepida said. 'Though there's so little one can do about it, except go to meetings. But I'm fortunate that my father and mother are for the franchise. And my father knows a lot of people.'

'Your father knows absolutely everyone,' Nina corrected.

Lepida gave her an indulgent smile. 'But it will be a long business, I'm afraid, to change minds so very set in their groove. What does your husband think about it?'

'Oh, Aubrey's a dear! And I've been working away on him for years now – like water, you know, on a stone. I don't think he quite *likes* the idea of women having the vote, but he does at least concede that it's just. He doesn't pontificate about women's brains being too small to grasp politics, and all the rest of the nonsense. But, then, darling Aubrey never does pontificate. Except for shooting and fishing, there isn't much that rouses him from his usual *lento*. And actually, when I come to think of it, fishing is such a somnolent business it actually makes him *lentissimo*, so it's really only shooting that agitates him. And poachers who spoil his shooting.'

'He doesn't mind you riding cross-saddle?' Lepida asked.

'He didn't like it at first, but when I pointed out to him how much safer it is, he came around. And how much better for the horses – if you don't watch them, the grooms *will* pull the girths so tight, to stop the side-saddle slipping over, that the horses end up with broken wind, as well as sore backs.'

'And what does Mr Cowling think about it?' Lepida asked, turning to Nina.

Nina felt her cheeks redden, and sipped her tea to cover it.

'Nina, you *have* told him?' Lepida pursued.

She had to answer. 'Not yet. I was going to, of course. I meant to. But, you see, I enjoy it so much, it's so delightful, that I couldn't bear to risk his saying no.'

'Why risk upsetting him over something he didn't need to know?' Bobby said. 'You didn't know, to begin with, that you'd even like it. But he'll have to know sooner or later. We'll have to think of a way of getting round him, because I'm determined to find you a horse that will carry you cross as well as side-saddle. That's why I haven't come up with one yet.'

'I wondered why it was taking so long,' Nina said.

'I did tell you it had to be absolutely right for you. I've heard of several suitable docile animals trained to side-saddle, but that's not what I want for you.'

Lepida put her cup down quietly in her saucer and said, 'Don't you think Nina needs to worry more about what her husband wants for her?'

There was an awkward silence. Nina said, 'I know I ought to tell him . . . ask him—'

'You married him, of your own free will,' Lepida said. 'You took on certain duties and responsibilities as a wife.'

'But to force women to ride side-saddle is so unreasonable,' Nina began. 'It's—'

'It's never right to deceive your husband,' Lepida said unemphatically.

Nina met her eyes. 'I know. But I'm so afraid he'll make me stop, and if he does—'

'Are you so afraid of losing a little bit of pleasure? He lets you ride.'

*Lets!* thought Nina. 'You don't know how lucky you are,' she cried. 'Your parents allow you to do anything you want.'

'Yes, I am lucky,' Lepida said. 'I don't want to marry, and I never will, and best of all I will never have to, because Mother and Father give me an allowance, and I'll inherit Father's fortune, which will give me freedom. But you chose your own fate, Nina—'

'Chose it? I had no money to inherit. What else could I do?'

'You could have been a teacher,' said Lepida.

Another silence. Yes, I could have been a teacher, Nina thought, but I didn't want to be. And as a teacher I would have been poor, and a drudge. Mr Cowling offered me an establishment. His money was supposed to make me free. He said when he courted me that I could do anything I liked.

She thought of how he had allowed her to move the establishment from Northampton to Market Harborough. How he was allowing her to furbish the house in the way she wanted. How he had readily agreed to buy her a horse. He was very kind to her. He wanted her to be happy. She should be grateful, she *was* grateful, but—

But he had the ultimate control over her, and it galled.

'I'm afraid,' she said in a low voice, 'that if he forbids me this, I shall hate him for it.'

The subject had to be changed. Bobby took a breath, and in a bright tone asked Lepida, 'What are the London fashions like this year? We are sadly out of touch down here. Has anything interesting come out?'

Lepida took the cue, and they chatted their way out of danger.

Heat in London was not like heat in the country. It stifled. And the smell of horses, which in general was a smell Richard quite liked, became overpowering. That was why wealthy Londoners always quit the capital in August. Parliament was in recess, the Season was over, and Scotland, the seaside, or the round of country-house visiting beckoned.

Those who couldn't get away made the best of it. There were, at least, wonderful parks in London. And the river. A steamer ride down to Southend, to walk along the prom in your best straw hat and eat whelks and jellied eels and ride back in the twilight was enough of a treat for those who didn't enjoy many.

There were even some well-to-do Londoners – usually those who had large gardens – who actually *liked* to stay in the capital, and claimed that London was only tolerable when it was half empty. Neither Richard's aunt Caroline nor his grandmother was among them. They were both going to the Côte d'Opale, and begged him to go with them.

'Even Giles is not such a slave-driver as to refuse you a holiday in August,' said Caroline. And when he declined, 'At least go down to Ashmore.'

'You want to close up the house,' Richard surmised. 'I suppose there are hotels. At least they'll be empty.'

231

'I don't take the whole household with me to France,' Caroline said, a little crossly. 'There will always be *someone* here, and of course you can use the house if you wish. But *why* do you wish? What can you do in London?'

'There is a woman in it,' said Grandmère, when he didn't answer. 'Depend upon it. *Cherchez la femme.*'

'But what sort of a woman stays in London in August?' Caroline asked blankly.

'One who can do no better,' Grandmère said. Richard whistled innocently. '*Dîtes moi, méchant* – it is not the girl, is it? *La musicienne?* Please tell me you are not so abandoned to *la folie* as that.'

*Oh, it's much worse*, Richard thought. *You can't imagine – or I hope you can't.* 'There is no woman in the case,' he said. 'I may stay up, or I may go down to Ashmore, I don't know. Or a friend might invite me on a jolly – who knows? Thank you for the invitation, but I don't want to go to France, even with two such *femmes adorables* as my aunt and my grand-mother.'

'There's no need to be satirical,' Caroline rebuked him.

He had been rebuked again in Golden Square, where Mrs Sands was looking fatigued. 'It is the heat, that's all,' she said. 'And it is galling that you, who could escape it, choose to remain here and suffer.'

'But I don't suffer,' he said. 'I never mind the heat. All those years in South Africa tempered me. Now *that* was heat. London simply doesn't have an idea of it.'

'You are wicked to remind me that you are a war hero, when I'm trying to be angry with you.'

'Don't waste your strength, *cara mia*. It's too much fag to be angry in this weather. Let me take you away from all this.'

'Don't talk nonsense. How can I go away with you?'

'Your pupils are all gone – no lessons until September – you told me so. And Chloë is away.' Chloë had been invited by the parents of a fellow student at the Royal Academy to spend August at their house in Surrey, an invitation Molly Sands had been eager to embrace for her daughter. 'So what's to keep you from it?'

'You know, Richard,' Molly said in a low voice. 'Don't torment me.'

'It's *you* who torment *me*,' he said, serious for an instant. 'I don't care that you were my father's mistress. What difference does it make?' He reverted to his usual tone. 'The old man is dead, and I don't know anyone who regrets him – not even you, if you're honest. He's gone, and I'm here – free, healthy, and over twenty-one. Seize me while you can, before some less worthy female pulls the wool over my eyes and tricks me into matrimony.'

She found it hard not to laugh. 'You are a very cruel boy. I was very fond of your father.'

'Fond of him you may have been, but you're not weeping into your pillow every night, if you ever did. Dearest Molly, you know I amuse you. Let me lighten the cloistral gloom of your day-to-day existence and take you somewhere frivolous.'

She was not laughing now. 'Brighton, perhaps? Or Maidenhead? To sign into a shabby hotel as Mr and Mrs Smith? You think little of me if you believe I would agree to that.'

He reddened. 'You think little of me if you believe that's what I meant.'

They stared at each other for a moment, two proud people. Then she sighed. 'I'm sorry, but you don't understand the difficulties faced by a woman in my position. As it is, Mrs Gateshill gives me suspicious looks when you visit too often.'

'Damn her impertinent eyes!'

'Damn all you like, but it is a fact of life. All women have to be careful, but women like me have to be more careful than most.'

'There *are* no women like you,' he said passionately.

233

'Fallen women are ten-a-penny, my dear,' she said sadly.

He dropped to his knees in front of her and took her hands. 'I won't let you talk like that about the most wonderful woman in the world!' He kissed her hands one after the other. 'You are not fallen! You are an angel!'

She looked uneasy. 'There's nothing special about me. I don't understand why you say that.'

He grinned engagingly – kneeling, his face was on a level with hers as she sat – and said lightly, 'There's no rule about it, you know. The little blind god fires his arrows completely at random. And, if you will forgive my impertinence in lecturing you, there is no point whatever in questioning *why* someone loves you, when you could just get on and enjoy it. Well, if you won't come away with me – and I was intending separate rooms, by the by – will you let me take you out for the day?' He got to his feet. 'A train to Henley, a picnic basket and a boat on the river. Now, don't say that doesn't tempt you.'

'It does.' She looked regretfully into his handsome face. If only things were different . . . 'Very well, you may take me to Henley. And thank you.'

'Go and put on something pretty, then, while I run out and secure a cab. Unless Mrs Gateshill will do it for me?'

'She's away,' Molly Sands said unthinkingly. 'Gone to stay with her sister for a week.'

With a great effort, Richard made no comment. 'Hurry up, then,' he said. 'Be ready by the time I get back.'

She determined to enjoy herself, and it was wonderful to be out of the house after so many weeks. Richard was the most attentive of companions, and had the earl's son's assurance that made everything fall effortlessly into place. The train journey was a novelty, through the baked August landscape, yellow fields and dark green hedges under a cornflower sky; plump hills, little villages, charming thatched cottages, rambling roses. It was all very pretty; and she felt pretty too – well, not pretty, she was too old for that, but attractive, in a beige shantung summer suit that she had hardly ever had the chance to wear, and a straw hat trimmed with artificial daisies.

Then, drifting down the river, reclining on cushions, was luxurious; watching the fine play of muscle in Richard's arms as, sleeves rolled up, he rowed with expert smoothness. How well he did it! How well he did everything. She indulged herself with gazing at his face as he concentrated on guiding the boat through the usual August river traffic. She no longer tried to see likenesses in his features to his father's. He was himself, and now she only saw that he was attractive – a good, firm face. A face one could love.

Once they had got past the crowds, Richard sought out a quiet bit of bank for them to settle on, under a large, spreading tree. He arranged the cushions from the boat and the rug that came with the picnic basket to make her comfortable, and she let him fuss over her, seeing it pleased him. The picnic, acquired from a hotel between the station and the river, was good: cold chicken, pork pie, tomatoes, buttered rolls, Eccles cakes, Battenburg cake, and fruit – peaches and grapes. The sun flickered through the leaves and threw dappled shade across their faces; the river chuckled a little against the bank with the occasional passing boat; four brown cows had come down to the water to stand knee deep, just far off enough to be a charming addition to the landscape.

'Talk to me,' Richard said, reclining on one elbow, a branchlet of grapes in hand. 'Tell me your life.'

'I think you've heard most of it already,' she said. The talk between them was always easy and satisfying.

'Not nearly most,' he said. 'You've never spoken about your marriage. Who, for instance, was Mr Sands?'

'Do you really want to know?'

'I really do. Expound, please.'

'Vancourt Sands was an importer of cigars. You may have heard of him,' she said.

He frowned. 'Vancourt Sands – of course I have. But I didn't know it was one person. I thought it was a company, like Mappin and Webb.'

'He was very much one,' she said, her mouth turned down. 'He was a lot older than me and not – not a very attractive character. My mother and father – I won't say they forced me into the marriage, but they urged me very hard. Van was rich, and they were not.'

'Was he unkind to you?'

'Not directly. He used me to further his business – that was what he wanted me for. I was beautiful in those days—'

'What do you mean, *in those days*?'

'Don't interrupt. Van's clients included the highest in the land, right up to and including the Royal Family, and to keep them sweet, and to recruit more customers, he held regular dinner parties – gentlemen-only dinners.'

'Oh? *Oh!*'

'Not what you're thinking. But I was the only woman there. My job was to welcome the gentlemen, to circulate among them in the drawing-room and see they were all comfortable, well supplied with drink. Flirt with them just a little and make them feel good. Then at the dinner table I sat at the head and kept the conversation going. I had to read up in advance about politics and world affairs and society gossip. "You must sparkle," Van would say. "You must scintillate, Molly." It was he who first called me Molly. Only when the cloth was drawn and it came to the cigars and port was I released, and could go to my room, usually with a headache. It was at one of his dinners, of course, that I met your father.'

'I think I had guessed that,' Richard said, a little stiffly. He didn't want to talk about his father and Molly in this context; but still he wanted to know. 'Did your husband . . .?'

'Pimp me to him?' she said brutally, but with a wry smile.

'No, he wasn't that bad. But he'd told me, long before, when the dinners first started, that if any of the gentlemen wanted to . . . that if the situation arose . . .' She shook her head, as if to clear it, '. . . I was to keep them in a sweet temper. The dinners must be a high spot in their calendars. They must look forward to it above anything. So I flirted and flattered. I'm not proud of what I was then—'

'It wasn't your fault,' Richard interrupted angrily. 'You were in no position to—'

'Refuse? But I did. I had propositions, many of them, but I treated them lightly and laughed them off. Until—'

She had no need to say *your father*. The words were like little darts to his heart. He had said all along that he did not care that she had been his father's mistress. But he had taken care not to think about what that really meant. Until now. Inwardly, he shrugged. He had *made* her tell him. He had to face up to it.

'So he knew about you and my father.'

'He approved of the situation. Your father was a valued client and had many friends. And he and I – Van and I – we didn't – we no longer—'

'I understand,' Richard said hastily.

'William was the only one,' she said, holding his gaze steadily. 'At least, on my side. On his side . . .' She shrugged. 'It's different for men.'

'It need not be,' he said hotly. She was silent. After a moment, he asked in a more normal tone, 'What happened to him – your husband?'

'He died. He was a lot older than me, as I said, suffered from bronchitis and had a heavy cough every winter. And one winter, it was too much for him. He developed pneumonia and died. Strange to think I was only married for five years. In retrospect it seems so much longer.'

'But then,' Richard frowned, 'he was very wealthy. Surely you must have been left a fortune.'

'Ah,' she said. 'I didn't mention that I was his second wife. And he had a son by his first wife, a grown man with a wife and child of his own. He left everything to Edgar. I appealed to him for help, for justice, but he said he would not spare a penny for a woman *such as I was*. He said he was sure I had plenty of paramours who would keep me.'

'I should like,' Richard said in even tones, 'to kill that swine.'

Molly shook her head. 'It was a long time ago. It hurt at the time, very much, but the memory of pain fades. I had my skill as a pianist, which allowed me to earn a respectable living. And your father was kind. He would have given me much more, but I was proud and wouldn't take it. After what Edgar had said, I had to prove to the world, or rather to myself, that I was not what he'd called me. I let William provide me with a house, but I would not allow him keep me entirely. Though I let him give me the occasional gift, for Chloë's sake.'

'Ah, yes, Chloë,' Richard said, and paused, not knowing how to go on.

'Chloë was two when I first got to know your father,' she said, and saw his brow clear. 'How long have you wanted to ask that?'

'No time at all,' he said blithely. 'I knew she was not my father's child. She looks nothing like him.'

'You are a very poor liar,' she said. 'It's something I like about you.'

He smiled. 'Now, really, that is not a logical statement, Molly Sands! If I were a good liar, you wouldn't know when I was lying, would you? And, by the way, you said it was your husband who started calling you Molly. What is your name really?'

'Oh dear. I was hoping you wouldn't ask. It's really quite unsuitable.'

'It can't be anything too bad,' he said. 'My second name

is Peregrine. I took good care the fellows at school didn't get hold of that, let me tell you! Come, madam, out with it!'

'If you must know, it's Mariamne.'

'But that's delightful!'

'No one – literally *no one* – could ever spell it. I was Marianne all through school.'

'It suits you much better than Molly. Mariamne was beautiful, and a princess. What more need I say?'

'You're such a fool!' she said, laughing.

'I shall call you by it from now on.'

'Do,' she invited, 'if *froideur* amuses you.'

'You can't frost me. You like me too much.'

'Sadly true.'

They fell silent, but it was a peaceful silence of accord. She took off her hat, and let the little wandering breeze cool her brow. Richard lit a cigarillo and lay on his back, watching the smoke coil up through the branches. A strand of hair had fallen on his forehead, and she wanted to brush it away, and kiss the place where it had been. Impossible! But just at that moment, less impossible than usual.

He caught her looking at him; he met her eyes, and sat up abruptly, putting aside his cigarillo. She felt herself blush. He was searching her face urgently, and she knew something difficult was coming.

He said it quite plainly, in a steady voice, like a statement of fact. 'I love you.'

'No, Richard,' she protested weakly.

'Yes. I love you. And I think you love me.' She didn't answer. Impossible! 'I am in such a damnable position,' he said. 'I love you, and I want to marry you, but I have nothing to offer you, no establishment. I couldn't support you, and so I can't ask you. But if I could, if I did, would you say yes?'

She was silent a long time. Then she said, 'I think that is a question that has to be asked to be answered.'

239

He looked hurt. 'Don't trifle with me! Do you think I'm not sincere? I mean it, every word.'

'I believe you,' she said. 'But it's you who are trifling with me. If you can't ask me to marry you – and I accept that you can't – you can't ask me to respond to a proposal that can never be made. It's cruel to expect me to.'

'Oh, damn,' he said wryly. 'You're quite right. I'm a fool and a cad – but you must forgive me on the grounds of inexperience. I've never asked a girl to marry me before.'

She flinched inwardly at the word 'girl'. 'You still haven't,' she pointed out lightly. 'And please don't take that as a hint that I want you to.'

'You're laughing at me.'

'No, my dear, at the situation. Which you must agree is closer to farce than tragedy.'

He took her hands and kissed them. 'You always make me laugh when I particularly don't want to. It's most unfair. And here I am, laying out my finest feelings for you to trample on, and you haven't even said *you* love *me!*'

'Nor shall I,' she said steadily.

'But you *do*,' he urged.

She freed her hands and looked away. 'You make it too hard for me, Richard. Everything is too hard.'

He was silent. Then, after a while, he said, 'We should go back,' and she was afraid she had hurt him, and that he was ending their day out of pique.

But when she looked at him enquiringly, he gave her a smile of purest sweetness, and said, 'The trains will get crowded when everyone comes off the river. We don't want to have to share a compartment. We should get away before the rush.'

Back at Golden Square, Molly let herself in with a latch-key and said, 'It has been such a lovely day – I don't want it to end.'

Richard followed her in and up the stairs, saying, 'I've no intention of letting it end. I mean to take you out to supper. There's a charming little French restaurant in Dean Street. You know the sort of thing – small tables, candlelight, unidentifiable cuts of meat disguised by quantities of garlic . . .'

She laughed. 'I especially like the garlic! But I'm not sure I ought to dine with you alone in a restaurant.'

'Are you under twenty-one? Do you need to ask your father's permission? Then don't be foolish.'

'I'd better change,' she said.

'It's not formal,' he said. 'They won't mind me in my blazer and flannel bags, and you look charmingly in that outfit.'

'If you don't mind, though, I will change. It's rather too light and summery. I might stand out too much.'

'As you please,' he said.

She went through into the bedroom, and Richard moved about the living-room restlessly, fidgeting with things. It had been a lovely day, but it had left him in a fret, unsatisfied. His blood was up, with nowhere to go. And then he noticed that her bedroom door had not caught when she pushed it closed, and was open a crack. He was suddenly cool, and the hair stood up on the back of his neck. He stepped to it, hesitated, then pushed it open.

She had her back to him, had taken off her jacket and blouse. Her chemise was a pale peach colour, edged with cotton lace. She was reaching up behind to unfasten her necklace, a simple gold chain. She froze when she heard him come up behind her, then dropped her arms. He stepped close, unfastened the catch, let the chain slip forward, and she caught it in a cupped hand. Then slowly, softly, he laid his lips on the warm nape of her neck.

She made a small sound, either of protest or despair. But her breathing had quickened, and he slipped his arms around her waist and moved his lips up the stretch of her taut neck to her hairline. Then she turned inside his embrace, and her mouth was his. He kissed her long and deeply. Her arms came up round his neck, he pulled her close against him, feeling the fantastic softness of her half-clothed body. He had loved her mind since their first meeting, but it was not enough. He wanted everything.

It was agony when she pulled back. 'No, Richard. No,' she said against his mouth.

He tightened his arms. 'Don't stop. Please, don't. My darling, my darling.'

She pulled his hands loose. He let her go, but not entirely – enough that she could face him, with a space between their bodies. But his hands remained at her waist. 'Why?' he said baldly.

'You know why,' she said, low and unhappy.

'I told you, that doesn't matter. God! I've told you and told you.'

'I'm too old for you. I'm old enough to—'

'Don't say it. Don't you dare say it!' He looked down at her angrily. 'Age is nothing. It's just a number. It doesn't mean anything when people love each other as we do. You think I'm a foolish boy, but you forget what I've seen and done. I'm old in experience. And you, you're fresh and lovely and timeless and immortal—'

'Oh, my dear, if only!' She stopped him, between laughter and tears. 'Have you thought how it would look?'

'I don't care what anyone thinks,' he said impatiently. 'I never have.'

'What about what Chloë would think?'

That gave him pause. Slowly he removed his arms from her, looked at her with a thoughtful frown. But then he said, 'I don't think she would care. Her music – it makes her different. I can't find the right words, exactly, but she isn't entirely of this world. She isn't a girl, really – she isn't any age.'

'I know what you mean,' Molly said, in fairness. 'But all

242

the same, she is my daughter, I am her mother, and she would be shocked.'

He pulled away from her, stumped to the door, put his arm up on the frame and rested his forehead on it. He was silent a moment. Then he said, 'If you don't want me, you only have to say it.'

She didn't answer. He felt her move up behind him. Then she put her arms round his waist and rested her head against his back. 'I can't say it,' she said. They were still for a while, just breathing. Then slowly he turned round and drew her against him, and she let him, rested against him, perilously safe.

At last, with a sigh, she released herself, stepped back, and said, in a steady, neutral voice. 'This must never happen again. If I can't trust you to behave, I can't see you again. Can I trust you?'

He looked steadily into her face for a long time. Then, as if he had had an answer to some unasked question, he smiled, and raising a hand, tenderly drew a thread of hair from her cheek and restored it to its place behind her ear. 'You know I would never do anything to harm you.'

'That is not an answer to my question,' she said, not quite managing to be stern – her voice shook just a little.

'It is all the answer you can have. And now, hurry up and get changed. All that fresh air has given me an appetite. I could eat a horse – and, given the tendencies of the French, I may well have to.'

He went back into the other room, closing the door behind him. She turned and looked at her reflection in the wardrobe mirror, and shook her head ruefully. He always made her laugh – that was the great danger. Laughter weakened your resolve. And she wanted to be weak: she wanted to have him. But she mustn't. She ought to send him away, tell him she wouldn't see him any more. But somehow she couldn't. She thought she would suffer for it in the end, but she couldn't.

243

# CHAPTER FOURTEEN

The Royal Yacht Squadron Gardens was where the *beau monde* gathered during Cowes week. There, a band played selections of popular music, there, people took tea at little tables to watch, and strolled up and down to be seen. The men wore white flannels, variously coloured blazers, and boaters with the ribbons of their clubs. The women were in voile, chiffon, taffeta, crêpe de Chine and *linon de soie*, and since the colours of the season were white, biscuit, champagne, pale green and pale rose, the effect was rather like a flock of moths being disturbed into fluttery motion. Hats were enormous, perched on top of high-piled hair, and frequently upturned like boats or fruit bowls so they could be filled with flowers and plumes and ribbons and lace rosettes.

Rachel was perfectly happy sipping tea, nibbling shortbread, and examining the ensembles with an increasingly expert eye. She had discovered that she adored clothes: she thought about them all the time, and was deeply happy that her mother, while not interested in fashion on her own behalf, was ready – indeed determined – to dress Rachel in the best possible style, with as many changes as the day required.

Despite the number of exceedingly well-dressed women passing before her, Rachel was satisfied with her present outfit. The style was for the waist to be tightly nipped in and emphasised by a belt, the blouse much decorated and falling loosely forward while the skirt was gathered, tucked and pleated to form a bustle and train behind so that, with the aid of a punishing corset, the body of the woman of fashion made a sort of S shape in silhouette. It made sitting difficult: one sat slightly sideways and perched on the edge of the chair. The piled hair and enormous hat took some skill to balance, and a gust of wind could spell disaster; but as dressmakers had often told Rachel recently, one must suffer for beauty.

Her *ensemble du jour* was a blouse of champagne voile with sleeves full to the elbow and tight below. There was a deep yoke of Swiss embroidery, a pelerine of coarse Cluny lace, and the skirt was of ecru crêpe de Chine with cross-way folds at the hem. Her upturned straw was worn fore-and-aft, and was filled with white plumes and white silk roses, the brim edged with daring narrow black bébé velvet for contrast. She was only sorry it was too warm to wear her darling little ecru coffee coat: coffee coats were absolutely the *dernier cri* this year.

Aunt Vicky had said Rachel was lucky to have such perfect colouring. 'Not everyone can wear these biscuit and champagne shades,' she said. 'They leave most women looking washed-out – unless they resort to maquillage.'

Rachel knew that she was in a very privileged position at Cowes. Aunt Vicky and Uncle Bobo were acquainted with the Kaiser, while her mother was acquainted with the King, her late father having been in his circle. And the Levens were the kindest of hosts, and knew just about everyone. So she was sure of being where the best people were, and seeing everything. From the deck of the *Tutamen* they had watched the Royal Yacht, *Victoria and Albert*, arrive, and come up to her moorings, which were agreeably close to *Tutamen*'s, and had seen all the distinguished guests, including the Kaiser, go on board to be greeted by the King and Queen, fresh from their visit to Ireland.

Rachel had watched some of the racing from *Tutamen*'s

deck, though it was not like watching a foot race or a horse race, where everyone went in a straight line from the start to the finishing post. It was hard to tell what was happening, with all the yachts going in different directions ('Tacking,' Lord Leven explained to her kindly, 'to get the best of the wind') and impossible to tell who had won. ('The Kaiser,' Lord Leven enlightened her, when the Schooners' Handicap finished. 'That's his racing yacht *Meteor*.')

'It's a good thing he's won,' Leven added, 'because it will put him in a good mood, and we're dining with him tonight at the King's table. He's not the easiest of people when he's put out about something.'

Rachel and Maud had not been invited to dine, but on the Tuesday, in the gardens, the King and Queen came strolling along, stopped to talk to Maud, and kindly asked for Rachel to be presented. It all happened so quickly she hadn't time to be nervous. She managed a creditable curtsy, and dared to peep up at the King's face. He looked exactly like his engravings in the *Illustrated London News* – tall, stout, white-bearded and jolly-looking, with very blue eyes. And – something the illustrations couldn't tell you – he smelt delicious. He asked her if she was enjoying herself, and said she looked very pretty, and she blushed, which did her no harm at all in the royal eyes. The Queen was fair and surprisingly young-looking; beautiful, but cool and remote. She did not speak to her. Her mother told her afterwards that the poor Queen was very deaf, which shut her out from normal society.

On the following day, they were invited with the Levens to tea on the Royal Yacht, and there Rachel met the Kaiser, or at least was mentioned to him, and curtseyed from a distance. He glanced at her briefly but did not otherwise acknowledge her or her mother. He was quite handsome, with the same blue eyes, but was not as imposing a figure as the King. He had a strange little waxed moustache that poked out to either side, and held himself very stiffly. There were half a dozen tables set out under a canopy on the after-deck for tea, and Rachel was at the furthest away from the royalty, but she was quite happy with her share of the honour. The tea was very good: little sandwiches – salmon, cucumber, and egg-and-cress – cakes with lemon icing, and fancy biscuits.

Best of all was that, because the Kaiser was at Cowes, lots of German nobles had come, like the Rantzaus, the Hardenbergs and the Schliebens, which meant that there were plenty of Rachel's previous dancing partners among their sons to flirt with. There were balls every night, at which she never had to sit a dance out; and during the day there were carriage rides and boat trips and picnics, and the daily strut in the Gardens, where her admirers could ask her to take a turn up and down with them, and everyone could see how popular she was.

Frittie Landau was there, and she still thought him the most amusing of her satellites. Unfortunately, Prince Paul Usingen had also arrived, and made a beeline for her and her mother, and bowed over their hands like – *like a fawning dog*, she thought.

'He's very rich,' said the American Nancy Ortenberg – she too had come with her husband, and joined Rachel at the tea table one day for a chat. Their eyes followed Usingen as he strolled past with Maud Stainton on his arm. He seemed to be talking to her urgently, but still broke off as they passed to doff his hat to Rachel and smile ingratiatingly.

'I suppose he thinks he's being charming,' Rachel said discontentedly. 'He really shouldn't smile at all, when his teeth are so bad.'

'Oh, Rachel, so cruel!' Nancy said.

'I can't help it. I hate him. Why does he keep hanging around me? I've never encouraged him. But Frittie Landau jokes me that he's going to make me an offer.'

'Frittie's a terrible tease,' Nancy said. 'But honestly, Rachel, if he did offer for you, would it be the worst thing in the world? Like I said, he's very rich. And you'd be a princess. I know my ma and pa would have loved me to be a princess. It was really hard work explaining to them what a landgrave is. I think they still don't really get it. If Manfred had only been a duke, they'd have known where they stood. They have dukes in Germany, though they don't spell them the same.'

'It would be nice to be a princess,' Rachel said, 'but not if it meant marrying Paul Usingen. He's so *old*.'

Nancy laughed. 'Then you wouldn't have to put up with him for long, would you? But he's not really that old – and I think he's rather sweet. Kinda like a hound pup, you know, all sad eyes and long floppy ears.'

Rachel burst out laughing. 'He doesn't have long floppy ears!'

'No, but he gives the impression of them. Still,' she gave Rachel a sidelong look, 'I suppose you've given your heart to Frittie Landau, and that's the end of that.'

'I like Frittie – he's good fun. But I don't think he's serious about me. Or not yet. And there's loads of time. I haven't even had my London debut yet. I definitely want to have a London Season before I get married.'

'Quite right. All the flirting and a lot of the dancing stops when you get married. But there are compensations.'

'Yes, a house of one's own, and a dear little baby,' Rachel said dreamily.

'Oh, Rachel, you're such a stitch!' Nancy said, laughing. 'There's a bit more to it than that.'

'Oh, I know. I mean, I suppose there is. But you're happy, aren't you, being married?'

'It's pretty much the way I expected it,' said Nancy, 'except that we don't go on the way Ma and Pa go on together – they're still real spoonies, and do everything together. But my Manny's a sweetheart, and no trouble at all. And I get to travel, which I love. I want to go *everywhere*! Manny says we might go to Russia next year. Half the Russian court are married to Germans, and Manny knows most of them. He's related to quite a few.'

'I'd like to see Russia,' Rachel said, impressed.

'Well, you can always marry Prince Usingen,' said Nancy. 'I'm sure he'd take you.'

Rachel made a face.

The origins of the Canons Ashmore Fair went back into history, at least to mediaeval times: it was mentioned in the records of the former priory. But there were some who believed it was even older than that, and that it had begun as a horse market in Roman times, when people from the surrounding areas brought in horses for the Legions to purchase as cavalry replacements. The British were known to be great horsemen and great horse-breeders, and their tough little mounts, ideally suited to the rough terrain, could go all day without tiring.

Though the High Street pubs, cafés and shops naturally hoped to benefit from the increased number of people flocking in, the main part of the fair took place on Poor's Field, a large meadow on the south edge of the village. It was here that the horse and cattle sales took place, and here also that the other attractions were set up: the merry-go-round, the coco-nut shy, the shooting gallery, the roll-a-penny; the tented freak shows; the boxing booth; the stalls selling produce and locally made goods; the food vendors and the beer tents. Each stall paid a tithe of its profits for the day to the church, which distributed the money to good works. And there was a series of light-hearted races – Gretna Green, egg-and-spoon, three-legged, wheelbarrow – with prizes donated by local tradesmen. And in the evening there would be dancing.

Kitty was surprised when the carriage that brought her, Giles and Alice to the show ground was met by a committee of the great and good, headed by the rector, with a brass band playing something celebratory – Alice thought it was meant to be 'See the Conquering Hero Comes', but it sounded as though one or two members were trying to play 'Rule Britannia' instead.

The rector was effusive. 'Such an honour . . . So delighted you have consented to open our fair . . . our humble endeavours . . . good causes . . . God's work comes in many forms . . . a few words to lift our hearts and set us on our way.'

'You want me to make a speech?' Giles said blankly, spotting a draped and decorated dais in the background, with people already gathering around it. He had not expected this.

'If you would be so kind. I know we will all take great inspiration from your thoughts on the occasion,' said Dr Bannister. 'Your late father and grandfather, sadly, found the date of the show too, er, challenging . . .'

Yes, thought Giles. Straight from Cowes to Scotland. They would never be at home in August.

'But records show your great-grandfather was a great supporter of our little fête. And we would deem it a great honour,' he added, turning to Kitty, 'if her ladyship would graciously condescend to present the prizes later.'

Kitty managed not to giggle, bowing her head to hide the twitch of her lips. She understood now why Hatto had insisted on dressing her so elaborately for what she had assumed was a private walk about some stalls at a country fair. It was her first experience of being a Great Person, and she felt utterly fraudulent. She was grateful for the very wide hat her maid had urged on her: it did give her a certain amount of cover.

Giles allowed himself to be led up onto the dais, like a French aristocrat mounting the scaffold, and managed to assemble a few suitable words while Kitty stood smiling at his side. There was enthusiastic applause, a small child presented Kitty with a posy, and then the villagers and visitors, all in their summer best, dispersed eagerly to get at the stalls, attractions and victuals.

Alice slipped away with them, determined to enjoy herself. Poor old Giles and Kitty, she observed, were going to be escorted by the committee. She decided to walk round the whole thing first, to get the lie of the land and choose what she might spend her money on, then go and look at the horse sale.

'M'lady,' somebody said, and curtsied to her, and she realised it was two of their own maids – Tilda and Milly – almost unrecognisable in their best dresses and straw boaters. All the servants had the day off to allow them to come to the fair. It was an annual treat for them, like the Boxing Day Ball.

'Are you having a nice time?' she said.

'Yes, thank you, m'lady,' they said in chorus, then hurried away, giggling.

Somehow, it was funny to see people in the wrong context, and she felt like giggling herself.

William wandered disconsolately about the various stalls, unable to enjoy them because Tabby had promised to come to the fair with him, but then at the last minute, just last night, had told him that she had to work. 'But I might be able to get off later in the afternoon. If I can, I'll come and find you. You don't need to go looking for me,' she had said.

He'd had grand visions of winning her a doll at the shooting gallery – he had quite a good eye – or perhaps impressing her by standing up for a round with 'Pugnacious Jack Pugsley, the Wycombe Wonder' (though William had never been a boxer and was rather afraid of fisticuffs, but it was hinted that, for half a crown, Pugnacious, a romantic at heart, would go easy on you if your sweetie was watching and even pretend to be knocked down).

Or he might take her on the merry-go-round where, sitting behind her on one of the galloping horses, he would be licensed to put his arms around her waist and perhaps give

251

her a squeeze. Even just strolling about the various stalls had offered the hope that she would let him hold her hand.

Listlessly he examined the stalls of local tradesmen, sampled a morsel of Shelloes pork pie and a sliver of Hillbrow cheese, expended six balls on the coco-nut shy without dislodging anything, and consoled himself with a half of summer ale at one of the beer tents. He bought himself a bacon and onion pastie and walked on, eating it. The crowds were growing more dense, and he almost bumped into Ellen and Mabel, walking together arm-in-arm, before he saw them.

''Lo, William,' Mabel said, giving him a grin. 'You got a bit of summing on your chin – looks like onion.'

He wiped his face vaguely with the back of his hand. Ellen glanced at him, then away again indifferently. She was pretty, and rumoured to be walking out with Tom Trapper, the chimney-sweep. William was troubled by an embarrassing memory of Speen and Hook telling him that, and then sniggering over some joke about a sheet of paper with a hole in it, which he didn't entirely understand and certainly didn't want to. He hated the way the two valets talked about women. He blushed at the memory, which caused Mabel's grin to widen, and caused him to remember, with further scalding, that they had said Mabel would do it with anyone, and had urged him to 'give it a go'.

'Are you having a nice time?' he mumbled, trying to be polite and rid his mind of inconvenient images.

'Yeah, prit' much,' Mabel said. 'Be more fun with a chap to show us round,' she added. 'Want to?'

'Oh, Mabel,' Ellen sighed disapprovingly.

'Never mind her,' Mabel said. 'You can take me in the Hall of Mirrors if you like. They say you see stuff in there that'll knock your eye out.'

William didn't want to go in the Hall of Mirrors with Mabel. With Tabby would be a different thing. But he was not often solicited by members of the female persuasion, and hardly knew how to refuse.

'I haven't got much money,' he mumbled stupidly. What he had, he wanted to save in case Tabby did make an appearance later.

'Well, you're no use to us, then, are you?' Mabel said, and shrieked with laughter. 'Go on, mutton-head, I'm not interested in you. I seen your mum, though, over by the gate. She'll look after you.' And the two walked on, leaving William feeling badgered and belittled.

And was his mother really here? If so, she could only have come to check up on him. She didn't approve of fairs – or of pleasure in general. Pleasure was the Devil's way of tricking you into sin: that was her belief. If you were enjoying yourself, something somewhere was wrong. He really didn't want to bump into his mother. But which way to go to avoid her? He turned on the spot, trying to look in every direction at once, in case he saw his mother's greenish-black best hat bobbing towards him.

What he did see – only a glimpse between heads and shoulders, but the eye of love was keen, and he was sure he was right – was Tabby's jolly straw boater decked with artificial cherries, and beneath it her golden hair, which was a colour different from everyone else's, so you couldn't mistake it.

She seemed to be on the arm of a man, but William was unable to see which man. Her boss, perhaps? Or her father? He tried to hurry after her, but the crowds were so thick they impeded his progress, and by the time he reached the place where she had been, she was long gone. Then he started to doubt he had actually seen her. He wandered on, from stall to stall, without purpose. If she *was* here, she had said she would find him, but in such a throng, would she be any more successful than him?

Alice examined the horses and ponies tied up for sale, which gave her both pleasure and pain: pleasure because she loved all horses, pain because some of them were so old and poor she feared for their future. She wished she had lots of money and could buy them all so they'd be safe and cared for. She stopped to stroke a very thin pony with a dull coat and hipbones that stuck out like a cow's, and it flinched away from her hand as though it expected to be struck. But then it sighed, and even leaned against her fingers a little, as if remembering better days.

'Lovely pony that,' said the exceedingly dirty man standing near it, who looked even thinner than his charge. 'Suit you perfect, miss. I can see you like him.'

'He's very thin,' she said disapprovingly.

'No, he's just lean and fit. You don't want no fat pony, miss, that'll lose his puff if you try to gallop. Fat ponies ain't healthy. Carry you all day, will this pony, up hill and down dale. Doesn't know the meaning of tired. Got more courage 'n a lion. Your pa here, miss? Get him to buy you this here pony, and you'll never regret it.'

'I'm sure I wouldn't,' Alice said, meaning something quite different.

'Starved,' said a voice beside her. 'And beaten too, if I'm any judge.' Alice glanced round and saw it was Miss Eddowes.

'It looks so sad,' Alice said quietly to her. 'I wish I could do something for it.'

'People who mistreat animals make my blood boil,' Miss Eddowes said. 'But judging by his appearance, the owner can't afford to feed himself, let alone a horse.'

'What will happen to it?' Alice asked fearfully.

'If the fellow's lucky, he'll get a few shillings for it from the knacker for its skin and bones.'

'It'll be killed?'

'Then its troubles will be over,' said Miss Eddowes. She looked at Alice, and read her thoughts. *Everyone says you're very rich. You could buy it. A few shillings would be nothing to you. You could feed it up and make it happy.*

'My dear Lady Alice,' she said, 'I doubt if anything much could save this poor beast. It's probably twenty years old, and riddled with disease into the bargain.'

'Oh, but—' Alice began. She felt tears gathering in her eyes and was angry with herself. She wanted to be calm and rational – that was the way to persuade. She knew instinctively that passion wouldn't do it with Miss Eddowes. She swallowed and tried again. 'I'm sure he was loved by someone once. See how he likes me scratching his head.'

Miss Eddowes looked a query. 'They don't give you an allowance up at the Castle.' It was half a question, half a statement.

Alice felt embarrassed. 'I never really have to buy things.'

'No, I suppose not. Your mother—'

'She's away. She was at Cowes, then she went to Scotland. I don't think she's coming back until the autumn.' There were a lot of questions competing for Alice's attention just then, foremost among them, *Why does my mother hate you?* But the pony gave a trembling sigh and eased its weight onto the other foot, and banished them all.

The owner spoke up again. 'This your ma, miss? She looks like a good judge of 'orses. Buy the young lady this nice pony, lady, what she's lost her heart to?'

'I'm not her mother,' Miss Eddowes said briskly. 'And this poor animal should be put out of its misery.' And she walked away.

Alice stood stunned, trying to think of a way out. Could she offer to buy the pony and promise to pay later, when she'd had a chance to beg some money from Giles? Or from Uncle Sebastian, more likely? But the man didn't seem like a local – she'd never seen him before and he didn't know who she was. So he'd want his money right away so he could go home. He'd never trust her for it.

Then a voice from behind her said over her head, 'Give you five bob for him.'

All the hair stood up on the back of Alice's neck. She knew that voice.

The owner's gaze tracked upwards to address a taller person. A hopeful look came into his sunken eyes. 'Lot of interest in this 'ere pony, guv'nor. Young lady's thinking of taking 'im. Twelve bob, I was thinking of asking.'

'Better think again, then. Five bob, and that's four bob more than it's worth.'

'I'd get eight bob from the knacker.'

'You'd never get it as far as the knacker. Take five bob before it drops dead and you're left holding a bit o' rope. Come on, I haven't got all day.'

And a moment later, the end of the dirty bit of rope that constituted a halter was in Axe's hand, the thin man had melted into the crowds with his two half-crowns, and Alice was staring up at her hero with a mixture of gratitude and bewilderment.

'Why?' is what she eventually managed to say.

He shook his head. 'Asking myself the same thing.' He scratched his head under his hat, staring at the wretched pony. 'How the dickens will I get it back up the hill? I must be going soft in the head.'

Alice laid a hand briefly on his wrist. 'You've saved a poor wretched creature from misery,' she said.

With expert and not unkind hands, Axe forced the pony's mouth open and looked at its teeth. 'Not as old as I thought,' he commented, letting it go. 'About fifteen. Maybe when it's fattened up, it might have a bit of work left in it. Few years, if we're lucky. I suppose that bloke couldn't afford to feed it.' He stood staring at it in silence, thinking. The pony had no energy to do anything but stand there, unaware of the changes in its fortunes.

Alice said, 'I'm so grateful to you for buying it. I couldn't bear the thought—'

He looked down at her. 'I know. I heard.' He coughed. 'Miss Eddowes – she's a practical person.'

Alice felt shy. 'I didn't know you'd be here,' she said.

'Everybody's here,' he said. 'Nobody misses the fair if they can help it. And I've got, er . . .' He cleared his throat. 'The church stall's selling some of my carvings,' he finished, looking shy himself. 'Some little things I made. Help out with the beetle fund.'

'Oh, how lovely! I must see them! But what are we going to do with the pony?'

'I been thinking,' Axe said. 'I thought of the stable behind the forge – there's a spare stall, and Mr Rowse'd let me use it temp'ry. But I'm not sure this old boy'd make it down the far end of the village on his own legs. So I'm thinking I should walk him round to the sexton's yard behind the church. Mr Gomperts lets me leave Della there. He'll let me put the pony under the cart shed with a bit of hay. I brought Della a feed down in the cart, and I reckon she can go without for once. Pony can have it, and if he don't drop dead from shock, I can keep him there a couple o' days til he's strong enough to go up the hill.' He scratched at the pony's neck and examined his fingernail. 'Could do with a good grooming as well.'

'You are so very kind,' Alice exclaimed passionately. 'And now I feel guilty for making you buy him. If I had any money, I'd pay you back, honestly I would.'

He smiled and shook his head. 'No need. You can come and visit him when he's up at my place, see how he gets on. You should think of a name for him as well. I'm no good at names. And now, I'd better get him moving.'

'Can I help?'

'No, m'lady, better you go and mingle. You don't want to be seen with this old scarecrow of a pony. Don't want people talking.'

'As if I'd care!'

'Go and enjoy the fair. I've got him,' Axe said imperturbably.

*　*　*

Moss had no idea why he had asked Ada to come to the fair with him. He hadn't known he was going to do it until the words were out of his mouth and, being Moss, it was issued less like an invitation than a summons. She would enjoy the fair a great deal more, he said, if she understood the background to it, the history, the traditions. And sweet, shy, pink-cheeked Ada had lowered her eyes and said, 'Thank you, Mr Moss,' in a whisper.

She looked even more enchanting in a grey skirt, white linen blouse and her Sunday hat of straw with a pink ribbon. 'Most suitable,' was all he allowed himself to say when she presented herself. There was a brake going down to take the servants, but he wouldn't subject her to the inevitable talk if they got into it together; and, besides, he wanted the length of the walk to have her to himself. He loved to talk to her. She listened so quietly, and he felt himself grow powerful and eloquent in her service. He wanted to educate her, so that she could Better Herself. She was too good to be a housemaid all her life. She was lovely and good, and with the polish he could give her, could raise herself to be a lady's maid, or even get a job in a shop – a lady's outfitters perhaps, or something genteel of that sort.

Actually, a different ending to her story was lurking in the back of his mind, but he couldn't yet bring himself to take it out and look at it directly. It was too beautiful, too precious, too delicate, like a butterfly's wing from which the bloom would vanish with too much handling.

On the way down the hill, they passed a hedge in which wild summer roses were having a second flowering. He stopped, picked a spray and, with a bow, presented them to her. She took them rather awkwardly, as though wondering what to do with them, and he said, 'Perhaps, pinned to your hat . . . They'd go so well with your pink ribbon.'

Between them, with one of her hat-pins, they accomplished this. The roses were already dropping their petals in the heat, and he was afraid they would be quite bare by the time they got down the hill, but he forgot the problem when a story came to his mind, which he took pleasure in relating to her.

'There is an old legend that the gods named the rose queen of all the flowers. This, of course, was in pagan times, when the people believed in lots of different gods, not the One True God we worship today, you understand.'

'Yes, Mr Moss.'

'Well, the legend says that the nightingale fell in love with the beauty of the flower queen, so much so that he flew down and tried to embrace her.' In his mind, he was the noble, the eloquent nightingale, she the exquisite, beautiful rose. 'Such was his passion, that he did not notice her thorns. As he embraced her, they pierced his breast, and drops of his blood fell on the ground.'

He paused. She frowned a little. 'Did—?' she began, and stopped, too shy to go on.

'Yes, my dear. Ask what you wish,' he said kindly.

'Did he die?' she managed.

'No, no! The legend is that where the drops of his blood fell, new roses grew.'

'Oh,' she said.

'A beautiful story, is it not?' She shook her head, just slightly, as though she were thinking. 'Don't you think it's a beautiful story?'

'I think it's rather cruel,' she said in a small voice.

'You are mistaken! The king of the birds and the queen of the flowers together created the lovely rose that we admire today. That is the purpose of the story.'

'Oh,' she said again. 'I don't understand things much,' she apologised. 'You know such a lot, Mr Moss. I think you must know everything there is.'

His heart swelled. 'Not everything,' he said playfully. 'I can't claim to have more than scratched the surface. But knowledge is power, my dear. You must take every opportunity of learning, just as I have all my life. You must Better Yourself, as I have.'

'I could never be like you, Mr Moss,' she murmured.

'I will help you,' he said. 'You have a young, eager mind, and I shall take delight in shaping it.' He searched for something new to tell her. 'The Canons Ashmore Fair, for instance – did you know it has been held every year for centuries past?'

'Goodness!' she said. 'Has it?'

'In mediaeval times there would have been jousting – a game in which two men on horseback charged each other, armed with pikes, and tried to knock each other off. I believe it is still done in some places, though not here, of course.'

'No, sir.'

'But it must have been very exciting to watch. Very colourful, with the knights in their armour, plumes in their helmets, and the horses covered with wonderful coloured cloths, called comparisons. You remember the picture I showed you, of the elephant in brightly coloured ceremonial robes?'

'Yes, Mr Moss,' she said dutifully.

'It's the same sort of thing,' he explained. 'But the elephant's robes are called a palladin, while on the horse it was called a comparison.' They walked on, down towards the village, and he unpacked more treasures of his mind and laid them before her. He had stored them up over many years, and here at last was someone worthy of receiving them. She would understand the fair better, and get so much more benefit out of the day. But it would not be all learning: he would make sure she partook of some of the more seemly entertainments, too. Perhaps even the merry-go-round. He could not compromise his dignity by riding on a horse or a cockerel, but he thought fondly of watching her go past him, seated on a galloping horse, her cheeks pink and her eyes sparkling with excitement, waving to him each time she passed in her innocent pleasure.

And when the ride stopped and he helped her down, she would look up at him with such warm gratitude, and he might take her hand for a moment – just to steady her, because she would be a little unsteady after the whirling about . . .

William saw Tabby at last, coming round from behind the furthest beer tent, which was set up against the boundary hedge of Poor's Field, beyond which was farmland and the looming back of Jasper Poor's big October barn. He was so pleased to see her, he did not think to wonder what she had been doing there.

'I been looking everywhere for you!' he exclaimed.

'Have you, then? Well, here I am,' she said, brushing down her skirt, and putting up a hand to feel her hair and push in a pin. It was such a feminine movement, it enchanted him, no less because raising her arm made her breast move delightfully under her blouse.

Her blouse – which, he noticed with faint surprise, was mis-buttoned, the topmost hole orphaned and hanging loose. And then he noticed her expression. She seemed to be distracted, as though thinking about something important, but at the same time angry. Her lips were pressed tight together, her eyes bright with it, her cheeks redder than usual.

'Are you all right?' he asked shyly.

'Course I am,' she snapped.

'Only you look upset. And you got your blouse done up wrong,'

She glanced down, then after a moment's pause up and into his eyes. Slowly her expression changed. The tight angry look went, and she smiled at him – in a rather strained way, but he was not particular. A smile was a smile. 'Look at me, so I have!' she said. ''Twas an old wasp, see, come buzzing around, and it crawled right down my neck. I was that scared, I pulled me buttons undone to get 'un out, and then I was in such a tizzy, I must've done it up all wrong.'

'It didn't sting you, did it?' he asked anxiously.

'No, 'twas just one of them old dummel wasps. They're dopey at this time of year.'

'But they can still sting you!'

'I know. That's why I wanted 'un out. But 'twas all right. Nice of you to worry about me, though,' she added, stepping a little closer and gazing up at him. 'Makes me think maybe you're a bit soft on me – are you?'

'More'n a bit,' he mumbled. Holding his gaze, she felt for her buttons, undid the top three, and rebuttoned them correctly. During the process he was able to look down the soft, secret cavern between her breasts, and his stomach turned to water. 'Much more'n a bit. I – I think about you all the time, Tab. I think you're beautiful and good and – and—'

She laid a hand on his arm. 'I like you too, William. In fact, I'm thinking we ought to start walking out proper. What do you think?'

'Oh, Tab, it'd be just – just—' He couldn't think of a fine enough word.

She slipped her hand through his arm, and turned with him towards the rest of the fair. 'That's settled then. You're my feller, then, and I'm your girl.'

'Oh, Tab!'

'And I tell you what, William. My mum's here somewhere. We ought to find her and introduce you to her. Make it all official-like.'

She glanced behind her, and he glanced too, automatically, but she tugged his arm, demanding his attention. 'What d'you think? Would you like that?'

'If you think it's right,' William said. He thought he'd caught a glimpse of someone else coming round from the back of the tent, but he hadn't really had time to see properly, and looking down at her and her soft lips and even softer bosom, spilling generously over the top of her blouse, every other thought was banished from his mind. Tabby Mattock wanted to walk out with him. With *him*! – the one Mr Speen called 'Daft William'.

Not so daft now, was he? Oh no!

He was walking on air.

# CHAPTER FIFTEEN

Despite being escorted around the fair, Kitty enjoyed the occasion. It was so good to be out and about, and to see people having fun. She even enjoyed the prize-giving, playing at lady-of-the-manor. Despite her title and fine clothes, it still felt like playing.

In the carriage on the way home, Giles said, 'Well, that's over for another year. We did our duty for a good cause.'

'Was it unpleasant for you?' Kitty asked. 'I saw you managed to get away from the committee at one point – with that tall, thin man.'

'That was Lord Shacklock,' Giles said. 'I forgot you've never met him.'

'But I know who he is. He owns Ashridge Park, and you bought his hunters.'

'That's right. I slipped away with him to have a look at one of his bulls. He breeds pedigreed shorthorns.'

'Not the one that killed the postman?' Alice put in.

'How do you know about these things?'

'Everyone was talking about it. Caesar – wasn't that its name?'

'The one at the show wasn't Caesar,' said Giles. 'It's a younger bull that he's selling.'

'Why is he selling it? Can't he have two?' Alice asked.

'Of course. But you have to sell your home-bred bulls from time to time and buy new ones from outside the herd, or

you get too much in-breeding. This young bull was a magnificent creature. A roan – they're the best. I almost bought it
myself.'

'Why do you want a bull?' Kitty asked.

'To improve our stock, of course,' Giles said patiently. 'The
tenants use any old bull to get their cows in calf, and even
if they wanted to, they couldn't afford a good one of their
own. But if I bought it, and lent it out to them . . .'

'But what difference does a good bull make?' Kitty asked.

'Stronger, healthier calves, which grow up into healthier
cows that give more milk. Better milk, too.'

'I see. So why didn't you buy this bull, then?'

'I need to talk to Markham and Adeane about it first. But
when the time comes, I shall certainly have a look first at
what Shacklock's got. That really was a beautiful animal.'

Giles had a dreamy look, as if he had fallen in love. Alice
thought of the animal she had wanted to buy, and shut her
lips firmly on any possible mention of it. Nothing about it
was beautiful – unless it had a beautiful soul. But there had
been love involved in that transaction, too. Love of a sort.

James Hook walked past the valets' room and, seeing Crooks
in there, turned and went in to do a bit of tormenting. He
was feeling restless and bored. When he had wangled his way
into being his lordship's valet, he had assumed there would
be a life of travel, parties, house-visits and such, where he
could throw a bit of swank and, not incidentally, make a bit
of money on the side. But his lordship didn't seem to want
to go anywhere, except around the estate day after day, which
gave no opportunities for a gentleman's gentleman to show
his feathers. It had always been his way to take out his
humours on those weaker than himself, so now he propped
himself at the end of the table, where Crooks was engaged
in polishing a pair of boots, and said, 'So, Crooky, you missed
the fair.'

'Don't call me Crooky,' the elderly valet said automatically.

'Bet you're cheesed off. Not much fun going on in this place to start with, and you go and miss a big slice of it.'

'I've been to fairs before,' Crooks said, rubbing in loving, rhythmic circles. He enjoyed polishing boots, seeing the high, mirror-like gloss slowly appear. It was an art. Young bucks like Hook hadn't the patience or the dedication. It was all rush and hurry and get-it-done-quick with them.

'I've had dinner before, doesn't mean I don't want another one,' Hook said. 'Must have galled you, having to go to Henley, that weekend of all weekends. What did the old fool want there, anyway? It's not his usual time.'

'You will kindly refer to my master in a proper manner,' Crooks snapped.

'Oh, I will, will I?'

'And I fancy a gentleman can go and visit his own house without asking *your* permission.'

'You *fancy*? Gawd, you bleat like an old nanny-goat, Crooky, and that's a fact! But there's nothing on in Henley in August. Full of day-trippers, I shouldn't wonder. What'd he go there for?' Crooks didn't answer. 'Look, I'm sorry I called him an old fool. He's a very nice gentleman, all right? So what did he go for?'

Crooks unbent slightly. If you didn't talk to your fellow-servants, you didn't get much conversation at all. 'He went to see what condition his house was in. A house that's not lived in much can get a bit neglected. There were a few things that needed putting right – a cracked window pane here and a slipped roof tile there. But he feels it needs smartening up. A bit shabby, he thought.'

Hook's ears pricked. 'Dickying up his house, is he? Oho! And why would he want to do that, I wonder? I smell a woman in it. Thinking of getting married, is he?'

'I should not be so impertinent as to speculate on the matter,' Crooks said loftily.

'Come off it, Crooky! You're as curious as an old woman when it comes to a bit of gossip about them upstairs. So don't set yourself up as better than the rest of us.' He glanced at the valet's hands, and said, 'You and your monogrammed brushes, and your special cloth! Who d'you think you are?'

'I don't think, I know. I am a gentleman's personal gentleman, and I know my place.' Glancing up, he saw Hook's sneer, and added angrily, 'You, however, do not know your place, because you're not worthy of one. And you are not a gentleman of any sort, whatever airs you give yourself. You're a jumped-up footman, and what you know about valeting could be written on the back of a postage stamp. I've seen the state you let his lordship's boots go out in, and it's a disgrace!'

Hook hadn't thought Crooks could rile him, but he didn't like being called a footman – those days were long behind him. 'I know a damn sight more about everything than you do, you old ninny! And before you talk about his lordship's boots, you should have a look at your own.' And before Crooks could anticipate the action, he reached a long arm forward and snatched the boot he was polishing from his hands. Fixing Crooks with his eye, he clamped his fingers round the back of the boot and pressed and twisted his thumbs on the highly polished surface. 'Look at this!' he crowed triumphantly, holding out the boot and pointing, jerking it away every time Crooks tried to grab it back. 'Fingermarks! Fingermarks all over! What sort of work is this? Mr Sebastian'll have a fit! There's a big old thumb print here, Crooky – greasy old thumbs everywhere! You're useless, old man!'

Crooks managed to secure the thing at last, and bent over it, almost weeping. It took hours of work to get rid of marks like that – days, even. Layers and layers of polish, lovingly applied and buffed to a glow like the gleam in a spaniel's eye . . . Any valet knew better than to lay a finger on the leather, let alone grab it and mash your thumbs about. It was a disaster! 'What have you done?' he wailed. 'What have you done?' Then he looked up, and for a moment there was a red glare of anger in his eyes that almost made Hook step backwards. 'You're a monster!' Crooks hissed. 'You don't deserve to live!'

'Shut up, you old fool!' Hook said, trying to sound contemptuous, but hearing it come out uneasy. 'It's only a boot, for God's sake.'

Crook continued to look at him a moment longer with raw hatred. 'I should like to kill you,' he said. Then he turned away, taking his wounded boot back to the table. 'Go away,' he said, low and hard.

And seeing no more fun to be had, Hook went. *Monster, am I?* he thought. *I'll give you monster.* He stalked on, thinking that this place was getting to be no fun at all any more. Maybe it was time he moved on, found another place. His present job wasn't up to his standards, and that was a fact. He was wasted on Ashmore Castle.

'Some sort of upset below stairs yesterday, wasn't there?' Sebastian asked Dory, as she sat hemming a new chemise for Lady Alice. He was playing very quietly, because the window was open and outside birds were singing. He wasn't following the music, really, just letting his hands wander, adapting the notes to the birdsong.

Dory looked up quizzically. 'What makes you think that?'

'I don't think it, I know it. I was intimately involved. Or, rather, one of my boots was.'

She sighed. 'That James Hook. He's always at the bottom of everything.'

'Crooks was almost in tears, apologising for the state of my left boot, though in justice I couldn't see anything wrong with it. He said there were thumb-marks on the heel but I couldn't see 'em.'

'Considering Mr Crooks was up half the night polishing

and rubbing and buffing, I should just about think there'd be nothing to see,' Dory said.

'So what happened?'

'Hook made the marks deliberately, just to torment Mr Crooks,' Dory said. 'I shouldn't tell you, because we're supposed to stick together—'

'But Hook doesn't stick together, does he?'

'No,' said Dory. 'So I don't feel like sticking by him. All the same, sir, I'd be obliged if you wouldn't tell anyone I peached.'

Sebastian laughed. 'Now, who would I tell? I don't talk to anyone but you.'

'And Lady Alice.'

'Lady Alice is as sound as a bell. But I wouldn't tell her about below-stairs shenanigans.'

'I wouldn't mind if they were just shenanigans,' Dory said, going back to her sewing. 'But sometimes there's quite an atmosphere. Mrs Webster was furious with Hook, but of course he's not under her, he's under Mr Moss. And Mr Moss . . .' She paused. It wasn't for her to peach on the butler. That was going too far.

Sebastian helped her out. 'I get the feeling that Moss isn't quite himself lately,' he suggested. 'Is he drinking?'

Dory looked up warily, but didn't answer.

'That's all right,' Sebastian said. 'I've been on this earth long enough to know that butlers always drink. It's part of their job, after all. When they open the claret, they have to taste it, to make sure it's sound. And when they decant it, there's always a little bit left at the end of the bottle. And if the port decanter comes back not quite empty, well, it can't be served up again the next day, can it?'

Dory took a few more stitches. 'I don't think it's drink,' she said at last. 'I think there's something on his mind. But I don't know what it is,' she added quickly.

'No,' he said. 'None of us can know another person's mind.'

269

He played a few phrases, then reversed them, and said, 'I have something I've been meaning to ask you.'

'Yes, sir?'

'When I visited my house last weekend, I noticed some things that need the attention of a good needlewoman. I wondered, if her ladyship and Mrs Webster and all other interested parties agree, whether you would come over for a few days and work your magic?'

She looked up. 'Would you be there, sir?'

'That's my intention,' he said. 'Crooks would come with me, of course, and I have staff there – a housekeeper, Mrs May, a maid, and an outside man – so you would have company. I thought of going next month, when the summer crowds are gone. The river is lovely in September. Fine walks for you in your time off.'

She thought of the word going round downstairs – that when a gentleman suddenly took an interest in his neglected house, it generally meant there was a bride in the offing. She had ignored the talk because she felt sure he would have mentioned it to her. But if he was making the house ready to receive a woman, she was happy for him.

'Would you be willing to come?' he asked again.

'Of course, sir. I go where I'm sent.'

He gave a little shake of the head. 'There's no coercion in the case. I thought you might enjoy the change – and the work does need doing. Needlework is not Mrs May's forté.'

'I'll come, sir, and gladly,' Dory said. She felt a little sad, because if he married he would go away, and she would miss these times, with her sewing, him playing, and both of them chatting. But mostly she felt happy for him.

The library was full of cigarette smoke by the end of the regular meeting with Markham, when Adeane was ushered in.

'You sent for me, my lord?'

'I'll be off,' Markham said, beginning to gather up his papers.

'No, stay,' Giles said. 'I want to put an idea to both of you.'

Richard pushed his chair back and stretched out his legs. 'Deal gently with him,' he advised the two men. 'It's an affair of the heart.'

Giles frowned at him. 'Must you always be so frivolous?'

'Yes, I'm afraid I must. Much as I sympathise with your tender feelings, I reserve my romantic inclinations for human females.'

Adeane was looking bewildered, and Markham gave a slight smile at Richard's whimsy. Giles explained about Lord Shacklock's bull at the Canons Ashmore Fair, and his thought about improving the stock of all his tenants.

Adeane immediately shook his head. 'Couldn't be done, my lord, not with one bull. He'd drop dead of exhaustion, having to go round all the farms and service everyone's cows.'

'In any case,' Markham said, 'the improvement would be desperately slow, just with one bull, given the poor stock you'd be starting with. It would be a decade at least before you'd see any results.'

'But wouldn't *any* improvement be a good thing?' Giles asked.

'Yes, but not at any price. It would be a terrible waste of a prize bull's – er – potential. If you really wanted to do something like that, you would need to start with half a dozen prize heifers as well, and start your own herd from scratch. Take one of the farms back in hand, say, and do the thing properly.'

'How would one take a farm back in hand?'

'Nothing easier,' Adeane growled. 'Just put the rent up, and chuck 'em out when they can't pay.'

Giles winced. 'That sounds a bit brutal.'

'Most of 'em are in arrears as it is,' Adeane said. 'Anyroad,' he went on disapprovingly, 'this estate's always been arable. Can't change it over to stock just like that.'

'Arable's finished,' Richard said. 'You know that. The price of wheat . . .'

Giles gave him an amused look. To think of his frivolous brother knowing the price of wheat!

'But beef prices are no better,' Markham said. 'With all that dead meat imported from America and Canada and Argentina, you'd never get a return on the investment.'

'What if it wasn't beef?' Giles said slowly. 'What about dairy cattle?'

Richard grinned. 'I told you it was love. That was a dairy shorthorn he saw at the show. You can't argue with the human heart.'

'I don't see any market for milk,' Markham said.

'So where do local people get their milk from?' Giles asked.

'Every farm's got a house cow or two, to provide 'em with their own milk,' Adeane said. 'Even if they had any to spare, who'd they sell it to?'

'What about the village?'

'Poor's dairy,' Markham said. 'You've probably seen the cart going round. Jasper Poor keeps a small herd, takes a few churns round the houses every morning, and that covers it.'

'What about cheese and butter?' Giles asked.

'Well, the farmers make a bit for their own use,' said Markham. 'What's in the shops is all imported.'

'*Imported?*'

'From Australia and New Zealand.'

'But that makes no sense!'

'Their costs are so low over there, and they can produce on such a scale, that even after it's shipped across half the world, it's still cheaper than anything our farmers can make in the small amounts they produce.'

'Suppose you set up a factory of your own?' Richard said suddenly. 'Did it on a large scale?'

'But where would you get the milk?' Markham said simply. 'And it would have to be good milk, high in butterfat.'

Giles shook his head. 'We've gone round in a circle. All right, I can see my idea isn't viable. But I still think there's something there. It just needs thinking through. This hand-to-mouth business benefits nobody.'

He remembered Mr Cowling saying farming had to be run like a business. He hadn't understood at the time, but he knew he was feeling his way towards an idea, though he didn't know what it was yet. But he thought of his tenants, scratching a living, each alone with his problems and debts; and the land, which every Englishman grew up to believe was all-important. Two wasted resources. There had to be a better way to bring them together.

'Improvements take time,' Markham said comfortingly. 'And you've already made a difference with the buildings and the tracks. And we'll start to see a benefit next year from the drainage schemes we're putting in hand.'

'Good effort,' Richard told him. 'But don't expect him to smile when his heart is broken.'


It was a hot day at the end of August when Axe Brandom's sister Ruth drove into his yard. He went to the pony's head, but there was no need – it seemed only too glad to stand still.

'He's sweating a bit,' Axe remarked.

'He's not used to that hill,' Ruth grumbled. 'It's a long way from the village.'

'I like it. 'Squiet up here,' said Axe. 'Shall I untack him?'

'Just tie him up and give him a bucket of water. I'm not stopping long.'

'But you'll have a cup of tea?'

'That I will.' Ruth climbed down, holding a basket. 'I've brought you a cake. And a jar of those pickles you like. And our Mary sent you some of her brawn. Seth sends his best.

And our Polly's started knitting you a scarf for Christmas. You're to act surprised when you get it. Mother's been showing her how to knit, but she's not very good at it yet, so it'll take her till then. She drops more stitches than she makes. Right, you see to Bramble, and I'll put the kettle on.'

She went inside, followed by a hopeful Dolly, who soon, however, came out disappointed. Ruth was thin and dark and brisk, taking after their mother, where Axe, large and fair and slow-talking, was more like their father. Ruth was practical and frugal, and not one to squander either food or caresses on a dog.

'So,' she said, when she emerged, 'let's see this famous white elephant of yours.' Axe feigned not to understand her. 'There's talk,' she said. 'Seems Lady Alice was mooning over some broken-down old pony on its way to the knackers, and you pranced in like a knight in armour and bought it for her.'

Axe didn't care for 'pranced'. He scowled. 'Didn't buy it for *her*.'

'Well, that's what it looked like. Where is it, then? Bring it out so I can see how a damn fool gets parted from his money.'

Axe went into the stable, and led the pony out. Two weeks of grooming and feeding-up had made a very different animal of it. Under the dirt, its coat had been revealed as bay, of a good, rich colour; and the hip-bones and ribs were now receding under a layer of flesh. The listlessness and misery had gone, and it stood normally rather than sagging at the knees with its head drooping. It was not, in any way, a distinguished-looking pony, but there was nothing basically wrong with it.

Ruth stared at it long and hard, with her lips compressed. 'What the devil were you thinking?' she said at last.

'It's not a bad bargain for five bob,' Axe defended himself. 'Nice-natured, too – easy to handle. I reckon I did all right.'

'I'm not concerned with whether you got your money's worth, you big gowk. You bought a pony for Lady Alice at the fair. For Lady Alice! In front of everyone. You couldn't even settle for winning her a coco-nut, oh, no, you had to buy her a blasted *pony*!'

'I told you, I didn't—'

'You were seen talking to her beforehand as well. And at the haysel up at High Ashmore. And now I'm told she's visiting you here, alone.'

'She just calls in when she's out and about, that's all. She likes to see the animals, and play with Dolly.' He thought for a moment before adding, 'I think she's lonely at home.'

'You're a damn fool! What d'you think you're playing at, having an unmarried girl visit you alone? And a girl from that family, what's more!'

'There's no harm in it. She's just a child.'

'Oh, to you, maybe, but not to the rest of the world. She's a grown woman, Axe Brandom. Marriageable age. That's what people see.'

'But I haven't done anything wrong,' he protested.

'Don't you understand? If there's a scandal, nobody will care about that. They won't ask what you did or even whether you did anything. The scandal will be enough on its own. You'll be chucked out. You'll lose your job, and you'll never get another one – they'll see to that. No one will touch you. And don't think any of *us* will help you, because if we did, *we'd* be damned along with you, and we've got our own families to think about. You've got to stop this, Axe, before it gets any worse. Make her stop coming here. And get rid of that pony.'

'Who told you she comes here?' he asked sulkily. Ruth telling him off had always made him feel six years old.

'I was told, that's all you need to know.' She read his expression as contrition, and softened slightly. 'Maybe there's not too much harm done yet. Just don't let her come here again. And don't get seen talking to her anywhere. You should have got married long ago,' she added, almost to herself. 'Too blooming handsome for your own good.'

There was an awkward silence. Axe broke it by saying, 'That kettle boiled yet?'

'Let's see,' she said. She looked around her with dissatisfaction as they walked towards the house. 'I don't like you being so far away. See how you get yourself into trouble? I wish you'd never taken this job.'

'It's a good job. Much better wages.'

'It'd need 'em, all alone up here like you are. What if you got ill?'

'I'm never ill.'

'What if you had an accident? Out in those woods of yours, what if a tree fell on you, and you lay there for days with no one coming? I worry about you.'

'Aaron Cutmore lived up here alone just the same, and I never knowed you worry about him.'

'Aaron Cutmore's not my brother,' said Ruth. But she slipped her arm through his and squeezed it, to signify forgiveness.

'Who told you?' he asked as they reached the door.

'Someone. You don't need to know.'

'Was it Josh?'

'Course it wasn't. If *he* knew, you'da been out on your ear long before now. You know what he's like about the Family. You better pray he never does find out, either. You better pray your Lady Alice never lets anything slip in front of him.'

'She wouldn't. She's sound.'

A snort of disbelief served Ruth as a reply to that.

# CHAPTER SIXTEEN

'I must say,' said Mrs May, at her most refined, 'that it's a treat to have you back here again so soon, Mr Crooks. Company of any sort's always welcome, but *superior* company – well!' She turned to Dory to explain. 'Most times when the Master comes, he only stays a couple of days, and he doesn't bring anyone with him.'

'How does he manage without a manservant?' Dory asked.

'Oh, he shaves and dresses himself all right. He's very handy. I just pop up at the last moment and do his studs for him. He could probably even manage them, if he had to. Very nimble hands, the master has, with all that piano-playing. And he doesn't dress up much when he's here, and no entertaining. Just a tweed suit, or flannels.'

'Mr Sebastian is sadly uninterested in sartorial matters,' Crooks said. 'It is a disappointment to me, my gentleman's appearance being, if I might put it so, the canvas upon which I practise my art.'

'That's a lovely turn of phrase!' Mrs May said. 'I don't know how you think of all those words, Mr Crooks. It's a treat to listen to you. And it's a shame you feel your talents are wasted. The master is a lovely person, but he's not one for fine feathers, it must be said.'

They were taking their midday dinner round the kitchen table: Mrs May, Mr Crooks, Dory, the house-parlourmaid Olive, and Joe, who did all manner of things, indoors and

277

outdoors. He was too multifunctional to be called gardener and too rustic to be called footman. He tended the garden, carried coal, cleaned silver, filled lamps, pumped up the water, even peeled vegetables when Mrs May was pressed for time, and dealt with such matters as a dead pigeon in the cistern or a wasps' nest under the eaves. He was a large, shy, fair young man, and rarely spoke, though he looked up when Mrs May made the remark about words, and almost seemed about to.

Crooks met his eyes and smiled encouragingly, making Joe blush. 'Well, at least I know that when I'm not here, Mr Sebastian's boots are in good hands. You do them very well, Joe.'

'I can't get 'em as glossy as what you do, Mr Crooks,' he apologised.

'It is an art,' Crooks admitted. 'But there are some tricks to it that I could teach you, if you liked.'

'There, Joe,' Mrs May encouraged. 'You could learn up Mr Crooks's secrets and become a valet yourself one day. Make something of yourself.'

'I don't know,' Joe mumbled. 'I'm not one for learnin'. I never was no scholard.'

'That's true,' said Mrs May cheerfully, collecting in the plates. 'Went to the village school, didn't you, Joe? But it never had much effect on him. Take the plates, Olive, and fetch the custard, and I'll turn out the duff. Currant duff, Mr Crooks, and there's a bit of hot jam to go with it.'

'Delightful,' Crooks said politely. There was a lovely Indian Summer going on outside, but Mrs May paid no heed to the weather when she cooked. The range meant it was always hot in the kitchen, so the seasons largely passed her by.

Wisteria House was a square, handsome, red-brick Georgian house, with a pleasant garden that ran down to the river. It was small after the Castle, only six bedrooms, but ample for a bachelor, especially one who was largely absent. During the regatta, the house was filled with guests, old friends staying for the week, and others coming in by the day to watch the river races from the garden. But apart from that, Sebastian didn't entertain much.

'Mrs May seems to keep it all in good order,' Dory said when, on the day after their arrival, Sebastian walked with her round the house to identify what needed doing. 'All this wood must take a lot of polishing.' As well as the furniture there was panelling, broad oak floors and a fine staircase.

'But perhaps . . . do you think it rather gloomy?' Sebastian asked. 'Would a lady like it, do you suppose?'

*A lady?* she thought. Was there something in the gossip after all? 'I wouldn't call it gloomy,' she said judiciously. 'Masculine, perhaps. But, of course, I couldn't say what any particular lady's taste would be.'

He deflected the implied question. 'Never mind, what do *you* think?'

'I think you had better show me what wants mending, sir,' she said firmly.

There were some tapestry chairs with frayed seats, curtains that needed new linings, some worn patches in venerable Persian carpets, an embroidered silk counterpane in a lamentable way. Enough to keep her busy for a couple of weeks, she thought happily. It was nice to get away from below-stairs bickering and factions.

'Come and look at this room,' he said, when they came back downstairs. 'I've never furnished it, not having need of it, but I'm conscious that there isn't a lady's sitting-room in the house. Do you think this would make a nice one?'

It was a square room on the corner of the house, not large, but with a bay window onto the garden. It wasn't panelled, being evidently a later addition to the house, but the wallpaper, brownish to begin with, was further dulled by ancient smoke.

'Supposing it to be redecorated and suitably furnished,' Sebastian went on, 'what do you think?'

'It's a pretty shape, and looks onto the garden, and you can see it gets the sun. I think any lady would love to have it for a sitting-room,' Dory said.

'Then I'll do it,' said Sebastian. 'I'm glad I asked your opinion. When it's done, you shall come back and tell me if I've got it right.'

Dory enjoyed her break from routine, the change of scene, new people to talk to, and the work was interesting, but she couldn't help feeling melancholy at the thought of his marrying and leaving the Castle. And she was anxious for him, too, because he was so nice and she wanted him to be happy; and to be happy he would have to marry someone who understood and valued him. She hoped very much that he had not fallen prey to some young thing who was only marrying him for his money, who perhaps regarded him merely as a necessary nuisance to be put up with on the way to prosperous widowhood.

'What's the matter with William?' Rose asked, more of herself than anyone else.

But Speen answered anyway. 'Daft William? Going dafter than ever. It's a medical fact – them as are a bit mental get worse as time goes on. He'll be running about naked with straws in his hair before you know it.'

Rose gave him a severe look. 'You've got a nasty tongue on you, Mr Speen. You mind you don't choke on your own spittle.'

Speen merely laughed and went on his way. Rose had been noticing William's air of abstraction for a while now, but this afternoon she had taken in the flowers for the dining-room table to find he had laid it for dinner with cutlery in the wrong places and half the things missing. And when she had spoken sharply to him about it, he had merely looked at her as if at someone waving from a distant field. She had had to physically drag him to a place-setting and point out with jabs of the finger what was amiss, and even then he had only said vaguely, 'Oh, yes,' and begun slowly to shuffle things into the right places. No shame or embarrassment. In previous times he would have blushed to the tips of his ears to be caught out and berated.

'But he doesn't look ill,' Rose mused, watching Speen's back recede down Piccadilly.

'Who don't?' demanded Cyril, scuttling out of the silver room with refilled salt and pepper pots.

'William,' Rose said. 'He's not been himself lately.'

Cyril sniggered. 'He's not sick,' he said derisively. 'Gurt lummox is in lu-u-urve!'

'Don't speak about your superiors like that,' Rose corrected him automatically, but Cyril, who modelled himself on James Hook, and more recently on Speen, was unreachable. *They've ruined that boy*, she thought, moving on towards the nap closet. She remembered when he had first come, a scrawny little fellow with ears at right angles and a scared deference for everyone older and taller than him – which was everyone below stairs. If he wasn't careful he'd be making himself unemployable before too long.

William, rearranging the knives and forks with one degree less randomness since Rose's intervention, moved in a dream. Tabby had introduced him to a new world of sensation which was so bewitching he could think of nothing else. For much of the time, he could hardly think at all. He had fallen in love many times, generally with every new maid as she arrived in the household, but it had always been a cerebral adoration, carried out at a distance, with the occasional foray into stumbled words of hope or a posy of flowers shyly thrust into a little hand in passing. He had felt a great yearning inside him, but for what he couldn't have told you. He had been very strictly brought up by his widowed mother, and she had discouraged him from making friends with other boys, with the result that he had not absorbed the basic facts and misconceptions that were commonly swapped in secluded corners along with purloined cigarettes. He knew females were different, and in a wholly delightful and mysterious way, but that was as far as it had gone.

After the first time with Tabby, in the hayloft of the Dog and Gun's stable, when he had been staring at her breathless and bedazzled, she had said to him, 'There! Now you're a man!'

Sometimes he felt like a man (and he understood, a little, the boastfulness and swaggering of men who presumably had long practised this occult art) but just as often he felt like a helpless fly in a spider's web, or a soap bubble rushing down a drain, or a bird that had jumped out of the nest for the first time and was wondering if it really could fly. Tabby was a sorceress before whom he abased himself, yet because she was a female, she remained to him a delicate, lovely creature he wanted to nurture and protect. On the whole his instincts were properly manly. He had fantasies of coming upon her besieged by gypsies whom he sent to the right-about with well placed fists or a large stick, after which she swooned into his arms, gazing up at him and whispering, 'My hero!'

But while she had him by the heart, the Thing They Did had him by an altogether more ancient part. He couldn't stop thinking about it, couldn't get enough of it. He wanted to be doing it all the time. He risked his job, and discovery, to get Tabby alone so that they could do it, and she seemed a willing collaborator. In barns, lofts, haystacks, behind hedges, even once standing up behind a tree, anywhere they could be unseen for a few moments – and he was so excited by her, it only took a few moments. Sometimes she would only do a Thing with her hand, but even that took him to the edge of a precipice of ecstasy over which he was only too willing to tumble.

He knew, dimly, that what they were doing must be kept secret, that it would not be approved of by his mother or the rector or any of those grown-ups he was accustomed to respect and fear. But he couldn't think of it as wrong. Tabby was his goddess, and a goddess couldn't do wrong. She was a lovely member of that loveliest phylum, womankind. Whatever she did must be good.

So he drifted through his work in a dream, and when, as today, he was alerted to the fact that he had made a mistake, he couldn't make himself care. Compared with being in love with Tabby, it was as inconsequential as a gnat on a bullock.

Maud Stainton went straight to Scotland from Cowes, as had been her husband's habit. In his case, it had been out of an eagerness to be fishing and shooting, and she had tolerated the weeks in Kincraig on the Spey because she had to, and because she did at least get to spend time with her adored brother Fergus, and with several cousins she never otherwise saw.

This year, she went for a rest. The months of continuous parties, balls and engagements – most of them in a foreign language – had been a strain, though the exercise had been undertaken from a sense of duty, and she regarded it as having been completely worthwhile. But she was tired now, and needed a rest before the whirligig started up again. And she gauged that Rachel was also tired, and needed time to step down from the merry-go-round and breathe.

Fergus, Lord Leake, liked to entertain at Kincraig, but he was lazy and preferred to leave the trouble of organisation to others. So while he had invited friends and relatives to stay for the sport, he did very little more than order his butler and housekeeper to arrange beds and food for them, and his head ghillie to arrange for them to go out after whatever fish or game they fancied. Balls and parties he left to other local families. A wealthy bachelor earl never lacked for invitations, and those in his house party would always be included; but there was no need for anyone actually to *go* if they didn't care for it. Maud emphatically *didn't* care for it. It suited her to stay at home and rest, to talk or listen to such company as didn't bore or annoy her, and to take a solitary walk every day for exercise.

The weather was perfect – soft autumn sunshine, golden light, a gentle warmth; a little misty in the mornings, chilly enough in the evenings to be glad of a log fire. She walked every afternoon, enjoying the autumn smell of leaves and woodsmoke, the low light on the purple hills, the golden ripples across the lake, and went home invigorated to tea, the best meal at Kincraig. Mrs McArdle was a dedicated baker, and always produced a grand spread of Scotch pancakes with cream and heather honey, scones, flapjacks, gingerbread, Melting Moments, Dundee cake, petticoat tails, butter tart, marmalade cakes, raspberry buns. She had very little interest in other forms of cooking, and what the sportsmen had managed to bag during the day supplied the other meals, prepared with the minimum of disguise. But Maud had never had much interest in food, so being faced mealtime after mealtime with the same grilled fish innocent of sauce followed by a pellet-speckled game bird served charred with boiled potatoes and cabbage hardly impinged on her.

After dinner she was happiest listening to Fergus talking about his very dull life, or recounting incidents remembered from childhood, or playing hand after hand of bridge with the sort of players who didn't care for conversation with their cards, followed by an early night, safe in the knowledge that whatever Rachel was doing, someone else – or rather a number of someones – was watching over her.

Rachel had also been to Kincraig often enough to know that it was best to fill up at tea time. And she, too, was tired from the long strain of engagements, though in her case being ready for a rest did not mean she wanted to stay at home and have early nights. Local balls and parties suited her exactly, because the young people she met were either cousins or people she had known all her life, the dances were all jolly Scottish country dances, and the other entertainments were parlour games or card games intended to amuse. She didn't have to impress anyone, she didn't have to be elegant and superior, she didn't have to fear doing the wrong thing and incurring a curled lip, she didn't have to wonder if any of the young men she whirled about with was calculating her qualities as a wife. She could romp, both indoors and outdoors, with dear, friendly people who just wanted to have fun. There were picnics and carriage rides, long walks with packs of dogs, boating on the loch; she let her hair down and hitched her skirts up, and forgot she was a dignified young lady, knowing that for a little while, her mother didn't care what she did.

And when, after a series of lighthearted races, she and the cousins flopped down in the heather to catch their breath, and her handsome cousin Angus dropped down beside her, what he tried to do was not kiss her but stick a prickly bit of heather down her neck.

It was all very refreshing.

Alice decided to call the pony Cobnut for its colour. Axe had no objection. When it came to naming things, he hadn't much imagination.

'He's doing so well,' she said. 'He's quite a different pony. I think he must have belonged to somebody who was fond of him, don't you?'

'Never thought about it,' Axe said.

'Oh, but you see the way he watches us, not anxiously, but in a friendly way. And the way he pushes his nose into me when I first arrive. He's been somebody's pet. I wish I knew his history,' she added. 'Why did they part with him? And how did he come to sink so low? I wonder if he belonged to a little girl, and she died in a tragic accident?'

'You ought to write books,' Axe said, amused, 'making up stories like that. What happened, then, when this little girl died?'

'Oh, her parents were so upset they couldn't bear to look at him, because he reminded them so much. So they sent him in to market, and he was bought by a dealer, who sold him to a tradesman, who worked him too hard until his health broke down. And then each time he was sold he went down a bit, until he ended up with that wretched man you bought him from.'

'The way you tell it, it sounds like real,' said Axe. 'It's a treat to listen to you.'

Alice was stroking the pony's head. 'If he did belong to a little girl, he'll be broken to saddle. Have you tried to ride him?'

'Now, how d'you think I could do that? He'd collapse under me, with my weight.'

'Shall I try him, then?'

'Do as you like,' he said agreeably.

She looked the pony over carefully. 'He's still a bit thin, probably not very strong. But I don't expect I'd be too heavy for him, not for a short time.'

'No, he'd carry you all right.'

'I don't suppose you've got a saddle that would fit him. I'll just try him bareback.'

'Want a leg up?'

'No, I can manage.' She smiled. 'I haven't done this since I was little, but you never forget, do you?' She leaned on the pony's withers and hitched herself quickly across his back. Axe was holding his rope, but Cobnut made no objection, only looked round at her curiously, then went back to stoically waiting. 'Give me the rope,' Alice said, and taking it, pressed her knees, and then her heels into the pony's sides. He walked forward a few steps, then stopped again. Increasingly urgent signals from her heels didn't induce him to move again. Not wanting to be harsh with him, Alice slipped down.

'Well, he's perfectly quiet, at least,' she said, leading him back to Axe. 'I can't tell if he's saddle broken or not, but he'd make a nice pony for a child to begin on. What do you mean to do with him?'

'Hadn't thought,' Axe said, taking the rope back from her. 'Feed 'im up, clean him up, that was as far as I got.'

She nodded. 'The trouble is, if you sold him, you wouldn't know what sort of home he'd go to. It would be awful if he got starved and neglected again, just when he was thinking he was going to be happy at last.'

He gave her a bemused look. Who knew so much went on in a horse's head? 'What'd *you* like me to do with him? Didn't cost me but five bob, so it doesn't matter too much to me.'

'I can't take him,' she said regretfully. 'I'd have to explain to Josh where he came from and—' She stopped, aware in an unspoken, complicated way, that this would not be a good idea.

Axe's conscience stirred. He had meant to do what Ruth told him, and tell Lady Alice she mustn't visit him any more, but somehow, when she turned up, he couldn't send her away. She was so open and straightforward and unsuspecting, he couldn't mar her innocent pleasure by suggesting to her what less pure-minded people would think. Suppose he gave her a hint and she didn't get it, and he had to spell it out? It would be horribly embarrassing, to him as well as to her. So he let it slide. But sooner or later, someone would say something, someone who mattered. And Ruth was right, he would get into more trouble than her. He *ought* to discourage her – but how to do it? And he would miss her if she didn't come any more. He had never felt lonely before, had never considered solitude as anything but a natural state, but she had brought something into his life, and he knew that, now he had had it, he would mourn it if it was gone.

Maybe, if he just let things be, she would naturally stop coming in time. She was at the age when things changed for young ladies. Other interests would fill her life, and she'd forget all about the woodsman's cottage, and Dolly, and Della, and the animals – and the woodsman himself. That was what ought to happen, what would naturally happen. He was nobody and nothing, and she'd forget him; and if it happened naturally like that, he would live with it. He'd still miss her, but he'd have to live with it.

'I can keep him,' he said, looking at her, because he was still licensed to do so, thinking how lovely she was, with the clean simplicity of a young animal, all her movements unstudied and graceful, her smile, the tilt of her head, the trusting, easy way she was with him. He'd had a fawn once that he'd brought home injured and looked after till it was sound. It had never been wholly tame, and he hadn't wanted it to be, because he'd always meant it to go back into the woods, but it had come to accept him, and it had turned its head to regard him when he went in to tend to it, a bit like the way Lady Alice turned hers to look at him now.

'Would you?' she asked, doubtful but hopeful.

'Once he's fit, I can work him. In the woods, same as Della. He can pull the lighter logs, or carry stuff for me. I can fit him up with a couple of saddle-bags, and he can carry my tools and my lunch and a bit of feed for him and Della and so on. He can be useful all right.'

She looked relieved. 'Oh, yes, he'd need to be that. I mean, he'd be happier working – and I'd worry if you'd paid money for him and it was wasted.'

''Twould never be wasted, Lady Alice, to save a creature from harm.'

'That's how I feel – not that I have any money, but if I did, I'd want to do good with it. And I know he'll be happy with you.' She stroked the pony's nose, and said, without looking up at him, 'But you never call me Lady Alice any more. Why did you call me that?'

His heart ached. He wanted to reach out and touch her,

just brush a finger along her cheek. But some things you couldn't touch, however gently, without damaging. Like a butterfly's wing. 'No reason. It's your name, isn't it? Same as his'un is Cobnut. Good name for him, that is. Once we've got him fed up a bit, so he's rounder. Toast Rack'd suit him better at the minute.'

She laughed, and the perilous moment was past. 'Oh, that's so unkind! Poor Cobnut! Anyway, you can hardly see his ribs now, so it isn't true.'

But still she didn't look at Axe. She'd felt something all right. She'd felt it.

# CHAPTER SEVENTEEN

Mr Cowling had been away a lot, about his various businesses. In between trips, when he was at home, he encouraged Nina to entertain and, obedient to his wishes, she had held several dinner parties, inviting the town's prominent people, whose names Bobby supplied. The bathrooms were finished, and everything put to rights. Mr Cowling was so proud of them he would rather have liked to have a grand unveiling, but as it was, he could not even boast about them to his guests. He only hoped that *someone* would make a murmured enquiry of the butler or housekeeper, be guided discretely to one of the new wonders, and later spread the word around the district.

Because of his absences, nothing had been done about acquiring a horse for Nina. But she was content to ride Bobby's, and Bobby was perfectly happy to lend a horse that would otherwise require exercising by a groom, especially when it meant she had company on her hacks.

Bobby brought by hand the invitations to the Harvest Ball she was holding at Welland Hall on the 20th of September. 'We always have one at the time of the harvest moon. It's not the official Hunt Ball – that was in May – but it's mostly for Fernie people. Everyone will have been getting their hunters up for the last few weeks, and there are bound to be horses they want to get rid of, so we'll hear all about them at the ball. Aubrey deplores the fact that everyone talks about horses all through the evening,' she added, 'but he knows we can't help ourselves. And, dear Nina, you and Joseph will dine beforehand, won't you?'

On the night of the ball, Mr Cowling gave Bobby's home his customary sharp inspection, and saw nothing to envy. Welland Hall was much larger, and was stuffed with furniture, pictures and artefacts that were obviously family heirlooms, while Wriothesby House was rather bare, neither he nor Nina having had anything to inherit. But though candlelight and a mass importation of flowers made a fine impression, he could see that underneath it was as plain and shabby as Wriothesby had been when they moved in. The fact that the Wharfedales didn't care a jot about that was, in his view, nothing to the point. Now that the bathrooms were finished, he intended to take the first opportunity to fill Wriothesby with modern furniture and comforts and show the neighbourhood how it was done.

He was relieved to see no one was wearing a tiara. He had wanted to buy Nina one in time for the ball, but she had told him Bobby had said it was not *de rigueur*. She hadn't told him how Bobby had laughed at the idea; she hadn't wanted to hurt his feelings. Mr Cowling had accepted at last that there was to be no tiara – at least, not this time – but had brought her back, from a quick trip to London, a very pretty hair clip, a spray of emeralds and diamonds to match her necklace. He had insisted on Nina's wearing it, and it did look very pretty. Nobody else had on anything like it, which made Nina feel uncomfortable and Mr Cowling feel proud.

The talk before they sat down to dine was all about hunting. Bobby, doing her rounds, apologised to Mr Cowling. 'I'm afraid this must be dull for you. Hunting people are the world's worst bores. Aubrey says we should be quarantined before any social event until we got it out of our systems. Come and talk to him now about something sensible and un-horsy.'

Nina was pleased to find herself seated at dinner between Bobby's brother Adam and a Lord Foxton who, despite being over sixty, was not only a keen huntsman but was handsome and a tremendous flirt, and knowledgeable about so many subjects he had no need to rely on horses to get Nina's attention. She duly impressed him with the depth of her own education and they had some very lively chat. It turned out that he had a passing interest in archaeology, and he was able to engage her on the subject of the Valley of the Kings and the intended expedition that winter. He had met Howard Carter at Didlington Hall, being acquainted with Lord Amherst, who was a keen collector of Egyptian artefacts.

Adam responded, when he had her attention, by flirting, which in turn spurred Lord Foxton to flirt too. At times Nina was besieged from both sides simultaneously, and could only laugh and enjoy it. Foxton, who had known Adam all his life, said, 'Give it up, young Denbigh! I can give you a field length's start and still get the brush.'

'We shall see, sir, when the dancing begins.'

Foxton grinned. 'Oh, we shall, indeed! I am considered the finest dancer in the county, Mrs Cowling. Young Denbigh here has a reputation as a toe-crusher. Many a young lady has believed he has himself shod with iron like his horses – an economy measure, I imagine,' he added, in a pretended undertone. 'I advise you to keep your own dainty feet far away from his.'

Mr Cowling, meanwhile, had tactfully been seated between two non-hunting guests – or, rather, the non-hunting wives of hunting guests. He did his best to engage the ladies in suitable conversation; but Mrs Hansom-Paige was one of those old-fashioned wives who, unless speaking about her own children, had no conversation, and could only listen and nod with a blankness of expression that would defeat all but the hardiest talker. On his other side, Lady Wyville presented a different problem. As one married into an old Leicestershire family, she resented having been put next to 'an industrialist'. As a friend of the departed Ampleforths she resented a parvenu's being able to buy Wriothesby House at all. And as a woman who had never been handsome, and whose marriage had provided a title but little money, she resented Mr Cowling's wealth, and Nina's acquisition of it though being nothing but pretty.

Her greatest resentment, however, was caused by the fact that whenever Mr Cowling was turned her way, he was also looking towards the place where Nina was sitting, and he plainly had difficulty in keeping his attention on his dinner companion. His eye and mind would keep straying to Nina, sparkling between two men who were, as was evident even to a man not skilled in the art, flirting with her madly. Lady Wyville might talk about local politics, corn prices, the strange incidence of earthquakes in the Midlands and Wales, the shocking number of Russians in London, or Singer Sargent's latest portrait, but Mr Cowling's heart was no longer in his replies, and even his, 'Yes, indeed,' and 'So true,' were being delivered over Lady Wyville's shoulder. She was not accustomed to such treatment – and from such a person!

When the dancing began, the company was joined by a large influx of guests invited only to the ball. The non-dancing set was given an ante-room and card tables where they could play bridge to their hearts' content. Mr Cowling was – as any friend of the King needed to be – very good at bridge, and though he danced neatly he would always sooner play cards; but where Nina was, he wanted to be. He secured a dance with her, and asked if she had enjoyed her companions at dinner.

'Oh, yes,' she said. 'But after a while they got rather silly. I suppose it was the wine. I preferred it when they talked about sensible things.'

That smoothed his ruffled feathers, and he was able to yield her with reasonable grace to Adam Denbigh, and to take over a lean woman who, having asked if he hunted and heard the negative reply, had nothing else to say to him, and allowed him to trundle her round in silence while he looked over everyone's heads for Nina.

Having seen that he was willing to dance, Bobby made full use of him, and as soon as he bowed thank you to one partner, she was presenting him to another.

The evening wore on, the atmosphere heated up, the dancing never flagged. At the supper break, he found himself obliged to offer his arm to a Mrs Anstruther, a hunting widow, who at least had conversation beyond horses. She encouraged him to talk about his business, exhibited an intelligent interest in shoes, and had some useful suggestions about a better way to make a riding boot. She then recounted amusing anecdotes and had him laughing at some of the absurdities of the hunting community. He found he was actually enjoying himself, though it did not stop him noticing that Nina, at another table, was surrounded by young and not-so-young men, and that her group seemed to be the liveliest in the room.

When dancing resumed, he hoped to catch Nina and dance with her again, but she was whirled away at once by one of her dinner companions, the one Cowling had labelled in his own mind as 'the elderly roué'. He was surprised to find himself dancing with Lady Wyville – she seemed just to appear in front of him in such a way as to make it impossible not to ask her. She danced stiffly and properly, and was hard to lead. He supposed she had commanded all her life, and after a few moments he gave up and let her guide him where she wanted.

The floor was crowded, the fun was gathering pace, and people seemed to be laughing a great deal. The determined impulsion of his partner eventually brought him to a spot where he could see Nina in the arms of Lord Foxton and laughing at something he had said. Foxton was holding her, Cowling thought, unnecessarily close, and was smiling down at her with a look he would have described as predatory, if he could have thought of the word.

Lady Wyville said, in a tone that suggested the exact opposite, 'You mustn't mind about Foxton. He is an abominable flirt, but there's no harm to him.'

'He seems to be enjoying himself,' Cowling said discontentedly as, reaching the end of the room, Foxton tightened his arm round Nina's waist and whirled her in an unnecessary double turn. 'Good dancer, too,' he added through gritted teeth.

'Your wife dances correctly,' Lady Wyville commented. 'She must have been well taught.'

Talking about Nina was always a temptation to Cowling, and he described the superior education she had had at Miss Thornton's school. Missing the contemptuous curl of Lady Wyville's lip, he went on to mention her bluestocking aunt who had brought her up when her soldier father had died.

When he paused for breath, Lady Wyville said, 'It seems she had little experience of good society before you brought her here. It must be pleasant for her to be in a position to make friends among higher echelons than she's accustomed to.'

Cowling was still working his way through this utterance, spoken like a compliment but sounding, to him, a bit like a put-down, when she went on.

'If I might inject a word of caution, you would do well to discourage some of her acquaintanceships. Lord Foxton may have a lamentable reputation when it comes to women, but I believe it is largely talk. He is no danger to a well-behaved woman. More importantly, his notions are sound. There are others, however, who might lead her astray. I mention it only in a spirit of neighbourliness.'

'I beg your pardon, ma'am,' said Mr Cowling. 'I have no idea what you're talking about.'

'Ah, I feared as much. I believe you are away from home

a great deal. You perhaps don't know what has been going on.'

Mr Cowling bristled a little. 'Are you suggesting that my wife—'

'I'm sure it was not at her own instigation. A young girl not entirely at ease in the social stratum in which she finds herself can easily stumble onto the wrong path. And there are those who see no harm in it. But what may be viewed as an eccentricity in a respectable widow like Mrs Anstruther – or even in Lady Wharfedale who, after all, comes from one of our very oldest families and has married into another – may not appear quite *comme il faut* in someone who is in, shall we say, a more *delicate* position *vis a vis* society, with her reputation still to make.'

Cowling, though concentrating hard, had found it difficult to keep track of the subordinate clauses and had been slowed down by the necessity of translating the French phrases. He arrived at the full stop several beats after her and without much idea of what she had said. But he gathered, at least, that she was saying Nina had done something she disapproved of.

He put on a little hauteur. 'I'm sure you mean to be helpful, ma'am,' he said, not now being sure of any such thing, 'but I don't care for innuendo. I'm a plain man, and prefer plain speech, and if you've heard anything disobliging said about Mrs Cowling, p'r'aps you'd tell me straight out what it is and who said it.'

*So that I can knock his block off*, he concluded internally.

She looked at him from an hauteur higher than his. 'If you think I am engaging in gossip, Mr Cowling, you quite mistake my character. I despise gossip, and those who propagate it. What I speak of is common knowledge, and it is only because a reading of your character suggests it is not something you would approve of that I presume to mention it, suspecting that you might not know, because of your frequent absences, what is going on.'

'What *is* going on?' he demanded in exasperation. 'What is this common knowledge that I don't know about?'

'Your wife goes out riding with Lady Wharfedale,' Lady Wyville said, happily abandoning syntactical complexity now she had got to the death blow. 'Sometimes they are accompanied by her brother, Mr Denbigh. The two ladies ride astride. It has quite shocked the neighbourhood. If you value your wife's place in society, you should forbid it. That's all.'

Cowling took the blow well; he was silent for a moment, then said, in a low voice, 'Who told you this?'

'One of my maids has a brother who is an agricultural worker. He has been hedging and ditching for several weeks in the fields around Gartree and the Gallows Road, and he has seen them pass – without himself being seen.'

Mr Cowling drew himself up. 'It seems to me, my lady, that what you've described is exactly what gossip is.'

Lady Wyville looked haughty, and was evidently about to say something crushing, when the dance came to an end and the music stopped.

'Thank you, ma'am,' Mr Cowling said stiffly, dropped her hand, bowed, and walked away. He went and found an empty room where he could stamp about for a bit, then took himself to the card room and watched the play while the last few dances of the evening went on, concluding with the post-horn gallop, which was accompanied by a lot of whooping.

He hung about in her bedroom, fiddling with things, while Tina unclasped her necklace, undid her buttons, and helped her out of her gown and corset. It was not his usual custom, and Tina grew nervous, sensing, as horses do, that a storm was coming. As soon as she had taken out Nina's pins, she said, 'Madam, do you want me to—?'

And Nina, who had been in a dream of pleasant tiredness, intercepted her anxious glance at the lingering husband and said, 'No, that's all right. You can go now.'

She took up her brush and drew it through her hair, watching him in the mirror. As soon as the door clicked shut, she put it down and turned, enquiringly.

Mr Cowling stared at her, unsmiling. 'Is it true?' he demanded.

She felt a flutter of nervousness. He had never looked at her like that before. 'Is what true?'

'Don't play with me! Is it true that you – that *my wife* has been riding about the countryside astride a horse? You and that Lady Wharfedale, riding about like men?'

Trump felt the atmosphere and slunk under the dressing-table.

'Not at first,' Nina said, trying to sound calm. 'Only lately. Bobby urged me to try it. She told me how delightful it was and – well, it's true! You can't imagine the difference it makes! It's quite wonderful.'

'Is it, then?' he said stonily.

'Please, Joseph, please don't be cross. There's nothing wrong with it, honestly.'

'Nothing wrong?' His anger rose. 'You've shocked the neighbourhood. Everyone's talking about it.'

She frowned. 'That can't be true – no one knows.'

'Oh, *someone* knows – and when somebody knows, every-body knows. It'll be all through the town. Whispering and pointing. You'll be shunned. We'll be cut – and after the trouble I've been to, to get you set up here, to get you into the best society. No one will want to know you now. There'll be no more invitations – they'll cross the road to avoid you. Is that what you wanted, eh? Is it?'

'But – I haven't done anything wrong. Honestly—'

'Honestly? Aye, and that's what hurts me most. You haven't been honest, have you, Nina?' His use of her name was like a slap across the cheek. 'You lied to me.'

'I didn't *lie*—'

'You kept it a secret from me, because you knew I wouldn't

like it. You deceived me. Have I deserved that? Have I treated you so shabby? Oh, I know who's behind it – that Lady Wharfedale! Thick as thieves, the two of you. I can see you now, heads together, laughing away at me, laughing at silly old Joseph Cowling, your foolish old husband – what a know-nothing! So easy to pull the wool over his eyes!'

'No!' she cried, agonised that he was so hurt.. 'Never, we never would! We didn't laugh at you. Truly, truly! We didn't talk about you at all.' Only once she'd said it did she realise how it sounded.

'No,' he said bitterly, 'I don't suppose you did. Out of sight is out of mind, isn't it? I dare say you never give me a thought once I'm out of the house, off to my work to earn the money to buy you nice things.'

She faced him, trying to hold his gaze steadily, though she was trembling inside. 'I *did* keep it from you,' she acknowledged, 'but it was only because I thought what you didn't know wouldn't hurt you, and I was afraid if I told you, you'd object.'

'Object?' His face reddened. 'I should think I would object! It's disgusting! It's indecent! My wife, riding astride? My wife, going about the countryside with her legs apart? Wide apart, with a horse between them?' He was shouting now. 'Oh, nothing to object to about that, is there? My wife with her legs on display to any man that cared to walk past? Nothing any man wouldn't be happy about there!'

'Nobody saw! Nobody was there! We only did it in the fields, not where there was anyone around. And the skirt covers the legs, just as it does side-saddle. It's not indecent. And oh, Joseph, if you only knew—'

'I don't care to know. You *knew* it was wrong, but you went on and did it anyway, behind my back.'

'But it isn't *reasonable* to object! And it's safer,' she brought out the justification eagerly. 'It's so much safer than sidesaddle. You can stop a horse if it tries to bolt – you know one can never stop a bolting horse when side-saddle because you have to carry your hands too high. And if it slips and falls, with a side-saddle, the chances are you'll be trapped underneath. If you care about my safety, you must see that.'

'I care about your safety.' His voice was lower, but tense with anger. 'And I care about your reputation. And your honour. Which is more than you seem to do. Well, there'll be no more of this. You are not to ride that way ever again. I forbid it.'

'You forbid it?' she said coldly.

'Yes, I, your husband, *I* forbid it. And since you're not to be trusted, I shan't be buying you a horse. No riding at all. The less you're seen around horses after this, the better. Maybe in time we can get back a bit of reputation, if you behave yourself from now on. And you stay away from that Lady Wharfedale. She adds nothing to your credit. I don't doubt she'll go on behaving like a hoyden and a trollop, but I won't have you tarnished with her brush.'

She stood quite still, staring at him, shocked at the storm she had unleashed. She had never thought it would be this bad. And the worst thing was that she could see, under the anger and the righteous indignation, the hurt she had inflicted.

She saw him with sudden appalling clarity, as someone quite separate from her. A man not old, but certainly not young. His hair was mostly grey. Where the whiskers were beginning to come through from the morning's shave, they glittered silvery. She saw the little broken veins in his cheeks. She saw the wisp of hair growing out of his nose. She saw the tired pouchiness under his eyes, and the slack flesh under his jaw. And she saw for the first time what a terrible thing it was to be married to a man she didn't love, had never loved. His stubby hands, with the large veins on the backs, were the only hands that would ever caress her. His lips, compressed in anger now, the only ones that would ever kiss her. By law and custom she belonged to him, wholly and for ever, and she had no idea what he was thinking or what he wanted. His authority over her was absolute. He could lock her up in an attic if he wanted. Those thick hands could curl into fists and hit her if he wanted. She didn't *think* he would ever hit her, but for an instant she shivered, imagining it. How much it would hurt! He was a stranger who owned her. She was the trembling puppy at the feet of a man with a stick, who held the rope that was tied round her neck.

'Joseph,' she said, quietly, pleadingly. He turned his face away for a moment, rubbing at his eyes. 'Joseph, please.'

'Haven't I been good to you?' he said, still turned away. 'Have I ever denied you anything? This house – you wanted to live here. Jewels. Bathrooms. Anything you've asked for.'

'I know,' she said.

Now he looked at her, searchingly, and under his scrutiny, she blushed. He thought of her, dancing and laughing with the young men at the ball. She would never laugh and dance with him like that. Deep down, and wordlessly, he knew it was not just the astride-riding that had let loose this rush of anger. It was the knowledge that comes at last to every old man who marries a young girl – that she does not love him. And for him, in particular, it was a bitter thing to know: that any one of those young blades at the ball could have served her better than he could, because of his damnable problem – his 'stage fright'! His mind touched it and winced away, as from a sore tooth. He loved her so much – but he could not bear to be ridiculous. She might break his heart – he had half expected when he married her that she would – but, damn it, *she must not laugh at him*!

The blood rushed to his head, and he stepped across the room and seized her by the arms. Before she could protest, he crushed his lips down onto hers. Her flesh was warm under his hands. She was wearing only a chemise, and her body was soft and flexible under it. By God, he wanted her! And by God, he would have her! She was his wife! And if she wanted to behave like a trollop, riding about the countryside with her legs apart, by God he would take her like a trollop! His hands were strong, the fabric was flimsy: he tore the clothes from her, and the feeling and the sound aroused him even more. He pushed her backwards onto the bed and went down on top of her. He fumbled briefly with his own buttons, but nothing now could break his mood. He freed himself, and without a thought he was in her, inside her, and doing what he had always longed to do, and never could. She did not resist. She lay submissive under him, and only at the end gave a little cry, like a whimper, and put her arms round him.

Afterwards he lay still for a long time, and as the heat receded from his brain, he thought of what he had done, and the triumph turned to shame. Under him, she gave a little sigh. In her ear, he whispered, 'Did I hurt you?'

She shook her head, then said, 'Can't breathe.'

He took some of his weight onto his elbow, and dared to look down at her, stroked the hair from her face. Her expression was unreadable. He wanted to apologise, but had just enough wit to know that it would be fatal – to him, if not to her.

'Nina,' he said instead. 'Nina. I love you.'

After a long moment, she said, 'I know.' She closed her eyes. There was a drop of moisture in her eye-socket. He wiped it gently away with the side of his thumb, not knowing if it was a tear, or sweat. He eased himself away, got up, turned his back, adjusted his dress, tried to think of something to say and failed, and went away to his own bedroom.

Left alone, Nina lay a long time without thinking. It was all too perplexing, too inexplicable, too . . . she hardly knew what. It might hurt too much to think about. Eventually, when words did come into her head, they were, 'So that's it. That's the thing husbands and wives do.' She could feel it was different. She had a used feeling where she'd never had a feeling of any sort before. And there was a stickiness. And a new smell. A brief echo of her aunt's lesson before marriage came up, and she shied away from it. And Giles's face came up too, briefly, and she shied away from that. She didn't want to think that it would have been different if he did it. She didn't want to be that person.

There was a soft thump as Trump jumped up on the bed, and she felt his hard warm body nudging itself under her hand. She let him crawl into the circle of her arm and, holding him, fell asleep.

Cowling was up very early in the morning and, unable to face seeing her, he went straight out to the factory, not even taking breakfast, leaving only a message with Mrs Deering that he would be there all day.

He was horrified at what he had done (yet in some deep place pleased and satisfied at his mastery). It was practically a rape (yet she was his wife and had a duty to submit to him). He longed to be reconciled to her, to cover her with kisses and bring her gifts (but she should learn who was master in the house and in the marriage bed).

Hopelessly at odds with himself, he walked the short distance to the factory through a sweet, misty morning, the trees beginning to gleam with gold amid the green, and the first fallen leaves like gold coins under his feet. A ghostly stem of cow-parsley poking up in the verge was draped in a spider-web that was hung with silver dew drops, reflecting the sun as it eased through the lifting mist. Sparrows erupted, bickering, from a hedge. Somewhere unseen a cow bellowed. His natural optimism began to reassert itself.

She was so lovely, so warm and soft and fragrant, and the sensation of possessing her body had been almost too wonderful to endure. If only – if only it was the end of his problem, the beginning of a new way between them, if only he could do it again! The thought came to him, like the sun breaking through, that she might at this very moment be pregnant. He might have given her a child. He longed for a child. He had done a bad thing, but perhaps good could come of it. He was reminded, foolishly, of the Lyle's Golden Syrup tin with its strange illustration of the dead lion and the bees. 'Out of the strong comes forth sweetness'. He had shown his strength to her – wouldn't it be wonderful if from that came forth the sweetness of a child?

Nina woke when Tina came in to attend to her fire, but she turned over, so the maid left her be, only letting Trump out, reckoning that a late night after much dancing should mean a lie-in. She did wonder about the master being in the bedroom. Even she, until recently nothing more than a housemaid, knew that gentlemen did not usually hang around in the room while their wives were undressed. The doors and walls in Wriothesby House were thick, and she hadn't lurked nearby to hear whether it was quarrelling or canoodling that was on Master's mind, but either way, Madam probably needed to sleep a bit longer.

Left alone, Nina wanted to retreat back into oblivion, but sleep abandoned her, and she was thrust into full wakefulness, with the memory of that awful row, and the subsequent action. Misery overcame her. She needed so desperately to talk to someone, to help her sort out in her mind what it all meant, but who was there? He had told her to stay away from Bobby, and even she knew that to rush straight to her would be provocative. And there was no one else. She felt lonely, miserable, guilty, self-righteous and small. And she didn't want to face him, imagining sternness and hurt.

The news that he had gone out early and would be out all day was a relief, and at the same time hurtful. He hadn't wanted to see her. But it left her free for the day, and she knew then where she had to go. When you're unhappy, you go home, because that's where they always let you in.

She collected her dog, walked to the station, and went to London.

Aunt Schofield took one look at Nina's face, and mentally cancelled the luncheon she had been going to. The fire was still alight in the morning-room. She summoned Minny to make it up and gave Haydock a specific instruction about refreshments. Nina had the look of one who had not breakfasted, and it was an intractable misery that could not be lightened by a stack of hot buttered toast.

She listened with her customary intelligent concentration to Nina's somewhat tangled account, and then was silent a while, allowing Nina to eat some more. Trump, who had had a walk at either end of the train journey, stretched his legs to expose more of his belly to the fire's warmth, and groaned comfortably.

'Well, Nina,' she said at last, 'I'm very sorry you've had this upset but, you know, I did try to warn you before you married that there would be difficulties. He is a much older man than you, from a different background, and it was not apparent that you had any tastes in common. Adjustment was bound to be uncomfortable.'

'But – you didn't try to stop me,' Nina said. 'You could have forbidden me.'

'You were no longer a child. I laid the problem before you, but you had to make your own decision. No one can live your life for you. You have to make your own mistakes, and learn from them.'

'So you think it was a mistake? To marry him, I mean?'

'I didn't say that.' She was silent a moment. 'You know, don't you, that you did a very wrong thing? You did something you knew your husband would object to. And you went behind his back.'

'But it's not *reasonable* to object to women riding astride,' Nina cried. 'And what right do men have, anyway, to dictate to us like that? It should be our choice!'

'Men run the world, Nina. They make the rules, they have control over us, and there's nothing to be done about it.'

'*Isn't* there? I'm surprised to hear *you* say that, Auntie.'

'I was lucky,' Aunt Schofield said. 'I married a man of intellect, who could be swayed by reason. But even he was a man, with a man's feelings, and there were things over which we struggled – and times when I had to submit. A woman *can* change things, but it has to be done gradually. You must never push them further than they can tolerate at one time. Your misfortune is that your husband is *not* a man of intellect, so you may have to work by even smaller increments. And you may never be able to make substantial changes in him.'

'So we are prisoners,' Nina said bitterly. 'Bound to obey every rule however foolish and petty and – and—'

'Inconvenient?' Aunt Schofield supplied coolly. Nina scowled at her, and she went on, 'Yes, women are prisoners – financial prisoners. Your father left you no money, so who is going to feed and keep you? I am a widow with just enough to live on, so I need answer only to myself. But I railed like you when I was young. It is hard, and I do feel for you. I wish I could help you, but I can't.'

But Nina was feeling better, just from talking about it to someone who understood. She hadn't told her aunt everything: she hadn't mentioned the denouement of the row, any more than she had spoken to her in the first place of the bedroom problem. She would have liked to, but she just couldn't. It was frustrating that women could not discuss this thing that was clearly so important and, if she understood correctly, fundamental to the continuation of the human race. She wished she could ask whether what he had done was the completion of the act her aunt had tried to prepare her for. She wished she could ask whether that episode made it more or less likely that he would do it again. Would the problem – if it was a problem – get better over time? Or worse? She felt lost, adrift in a sea of uncertainty, alone on a ship that she didn't know how to sail, knowing only that there were no charts, and no land in sight.

Slowly she ate the last piece of toast, and licked the butter from her fingers. She was young, and it's hard for the young to feel hopeless for long. 'Thank you for listening to me, at any rate,' she said.

'Oh, my dear,' Aunt Schofield said sadly.

'I wish I knew what to do,' Nina said. 'Is there *anything* you can tell me, anything I can do in a practical way to make things better?'

Aunt Schofield thought. 'You can apologise. An apology always goes a long way. And I'm sure that Mr Cowling does love you. This early in the marriage, he will probably be eager to forgive you.'

*But I don't want to be forgiven*, Nina thought resentfully. *There's nothing wrong with riding astride.*

Aunt Schofield read her thought easily enough – it was written on her face. 'The good thing about an apology,' she said, 'is that it doesn't always have to be specific. You were not wholly in the right, you know.'

'You mean I should just apologise for having kept it from him? I suppose that was bad. And I *am* sorry I hurt his feelings.'

'Yes, but you needn't go into details. Just say you're sorry and ask him to forgive you. Let his generosity do the rest.'

He was at home when she arrived back. He had come in, found her gone, and had panicked for a moment, until Mrs Deering had told him she had gone to London to see her aunt. Then relief had been followed by regret and shame, and a simple longing for her. But, left alone, he had begun to wonder what she was saying to her frighteningly clever relative. Was she telling her *everything*? Was she crying? Was her aunt shocked? Would she tell Nina to stay and never return? No, she wouldn't do that – surely not! But if Nina told her everything – *did* women talk about such things? – would Mrs Schofield think him less of a man? Would she speak scornfully about him to Nina? Would they *laugh* about him?

It was not a long time, between his getting home and her arriving, but it was long enough for him to go through a range of feelings and internal arguments. By the time Trump ran in to stand up on his hind legs for a caress, heralding her entrance, he was thoroughly confused and hardly knew whether to be angry or contrite. So he said nothing, and schooled his face into immobility.

She came in looking tired, which plucked at his heart-strings, and came straight up to him, looking up under her eyebrows, like a child, and said, 'I'm sorry, Joseph. Please forgive me.'

Just for a moment, he didn't know what to say, and while he hesitated, she brought out from behind her back a box, which she presented to him. 'Carlsbad plums,' she said. 'I know you like them. I went to Fortnum's for them. To say I'm really, really sorry.'

He wanted to cry, he wanted to sweep her into his arms, he wanted to ask if she thought he could be bought off with a box of sweetmeats. He wanted to kiss and forgive her, he wanted to beg her to forgive him, he wanted to demand her future obedience. And in the turmoil, he could say nothing. He took the box with a gruff 'Thank you,' and turned away, saying, 'You had better go and change for dinner. It's time.'

At dinner, they both tried to behave normally, each hoping the storm had passed, neither entirely sure what they should be thinking. Conversation was stilted. 'How are things at the factory?' 'How was your aunt?' It faltered and ran out, and they ate mostly in silence. After dinner he excused himself, saying he had business to attend to, and went to his study. She read a book, and went early to bed, exhausted by all the emotions.

She was almost asleep when he came to her room and got into bed with her. She tensed, listening to his breathing.

At last he said in a low voice, 'What did you tell your aunt about me?'

'Nothing,' she said. 'Not – I told her what I'd done, and that you were angry, that's all.'

Another silence. Then: 'I suppose she took your part.'

'She said I was in the wrong.'

He felt relief, and a resurgence of power. 'So you were!'

'I'm sorry,' she said again, very low. 'I'm sorry I hurt you.'

*Yes, you did, by God!* he thought with a last surge of anger. His blood rushed up, he had a brief, quite surprising image of her naked on a horse, like Lady Godiva, her shame covered only by her hair, and with a sort of growl he rolled over onto her, and for a second time consummated his marriage. This time he fell asleep afterwards, still in her bed, with a heavy, possessive arm across her. Dead tired, she slept too, but when she woke at dawn he had gone.

# CHAPTER EIGHTEEN

He was there at breakfast when she went down, slowly consuming eggs and sausages. He had the newspaper open, but put it aside as soon as she came in. He smiled tentatively at her, as if unsure how she would respond. She smiled with relief, and said, 'Good morning.'

He jumped straight in. 'I have to go to Leicester for a few days, on business. Would you like to come with me? I usually stay in lodgings when I'm there, but we can stay at a hotel, and you can look around the place while I'm busy. There's some fine shops and old buildings. I won't need Decius with me all the time – he can show you around. And he can take you to Wigston to meet his family if you'd like.'

'Oh, yes, I would,' Nina said. 'He's always talking about them.'

'Aye, they're a rum lot, those Blakes. Think the world of each other. It's pretty to see, family feeling like that,' he added wistfully.

'I never had brothers and sisters either,' she said, and he was touched that she had read his thought.

'So you'll come.'

'Yes, please.'

Nina was thinking that it would be good to get away for a few days. Bobby wouldn't know about the quarrel, and would probably come calling. Would Nina be forced to deny her? That would be awful. Were people really talking? Would she be stared at or shunned if she went out walking? Problems would have to be faced, but she would prefer to put them off for a bit until she'd had time to think properly.

And then she realised that Mr Cowling – who had never invited her on a business trip before – was probably thinking just the same things.

They stayed at the Grand Hotel in Granby Street. Mr Cowling took his man, Moxton, but said that Nina didn't need to take Tina if she didn't want to – the Grand would have chamber-maids accustomed to act as temporary ladies' maids.

The Grand was a new hotel, very ornate, built in the European Renaissance style in red brick with white copings, white pinnacles, and a dome and lantern on top that made it look like a wedding-cake. Inside there was everything you could want in the way of moulded and painted ceilings, gilded woodwork, elaborate plasterwork, marble fireplaces, vast mirrors, onyx pillars, glittering chandeliers, opulent carpets in rich colours. There was a magnificent central staircase lit by the glass dome high above, and enormous public saloons with every facility offered to the guests, including a coffee room and a palm court. Nina was struck dumb when they first entered at the sheer size and magnificence of it all. It didn't seem real. Her hand was through Mr Cowling's arm, and he pressed it against her ribs. She thought it was for her reassurance, but when she glanced up at him, she saw that he was looking about with his 'Now this is something *like*!' expression; and she realised that this was how he would like his own house to be. She understood then what a wrench it had been for him to go along with her desire to live in Wriothesby House without completely redesigning it. He had made a noble sacrifice for her.

He was not at all intimidated by the Grand's glories, strode masterfully, commanded pages, and behaved as though born to such extravagances. Nina was glad of his self-confidence,

311

feeling she might really get lost in this vast palace, both physically and spiritually. He had taken a suite, with a bedroom, sitting-room and, wonder of wonders, a bathroom, all for them. It was decorated in pink and white and gold, and the furniture was 'one of those French Louis, fifteenth or sixteenth, can't remember,' said Mr Cowling, but all brand new, of course. And on the round table in the sitting-room there was an arrangement of fruit in a sort of urn like a Bacchic cornucopia, which was all of two feet high and was topped with a bunch of black grapes that tumbled artistically down the side.

'Well, I think we can scrape by all right in here, don't you, Mrs Cowling?' her husband said for the sake of the page-boy, and sent him away with a tip that made him blink.

Nina was torn between a desire to giggle madly, and the conviction that her clothes were not nearly good enough for the place.

It was a happy few days. The bit she liked best was being taken by Decius to meet his family, whom she instantly loved. His father was the dream of a rector, tall and lean and scholarly, white-haired and white-bearded, with a mild, sensitive face and clear-sighted blue eyes – you felt that he would see right through you at first glance, recognise all your faults and failings, and forgive and love you even so.

Mrs Blake was motherly and brisk, so fast-moving it was hard to get any clear picture of her until you'd been tracking her for a while as she darted back and forth attending to things. But when you spoke to her she really looked at you, and then you saw where Decius had got his exceptional good looks. She was beautiful. As well as brisk and busy she was very gay, and laughter seemed to spring up around her, like flowers springing wherever Persephone trod.

Nina never did entirely sort out the various brothers and sisters and their spouses and children. There were a good many of them around, and others came and went during the day, and they all seemed very handsome and good-humoured, ready to pet and admire Nina and interested in everything about her. They sat down to a meal at a very large table and Nina calculated there were about twenty there, not counting younger children who had their own table and ran back and forth helping, and even smaller children who sat on laps at the table and were charming and well-behaved, and followed the conversation with their big eyes. Nina had the place of honour next to the rector, and had a very interesting talk with him about Greek and Roman mythology. Decius, on her other side, encouraged her to ask the elder Mr Blake about the legends of Atlantis, one of his interests, and he told her all about Pliny's account and various pieces of evidence that it was not a myth but had actually existed.

The time flew past, and Nina was sorry when it was time to go.

'But you'll come again, my dear?' Mrs Blake said, embracing her like a mother. 'We'd love to see you. And remember, we can always find a bed for a friend, if you don't mind not being luxurious.'

'What are your plans for tomorrow?' Mr Blake asked, shaking his son's hand vigorously.

'Haven't any at the moment,' Decius said. 'I'd like to show Mrs Cowling some of the countryside – it's pretty at this time of year. We could hire a carriage, I suppose.'

'You should take her to Evington Manor,' said Mr Blake.

'Oh, yes – there's a breakdown sale there tomorrow,' said Mrs Blake. 'Poor Lord Stoughton is all to pieces and everything's to be sold. But the grounds are so pretty, with the Washbrook running through, and the ornamental lake, and the flower gardens. And it will be the last chance to see the interior, before everything goes.' She turned to Nina. 'Evington was accounted one of the finest houses in Leicestershire, and Lord Stoughton was a great collector. It was open to the public at certain times, and always very popular with visitors.'

'His father's debts undid him, poor man,' said Mr Blake. 'A tragedy to see such a lovely place go under the hammer. And his library! I would love to go there myself tomorrow and bid for some of his books—'

'But I told the rector, if he brought one more book into this house I would run away,' Mrs Blake said, laughing affectionately at her husband. 'You can positively see the walls of this house bulging from the outside. One more book would burst it like a paper bag.' Her husband shook his head smilingly at her exaggeration.

'I've never seen a sale like that,' Nina said. 'It does sound so sad. Do they really have to sell everything?'

'Everything. Furniture, carpets, paintings, silver, clocks – books,' said Mr Blake. 'All the animals, too, but they went last week. And the house itself and the land go under the hammer next week. They're so heavily mortgaged, it's said he'll only just clear his debts. Heaven knows how the poor man will live.' A thoughtful look came over his face, and his eyes grew distant.

Decius looked at Nina and winked. 'I know that look – it means a sermon is brewing. Poor Stoughton's ill-fortune will be turned to good account from the pulpit on Sunday.'

Mrs Blake slapped his wrist. 'Don't be naughty. As if your father would ever exploit an unfortunate!'

Mr Cowling invited Decius to dine with them at the hotel that evening. He was glad to see Nina so animated, though at the same time wistful that it was with Decius, not with him, that she was having such a good time. He had been pleased to see how impressed she was with the Grand, and hoped she might have taken some ideas about how the inside of a gentleman's house ought to look. He had his dissatisfactions, too. For one thing, though Leicester had fine shops and she had used a whole morning going round them, she hadn't bought anything, despite his giving her a fistful of banknotes and telling her to charge anything she fancied. But not so much as a pair of silk stockings had she bought for herself!

And though they were sharing the same bed in the hotel, he hadn't managed to repeat his recent happy performance. The anger that had stiffened his sinews and summoned up his blood had disappeared down some spiritual rabbit hole, leaving him tangled in the old, debilitating love and yearning. She was so beautiful, so fresh, so young and untouched, so fragrant, so clever, so entirely lovely that he did not, never could deserve her. Approaching her in bed made him feel again like a gross and ugly old satyr. It was of no use to tell himself that she had chosen him, that she was his wife – or even that he had managed it before. Whenever he tried to bring her the proud flower of his adoration, it wilted during the approach.

The superb dinner in the magnificent dining room of the Grand cheered his spirits somewhat, and he was pleased and touched when Nina told him that she had asked Decius to show her the cobbler's shop in Wigston where he had begun his career, and the shop opposite where he had first set up on his own.

'The cobbler's is a lady's dress shop now,' she told him. 'But your shoe shop is still a shoe shop.'

'Of course it is,' he said, amused. 'I still own it. Did you think I'd part with the place that gave me my start?'

'But it doesn't say Cowling over the door,' she objected. 'It says J. Clarke.'

'No, because I let it to a chap and he wants his own name there, which is fair enough. But he sells Cowling and Kempson shoes. While I live, that shop will always sell shoes.'

She smiled at him. 'I think that's lovely. It can be like your auriga, for when you are the King's right-hand man and he makes you a duke.'

Mr Cowling laughed. 'I don't see that happening,' he said – though he had secretly thought that a barony wasn't out of the question. 'What's an auriga when it's at home?'

Decius answered. 'When a Roman general had a public celebration for one of his victories and was driven through the streets in front of the adoring crowds, the auriga stood behind him in the chariot and whispered in his ear, "Remember you are mortal." So that he didn't get too big-headed and offend the gods.'

Mr Cowling felt peeved that they both knew that, and he didn't. He hadn't had that sort of education. Of course Decius had – you'd expect it – but it was galling that Nina knew about this whispering chap too. 'Oh, you think I'm big-headed, do you?' he said sourly.

'No, of course not,' Decius said hastily.

Nina reached across the table and touched his hand. 'You're the most modest man I've ever met,' she said. '*Too* modest. And kind, and generous.'

He was placated. 'Hard to be generous to someone when they won't buy anything. All those shops you went to yesterday – couldn't find anything you liked?' he teased. 'Got too grand for them, eh? Maybe it's you that needs this chap in your ear.'

It was such a good opening that Nina couldn't waste it. She told him eagerly about the Evington Manor sale, said that Decius was willing to take her there, and added breathlessly that if he didn't mind, she would like to look out for some pieces of furniture.

Mr Cowling scowled. She had already shown how much she liked the Blakes's ramshackle old place, and in his mind Evington – which he had never visited – took on the same aspect. They wouldn't be selling up if they weren't broke, and broke people didn't have nice things. And after he'd brought her to the Grand, which was said to be the finest hotel in Europe, specifically to show her what was what!

'No, no,' he said. 'I'm not having it! Buying up broken old

316

second-hand things for my house, what do you take me for? Scratching around like a cock on a dung-heap for somebody's left-overs – aye, even if that somebody is a lord! I know a bit about Stoughton. His father was a gamester, got himself into debt, and his son hadn't got the gumption to pull himself out of the mire. Pallid youth with watery eyes and no chin – all the stomach bred out of him. Well, I'm not having his old cast-offs! I've told you, Nina, buy new things. You can spend as much as you like. Go up to London and fit out the whole house at Maples.'

Decius stepped in before she could reply, speaking quietly and thoughtfully. 'I can see why you might think that, sir,' he said, 'but in fact, the interior of Evington has always been accounted the finest in the land – finer than Blenheim Palace, I've heard it said. As for things being old, their antiquity is part of their value. Like Greek and Roman statues, for instance—'

'Aye, and I've seen enough of them, too. Dingy and stained, some man with a chipped nose and some woman with her arms knocked off!'

'Well, they were ill-treated by the Greeks and Italians before ever they were brought to England. But the furniture at Evington's not like that. There are some beautiful pieces, made by the finest craftsmen of their time, absolute masterpieces. And those craftsmen made very few of them, so only the richest and most distinguished people could afford them – and having bought them they made sure they were lovingly cared for. You would not find a scratch or a scuff anywhere. And fine wood – as you know, sir – improves with age. It gains a deep patina from the years of polishing that you'll never find in new furniture.'

Mr Cowling had listened suspiciously, and now looked at Nina. 'Is this what you want? When – mark me, now – you could have anything in the world?'

'Well, I would like to see what's there,' she said cautiously. 'And if there was anything that I *really* loved . . .'

317

'Naturally I was only thinking of the finest pieces, sir,' Decius said. And, knowing his employer, he added, 'Of course, pieces like that would cost a great deal more than new furniture—'

'Oh, would they?' Mr Cowling said derisively. 'Pay a lot for this patina, do you?'

'And for the original craftsmanship. A piece like that is unique, like an Old Master painting. No one else in the country will have one like it. While Maples' things are made in large numbers and many people will have identical pieces.'

Mr Cowling considered. He knew his Decius too, and he knew he was being manipulated. The Prince of Wales had furniture from Maples, and it was good enough for him and Princess May. On the other hand, to have a really rare object – he knew the value of that. Something there was only one of. That added to a man's reputation. But would the sort of folk he invited to his house in Market Harborough recognise a thing like that when they saw it?

But Nina was looking at him hopefully. He had wanted her to buy herself something that pleased her. He'd been thinking more of a hat or a trinket or a fur tippet, but if this was how it had to be . . .

'All right, then,' he said, and enjoyed seeing her face light. 'But no rubbish, mind!'

'I'll only be looking at the finest pieces,' Decius said.

'They'll probably cost too much anyway,' Nina said.

Cowling looked stern. 'If you want it, you buy it. What am I, a pauper? I can afford anything Lord Stoughton's got to sell. Mark me, Decius, if Mrs Cowling wants something, she's to have it, no matter what it costs.'

For once in her life since she had met him, Nina took Mr Cowling at his word, and spent his money. She bought a walnut chest of drawers and a bow-fronted dressing-table for her bedroom, an elegant sideboard and a serpentine serving-table for the dining-room, and a breakfront bookcase, a secretaire, a pair of demi-lune side tables, and a very pretty rosewood sewing table for the drawing-room. She had been tempted by a chest-on-chest and a wardrobe for Mr Cowling's bedroom – the wardrobe in particular appealed to her, having four drawers in the middle section concealed by the doors – but despite long deliberation with Decius she could not be sure he would want them, immaculate though they were, rather than new things from Maples.

Mr Cowling's comment, when he saw the bill, was, 'You didn't get very much in the end.' But he was impressed with the total price, and pleased that she had bought a sewing-table just for herself: that seemed properly feminine. Decius was arranging with a carrier for the things to be delivered straight to Wriothesby, and he reserved final judgement until he actually saw them. But it had certainly made Nina happy – her shiny eyes and smiling cheeks were a treat to see.

He held her in his arms that night while she fell asleep, and thought about what they were going home to. The test would be on Sunday, at church – their first public appearance in the town since the ball. Would there really be a big scandal? How much influence did Lady Wyville have? Well, if anyone tried to snub his Nina, they would have him to answer to!

Scandals died down over time, he knew that. Today's newspaper wrapped tomorrow's fish, as the saying was. He listened to her gentle breathing and felt sorry that he had forbidden her to ride, when he knew she loved it so much. He thought of her as a little girl in India, riding about on her pony. Of course, children rode across, but it was simply not right for a grown woman. He stood by that. He had been right to stop it. But, at some point, when the fuss had died down, if there was a fuss, he ought to let her ride again, as long as it was side-saddle.

Unless, of course, he thought as he drifted into sleep, unless she was with child. Then she wouldn't be riding anyway, and the problem would solve itself. He slept, and dreamed of a little child toddling beside him, holding his hand. In the dream he couldn't turn his head and look down, so he couldn't see it clearly, didn't know if it was a boy or girl. And at some point its hand slipped out of his, and he seemed to be carried helplessly forward by some imperative, leaving the little one behind.

It was another fine day on Sunday. Mr Cowling supervised Nina's outfit, to make sure she was killingly smart, aware that there must be nothing apologetic about their appearance. Best hat, he decreed, newest gloves, pearls. He had himself turned out equally nattily, and even went out into the garden and found a late rose, just opening, for his buttonhole.

It was after church, when everyone poured out and stood around to chat, that the test would come. And, yes, there were some stares. Lady Wyville exchanged the merest, coldest nod, then stood at a little distance, gathering a clique around her. Heads together, they talked in low voices, and Mr Cowling was convinced it was about Nina.

On the other hand, Sir Bradley Graham, the immensely popular local MP, came straight up to the Cowlings and engaged them in friendly talk, and was soon joined by Mrs Anstruther, Mr and Mrs Burham Andrews – wealthy philanthropists and hunt supporters – and Lord Foxton. The Crawfords inched up shyly and were absorbed. Mr Cowling was also pleased, as the lower orders began to stream out, to see how many respectful doffings and bobs he received from the workers at the factory.

Nina reckoned the groups were about equal in size. Mrs Anstruther, seeing the direction of her glance, stepped closer and said in a brisk, practical voice, 'Never mind them, Mrs Cowling. They are the past. *We* are the future.'

'We are?' Nina said, startled.

'History teaches us that the world moves always towards

greater liberality, greater openness.' She made an expansive gesture with her hands. 'Those who resist are doomed. Extinction awaits them. We are in a new century, on the brink of great change. We must not stand in the way of progress.' She lowered her voice and added, 'And we must have fun.' Then she patted Nina's arm briefly, and turned away to talk to Major Cazenove.

The crowning moment was when Lord and Lady Wharfedale, who had been delayed talking to the rector in the porch, came out and joined them, bringing the rector with them. He was very well respected in the town, and his opinion mattered.

Having spoken to the rector, Mr Cowling turned to the Wharfedales. He drew a step closer to Nina and looked at them with a little reserve, to which Bobby reacted with her usual impulsive warmth. She seized his hand, looked up earnestly into his face and said, 'Ah, now, don't frost me! You are right, it was all my fault. I was so eager to have a new recruit to the cause that I persuaded her to go against her conscience, and that was very bad of me. I confess it freely. And Aubrey has already given me such a scolding, you needn't fear I don't know the error of my ways. I am quite repentant and beg you to forgive me.'

'Now, then, Lady Wharfedale,' Mr Cowling began awkwardly, not knowing how to deal with this approach.

'You mustn't be angry with Nina! And please don't forbid her to be my friend. I expect you think I am a bad influence – yes, I can see it in your face! – but it's only because I'm so passionate about the well-being of women, and I'm sure that must be something you care about too.'

'Now, Bobby,' Lord Wharfedale said, 'don't start badgering the poor man. Mr Cowling,' He offered his hand and shook Mr Cowling's vigorously. 'We have two eager, passionate young women for wives, and how shall we handle them?'

'Passion is one thing . . .' Mr Cowling began doubtfully.

Aubrey smiled and jerked his head towards the opposite

camp. 'When you look at the alternative – closed minds, bigoted ignorance, a refusal even to consider change – then a little passion, even if sadly unregulated, becomes attractive. You, sir – I've heard about your innovations at the factory – you are a man who embraces the future, a man who gets things done. I admire that tremendously.'

Mr Cowling was eyeing Wharfedale cannily, suspecting he was being buttered like a crumpet. 'Thank you, my lord, but I can't see how all that fits with the case in point. This business of riding across—'

Wharfedale nodded. 'It's all part of the same thing. Those people—' Another nod towards the Wyville party, 'have closed minds. In the absence of rational thought, they can only cling to old prejudices, that riding cross-saddle is not *decent*. They cannot absorb the scientific argument, they balk at actual facts and empirical proof. They are,' he added with a smile that invited Mr Cowling firmly into the scientific camp, 'the flat-earth believers of the modern world.'

Mr Cowling was still resisting the implied flattery. 'Facts and proof about *what*?' he demanded.

'About the health benefits and vastly improved safety of the modern method of riding for women.'

'You think they're facts, do you?'

'I know so.'

'Well, sir, I shall have to think about it,' Mr Cowling said.

Bobby, meanwhile, was talking in a low voice to Nina. 'Oh, my dear, I'm so sorry I got you into trouble. I've heard what that dreadful Wyville creature is saying. I only invited her to the ball because her late husband was a sort of cousin of Aubrey's, but she's always been a poisonous woman, eaten up by jealousy, and I shall be sure to keep her at arm's length in future. I'm so sorry you've been caught in the cross-fire, but you mustn't mind her. This horrid talk will soon die away, *especially* if we all stick together. Margot Anstruther has been an absolute rock in mobilising the hunt people to rally to our side, even those who weren't keen on the riding-astride thing. And I'm *sorry*, dearest Nina, that I encouraged you to go behind your husband's back, which was very wrong of me. But my darling Aubrey will talk him round. He could talk the birds down from the trees. He's given me my scolding and I'm suitably contrite, but he's completely on my side – the dearest, loyalest old hound you can imagine! Was Mr Cowling dreadfully angry? He doesn't seem to be now. He looks at you with the greatest fondness.'

'He *was* angry,' Nina said, 'but I told him how very sorry I was, and that I would never do it again.'

Bobby looked alarmed. 'Never ride astride again?'

'Never deceive him again. That was really wrong.'

'Oh, yes, I know. But, Nina, you don't mean to go back to side-saddle?'

'At the moment, Mr Cowling doesn't want me to ride at all.'

Bobby considered a moment, and then said, 'I'm sure that's just shock, because of that hateful Lady Wyville and the trouble she's caused. This horridness will pass, and he'll relent, I'm sure of it.'

'I wish I were sure,' said Nina.

'Just give it time,' said Bobby. 'And meanwhile we shall be exemplary friends, and avoid all talk of horses and riding in his presence. But it's not long until the season starts, so I do hope his powers of healing are swift, because I absolutely *must* have you hunting beside me this year – even if it is side-saddle.'

'I don't even have a horse.'

'If Mr Cowling comes about in time, we shall get you a hunter of your own, but at any rate, you shall ride any of mine you choose. You *shall* go to the ball, Cinderella!'

'As I remember,' Nina said, 'that ball didn't end well.'

'But she married the prince in the end. It all came out right,' said Bobby.

★　★　★

Two days later the Cowlings dined at Welland Hall. It was a pleasant occasion, with just the four of them – though the Wharfedale children were brought down to the drawing-room to say goodnight. Mr Cowling loved children, and chatted to them pleasantly, watching Nina out of the corner of his eye with the vague hope that having children might somehow be contagious. The Wharfedales were good company, and had plenty to talk about, and nobody mentioned the side-saddle controversy or talked about horses at all, so it all passed sweetly.

This was followed by a return dinner at Wriothesby House, with the Crawfords as the other guests, and that was pleasant too, with entirely different but still not horse-related conversation. Mr Cowling was impressed with Wharfedale's intelligent questions about manufacturing processes. The furniture from Evington had been delivered and arranged, and the Wharfedales used the licence of being close friends to comment on and admire the new pieces. Mr Cowling had inspected them all closely when they arrived and had to admit there was nothing shabby about them; and he was especially pleased when Mrs Crawford broke her usual silence on arrival in the drawing-room and said, in a soft voice he might have missed had he not been attending to her, 'How lovely this room looks, Mr Cowling. So spacious, and not crowded like so many rooms. I hope you don't mind my saying so,' she added with an anxious blush.

Then there was a card evening at Welland Hall, with five tables of bridge and an elegant supper, and then a musical *soirée* at Peasedale, Sir Bradley and Lady Graham's place. Mr Cowling enjoyed everything, and reflected that this was what he had always wanted for them, to be accepted into the society of the local nobs. He wanted it for himself, to advance his place in the world, but more especially for Nina, who had her way to make. There was still some factionalism and whispering in the town, but he was able to ignore it, and hoped it would soon die away.

He was not to know of the heroic efforts of Bobby in persuading her circle not to talk in his presence about the upcoming hunting season, reasoning that a period of convalescence was needed for Mr Cowling's sensibilities to heal and harden over.

Meanwhile Mr Cowling waited, with bated breath, for news from Nina. He worried that, young and innocent as she was, she wouldn't know the signs – but surely her maid would. It was a commonplace that a lady's maid was always the first to know when she was carrying. Monthly matters, even in the stratum in which he had been born, were always handled well out of the ken of menfolk, so the first he would know would be when Nina came to him to tell him he was to be a father.

He imagined the scene fondly at night as he drifted to sleep – how she would look, shy, happy, bright-eyed, a little pink from having to discuss something of such intimacy. He almost could not bear to think about what he would feel. Could the human heart hold so much happiness without actually bursting? He wanted a child so much – a child of Nina's. He thought of his dream, of the small hand in his. A son, a son to follow him into his business. Of course, a son would be best, but if it was a little girl – a girl who looked like Nina – who would sit in his lap and wind him round her tiny fingers . . . He saw her playing with his pocket watch, head gravely bent, saw himself kiss her golden curls, saw her look up and laugh, tiny white teeth and rosy cheeks . . . He would love her just as much as any boy. So much love waiting for her. A man could die of so much love . . .

He waited, aching with hope. September turned to October and the leaves began to fall, but still the news didn't come.

# CHAPTER NINETEEN

The new walled garden was finished and planted, and Kitty was deep in plans with Peason for the succession-houses; and early ideas for the pleasure-gardens on the other side of the house.

The news that Lady Stainton was on the way back jerked her out of her happy reverie. She had changed things in the house! She was so nervous with guilt that when the dowager finally arrived, she was positive she was examining everything with a furious eye, and would at any minute explode and demand to know what Kitty had been *thinking*.

In fact, Maud paid little attention to her surroundings, and did not notice that Ashmore Castle was looking unusually clean and polished. Kitty had not dared to touch the dowager's room, apart from having it cleaned as usual, so nothing had been moved or altered, and the carpet and drapes were the same worn and faded ones she had left behind. She didn't notice those, either, only felt vaguely glad to be back at home and out of the public eye.

Miss Taylor noticed, of course. Her gimlet eye took in every detail: the repaired rail on the great staircase, the newly painted walls above the panelling of the great hall, where decades of woodsmoke had been vanquished by cream distemper, the soft lustre and lavender smell of polished wood, the newly discernable colours of cleaned carpets. She noticed, but said nothing, calculating what and when to communicate to her mistress, how to turn the situation to her own account. When she went downstairs, she noticed Moss's vague and woolly mien, and wondered if his drinking had got worse. She noticed the new cockiness of Hook, and the increase of daftness in William, and wondered if there was a connection. But she held her tongue.

'You've been away a long time, Miss Taylor,' Mrs Webster observed, as she brought down an armful of linen to be washed. 'Eight months, I make it – apart from the short visit when the baby was born. You'll notice changes, I dare say.'

She meant changes in the baby, and she was only making polite conversation. But Miss Taylor said, 'Yes, I can see that while the cat was away, the mice had a fine old time playing. And I suppose you didn't exert yourself to stop them.'

Mrs Webster raised an eyebrow. 'Are you referring to her ladyship as a cat, Miss Taylor? I don't think that's proper language from someone of your station.'

Miss Taylor was unmoved. 'You may think the sceptre has passed, but you'll find yourself thinking again. And I know perfectly well that it doesn't stop at a lick of paint and a tin of polish. I saw the look on her young ladyship's face. We shall see what her ladyship thinks when she finds out.'

Miss Taylor was hoping that something had been done that would exasperate the dowager sufficiently to drive Kitty back into her shell. She would never have admitted it to anyone, but she was apprehensive. If the young ladyship did grow up and take over the house, what would happen to Miss Taylor's mistress, and by extension to her? The horrid spectre of the Dower House beckoned – and the even worse fate of seeing the dowager drop out of society and Miss Taylor become personal maid to an old lady who never went anywhere or saw anyone. She had no confidence that retirement from the world would sweeten the dowager's temper. Maud Stainton would be a sour old lady if ever there was one.

★ ★ ★

While Rose and Hatto between them unpacked Rachel's luggage, she grabbed Alice and towed her to the schoolroom for an exchange of news.

'I'm glad to see nothing's been changed in here,' Rachel said, looking around eagerly. 'And it still smells the same. Looks smaller, somehow.'

'That's because you're taller,' said Alice.

'Am I really?' Rachel was pleased. 'You haven't changed a bit, dear old Alice. Come and sit in the window-seat. I've so much to tell you!'

Alice obeyed. The fire hadn't been lit today, but it was still warm outside, and the sun was only just off the window. She noted how Rachel sat, smoothing her skirts under her and arranging her hands and feet just so. She was definitely a young lady now. Alice felt a stab of loneliness. 'Don't tell me,' she said, only half humorously, 'you're in love.'

'Oh, no, not yet,' Rachel said. 'I'm having too much fun to settle for one person. Mama said – and I agree with her – that we shouldn't even consider any offer until I've had my London debut. I am out, to all intents and purposes, but the London market is so much greater, and just having a debut there increases your attractions to the best candidates.'

'Candidates?' Alice queried.

Rachel looked a little lofty. '*I* am the pursued, *they* are the pursuers. That's how it ought to be. I am an earl's daughter from one of England's oldest families. They make their applications, and I choose between them. Or Mama does.'

'But what about dowry? Doesn't that count?'

For an instant Rachel looked uncomfortable. 'I shall have a dowry,' she said. 'Giles will provide one. We don't know how much it will be, that's all. But Mama says even without a penny, I'd be a catch—'

'I bet Mama never said anything so vulgar as "catch"!'

'Well, that's what she means. However much my dowry turns out to be, I'm a most desirable match.'

328

She seemed to want reassurance, so Alice patted her hand. 'You're so beautiful, you're bound to be. How were things in Scotland?'

'Oh, such fun! I thought it might be dull after Germany and the South of France and the Isle of Wight – oh, did I tell you, darling, that I was presented to the King and Queen there *and* the Kaiser?'

'You did, in your letters. You said the King smelt nice and the Queen was beautiful and the Kaiser was a funny little man.'

Rachel put her hands to her cheeks. '*Never* show those letters to anyone! It sounds so childish. The Kaiser *is* a bit strange, but he's very good-looking, with lovely blue eyes. But even when he tries to be jolly, there's a sort of air about him – as if he might suddenly bite you. We had lovely dinners in Cowes, and lots of dancing. Trips that were the greatest fun. And fireworks on the last night – they look so gorgeous when they go off over the sea. You can see all the colours reflected in the water.'

'What made Scotland nice, after all that?'

'Not having to be on show all the time. Chatting with the cousins and going for walks and playing silly games. But after the first week, Uncle Stuffy thought we would all be bored and started accepting invitations, so we were going to dinners and having people over in return. And every evening seemed to end in dancing, but not dancing like in Cowes. Scottish country dancing – such a romp!'

'You enjoyed it?'

'Well, it can get a bit wild, and one's hair does tend to come adrift, but it's fun. And the boys one dances with are different – not always trying to impress you, just pleasant and jolly. And, I suppose it's all the outdoor sports, but one noticed how strong and healthy they were. Different from drawing-room boys.'

For a moment there was a pensive, almost dreamy look on her face.

Alice said, 'You've got a secret! Tell me.'

Rachel came back to earth, and giggled, her cheeks pink. She leaned close to Alice, though there was no one to hear, and said, 'I've been kissed!'

Alice was not immediately impressed. 'But you did a lot of kissing with Victor Lattery last year. At least, that's what you told me.'

'Oh, but I was a child then. It was just play – it didn't mean anything.'

'You cried like anything when he went away. You wanted to marry him.'

'I wish you would forget about that. I tell you, it was nothing. And Victor was just a boy. Now I've been kissed by a man.'

'Oh, Ray!' said Alice affectionately. 'Well, what was it like?'

'It was . . .' Rachel paused, remembering. 'It was different from what I expected. But so nice. I'll tell you how it happened.'

Their mother's Aunt Cecily, who was only a few years older than Maud, had married a Scottish landowner, Gordon Tullamore, who had a great fortune from coal mines. Their children had always been known as the Cousins, and Tullamores and Tallants had been meeting all through their childhood. The eldest, Angus, was twenty-five and learning his father's business. They had played together as children, but Rachel's appearance at Kincraig in her new grown-up guise seemed to make him see her differently. When they were romping and playing games as a family, she caught him watching her all the time – only when she looked at him, he'd look away and pretend he hadn't been. But when the outside engagements began, and there was dancing, and other young men showed their eagerness to be dancing with her, Angus seemed not to like it.

'He was always wanting to dance with me, and got quite cross when I danced with anyone else – though he tried to hide it, of course.'

'He was jealous?'

'Well,' said Rachel modestly, 'I did wonder about that. Then one evening at Alvie Castle, I was dancing with Johnny Etteridge, who was being awfully silly and flirting with me madly, and when the dance ended, Angus came up and told Johnny he was making a spectacle of me and ordered him not to dance with me any more. Johnny just laughed, which made Angus even angrier. I was afraid they were going to fight each other.'

'How horrid!' said Alice.

'Well, I thought if I wasn't there they might both calm down. I was feeling hot, anyway – you do jump about an awful lot with Scottish dancing – so I went into the conservatory to cool down. Alvie has the most splendid one – they call it the orangery, and it runs all along one side of the house, and it's full of marvellous trees and shrubs and things. And, anyway, while I was walking about there—'

'Let me guess, Angus came in. Oh, Rachel, did you plan it?'

'No!' Rachel exclaimed indignantly. And then admitted, 'Well, actually I thought Johnny Etteridge might come in, and I wasn't sure how I felt about that, but I thought I might as well see what happened. But it was Angus who found me, and he wasn't flirty at all, but serious and rather upset-looking. And it made me feel awfully queer inside because, well, you haven't seen him for ages, but he's really grown-up now, and awfully handsome. I got a strange, fluttery feeling in my stomach. I tried to hide it – told him he couldn't tell Johnny off like that. I said, "You're not my father," and he gave me such a look, and said, "No, thank God." I said, "What do you mean by that?" And he said, "The last thing I want is to be a father to you." And then he took me in his arms, and kissed me.'

Alice was imagining the scene, only, of course, with herself in the place of heroine. And the hero . . . She couldn't bring

Cousin Angus's face to mind, but she gave him a tall, powerful body, with big, strong hands which were at the same time delicate in their touch, and a fair face with outdoor ruddiness, and tousled reddish-gold hair, and blue eyes. And a faint delicious smell about him, of leather and wood-shavings and a particular clean, warm male smell . . .

She found she had closed her eyes. 'What was it like?' she asked, without opening them.

'When his mouth first touched mine, it was like an electric shock. It's so *intimate,* you know, and – and like something that's, oh, sort of forbidden, and dangerous, and you oughtn't, but you want to anyway. But it went on for a long time, and after a bit it was . . .'

Her voice trailed off. Alice opened her eyes. Rachel was staring into space, and Alice couldn't read her expression. It almost looked *sad.*

'My first proper kiss,' she said, 'with a real man. Angus – he's not a boy, you know, he's a real, serious grown-up. And I could feel he was serious about kissing me.'

She stopped, remembering. She had felt quivery and sort of – hungry: wanting something, but not really knowing what it was she wanted. It had been disturbing. All this year she had been enjoying her mastery over the young men who flirted and danced with her and obeyed her every whim, vying for her smiles. But now suddenly with Angus she had felt weak. She felt she had no power over him. She didn't entirely like it – but it was strangely exciting.

'Yes?' Alice prompted. 'Then what happened.'

Rachel shook herself. 'He asked me to marry him.'

Alice was impressed. 'No! Not really?'

Rachel remembered how he had held her, how he had looked down at her, almost grimly, as if he wanted to shake her. 'I don't want to be your father,' he'd said. 'I want to be your husband. Will you marry me, Rachel? Say yes, and I'll kiss you again. You need kissing – and by a man, not silly

332

boys like Johnny Etteridge. Say yes, and I'll kiss you until you swoon.'

She didn't tell Alice any of that. The gulf between her, now a woman, and Alice, still a girl, was too great. 'Yes, he did,' she said.

'And what did you say?'

She had looked up at him for a long time, weakening all the time under his gaze, and if he had smiled at her, she would probably have said yes. But he had gone on looking at her with that stern determination, and she had become aware that his gripping hands were hurting her upper arms. She had lowered her eyelids and said, as scornfully as she could, 'Marry you? Even if I wanted to, Mama would never allow it.'

'But you *do* want to?' he had insisted, not as if it was a question.

Now she answered Alice. 'I told him I wanted to have my London come-out before I even *thought* about marrying anybody. And then I ran away, back into the ballroom. I avoided him for the rest of the evening – but I could feel him watching me all the time.' *And of course,* she thought, *I was right – Mama would never even consider him. I'm to marry a duke or a prince.*

Alice, still thinking about the kiss and the tall, strong hero who was not really Cousin Angus, said, 'Daisy says that the man who gives you your first kiss steals a bit of your soul, and he owns that bit of you for ever.'

'What vulgar nonsense!' Rachel said robustly, though Alice could see she was a little shaken. 'Servants' talk. What does Daisy know about anything?'

'You don't think there's any truth in it, then?' Alice said, more to be provoking than because she thought so.

'I mean to have a good many more kisses before I choose my husband. How will I know I've got it right if I've got nothing to compare with?'

'*Mama* will choose your husband, not you,' Alice pointed out.

Kitty's carefulness in not changing Lady Stainton's room did her no good, because when Maud came down to the drawing-room she noticed the sheer contrast with the room she had just quitted. Everything gleamed: there was new upholstery on chairs and sofas, what she took to be a new carpet (actually just cleaned so that you could see the colours again) and, most noticeable of all, the new curtains. She stared, and her nostrils flared. 'What *have* you done?' she demanded.

Kitty was scarlet and tongue-tied. Alice, noting the direction of her mother's gaze, said, 'Oh, the curtains? Aren't they splendid? They're actually the same as the old ones, only you'd never know.'

Kitty rushed into explanation. 'We unpicked the hem so that we could see what colour they originally were, and then we matched the material exactly. They really are the same, you know, only now they're nice.'

Lady Stainton looked at her with faint contempt. 'To expend so much thought and energy on a *curtain* verges on the vulgar.' She looked around her with disapproval. 'All this newness. It looks – like a suburban bank clerk's parlour.'

Sebastian smiled. 'My dear Maud, I cannot persuade myself you have ever seen the inside of a suburban bank-clerk's house.'

Giles intervened. 'Are you home for good? Will you be hunting this year?'

'We are settled here,' Maud said. 'Except for the preparations for Rachel's coming-out and presentation. We shall have to go up for fittings, consultations for the court dress, and I should like to introduce her at a few of the Little Season events. I assume you will be entertaining here between now and Christmas, and that will be useful in showing her. And of course I shall hunt. How is my horse going?'

Alice answered. 'We brought her up two weeks ago and I've been exercising her. She's going nicely. Mama, am I to be brought out next year as well?' She would be eighteen in March, and though she didn't want any of that débutante fol-de-rol, she thought she'd better be prepared, if it was to happen.

Maud looked at her as if she had only just noticed she was there. 'I can't concentrate on bringing out two daughters at once,' she said. 'Rachel must be given every chance – she is the one with prospects. She can look as high as she likes. You—'

She examined her youngest daughter, and perceived that she really had grown during the year, and was clearly no longer an absolute child. But she had the manner of a child, the undisguised straightforwardness that would not show well in ballroom or soirée. If she left her another year, she would be nineteen, old for a debut. On the other hand, what sort of marriage would suit a girl like Alice? Would she shine in high society? Surely a rich country gentleman with plenty of acres and horses would be enough for her – a baronet or knight, or even a plain mister if it was a good, old name that would not disgrace the family. She might meet that sort of person at home, or going round the country-house circuit. Would a formal come-out, let alone Presentation, really be necessary? It wasn't the expense that deterred her, but the actual process. She had enjoyed showing Rachel off, though it had been exhausting; but Rachel fell in with plans, and was rewarding to dress. The idea of dragging a reluctant, always dishevelled Alice around the ballrooms and drawing-rooms of the Ton was repulsive.

'I dare say we shall have Rachel's wedding to attend to next summer, but you might meet someone there, or during country-house visits. I don't see that a formal debut is necessary for you. Linda can chaperone you to one or two balls during next year's Little Season if necessary. Once Rachel is back from her honeymoon, she will be entertaining at the highest level, and I'm sure will help you, if you haven't already had an offer by then.' Her eyes narrowed. 'You haven't formed an attachment, I trust?'

'No, Mama. How could I? I don't go anywhere.'

'Don't be pert,' said Maud automatically. 'That sort of attitude will never get you married.'

'I don't want to get married,' Alice said.

'Well, I don't suppose Giles wants to have to keep you for the rest of your life,' Maud retorted. 'Or Kitty.'

The last was so obviously an afterthought that Alice felt indignant on her sister-in-law's behalf. Kitty's head was down, her face invisible as she fondled the ears of Isaac, whose head was in her lap. Of course it hurt that Maud barely acknowledged her existence, but she so much preferred it to being the object of her attention.

Having to mention Kitty reminded Maud of something much more agreeable. 'How is my grandson?' she asked.

Giles answered, while Sebastian caught Alice's eye and they exchanged a look. It was so typical of Maud that Louis was always her grandson, never Kitty's or Giles's son.

Rumour below-stairs that Mr Sebastian was about to marry grew thin from lack of nourishment and finally died. No one could put a name to the putative lady, or even any place he had gone where he could have met her. Interest in him died away. He was just old Mr Sebastian who liked his claret and his cigars, whose life seemed a simple circuit between fireside chair and dining-table. Even his piano-playing – the only difference between him and any other old gentleman – wasn't in itself *interesting*, any more than his occasionally playing billiards was. It was just what upstairs folk did.

But for the two closest to him, it remained a matter of unspoken speculation. After that first visit, when he had taken

Crooks and Dory, he had been back to Henley on several occasions, and up to London twice, but on those trips he had taken no one. It was a fact that he went away more often than before. Dory didn't now think there had been anything in the rumour; but she feared any change. What if he were planning to move out, and live permanently in Henley? She imagined life at the Castle without those precious interludes of music and conversation, and it looked bleak, a featureless desert of work. Such was the usual life of a person in service, but having had something more would make that reality harder to bear.

Crooks's fears were more basic. When his master went away, these days, he said, 'It will only be for a couple of nights. I can manage without you.' Crooks was too good a servant to protest – but he was rattled. And there were the London trips to take into account. Mr Sebastian rarely went to London, and when he did, he always took his manservant with him. Now he had gone twice alone. Crooks had imagined Mr Sebastian pottering into Boodles or Mappin's to buy a ring, and he could not now get rid of the image.

The thing all valets knew was that when a gentlemen married, if his new wife took a dislike to his manservant, he had to go. This was more likely when the gentleman was of a fixed bachelor persuasion. Wives liked to put their own stamp on a household, and confirmed bachelors and their valets tended to get into settled ways that could make the new wife feel shut out. Jealousy and pique were usually followed by the dreaded new broom, and the valet, with his proprietary intimacy, was the first to be swept clean.

When the old earl had died and Crooks had become a masterless dog, he had thought his life was over. Then by a miracle he had been brought back from despair to the safe haven of Mr Sebastian's service – undemanding, comfortable, and, he had felt entitled to assume, permanent. Now he was nervous. *Something* was up, he knew that deep in his bones; *something* was going on. And whatever it was, if Mr Sebastian was keeping it a secret from Crooks, that could only bode Crooks no good – no good at all.

# CHAPTER TWENTY

William was having a smoke out in the yard with Cyril when one of the stable-boys came in, looking furtive.

'Here, you, William – there's someone wants yer.'

William straightened up, frowning at the grin on the grubby face. He was first footman now, a position that should be accorded respect by mere dung-shovellers. 'What way is that to talk? You got a message, you deliver it proper.'

'Ho, yuss, yer lordship,' the boy mocked. 'Yer presence is required out there,' he jerked his head, '*hif* you'd be so kind.'

Cyril sniggered. William tried to frown at him and at the boy simultaneously. 'Is it Mr Giddins wants me?'

'Naw – what'd the boss want wiv a waspie?' The stable hands called the footmen wasps because of their striped waistcoats. 'It's a *laydee* wants yer – and quick about it!'

'Ooh, a *laydee*!' Cyril mocked. 'William's a great one for the *laydees*!'

'It's prob'ly my mum,' William said hastily. 'Is she all right?' he demanded of the boy.

'It ain't yer *ma*,' the boy said with an indescribable leer, and disappeared.

William hurried out of the yard, and as he rounded the corner he saw a figure lurking behind the big bush that grew by the stableyard gate. An arm came out and beckoned him urgently, and he recognised the bottle-green velvet sleeve of Tabby's favourite jacket. He joined her behind the bush, his loins giving a now-familiar surge of welcome. 'Tab,' he said. 'It's lovely to see you, but I *can't* do it, not here. Anyone could see. And I can't go anywhere – I'm on duty.'

Tabby fastened her hand round his forearm as if to stop him fleeing. 'I've not come for that,' she said sternly. 'Lord, how your mind does run on one thing! I want to talk to you.'

'Can't it wait? I haven't got long – I was just having a fag.'

'No, it can't wait. I got to talk to you now.' She looked up into his eyes, dragging them back from their natural propensity to slither down her cleavage. 'I'm in trouble.'

'How's that?' he asked nervously, but wanting to help. She was his girl, after all. 'It's not old man Corbie, is it? Is he having a go at you again?' Corbie had told Tabby off for sneaking out of the bar to see William, and he felt both indignant and guilty.

'It's not Corbie,' she said impatiently. 'This is serious, William. Will you just shut up and listen?'

'Course,' he said, slightly hurt. He folded his arms and ostentatiously closed his mouth.

His silence seemed to put her off. She chewed her lip, her eyes shifting away from his face and back. Finally, she said, 'I'm expecting.' The news didn't seem to register with him. She tried again. 'I'm having a baby.'

'Oh,' he said. He stared, his brain obviously working slowly through what was, after all, a short sentence.

She grew impatient. 'Is that all you've got to say – oh?'

'Well, I don't know,' he said stumblingly. 'I've never – no one never – a baby?'

'Yes, a baby. So what're you going to do about it?' This was obviously too complex a question for him. She simplified: 'You and me, we've got to get spliced. Before the baby comes.'

'Oh,' said William again. 'Married?' He'd got there at last. 'But—'

'Don't you "but" me, William Sweeting,' she said in low fury. 'We got to get spliced, and that's all about it! You had

340

your fun, and fun don't come free. Got to be paid for. I'm not having this here baby out of wedlock, with everyone pointing at me, while you get away scot-free—'

He caught hold of her arms. 'Tab, Tab, I don't mean to. I don't want nobody pointing at you. And this baby . . .' A soppy look crossed his face. 'A real baby? I'm going to be a dad?'

'It's real all right,' she said grimly. 'So what're you going to do?'

The soppiness faded. 'But, Tab, I don't see how I can marry you. I'd never be allowed. You can't be a married footman. And I got to live in. Footmen can't live out.'

'You know all that, when you've never asked?'

'But I do know,' he said anxiously. 'It's the truth. Honest, Tab, I wouldn't lie to you. I'd never get permission to get married. I'd lose me job, and then what?'

'You'll have to get a different job,' she said remorselessly. 'You've got to support me and the baby. I can keep working at the Dog for a bit—'

'I don't want my wife working behind a bar,' he said, because it seemed like the sort of thing a proper man would say.

'Your wife? So you do want to marry me, then?'

'Course I do. *Course* I do. And a baby! You and me and a baby, like a proper family. It'll be smashing!' He thought of being able to do those things Tabby had shown him *all the time* – and in comfort. What joy! 'But it'll take some thinking about. I mean, what other job could I get? I don't know anything else. I've always been in service. And I'm getting on at the Castle – first footman now, and if Mr Moss retires one day, I bet I'll get made butler. If I leave I'll lose all that.'

'Well, I can't help it. We've got to get married.'

'And where would we live?' he went on, following his own thoughts.

Tabby had an answer. 'We could live with your ma first

off, till you'd got a bit saved. Then we could rent a little place. And as for jobs, you know how to serve drinks and wait tables. You could be a barman or a waiter. They always want people at the Crown – smart people for the carriage trade. You'd be grand at that. You know how nobs like things done – and you're good-looking. If that Horace Dawkins can get a job there, with a face like a squashed tomato, they'll jump at you. He's got half his teeth missing.'

'Oh, I don't know, Tab. It's a big change—'

'Well, what d'you think it is for me? But it's got to be. You just get your head around it, William Sweeting, because this is going to happen. Now, I could have a word with Mr Millet down the Crown, but it'd come better from you. Don't want him to think you're going to be hen-pecked, do you?' The truth was that Millet knew too much about her, and a word from her wouldn't secure a dog a scratch behind the ears, but she couldn't tell him that. 'You want him to think you're a proper man, don't you?'

'I am a proper man,' William said, drawing himself up. 'And I will see you right, Tabby. But you got to give me time. I got to think about it. I got to sort it out.'

'Well, don't take too long about it. I ain't *got* time. Babies don't hang about.'

'No, I won't. But I got to think things out. And, Tab, don't say anything to my ma. Don't go round there and talk to her.' Her eyes narrowed suspiciously, and he hurried on, 'Only, she can't take a shock. She has these funny turns if she gets upset. I'll have to break it to her gentle, in my own time. And don't say anything to anyone else about the baby, because you know how things get round, and if she hears from someone else . . . But I'll look after you, Tab, I promise. Only I've got to do it right. You've got to give me time.'

She stepped closer, and lifted her mouth for kissing. 'All right. I trust you, William. I know you love me. And when

342

we're married, I'll make you the happiest man in the world. *You* know what I mean.'

He did. He surged again. If only he was free now . . . But when they were married, oh, they could do it every night. When he got back from work. He gulped, thinking about that. He'd always been in service and it had never bothered him, the lack of freedom. But thinking of doing a job that you left in the evening to go home to a separate place where no one was watching you – well, it was exciting. Frightening, too. But exciting.

Mr Cowling watched Nina smiling over a letter, reached for the marmalade, and said, 'Something interesting, my love?'

'It's from Kitty.' She looked up. 'She says they're all going to London next week. Rachel's going to be shown off in the Little Season, and Giles has business, and everyone else is just going to have some fun. They'll be staying at Lady Manningtree's.'

'Funny coincidence,' Mr Cowling said. 'I was just going to ask you if you'd like to go to London for a bit.' Her face lighting up was his reward. It wasn't entirely fiction – he did need to go to London on business, but hadn't begun to think about when. But he thought he had heard a note of wistfulness in her voice. 'Decius can find us somewhere for a couple of weeks. I don't like to make you stay in a hotel all that time.'

'I don't mind where I stay,' she said, 'but it would be lovely to go. Can we go to the theatre and things like that?'

'Anything you like. And I'm sure if you tell your friend Kitty there'll be invitations from them, too.'

'I don't know about that,' Nina said doubtfully. 'I expect everything's been arranged. But I'm sure we can manage to meet somewhere. Perhaps have tea together.'

'You write and tell her straight away,' said Mr Cowling.

He crunched up his last piece of toast and stood up. 'And I'd better get on and arrange things my end.'

'Sit up straight, Alice. Do not slouch.'

'Or you'll never get a husband,' Alice muttered.

'What do you say?' asked Grandmère sharply.

Alice straightened herself hastily. 'That's what they always say: "Sit up straight or you'll never get a husband".'

'Me, I do not talk about husbands. I wish you will not slouch because it is disagreeable to look at. Also, it is not *comme il faut* to show so clearly that you find it a bore to visit me.'

Alice was instantly contrite. 'Oh, no, truly, Granny, I love to visit you. It's London that's a bore. There's nothing to do.'

Grandmère looked amused. 'Some might say that London has more things to do than one can have time for.'

Alice made a rather French popping of the lips that she had caught from her grandmother. 'London things!' she dismissed them. 'Theatres and art galleries and *dancing*. The only green is the parks, and what can one do in a park?'

'Whereas at home you can disport yourself over green fields *comme une femme sauvage*. And that pleases you?'

'At home, no one cares what I do,' Alice said simply.

'That, I fear, is the truth. But, *ma petite*, that cannot go on for ever. Life lies in wait, like a wolf at the door.'

'"The Assyrian came down like the wolf on the fold, and his cohorts were gleaming in purple and gold,"' Alice quoted.

'Very pretty. Where do you have that?'

'We used to have to recite poetry for Papa when we were very young. That's the only bit I can remember now. I used to love the name Sennacherib – it sounds like crunching up chop bones.' She sighed. 'I wouldn't mind so much if life was going to arrive gleaming in purple and gold, but I have a horrid feeling it's going to be just an ordinary grey old wolf – probably with a mangy coat and dog's breath.'

Her grandmother laughed. 'Poor little one! I fear you are right. But your imagination will save you. There you shall romp in the green fields always.'

Alice was about to say she'd sooner do it in reality, when the door opened, and Richard came in, closely followed by the butler, Chaplin, who had wanted to announce him properly but could not beat him up the stairs.

'Thank you, Chaplin. We shall have tea. And so,' Grandmère turned up her face to receive Richard's kiss, 'tell me about your protégée.'

'What is a protégée?' Alice asked

'Do they not teach you *any* French?' Grandmère complained.

'There is no "they", Granny. I haven't had a governess for years.'

'Hmm. In general, I am not in favour of too much education for females – it takes off the natural bloom – but there are some things that are merely a matter of civilisation.'

'Like sitting up straight,' Alice said.

'And speaking French,' Richard added. 'Or at least understanding it.'

'You are both wicked creatures to tease your poor frail *grandmère*.'

'You, frail?' Richard exclaimed. 'You're made of pure steel, and you know it. You will outlive all of us.'

'*Oh, j'espère que non!*'

'But what is a protégée?' Alice persisted. 'Is it the same as a prodigy?'

'In this case, yes,' Richard said.

'Like the infant phenomenon in *Nicholas Nickleby*?'

'She's no infant. But she has astonishing talent for a young woman. And protégée is from the French, as you ought to know, my ignorant little savage, and means "protected person". But she's not my protégée, she's Grandmère's. And Sir Thomas Burton's.'

'Oh. She's musical, then,' Alice said.

'She plays the piano like – like – well, you have to hear her to understand.'

'But who is she?' Alice demanded.

'Her name is Chloë Sands. Remember that, because she'll be famous one day.'

'And how do you know her?'

Grandmère stepped in. 'It is not *comme il faut* to ask so many questions, *cherie*.' She turned to Richard. 'All is well for the first recital? I have not seen Sir Thomas for a day or two. *Il n'y a pas de problèmes?*'

'Only some severe pre-performance nerves when I visited this morning.'

Grandmère frowned. 'She has always struck me as a supremely confident young woman. But once she begins to play, she will forget all but the music.'

'Not the prodigy's nerves, *ma chère*, the mother's,' said Richard. 'Miss Chloë already thinks about nothing but the music. It is her mother who is in shreds. I recommended a glass of Wincarnis and a cold flannel to the head.'

'You are a very wicked boy. Some nervousness is natural in a mother at such a time. But it will all go splendidly. When Sir Thomas puts on a concert, *tout le monde fait attention*. There will be no empty seat.'

Richard nodded. 'I've secured tickets for everyone at Aunt Caroline's, and she's warned her friends that they absent themselves at their peril. Mother isn't entirely happy. She dislikes concerts – and dislikes even more to be dragooned. "Who is this *person*?" she booms – person, being, as you know, Granny, the worst insult she can bestow.'

'But she will be present,' Grandmère said. It was not a question.

'Sheer curiosity will bring her,' said Richard. 'She can't understand what I have to do with music. She suspects some ulterior motive.'

'She will be there because I will tell her to be. And because it will be a very important event of the Season.'

'Do I have to go?' asked Alice, who had followed the exchanges like someone watching tennis.

'You do. But you'll enjoy it,' said Richard, patting her arm. 'I didn't think I liked music until I heard Chloë play. It's like nothing on earth.'

'Are you in love with her?' Alice asked suspiciously.

'Too impudent,' Grandmère rebuked her.

But it was Richard's laugh that convinced her. 'No, I certainly am not.'

*She must be more than usually plain, then, poor thing*, Alice thought. And said, 'I suppose a pianist must be something like a ballet-girl or an actress?'

'No, nothing like,' Richard said, a little tautly.

'Good. Because I overheard one of the grooms saying something about Papa liking actresses and ballet girls and—'

'That's enough from you, miss,' Richard said. 'You ought to know better at your age than to repeat grooms' talk.'

'I wouldn't, to anyone else,' Alice said.

Grandmère thought it time to change the subject. 'I hope you are to be fitted with some new gowns while you are here. Your hems are too short.'

'I've outgrown everything,' Alice said. 'I don't mind.'

'*I* mind,' said Grandmère. 'I cannot have my granddaughter appear in public like that.' She waved a hand. 'I shall speak to Maud.'

'She's awfully busy with Rachel.'

'Then I shall speak to Caroline. You must have a new gown before the concert. I mean you to sit beside me, and all eyes will be on us.'

'Ah, the concert of the unearthly pianist!' Alice said, with a sly look at Richard. 'Does she have wings?'

★   ★   ★

How Linda learned that the Castle Staintons had gone to London was uncertain, but she arrived the day after they did, and it was only fortunate that she did not bring her husband, children or a maid, because it would have puzzled Lady Manningtree how to accommodate them all. 'How lucky to find everyone here,' Linda said brightly. 'I have some business to attend to which necessitated coming up, but now I see it's a family gathering, I shall stay for a day or two. What's the occasion?'

'No occasion,' Caroline said. 'Giles has business, and Rachel is to be shown at a few parties—'

'Oh, I can help Mama there. I know she doesn't care for such things. I can chaperone Rachel and save her the trouble,' Linda said eagerly.

'You can offer,' Caroline said, 'but I don't think she is minding it this time. Rachel has taken very well so far. She's certainly rewarding to show.'

'Well, she's pretty,' Linda said, somewhat sourly. 'But she may find the lack of dowry holds her back – unless Giles has relented at all. He seems very reluctant to part with any of the fortune he married.'

'If I were you,' Caroline said mildly, 'I would not use that tone – or those words – around him. Honey catches more flies than vinegar, Linda dear.'

'You'd be vinegary, Auntie, if you had my problems. And he *ought* to continue Papa's allowance. He has an obligation to respect our father's wishes. Family is everything.'

'All I'm saying is that if you ask him, ask nicely. But don't expect too much. He has a great many drains on his finances with the estate.'

'Oh, the estate,' Linda said dismissively. What were acres and farms compared with blood relations? she thought. 'Did they bring the baby?' she asked, on the back of that idea.

'Yes. He's in the nursery – do you want to see him?'

'I suppose so. She's lucky she had a boy first time. If I

hadn't had a girl first I wouldn't have had to have two. Half the trouble and half the expense.'

*Poor Gerald*, Caroline thought. She had begun by thinking it callous of Linda to leave him behind with the children (presumably to save on the railway fares), but now she thought he was probably relieved to be rid of her for a while.

Vogel, the Staintons's banker, had offered to attend Giles in Berkeley Square, but he had preferred to go to the bank, and when he said he was going to discuss the Harvey's Jam business, Kitty asked shyly if she could go with him.

'If you want to, of course,' Giles said, surprised. 'But it will be dull, you know – talk of money and business and so on.'

'But I should like to understand where the money comes from,' Kitty said. 'I always knew I was an heiress, but at home no one would tell me anything more than that. Mama used to say talking about money was vulgar, but it can't be, with a banker, can it?'

He laughed. 'No. What else would you talk to a banker about? Certainly Vogel is a very dull dog. I don't think you'd get very far with chat about balls and dinners and plays and so on.'

'So I can come?'

'Of course,' Giles said. Despite the words, there was the faintest impatience in his tone. But it was her inheritance, and she wanted to know, so she didn't back down.

Vogel was a tall, thin man, with a long, sharp nose on which gold-rimmed pince-nez perched like some exotic but very tame bird. Behind them, his eyes were large and blue and heavy-lidded; his hair was fluffy and white, curling like feathers, and left the front of his head shiningly bare. He looked frighteningly intelligent and serious, which was what you would want in a banker, but his wide, thin-lipped mouth stretched into a charming smile as he greeted Kitty, and she didn't think him at all a dull dog. When she said hesitatingly that she wanted to understand her inheritance, he said that it was a very good idea, and that he was a great advocate for females to understand finance. 'They, after all, are so often the victims of financial accident or mismanagement – far more than men are, because there's so little they can do about it. I shall be happy to tell you anything you want to know, Lady Stainton.'

The story behind Harvey's Jam was an interesting one, he said. 'Your great-grandfather, Josiah Harvey, first came to Cambridgeshire to farm in 1817. It was just after the Napoleonic Wars, and there was an agricultural slump. Corn prices were very much depressed, so he went in for market-gardening, and did quite well. Then in 1847 the railway came to that part of the country. Josiah took the opportunity to acquire a large piece of land to grow fruit, which of course he could transport quickly to London by rail and sell at Covent Garden.'

Vogel looked enquiringly at Kitty, to see if he was giving too much detail. She said, 'Please go on. I knew nothing of all this.'

'Very well, your ladyship. The business was thriving, and whenever there was an adjacent parcel of land for sale, Josiah bought it and expanded. By 1873 he had two hundred and fifty acres under production. He also had two sons, your grandfather John and your great-uncle William. They were the ones who accompanied the fruit up to London to sell it, and they reported to their father that it was mostly jam-makers who were buying it. That year happened to be a bumper year with a very heavy crop, so they persuaded their father to let them try making a batch of jam, and selling it. It proved so popular that two years later they built a factory next to the railway station and went entirely into jam-making.'

'I never knew my grandfather,' Kitty said. 'I think he died when I was quite small.'

Vogel nodded. 'By the 1880s, the company had expanded into making marmalade, so as to be able to keep a permanent workforce, rather than laying them off in the winter. By the 1890s they owned five hundred acres of land, and had added clear table jellies, custard powder, lemonade, and mincemeat for the Christmas market to their products. It was a remarkable tale of success. When your grandfather died in 1890, everything went to your great-uncle William, and he, being unmarried, left it to you.'

'I never knew him either,' Kitty said sadly. 'I remember my father telling me he had died, but I never met him. I seem to have been unlucky with my relatives.'

Vogel bowed. 'In that sense, yes. But the company continues to flourish. When your grandfather died, your great-uncle took on the son of a family friend, and trained him up to manage the day-to-day business. Charles Logan is a very able man and runs everything efficiently. It was he, I believe, who came up with many of the new ideas the company has pioneered. And he has now come up with another one, which is what I wanted to put to you today.'

He looked at Giles at this point, and Giles nodded and said, 'Carry on.'

'Logan believes the company should be exporting its products, which would mean a very significant expansion – and also, of course, a large increase in profits. To take full advantage of export markets, he believes the jam should be put into tin cans, rather than glass jars as at present. Cans are much lighter than glass; and glass, of course, is breakable, which is a consideration when the goods are travelling long distances, perhaps over rough terrain. And if you were providing jam on a large scale, say to the army, the navy, ocean-going passenger vessels, foreign administrations and so on, you would want to sell it in larger units. The domestic market, I understand, is mostly for a two-pound glass jar. That would not go far when catering for a company of soldiers: you would want your jam in a ten-pound container.'

'I see,' said Giles. 'A ten-pound glass jar would be heavy and unwieldy.'

'And if it breaks, it's a lot of jam to be wasted.'

Giles saw the point. 'The company cook couldn't scrape it off the floor and use it, for fear there would be shards of glass in it.'

Vogel permitted himself a small smile. 'Precisely.'

'Would they do that?' Kitty asked, slightly shocked.

Giles smiled at her. 'My dear Kitty, I do advise you not to enter a kitchen while it is actually preparing food. You would never eat again. So, Vogel, what is the catch to this plan of Logan's?'

'No catch, my lord. Simply, it requires a large investment to build and equip the canning factory. Logan also wants the business to make its own tin cans – it has always been self-sufficient and, of course in the long run, it would mean more profits for Harvey's than if cans were being bought in from elsewhere.'

'I see. And how much would it all cost? How much does Logan want me to invest?'

Vogel mentioned a sum. To Kitty it sounded enormous, but she knew she had no idea of how that related to anything commercial.

Giles, it seemed, also thought it large – too large. He shook his head. 'No,' he said. 'I can't agree to that. It's too big a slice of our capital.'

'It *is* a lot, but I believe the investment very sound, and certain to yield substantial profits longer term. There is a limit to the potential for expansion in the domestic market, but the world is effectively limitless. Even to secure a contract with the British army would be a major coup.'

'Perhaps so,' said Giles, 'but I have a great deal to do on the estate, which will require large capital investments. I'm sorry.'

'I'm sorry too,' Vogel said thoughtfully. 'I understand your

352

priorities, my lord, but it would be a great shame to miss an opportunity like this.'

'Can't it be done some other time?'

'The market is ripe for it now. If we do not seize the moment, some other firm will certainly do so, and it will be harder to make an impact when in competition with another company, rather than playing in an open field. And Logan – he is energetic, ambitious, full of enthusiasm. I fear if he is thwarted of his plans, he may leave the company, and he would be a great loss.'

Giles frowned. 'Do you seriously suggest I would make a decision based on the career plans of an employee?'

'Of course not, my lord. I merely suggest that all the stars are in alignment at this moment. There is a tide in the affairs of . . .'

*Jam?* Giles anticipated. He shrugged. 'No, I'm sorry, I need the capital for the estate.'

'Then I wonder if there might be someone else we could bring in, someone looking for a good investment opportunity? Of course, they would take a share in the profits. And they might also want a say in the running of the company, so it would have to be someone you trust – someone who would take the business in the right direction.'

'The only people I know who have that sort of money,' Giles began, thinking hopelessly of Lord Shacklock, but at that moment he caught Kitty's eye, and her thought seemed to leap the gap into his mind. 'Have you ever come across a Mr Cowling – Joseph Cowling?'

'Of Cowling and Kempson, the shoe manufacturer?' said Vogel. 'I've never met him, but of course I've heard of him. He is known to be a very shrewd businessman – the King relies on his financial advice. Do you know him?'

It was Kitty who answered. 'Yes, we know him. He married my closest friend.'

★　★　★

353

Forbes, the Manningtree butler, was plainly on the verge of regretting that Lady Stainton was not at home, when Kitty came down the stairs, almost running.

'Dearest, dearest Nina! When Hatto said you were downstairs I had to come, in case you thought I didn't want to see you, but I really *am* just going out, and I daren't be late! Oh, it's lovely to see you! How are you? You must come and see my baby! But, oh dear, I'm engaged every *minute* this week. It's wretched!'

Nina laughed. 'Wretched, is it? Oh, the miserable life of the fashionable lady!'

Kitty laughed too. 'But you know what I mean. I'd much sooner sit and coze with you, but all these things have been arranged and one can't not go – especially when it's my mother-in-law who's done the arranging.'

'No, I quite see that. I wouldn't dare cross her either.'

'Next week will be better – not so busy. But I want to talk to you *now*, today! We can't even have tea, because I have a fitting this afternoon, and then there's the concert, or recital, or whatever it is, at Lady Leven's.'

Nina brightened. 'We are going to that, too.'

'Are you? Well, of course *you* are musical – I'm sure a talented new pianist will be a treat for you. I'm rather dreading it, though Richard knows her and says she really is wonderful. It was going to be here originally, but once Sir Thomas persuaded the King to look in, too many people wanted to come to fit in the drawing-room. So Sir Thomas asked Lord and Lady Leven for the use of their long gallery – you know, where we went to the art exhibition – because they are great patrons of the arts, music as well as pictures. How is it that you are coming?'

'Mr Cowling knows Lord Leven – and the King of course. They're all in the same circle.' Nina smiled impishly. 'I think Mr Cowling is rather dreading it, too – he's not musical – but he wouldn't let the Levens down. He suspects a subscription is going to be taken up – that's usually why he gets invited to things.'

Kitty looked slightly shocked. 'Oh, I'm sure not! The pianist is Sir Thomas's protégée – he's paying for everything. I'm sure it was just a friendly gesture on Lord Leven's part. It's going to be very grand, with a reception afterwards, and the newspapers will be sending people, so there'll be photographs in all the papers and magazines.' The hall clock struck the three-quarters. Kitty glanced at it. 'Oh dear, I really *must* go. But I'll see you at the reception tonight, and we can make a plan. I'm determined to have a whole day with you, if it can be managed' She darted a kiss at Nina's cheek. '*Dearest Nina!*' And she was gone.

'I'm not even to be allowed to turn for her,' Molly Sands said to Richard, when they met for a moment in the great hall of the Levens' mansion in Portman Square. 'Sir Thomas has got one of his students to do it – a young man who is altogether too handsome for a mother's peace of mind.'

'Does she need the music?'

'Not for the solo pieces – only for the quintets.' She sighed. 'I suppose he thinks a slender young man in black and white will look tidier in the background than a fussing mother.'

'You never fuss,' Richard said. 'But I agree that you wouldn't disappear into the background. You are altogether too striking, Mariamne. Sir Thomas is right – you would draw too much attention from Chloë, and it is her night after all.'

'You say very foolish things,' Mrs Sands said severely. 'And if anyone should hear you calling me by that ridiculous name—'

'There's no one within earshot. Though it's not ridiculous,' Richard said. 'Is Chloë nervous? Considering all the grand people who will be here, not least the King . . .'

'She was a little nervous yesterday, but she was quite calm

355

this morning. She says the music is the only thing that matters, not the rank of the people listening. I don't know how she does it, when so much hangs on it.'

'Does it?'

Mrs Sands frowned. 'Sir Thomas has put such a lot into this occasion. If it didn't go well, I'm afraid he would drop her. His pride, you know – he'd feel she'd made a fool of him.'

'Hmm,' said Richard. 'Oh, it seems people are moving. Can I show you to your seat?'

He crooked his arm for her, but being jostled just at that moment by a general movement of people, she took it rather too high up, and he winced. She gave him a concerned look. 'Is it still troubling you?' He had broken his arm and shoulder badly in a motoring accident the year before.

'Comes and goes,' he said dismissively. 'I tried taking a gun out last week and the shoulder didn't like it. Oh, look, here are the principal girl and boy of tonight's pantomime! And Sir Thomas, too – the Demon King! If he's popped up, there must be photographers about . . . Ah, yes, there, just come in behind us.'

The group had appeared on the landing where the wide staircase branched left and right, a natural stage setting for being photographed from below. Sir Thomas looked magnificent and important as he always did in evening clothes. He gently inserted himself between Chloë and the young musician who was to turn for her, pushing the latter backwards out of the way, then stood beaming proudly with a proprietary arm around Chloë's slender shoulders.

'He looks like the fond papa at a wedding,' Richard said. Mrs Sands did not laugh, and he glanced at her.

She was frowning. '*How* fond, that's what I worry about,' she said. 'I've learned recently that he has a – a reputation, where young women are concerned.'

Richard had known about that from his grandmother for a long time.

Having waved genially with his free hand, Sir Thomas now looked down into Chloë's face, making a pretty vignette for the photographers. He did look particularly fond, Richard thought, and not altogether fatherly. 'Has she said anything about him in that respect?'

'No, but I don't find that reassuring. She has a foolish way of trying to protect me from life's unpleasantnesses.'

'Not foolish at all – I would do the same if I was allowed. But I'll have a word with her, if it would help. She might tell me things she wouldn't tell you.'

'Oh, please, would you?'

Chloë played, as far as Richard could tell, perfectly. He was transported by one or two of the pieces, and even in those he found less engaging, he marvelled at how her fingers danced and rushed over the keys. How could anyone *do* that? The audience seemed to receive it all very well, and applause was long and hearty. In the interval, the King asked for her to be presented, and chatted with her for a few minutes before leaving for another engagement. He was a connoisseur of female beauty, and Chloë was looking ethereally lovely.

After the second half, everyone went downstairs from the long gallery to the first-floor saloons, which had been thrown together for the occasion. There was a buffet supper, and waiters circulated with trays of champagne.

Richard watched for his chance. Sir Thomas was sticking close by Chloë's side, talking to various patrons and aficionados, but when Lord Leven came up to speak to him, his attention was diverted enough for Richard to dart in and draw her backwards into the shadow of one of the great red velvet curtains that masked the tall windows.

'We won't have long,' he said, 'so I wanted quickly to say that you were wonderful – which you will have heard from everybody else tonight already.'

Close up, Chloë looked very tired and rather pale, but she

managed a smile. 'I'm glad you were there,' she said, 'to keep Mother calm. She does worry.'

'She's not worried about your playing, which we all know is magnificent. She does worry, though, about Sir Thomas. As do I – I don't like to see him draping himself all over you.'

Chloë gave him a direct look. 'Richard, what are you saying?'

'He has a reputation – you may not be aware. My grandmother knows him very well—'

'Your grandmother, his mistress of many years,' she said, as unemphatically as if she was talking about bread and butter. 'Did you think I didn't know? Everyone does.'

'Well, they're more like old friends now,' Richard said hastily, 'but it doesn't mean she doesn't see what goes on. I just wanted to be sure that he hasn't – hasn't upset you in any way.'

She gave a small, tired smile. 'I won't pretend not to understand you. There's talk in the Academy, too. There was a flautist last year, Sylvia Anderson. She left in a hurry, and no one's heard of her since. And before that there was a violinist. But you needn't worry about me, Richard. I can take care of myself.'

Richard persisted. 'Has he made any – er – *moves* towards you?'

'He is very kind to me. And, I think, very fond of me. Sometimes it worries me. But he has never behaved improperly in any way. I think,' she added hesitantly, 'he's a little afraid of me.'

'I can understand that,' Richard said. 'You frighten me a bit, when you play. Well, as long as it stays that way – but if there's ever anything that makes you uneasy, you'll let me know?'

'And you'll ride to the rescue? And slay the dragon with your sword?'

'If necessary.'

'And ruin my career.'

'Your career is not as important as your comfort and reputation.'

She shook her head. 'Only someone who is not a musician would say that. But, really, don't worry. He doesn't mean me any harm. And I can handle him.' She glanced away. 'He's looking for me. I must go. Thank you, Richard – you're a dear.'

She patted his hand and slipped away. Her hand, as he had noted before, was hard and strong – when he saw her playing the piano, he always thought uneasily that she would have no difficulty in strangling a man with those hands. It was one reason why he had never been affected by her beauty. He knew she already had a following of hopelessly love-struck young men at the Academy, but he was immune to her. He admired her and respected her, but he had always felt there was something slightly inhuman about her.

# CHAPTER TWENTY-ONE

Decius had found a flat in St James's Square, handy for Mr Cowling's clubs, where he did a lot of business, and for Jermyn Street and Piccadilly, where a great many gentlemen's outfitters were located. The new section of the Market Harborough factory had started operations, and he was eager to promote the art-silk socks and get them into the shops.

Decius had had to rent it for the whole quarter, but Mr Cowling did not regard the cost. It was on the first floor, with good high ceilings, long windows and fine plasterwork: a large drawing-room, a dining-room, a bedroom, a dressing-room, and a bathroom. The flat had gaslight, and there was running cold water into the bath, though hot water, if wanted, still had to be brought up. There was a resident housekeeper downstairs, and a porter who carried up coals and water and dealt with any running repairs, and there were bedrooms in the attics for the personal servants of the renters – they had brought Moxton and Tina. As for food, anything could be ordered in from the multitude of local restaurants if they wanted to eat at home.

'It's quite comfortable, at least, for a short visit,' Nina said, as she and Kitty pushed the perambulator around the gardens in Berkeley Square, with Trump running ahead and exploring.

It had seriously agitated the nursery staff that her ladyship wanted to take the baby out herself. Nanny had quite modern views, and thought it good for babies to get fresh air every morning, but mothers were meant to occupy only a decorative role in the child's life, after the essential one of giving birth. The day-to-day care of a child belonged in the hands of the professional, and even after Kitty had put her foot down and asserted that she *would* push the baby-carriage herself, they had still wanted nursemaid Jessie and a footman to accompany her, walking a pace behind and ready to jump in and extract little Lord Ayton at the first hint of disaster. It had taken all her persistence for Kitty to veto that.

'I don't know what they thought I was going to do,' she had grumbled to Nina when they met in the gardens. 'Crash the perambulator into a tree, I suppose.'

'Or abandon it, screaming, when approached by a large dog,' Nina had improvised.

'Be sure you choose your own nursery staff when your turn comes, so you can make it plain who is in charge,' Kitty advised. She gave Nina a hopeful look. 'I suppose you're not . . . ? I mean, is there any sign?'

'No,' said Nina. 'But I haven't been married a year yet.'

Kitty sighed. 'I was pregnant within weeks. It would have been nice to have enjoyed things a bit first. But,' she brightened, 'Louis is such a glorious baby, one can't repine.'

The great plane trees in the garden were turning, and enormous bronze-edged, yellow leaves were drifting down and spangling the emerald grass. A sailor-suited child ran past them in deep concentration, bowling a hoop with a stick. A squirrel skittered across the path in front of them with some kind of nut in its mouth, almost under the nose of Trump, who was too surprised to chase it until it was already safely up a tree. They left him barking in a face-saving way and walked on.

Nina had been describing the rented flat. 'Did I mention that Mr Cowling said he's going to sell the house in Northampton? He says since I don't like it, he can stay in an hotel when he has to visit the factory there. And he's thinking of taking a place in London, so that we can come up whenever we like. He doesn't like the idea of my staying in hotels.'

'Will you like that? Coming to London, I mean?'

'Market Harborough is very nice, but one wants a change now and then. And there's so much to do in London. It's been fun going to the theatre again.'

They had seen *The Man From Blankley's* – a very complicated play full of mistaken identities and mysterious strangers – and *The Orchid*, a romantic musical comedy, which Mr Cowling had loved, though Nina would have preferred something weightier to stretch her mind. They had also seen *La Bohème*, which she had loved though it had tried Mr Cowling's patience, and *La Fille Mal Gardée* at the Royal Opera House, which they'd both enjoyed.

And still to come was Gounod's *Faust*. Kitty, Giles, Richard and Alice were going to the same performance. 'Richard says it's a great pity that Caruso is in New York this autumn, because his performance last year was beyond compare.' Kitty wrinkled her nose. 'He says that sort of thing, now he's become a musical expert. Alice says he's shockingly bogus, because he never cared a jot about music until last week. Mother-in-law deplores slang, and tells Alice to mind her language, and Alice says if they'd only leave her at home they'd never have to hear her speak again, slang or otherwise. She hates London, poor girl – though she's probably the most musical of all of us. She did actually enjoy the recital at the Levens', while Rachel had difficulty in staying awake.'

'They're not going to *Faust*, Rachel and Lady Stainton?'

'No, there's a card evening at Lady Vaine's that important people are going to be at.'

Nina laughed, and slipped her hand through Kitty's arm. 'Aren't we lucky that we don't need to meet important people any more? The great advantage of being married.'

'Well, we don't *need* to,' Kitty allowed, 'but you still do.

Mr Cowling seems to know everyone. All the parties you've been to this past week! And much cleverer people – people who actually *do* things, rather than just people with titles, like Mother-in-law knows. I often think Giles would prefer Mr Cowling's circle. When I see him trying not to yawn at some of the receptions and dinners we go to, it makes me glad I don't have a brain.'

'Darling Kitty, you do have a brain, and a very good one,' said Nina. 'Otherwise you wouldn't have been one of Miss Thornton's "special girls".'

'You're very loyal,' Kitty said with a fond smile, 'but you know I'm not brainy like you. Oh dear, that's another slang word I've caught from Alice. Mother-in-law would have a fit.'

Mr Cowling received Giles at the St James's Square flat. He would have met him anywhere, but Giles had said he would wait on him at home, secretly wanting to see the place where Nina was living so that he could imagine her there.

They had met several times since he came to London, though their exposure to each other had been brief in every case – the merest exchange of a few words at a social gathering before the crowds parted them. It was safer that way; but there was a devil in Giles – buried, but not quite deeply enough – that wanted to push against the barriers of safety. The confines of his life and the straitjacket of responsibility irked him. His devil wanted to cut loose, take mad chances, and run – that most of all. The estate held him back. His duty to the estate. Without that, he could have married Nina, and they could have lived as best they might, as travellers, explorers – citizens of the world. When he sat in Lady Something's drawing-room, balancing a cup of coffee on his knee and listening to the meaningless chatter all around him, like the sound of flocking finches, he sometimes had a sensation of looking down at himself from above and wondering how he had ever come to this.

But he would do his duty. A further meeting with Vogel had convinced him that the canning idea was worth pursuing, and an approach by Vogel to Decius Blake had resulted in a message, in Cowling's large, assertive hand, saying that he would meet him anywhere, at his pleasure. It was only this morning, as he was about to set off, that he heard Nina would be calling for Kitty at the same hour.

In St James's Square, he learned that it was intentional. 'Much better to discuss business without the ladies being present,' Cowling said as Giles was shown in. 'Can't concentrate on what's important if you're worried about boring the fair sex – besides talk of money having a coarsening effect, which one wouldn't want them exposed to.'

'Quite,' Giles said, with a slight mental reservation that he would have been able to talk about *anything* to Nina. Of course, if he had married her, there would have been no money to talk about anyway . . .

Mr Cowling was eager to show off the flat, while simultaneously seeming nervous that it was not good enough for his lordship. 'A pretty aspect, and nice big windows – and the rooms are a good size. Of course, it's only temporary – one can put up with a lot when it's only for a few weeks, and normally I wouldn't think of a flat of this sort, without one's own servants. But it's all kept spotless – Mrs Rice sees to that, and she employs good girls.'

Giles was embarrassed by the topic. 'I know you're a busy man, so perhaps we should get down to business. I wonder if you've had a chance to think about the plan Vogel put to your man?'

Cowling seemed relieved to be rescued. 'Aye, brass tacks, that's the ticket! Well now, it seems Harvey's jam is doing very well – a thriving business, though I should have to make a trip out to the factory and see for myself, have a look over the ground plans, and the books. And talk to this Charles Logan of yours. Vogel thinks he's a sound chap, energetic and full of ideas. As to the basic plan, it seems a good 'un. Jam in cans for the export market. I like the scope it opens up – the army, the navy, the colonies. Army barracks in India. Hospitals. Big schools. Local government. The sky's the limit, lad, that's what I like about it. Think big! And get in first! You want the name Harvey's to spring to mind whenever anyone mentions jam. And that's anywhere in the world, mind you! Think of a rancher in South America or an explorer in darkest Africa going to buy jam for their trip: you want 'em to be saying, "And I'll have a tin of Harvey's to take with me," Not jam, note, but Harvey's.'

He spoke with such enthusiasm that for a moment Giles was seduced, and found himself feeling excited about the prospects. Expand all over the world! Harvey's jam everywhere! The sailors on a British warship eyeing the Harvey's tin with affection as it was opened for breakfast! Indian clerks in a Bombay government office spreading Harvey's strawberry on their canteen toast! A tin of Harvey's in the covered wagon rattling behind the cowboys driving herds across America! And why stop at jam? They did mincemeat – why not Christmas puddings? They did lemonade – why not ginger beer? Cakes, biscuits, tinned food of all sorts – there was no limit to what they could sell, and where.

'By Jove!' he exclaimed.

'Aye, you see it now,' Cowling said, smiling. 'Vogel's a good chap, but not inspirational – not that you'd want that in a banker. But now you've seen it, you'll be thinking twice about letting anyone else in on it. I couldn't understand why you didn't want to use your own capital, and keep all the profits to yourself. But I'll tell you what, lad – my lord, I should say – if you want to change your mind now, there'll be no hard feelings, our wives being best of friends and all that. I shan't hold it against you, though I think it's a grand opportunity.'

The excitement faded. Of course, it was the idea of the wide world that had fired him up: geography, not commerce.

The question of whether the world got its jam from him or someone else interested him not at all.

'I haven't changed my mind,' he said. 'I understand that it's a good investment, in business terms, but I can't commit my capital when I need it for other things – things that are closer to my heart. And frankly, Mr Cowling, I would like to have your expertise and enthusiasm behind it. You are the sort of man who would get things moving and make a success of them. And if you make a handsome profit in the process – well, that's only fair.'

Cowling was eyeing him during this speech as if trying to get to the bottom of his character. 'Well,' he said, after a pause for thought, 'let's put things in train and see where we get. Financial details I can discuss with Vogel – he'll see you straight. But I'm known throughout the land for fair dealing, so you needn't hold back from trusting me. And you've come to the right man. I don't know if Nina's mentioned it, but I've been involved in building an extension to the factory in Market Harborough, all new machinery for making art-silk socks. So I know a bit about setting up for a new product, getting the machinery in, training the workers, sorting out the market and the transport and so on.'

'No, Nina didn't mention it,' he said painfully. 'But I've hardly spoken to her.'

In Berkeley Square, Kitty and Nina were also talking about jam. 'Giles thinks there's no one better to approach than your Mr Cowling,' said Kitty. 'And if he does decide to go along with it, it will bring our two families closer. I'd love that.'

'He's a very good businessman,' Nina said. 'Everyone says so.'

'And if it all goes as Vogel seems to think it will, it will make us very rich. That will be nice. I should like Giles to be able to do all the things about the estate he wants to do. Not that Harvey's isn't doing very well already. I was surprised at how much money it makes. I'm glad,' she added, 'that I've been able to do that for him – bring him my money. All those years, when Mama kept telling me I was an heiress, I never really thought what it meant. And of course, I never had the spending of it. Now it's all Giles's. It makes me happy to think that I've helped him.'

She was staring away across the gardens as she spoke, and Nina looked at her, detecting a hint of wistfulness in the tone. 'You are happy, aren't you?' she asked at last. 'It's what you wanted – to be married to Giles, and have a child.'

'Oh, yes,' said Kitty, eyes on the horizon. 'Of course I'm happy. It's just – it's not what we imagined, is it? I suppose it never is. We tell ourselves stories . . . What exactly does "happy ever after" mean, anyway?' After a pause, she added, 'You're happy too, aren't you? With – your Joseph.' She made herself use the name, though Nina never seemed to.

Nina thought of the terrible row over riding cross-saddle, and the question mark that still hung over whether she'd be allowed to ride again, or hunt. Getting away had pushed the problem aside, and Mr Cowling had been genial and kind in London, and hadn't so much as hinted at the past upset. What would happen when they went home?

Kitty might think the jam scheme would bring their families closer, but they were still separated by distance both literal and social. Day by day, they could not be friends, as Nina had been with Bobby Wharfedale. She found she could not tell Kitty about the quarrel. She wanted to, but she couldn't.

She glanced down into the pram, at little Louis, who had woken up, but was still drowsy, gazing up contentedly at the fringe of the hood as it shook with their movement. If she had a baby, everything might be different. But there was no baby – and what if there never was? She would have to find something else to occupy her mind. Keeping house and giving dinners would not be enough. If Kitty lived as close as Bobby

Wharfedale, she might have been able to talk to her about it all, but she could not unburden to a long-distance friend. In another week, they would be back to writing letters.

'Yes, I'm happy,' she said. 'As you said, it's not what we expected. But, then, I'm not sure I expected anything in particular.'

Except that if Giles had not needed money, they might have married, and lived a life of travel and adventure. He would not have wanted to stay in England, she knew that. Digging in Egypt, first off – but what else? Africa? India? It wouldn't have mattered where, because they would have been together, sharing minds . . .

But she mustn't think like that, especially with Kitty walking right beside her. She shook the thoughts from her mind, angry with herself. 'It's lovely that you brought your baby to London with you,' she said, for something to say.

'I couldn't bear to be parted from him,' Kitty said. 'I can't understand how Linda can care so little for hers. She never minds leaving them. I think she's almost glad to.'

'Some people are not motherly by nature,' Nina offered.

They had reached the gate, and passed through onto the pavement. Nina looked round vaguely for Trump and saw him a little way off, nose deep in a tuft of grass.

'And they do have terrible money troubles, Linda and Gerald. I don't know if you knew, but Giles's father used to pay her an allowance, which stopped when he died. She keeps asking Giles to restore it, but he feels it's her husband's duty to support her. He has to find dowries for Rachel and Alice, and that's worry enough, on top of bringing the estate back into order.'

They had to cross the road to get back to the house, and it was busy with traffic. They paused at the kerb. Trump caught them up and stood at Nina's heel. 'Oh, look,' she said, 'there's another motor-car. That's the third one I've seen this week.'

368

'They're dreadfully noisy,' Kitty said. 'And the smell is horrid.'

'But it must be fun to ride in one. I'd like to try.'

'Every time I see one, I think about poor Richard's accident. He almost died, you know. And it changed him.'

'Has he—?' Nina began. But at that moment, the motor-car they were watching made a tremendous noise – back-firing, she thought it was called. At any rate, it was a noise like a gun shot, or a firework exploding, made just as it was passing a horse-drawn gig. The horse was so startled, it went up in the air on its hind legs, and then, in a panic to get away, dragged the gig round and mounted the pavement. The motor-car backfired again: the horse, checked by its driver, and blocked by the perambulator, reared again in terror.

Nina didn't stop to think. She flung herself between the horse and the pram, catching the bit-ring and throwing her weight against the horse to bring it down and make it back a step. She heard Trump barking, there were shouts and protests all around, and someone screamed – she hoped not Kitty – but she had the animal now, her weight stopping it from rearing, while being hemmed in on all sides stopped it bolting. She fixed its rolling eye with her own and spoke to it in calm, soothing tones. 'All right, all right, old fellow. It's all right. It's only a noise. It won't hurt you.'

Quivering, the horse pulled back for a moment, jerking at her hands; and then gave in, dropping its head, relieved to have someone take charge, and let her stroke its cheek and neck. 'Poor old thing,' she said. 'Easy now.' It pushed its nose into her, trying to shut out the world, and gave a great trembling sigh.

The driver had jumped down, and was protesting volubly; a crowd was gathering, and any number of them were trying to help – the men wanting to take the horse from her, the women fussing over whether Louis was hurt (he wasn't even startled), and everyone in general having an opinion over what should happen next, from hot sweet tea for the heroine to summoning a policeman to prosecute the motor-car driver.

Kitty was white. In some odd reaction she had picked up Trump, who was wriggling madly trying to get to Nina. 'You were very brave,' she said to Nina, her voice vibrating with shock. She had seen the horse rear over her child; she had imagined the hoofs coming down and crushing him. Nina had acted, had done the thing that had to be done, with no time to think, so she was not shocked, only embarrassed at being the centre of attention. She was very glad when two footmen, despatched by Forbes from across the road, came and parted the crowd and escorted them back to the house.

Everyone was out, so Nina was able to divert attention from herself to Kitty, who was shaking, by telling Forbes to bring her a glass of brandy. And then the news of the incident penetrated to the nursery, and Nanny and Jessie came steaming down into the hall in wild alarm, to check on the condition of their baby and to extrapolate from the incident the folly of ever allowing a mother to take a baby out unattended.

Giles had just turned into Piccadilly when he was hailed.

'Ayton – I say!'

He turned. 'Wolski! How are you?'

'Good to see you! But I forgot, it's Stainton now, isn't it? Baxter said he saw you down at Ashmore, looking quite the earl!'

They clasped hands. 'I don't mind what you call me. You're in England? I thought you'd gone out with Carter.'

'I did – I was. I've just come back for a visit, do some business, collect some supplies. I say, what luck to run into you! Are you going somewhere, or have you time? My club's just round the corner. We could toddle round for a drink and a natter.'

'I'd like that,' Giles said. To meet Max Wolski, an old friend and another archaeologist, just when he was feeling very unlike himself, with a head full of finance and jam and factories and export plans! They turned together and strolled back down St James's Street. 'How are things going over there?'

'Oh, great guns!' said Wolski. He was a tall, thin, swarthy American, with thick black hair, and an outdoor tan. Giles always thought that, apart from his height, he could be Egyptian. 'You've heard about KV60, I suppose?'

Giles shook his head ruefully. 'These days, trapped down in the country, I don't hear about anything but crop yields and milk fever.'

'But you're here now?'

'Escaped for a couple of weeks, that's all. What about KV60? Did you find anything?'

'It seems it was ransacked, probably in antiquity, but it did contain two female mummies, and some mummified geese.'

'Geese!'

'A handy snack in the afterlife for our royal ladies, I imagine.'

'What sort of condition are they in – the females?'

'One's very well preserved – still has her long red hair, and she's lying in a coffin base. The other not so well – an older woman, quite obese. Not much in the way of funerary objects, and no clues as to their identity. But they both have the left arm flexed across the body, which as you know—'

'Is the sign of a royal woman of the Eighteenth Dynasty. Max, you don't think it could be—?'

'Hatshepsut? Well, of course the idea always crosses your mind. But we didn't really have time to go into it. Carter took the geese for investigation and resealed the tomb, because we had bigger fish to fry.'

'KV20?'

'Yes, of course. And we're on the brink of marvellous discoveries. You know it's never been explored beyond the first chamber—'

'Because the corridor is blocked.'

'Yes, and the fill is rock hard. It's been the very devil to get through. And there are five descending corridors, very distinctive . . .'

They turned into the club together.

Giles walked home, his mind far away. The soft damp air of England, the London traffic, the smell of soot and horses, the people brushing past him in their multitudes, barely existed for him. He was in a place of sharp, direct light, dry air, the susurrus of sand and the papery whisper of palm trees, the clink of hammer on stone, and the intense, focused concentration of minds on a time far distant from the modern world.

Max Wolski had said, 'Come back with me! Carter would love to have you. There's so much to do. Baxter's there, and the Portwines – all the old gang. The fun is just beginning. You could come, couldn't you? I mean, what's to stop you?'

And he had said, 'I can't.'

'Lord, just pack a bag, old boy!' Max had said, clapping his shoulder. 'You were born for this – I remember Percy Newberry raving about you. A born Egyptologist, he said. Wrap up your affairs, pack a bag, and head for the station. What's to stop you?' And he had laughed. 'You're the earl now – earls can damn well do as they please, can't they?'

Giles positively *ached* with longing to go. And it was true, wasn't it? He was his own master. The estate was beginning to run more smoothly – and Markham and Adeane knew what to do. They hardly needed him. And he could leave Richard as his deputy. There was money now, enough to keep things ticking over.

He wouldn't need much for a trip to Egypt – living was so cheap out there. He had done his duty – damn it, he'd done everything expected of him! Married, brought in money, got an heir. It was time he did something for himself. His father had spent his whole life indulging himself. Giles wasn't asking for his whole life, just a little bit, just a break from it all, just *something*. KV20 was a royal tomb, one of the earliest. Probably the burial place of Thutmose I. Suppose there were intact sarcophagi in there? Identifiable mummies? And what of KV60 – was that really Hatshepsut, the female pharaoh, who wore a false beard as a sign of rank, and reigned successfully for such a long time? Why had Carter closed it up again? There was so much to find out. He *had* to go. No reasonable person could deny him.

He ran up the steps at the front of Aunt Caroline's house, and the door opened just before he reached it, in the unsettling way he had not yet quite got used to. He could tell from the suppressed air of excitement that something had happened, and pretty soon he was enveloped in a confused story of how a mad runaway horse had almost killed his wife and child, and how Mrs Cowling had thrown herself under the horse without regard to her own life and saved them both. It took a bit of untangling before he understood that Nina was not actually dead (something that seemed to be mildly regretted, though he realised it was only for the sake of the narrative and not because anyone wished her ill) and that no harm had come to Kitty or Louis either.

In the drawing-room he found Kitty reclining on a sofa with Alice sitting nearby and Aunt Caroline on the other side clutching a smelling-bottle (how traditional of her, he thought). And on the other side of the fireplace, Nina was still there, Nina, seeming to attract all the light in the room to herself, leaving everything else in dusk.

'Now what's this I hear?' he said. 'Runaway horses and acts of bravery? People snatched from the jaws of death?'

'It was nothing of the sort,' Nina said stoutly, looking at him as if feeding something inside her that had been starving to death. He knew that was how she felt because he felt the same. 'Everyone's making such a fuss. All that happened was that a horse was startled by a motor-car making that exploding noise. It reared up, and I caught its bridle and held it so it couldn't bolt. No one was ever in any danger.'

'It was rearing up right over the perambulator,' Kitty said faintly. 'I thought it was going to kill Louis. Nina saved our son's life, Giles. She was so brave.'

'Please, Kitty, don't talk like that,' Nina said. 'I wasn't brave at all.'

The other three women started to talk at once, Trump helpfully added some barking, and into the scene rushed Richard, crying, 'I seem to have missed all the fun! What's this I hear, about you jumping onto a runaway motor-car and stopping it from killing hundreds of pedestrians? How did you learn to drive a motor-car, Mrs Cowling? You are a dark horse!'

'It was nothing of the sort—' Nina began desperately.

Giles began to laugh. 'No use, you'll be a heroine despite yourself!'

'One thing is sure, you'll have to stay here for now,' Richard said. 'There's a crowd gathering outside and I saw newspaper reporters.'

'Of course she must stay,' Giles said quickly. 'We ought to have a celebration dinner. What did we have on tonight?'

'The Richboroughs' ball,' said Aunt Caroline.

'They'll never notice if we're not there,' said Richard. 'It will be an unholy crush anyway'

'Maud will want to take Rachel.'

'They can go – and Linda too. The rest of us will dine at home and give thanks for the preservation of our loved ones. What were you doing this evening, Nina?'

'*Man and Superman* at the Royal Court,' said Nina. 'But I don't think Mr Cowling much wanted to go. Shaw, you know – requires a lot of concentration.'

'Good, then you won't mind if I send word round to St James's Square and tell him to come here instead?' He anticipated her objection. 'Don't worry about changing – we shan't dress.'

'Excellent idea!' Richard said. 'We could do with a cosy night in, after all this gallivanting. I'm sure we're all worn out with gaiety! And Nina shall tell us in blood-curdling detail exactly what happened and what was passing through her mind as she looked death in the face.'

'You all joke,' Kitty said, 'but she was very brave.'

'I *wasn't* brave,' Nina asserted.

'You *were*!'

'Oh, this is going to be fun!' said Richard.

And Giles had forgotten for the moment all about Egypt.

Crooks had taken over the table in the corner of the ironing room, which was rarely wanted in the evening, and was installed there with Sam and his copy of the Good Book. It wasn't ideal for teaching reading, with so many long words and with the print being so small, but it had the advantage that Sam already knew a lot of the passages by heart, having heard them in church every Sunday of his life. And a lot of the stories were familiar, too, from Sunday-school. If he stuck to the better-known bits . . . Sam wasn't showing much progress so far, but one thing Crooks had in quantities was patience. He was willing to go on for far longer at a session than Sam was.

A shadow passed the door, and Crooks's heart sank when he saw it was Hook, stalking past with a jacket over his arm, doubling back when he saw them. His bulging eyes surveyed the scene. His face was so thin you could see the muscles in it move as he assembled an unpleasant grin.

'Oh, very cosy!' he said. 'What d'you call this, then?'

'I'm teaching Sam to read, as you very well know,' said Crooks, trying for dignity.

'I know what *you* call it, Crooky. I was talking to Sam.' Sam looked up, and blushed automatically. Hook's expression had that effect on a lot of people. 'You want to watch him, Sam, my lad. He does you a favour, you have to do him one back – that'll be expected.'

Sam only looked bewildered. 'Mr Crooks is being kind—' he mumbled.

Hook cut him off. 'Oh, I'll *bet* he's being kind. Kind of this, kind of that. Kind of queer behaviour from an old man, isn't it?'

Crooks mottled. 'What business is it of yours? Go away and leave us alone.'

'I dunno what he says he's teaching you, Sam, old chum,' Hook said with a salacious wink, 'but you're not the first. Oh, no, not by a long chalk. Very keen on teaching stuff to young men, is Mr Crooks.'

'What are you implying?' Crooks said angrily.

Hook ignored him. 'Just make sure he keeps both hands on the table.' He waggled his hands in the air. 'Adam and Eve and Pinch-me, eh?'

'How *dare* you!' Crooks cried, almost inarticulate with rage. 'How dare you come here with your disgusting insinuations—'

'If the cap fits, Crooky,' Hook began. 'We all know—'

But Speen had appeared in the doorway behind him, and said sharply, 'That's enough.'

Hook turned in surprise. 'What?'

'I said, that's enough. You're always riding him. Leave the poor old devil alone.'

'I'll remind you, *Mister* Speen,' Hook said angrily, 'that I am the senior valet in this house. My master outranks yours, and I outrank you.'

'Oh, give it a rest, James,' Speen said indifferently. 'Rank this and rank that. We all put our trousers on one leg at a time. Just leave Crooks alone. Nobody likes a bully. Go on, go about your business.'

And he stood, calmly but implacably, until Hook gave a snort, turned on his heel, and went. Speen, his face expressionless, gave Crooks a nod and walked away too.

After a moment, Crooks said, 'I think we'd better stop for tonight.' Sam, his face red, scrambled away hastily without meeting his eye, and Crooks closed his precious Bible and wondered whether there would ever be another lesson. He hated Hook, with his crudeness, his libidinous mind and his spitefulness. Hated him and wished him dead. He had been in two minds about Speen, and he didn't much like being beholden to him. But Speen had done the right thing this evening – and no one else seemed able to get the better of James Hook.

Tabby was getting impatient.

'I will marry you, Tab,' William said, 'but I got to sort things out.'

'It's all right for you,' she said angrily. 'You're not the one swelling up like a balloon. You're not the one that'll have fingers pointed at you.'

'No one's going to point a finger at you, not if I have anything to do with it,' William said stoutly.

'Well, but what *are* you doing about it? Cos this baby won't wait for ever.'

'I been looking for another job,' he said. 'But it's not that easy. You know this place – everyone knows everyone, and all the jobs're being done by somebody already. I've tried the Crown and the Royal George. There was nothing doing. That Ippy Cobham just laughed when I asked her dad for a job, then whispered to him, and he grinned and said I'd have to sort out my problems on my own. And I've asked around the village, but no one wants an extra hand. Most wouldn't even listen to me. But Mr Peascod's housekeeper said I ought to go to London and sign on with an employment exchange. Maybe we ought to think about going away. There'd be bound to be more jobs in London, stands to reason.'

'But I don't want to go away,' Tabby objected. 'I've lived here all my life.'

William sighed. 'I don't want to either, and there's my ma to think about. But maybe that's the only way. I could go on ahead and find something, and get some lodgings, and then send for you when I was settled.'

'Oh no you don't!' Tabby said. 'You're not running out on me!'

'I never said I was running.' William was hurt. 'I'm going to do the right thing by you, Tab. I'm standing by you, but I got to have a job. Don't you trust me?'

She burst into tears. 'You don't know what it's like. People'll say I'm a loose woman, just because I was overcome with love for you.'

He put his arms round her. 'I love you too. And we'll get married, I promise, and we'll love this baby, don't you fret.'

She stopped sobbing and dried her eyes on her sleeve. 'I've got to start getting things for the baby, William. Get ready, like. And my clothes won't fit me much longer. I need some money.'

'I got a bit left out of last month's wages, you can have that. And when my next month comes in, you can have it all – or nearly all. I can give you two pound ten.'

Her eyes narrowed. 'First footman at the Grange gets four pound a month.'

'I only get three,' William said sadly. 'And I got to give my ma something.'

'I reckon the master's getting restless,' Hook said at dinner, heaping potatoes onto his plate and passing the dish on.

'What makes you think that?' Rose asked, wondering how he stayed so rake-thin when he ate so much. Probably worked it off in spite and bile, she thought.

'His bedside book. Always a good clue, that is, to the valet that knows how to read it.'

'I didn't know you could read,' Speen said with mock interest. 'When did you learn that, then?'

378

'Read the clue, is what I mean,' Hook said, glaring at him. 'And since he got back from London, he's had this old book beside the bed by some bloke called Belzoni. All about the pyramids, temples and tombs of Egypt and – some other place, Nubbly or something.'

'Nubia?' suggested Mrs Webster. 'That's next door to Egypt.'

'Could be that,' Hook admitted.

'Ah, Egypt!' Moss exclaimed with a sigh, gazing down the table at Ada, who was daintily crunching a piece of crackling. 'The pyramids! The mighty Nile! The great Cleopatra! Most beautiful woman in the world, you know, Queen Cleopatra. The Emperor Julius Caesar fell in love with her at first sight, as did Mark Antony, who was a great Roman general. She used to bathe in asses' milk—'

'How d'you get milk out of an ass?' Hook interrupted impatiently.

'You ask him to pass you the jug,' said Speen. 'Pass it down, will you, Mr Hook, there's a good chap?' Hook gave him a furious look.

'All domestic mammals can create milk, not just cows,' Moss said, momentarily diverted from his course. Knowledge of all kinds was his resource, and distributing it his prerogative. 'Many primitive peoples drink goat's milk instead of cow's. Even, I believe, sheep's milk in some places.'

'Sheep's milk, fancy,' murmured Ellen politely. She quite liked learning new facts. She thought it was posh, knowing things.

'Asses are donkeys, aren't they?' said Mabel. 'I couldn't fancy drinking that. Mr Gregory has a donkey up at Shelloes, and it don't half pong!'

'That was because of the pigs,' said Doris. 'It's always getting into the same field with 'em and getting pig mess on it when it rolls.'

'*Asses' milk*,' Moss said emphatically, regaining attention, 'was considered to be an aid to beauty. I believe all the lovely women of the eastern world used it: the Queen of Sheba, the famous obelisks of the sultans—'

'Odalisques,' Mrs Webster corrected.

He ignored her. 'It was said to soften and whiten the skin.' His eyes drifted back of their own accord to Ada, who was as white as a lily. 'Fine ladies used to anoint their bodies with exotic ungulents . . .'

He saw Ada's lips form a pleasantly shocked O at the mention of bodies, and missed Mrs Webster's patient correction.

Speen, who knew what an ungulate was, smirked. 'And now we're back to the asses,' he commented to his plate.

'But Cleopatra was the most beautiful of all,' Moss went on for his audience of one. 'They say her face was so lovely it could launch a thousand ships.'

Mrs Webster rolled her eyes and gave up.

'How did that work, then, Mr Moss?' asked Ellen, genuinely puzzled. 'I thought they used a bottle o' champagne.'

Moss was puzzled himself, but could not, of course, admit it. 'It's a metaphor,' he said kindly.

Ellen was plainly about to ask, *What's a metaphor?*

Hook intervened loudly. 'My point *being*,' he said, 'that I wouldn't be surprised if the master wasn't to bolt one of these days. He had a letter from some old university friend of his that's going out to Egypt to dig up tombs, and I bet he's thinking of joining him. He's been staring at nothing a lot these last few days, and you know what that means.'

'How do you know about the letter?' Speen asked, beating Mrs Webster to it.

'I saw it. He's using it to keep his place in the book.'

'But how d'you know what it said?' Speen asked nastily.

'Please tell me you didn't read it,' said Mrs Webster.

Hook flushed angrily at being caught out. 'Of course I didn't. What do you take me for? It – it fell on the floor when

I moved the book, and I couldn't help seeing a few words when I picked it up.'

'Oh, Hooky, you've done it now,' Speen murmured.

Crooks, a little slow off the mark, caught up. 'A gentleman's gentleman reading his master's private correspondence? I can't believe it! I simply cannot believe any personal servant would be so debased as to do such a thing!'

'Or, at least, not so stupid as to blurt it out in front of everyone,' Speen said, for Hook's ears alone.

'Oh, come off it, Crooky,' Hook lashed out angrily. 'I bet you did your share of snooping – before you got demoted, that is.'

'How dare you! I wasn't—'

'Be quiet, all of you!' Moss commanded. He glared from one valet to another. 'What sort of example is this to set to the lower servants?' Silence settled over the table, except for the rather noisy chewing of Wilfrid, down the far end, who had adenoids and ate with his mouth open. *And we were having such a nice, civilised conversation about antiquities*, Moss thought sadly, *and the girls were learning so much*. He sought for another subject. India might be too inflammatory, and too close to Egypt. He settled on milk. 'Turning milk into cheese is an ancient craft, practised by the earliest humans. It is believed to have started with the Sumerians of Mesopotamia.'

Peaceful eating resumed. Ada was daydreaming about bathing, not in milk, which she thought would be a bit nasty, but in hot water, scented with bath salts, which she had seen in an advertisement. In her dream she arose from the bath and dressed herself in a flowing silk gown, and was brought a bouquet of roses by a tall, handsome man who bore a strong resemblance to George, the third groom in his lordship's stables . . .

Speen dissected the black bit carefully out of a potato, smiling to himself in a satisfied manner.

Hook glared at Speen sideways under his brows, viciously smashing his potato into his gravy and vowing to get his own back. That was two grudges he had now, and Hook was good at grudges. That Speen thought he was *so* clever. But everyone had secrets, and Hook was the man to find them out. He'd get him back, you could count on that!

# CHAPTER TWENTY-TWO

On a warm, misty November day, Dolly bounded up to Alice, her hindquarters vibrating madly, her stubby tail a blur.

Axe straightened up from reaching under Della for the end of the girth, and the flush of his face could be attributed to his having been bending. He waited for Alice to speak, and when she didn't, seeming fully occupied with receiving Dolly's raptures, he said, 'Thought you weren't coming any more.'

'I've been in London. For ages and ages.'

'Did you have a nice time?' Axe asked politely.

'No! I hated it.' He waited, unspeaking, watching her. Finally she looked up, then stood up. 'I like to be here,' she said. 'Everything feels . . . right, when I'm here.'

Dolly had sat down by her feet. She hoisted a hind leg and scratched behind an ear, then lay down, crossing her paws, looking content. Axe, troubled, thought of Ruth's strictures. He'd thought that being in London for a month would break the habit, that she would discover new interests, or simply forget. But here she was, and there was no doubting she was no little girl any longer. He ought to send her away. Instead of plaits, she had her hair coiled up behind, and it exposed the planes of her face. No, not a child any more. It was not right, it was not appropriate, for a young lady of the house to be hanging around the woodsman's cottage. But just seeing her again had produced a feeling of contentment in him that he had not been aware was missing. He felt, like Dolly, that all was now well.

Alice broke the silence at last. 'Are you going up to the woods? With Della?'

'That's right,' he said. Then, 'Want to come too, bring Cobnut?' It didn't even seem like a decision.

Her face lit. 'Yes, please,' she said.

The stay in London had been good for Nina. Apart from the plays and operas, apart from seeing Kitty (and Giles), she had had lunch with her aunt, along with some of her aunt's academic friends, which had been very pleasant. She'd had a very happy afternoon with the Morrises, Mr Cowling joining them for tea, and Mawes drawing her madly all through, and then she and Lepida had gone on to a lecture at University College about atoms, beta rays and electrons. She hadn't understood very much of it, but it had made her feel connected to a larger world. After the lecture, she and Lepida had been met by Mr Cowling and Decius, who took them to supper. They'd had a very merry evening, and Nina was glad to see her friend getting on so well with Decius. Even Mr Cowling said afterwards, privately to Nina, 'I think our Decius took a shine to that young woman.' Though he spoiled it a little by adding, 'I suppose she reminds him of his mother – she's a blue-stocking, too.'

She was happy to get home to her lovely house; to be greeted so warmly by motherly Mrs Deering; to see how her nerines were doing. She straight away took Trump out for a long walk – like her, he had found London confining after the wider spaces they were used to. The November air was a little foggy; the trees were half bare, wanting only a rain-storm or a strong wind to strip off the last leaves. The autumn smell reminded her that the hunting season had started, which reminded her of the uncertainties that hung around her. It would have damped her pleasure if she had let it; but London had given her a new perspective. There were more things in life than horses – though naturally in a town like this they would seem important. But, as Aunt Schofield had said, she had gone into marriage with her eyes open, and it would be childish now to repine. She must make the best of things, and not make an enemy of her husband.

It was as well that she had her thoughts in good order because when she got back to the house, just as it was getting dark, she learned that Lady Wharfedale had called and left her card, and Mr Cowling, who came into the hall to meet her, was in an odd mood. Nina would have called it uneasy, if it had been anyone other than the supremely confident Mr Cowling. Still, he looked at her a little sidelong, as if she were a strange dog that might or might not bite.

But what he said was, 'Did you have a nice walk? Did you meet anyone?'

'Very nice, thank you. No, no one.'

'You must be cold. Come, come into the drawing-room. The fire's got up nicely now.'

She wasn't feeling cold, but she let him fuss over her, ushering her to the best seat by the fire, questioning if her feet were wet, bringing her a glass of sherry. The room looked rich and cosy with the curtains drawn and the firelight gleaming on the fine old furniture. Gas lighting was all very well, but there was something very comforting about this time of day in late autumn and winter, when it grew dark outside and the servants brought in the lamps and closed the curtains and settled you in for the evening.

Watching him pouring his own glass, she reflected that she never knew what he was thinking. Still, he must have seen the card on the tray in the hall, even if Mrs Deering hadn't mentioned the visitor to him. She went straight to the heart of it. 'If you don't want me to be friends any more with Lady Wharfedale, Joseph,' she said, thinking that using his name would please him, 'I won't be.'

He sat down on the sofa, catty-corner to her, and said, 'My dear! There's no need . . . I don't want you to be unhappy. I never liked having to – well – forbid things. But I've been on this earth longer than you, and I understand its ways better. And I couldn't have you careering away into trouble and not stop you. What sort of a husband would I be if I didn't look after you?'

'I know I did wrong in keeping things from you,' she began.

But he leaned forward and took her hands, stopping her. 'That's all over and done, now. No need to bring it up again. And I warrant you, when we go to church again, it'll all have been forgotten.'

Nina brightened. 'So, then, it will be all right if I go hunting this season? I'll ride side-saddle,' she promised hastily. 'Bobby will lend me a horse.'

Her hands were dropped. Mr Cowling looked troubled again. 'No. That won't do. When I said it would all have been forgotten, that doesn't mean folk can't be reminded. It's too soon to start stirring things up again. I don't want you hunting this year. Maybe by next winter, things'll be different – we'll see. But for now, you'd better leave horses alone. If people don't see you on a horse, they'll forget quicker. And anyway,' he added, trying to read her expression, 'it's dangerous, is hunting. I hadn't properly thought before, but folk get hurt all the time – killed even. Wasn't your friend Kitty's father-in-law killed out hunting? I don't want to lose you, my love. I'd never have a quiet moment if you were out there risking your life.'

Nina thought his arguments illogical. 'But thousands of people go hunting and *don't* get hurt. And why would it be any different next winter?'

He frowned. 'I'm not going to debate it with you, Nina. That's my decision. No horses, no hunting. That's final.'

Nina looked away, embarrassed. It seemed somehow odd to be told such things – and in such a manner, as of a stern father – by someone she had shared a bed with. It was, she supposed, a consequence of marrying an older man. If she had married a man of her own age, they would probably have quarrelled like children.

'Then I suppose I can't see Bobby Wharfedale any more? You won't want me to be friends with her.'

'I never said that.' Mr Cowling thought for a moment. Lady Wharfedale might not be the best influence on Nina, but she was a leader of society and an important person in Market Harborough. And he was conscious that Nina needed a female friend of her own age. She was hardly more than a girl, really, and girls needed other girls to chatter and giggle with. He didn't want to come the tyrant over his young wife and see her wilt, like a flower starved of water. 'I don't see any harm in your being friends with her. I know you like her, and she obviously likes you. It was civil of her to call the first minute we were back. No, you go ahead and enjoy your friend's company. Just keep away from horses for now.'

Nina thanked him; but was remembering that Bobby hunted three times a week in the season. Horses were such a big part of her life through the winter months, Nina wondered if she'd have much time to spare for a non-riding friend.

Giles walked up the hill from the station. Two days largely spent travelling, and two days in the company of Mr Cowling, looking over the factory and the plans, had left him in a state of mind to enjoy the solitude of a walk and the peace of the green hill. He was nearly home when the dogs, wandering aimlessly about the hedgerows, found him, and bounded up with swinging tails and gleaming eyes and hard jabs of the muzzle into his tender places to show their joy at the reunion. They circled him wildly, then led him straight to Kitty, who was walking in what passed at the Castle for a garden. Her face lit, too, when she saw him, and he warmed for a moment with affection.

'Come for a ride with me,' he said. 'There's time before it gets dark.'

'Just a ride? You're not going to meet Adeane or inspect a barn roof or anything?'

He laughed. 'Just a ride. Purely for pleasure. Would you like?'

'I would like,' she answered, laughing too.

They changed, ordered the horses, and half an hour later set off up the hill. By unspoken consent they cantered for a long way along the crest, then turned back at the walk, the horses blowing and steaming in the misty air. The declining sun was swollen and red; a scarf of starlings swirled across the sky and draped itself over the treetops for the evening assembly.

Riding side by side on a broad path was a pleasant way to have a conversation. Giles glanced across at his wife and thought she looked pretty, her dark curls netted under a saucy tricorn hat, the chilly air bringing colour to her cheeks. 'You're a good rider,' he said. He had talked of horses with Nina from the very beginning, but they hadn't seemed to be a large part of Kitty's growing-up. 'Where did you learn?'

'On Hampstead Heath,' she said. 'I know country people think Hampstead is part of London, but there's lots of open country. Papa thought a lady should be able to ride properly, and had me taught. But anyone could ride well on Apollo,' she said, stroking the golden neck.

'I'm glad you like him.'

Kitty glanced sidelong at him, and judged that he was in the mood for conversation. 'Tell me about your trip,' she said. 'How was Cambridgeshire?'

'Very flat,' Giles said. She didn't laugh, as Nina would have done, but looked at him seriously, receptively. 'The factory is astonishing, almost like a self-contained village. They grow all their own fruit, apart from the lemons and oranges, of course. They have their own electricity plant, their own sawmill, they have carpenters and blacksmiths and coopers, they have a building department – which will make putting up the new extension easier. Logan, the general manager, was training as an engineer when your great-uncle recruited him, so he's interested in that side of things. He has a chief engineer on the staff, a fellow called Ingram, who has already designed machines for sorting the fruit and sterilising the jars, and he showed us a lot of drawings he and Logan have got together for the canning machinery, including making the cans themselves. They've thought it all out, the two of them. Cowling was very impressed. He liked the fact that they'd got the whole scheme together before they came asking for money. He says it's rare to find youthful enthusiasm allied to solid common sense.'

'I expect he had it, when he was getting on,' Kitty suggested. 'People tend to praise the things they like in themselves.'

He raised his eyebrows at her. 'That's very perceptive of you.' She blushed with pleasure at the compliment. 'At all events, they impressed me so much I was half sorry I wasn't doing the whole thing myself. But it's easy to be overwhelmed in that sort of atmosphere, with the machines thundering away, workers dashing back and forth, and all that commercial endeavour all around. As soon as I got a proper distance between me and it, I knew I'd made the right decision. Cowling is the man to make sure it goes as it should, and there'll be plenty of profits to go round. I don't begrudge him his share. Even without the canning operation, Logan has lots of schemes for expansion into other lines; and the lines he already has are very profitable. I had no idea jam was such a big thing, but it seems people can't get enough of it.'

'I'm glad it's making you lots of money,' Kitty said.

'Us,' he corrected. 'Making us lots of money. And young Louis. He'll be the King of Conserves one day; the Emperor of Marmalade.'

389

'And you'll still have the capital intact to put into the estate,' she said.

'Most of it, yes. I am putting some into the canning scheme. Vogel advised it. But best of all is a stream of income that should increase, unless something goes terribly wrong.'

The fat red sun snagged itself in the net of the bare tree-tops; it got suddenly, noticeably colder. The shadows were long and blue, and there was that wintry sense in the air that one should be getting indoors before it got dark. 'We'd better take the short way home,' said Giles.

They turned downhill

Kitty felt so comfortable with him, she said, 'Will you come up to the nursery when we get back and see Louis having his bath?'

He concealed a smile. 'What red-blooded man could resist an invitation like that?'

'I know you're joking,' Kitty said, 'but will you? I sometimes feel men don't have any of the pleasure of having children, just the worries about money.'

'It is a very great pleasure to me to have a son,' he assured her.

'I'm glad Louis was a boy, for your sake,' Kitty said. 'I know you had to have an heir. But I would love to have a girl as well, though.' She pondered a moment. 'Or another boy. I wouldn't mind.'

There was a wistfulness to her tone that tweaked his conscience. He hadn't visited her bed in longer than he could remember. There was so much else to do. 'Would you like another child?' he asked diffidently.

'Of course,' she said, surprised. She went on carefully. 'I always thought it was intended. What is it Richard says? An heir and a spare. But—'

'Yes?'

'I'd like lots of children. If they're yours.'

The tweak became a twinge. He tried to joke it off. 'They had better be mine, Lady Stainton!'

And this time she only looked at him, a look so full of love and longing and doubt and resignation, if he had been a dog he'd have thrown back his head and howled.

Warner's Rents was a row of cottages at the south end of the village, on a back lane that bordered Poor's Farm. They looked picturesque, with their thatch and crooked chimneys, especially now, with a soft snow falling, capping the roof trees and the chimney tops, the grey gloom of snow clouds making the small windows glow with the lights inside. An artist could have made a very pretty picture of it.

In reality, the brick floors were laid straight onto earth so they were damp, the wattle-and-daub walls were too thin to keep out the cold. The ancient green glass of the windows let in too little light, and the thatch needed renewing, and harboured rats. The rents were too low for old Warner to afford to do repairs, and they were too badly in need of repair to command a higher rent. So cottages and tenants rotted gently together.

Mrs Mattock opened the door to number five, and surveyed the bundled-up figure on the doorstep. A jaundiced eye took in the swollen belly and the carpet bag in one hand.

'Oh, it's you,' she said.

'Hello, Ma,' said Tabby. 'I've come home.'

'Lost your job?'

'Corbie don't want me this shape,' Tabby said. 'Damn the old blood-sucker! Afraid I'll drop the kid in the public and scare the customers.'

'What happened to your feller, then? The soft one you had at the fair. You said you could wind him round your thumb.'

'I'm working on him,' said Tabby. 'Takes time.'

'You ain't got time.'

Tabby agreed, but she didn't want to talk about it now.

The chill was striking upwards through the inadequate soles of her boots. 'Let us in, then. I'm starving cold.'

Mrs Mattock considered. 'There's that do-good woman in the village, Miss Eddowes. She does with females in trouble.'

'I won't need to go to her. I can handle William.'

'So's you know, you can't have that baby here.'

'It won't come to that. Let us in, for gawd's sake. Can't stand out here all night.'

Mrs Mattock stood back. 'Come on, then,' she said resignedly. 'Don't know why you get yourself mixed up with these fellers. No good never come to no woman from no man. Making babies and smacking you around, that's all they're good for.'

Tabby went into the familiar sour, dark house, with the familiar sour, dark litany rising and falling behind her as Mrs Mattock went about filling the kettle and pushing it over the fire. She wondered if her mother had ever been young and in love. Or even young and happy. She couldn't imagine it, somehow.

Balcombe House was in the centre of Market Harborough, on one of the roads that led out of the market square, a handsome, symmetrical Georgian house, flint-knapped, with a red brick trim. There were steps up to the front door straight from the pavement, and a railing that defended the narrow pit that gave light to the basement windows. The door was answered by a very elderly butler, who took their cards gravely, and begged them to come in, saying that her ladyship was at home and would be pleased to receive Lady Wharfedale and Mrs Cowling.

Bobby had told Nina that she had met the new arrival in Market Harborough, found her charming, and was anxious for Nina to meet her too. 'She's a single lady, so it's especially important to make her welcome to the town. And I know you'll like her.'

392

The hall was dark with well-polished wood – floorboards, panelling and staircase – but they were shown into a parlour that had been painted a light colour and sported modern furniture. There were few ornaments, and only a couple of paintings, which from Nina's cursory glance looked daringly modern. They were not afforded long to inspect them, because the lady of the house came in almost immediately, and greeted Bobby warmly.

'Lady Wharfedale, how kind of you to call!'

'Lady Clementine, may I present my very dear friend Mrs Joseph Cowling, of Wriothesby House? Nina, Lady Clementine Leacock.'

Nina shook hands with a very tall, thin lady in her thirties, with soft fair hair, a pale face and large pale blue eyes, which together gave her a rather failing look, as though she had suffered all her life from ill-health. But her handshake was firm, and her expression keen.

'Mrs Cowling, delighted to meet you. Wriothesby House? Isn't that the beautiful Queen Anne house just on the edge of the town? I so admired it when I went past. Please, sit down, and may I offer you some refreshments?' She nodded to the butler, who needed no more instruction, but shuffled away.

This sort of first meeting was usually attended by rather desultory, awkward conversation; but Bobby didn't seem to know what it was to be shy, and she talked so naturally about local affairs, the weather and other easy topics that Lady Clementine, who seemed at first rather reserved, quickly relaxed, and the visit went on to double the conventional fifteen minutes.

She returned the courtesy to Nina the following day, where the friendship was further cemented by Trump, who broke any remaining ice by trying to get onto Lady Clementine's lap, and not being rebuffed.

'He's a fine fellow,' she said. 'I always had dogs when I was a child in India.'

393

'You lived in India?' Nina asked.

'Until I was eleven. I was born out there. My father was on the governor general's staff.'

In no time, they were telling each other their life histories. Lady Clementine's father was the Earl Leacock, with a lifetime in the diplomatic service. Though they had not been in India at the same time, their lives and experiences had been so similar that soon they were chatting like old friends, exchanging fond memories and recounting anecdotes. Fifteen minutes turned into an hour this time, and by the end of it, it was 'Please won't you call me Clemmie?' and 'May I call you Nina? I feel as if I've always known you.'

The difference in their ages did not seem obtrusive. Clemmie was in some ways young for her age, while Nina, because of her education, was older. Clemmie had been educated along old-fashioned lines, later improving it by reading, but Nina's education had been deeper and wider.

There was also an innocence about Clemmie, perhaps because she had never been married.

'I was so tall, you see – taller than most of the men – and it made me shy and awkward. My mother had been a great beauty, and I think I was a disappointment to her.' Eventually, she fell in love with a young subaltern. 'I liked him at first simply because he was taller than me. But then I came to appreciate his other qualities. Jeremy wasn't high-born, but he was from a good family, and I think my parents were despairing of me by then, because we were allowed to become engaged.'

He had been killed on the North West Frontier before they could be married.

'After that, Mother kept pushing other potential matches at me, but I never wanted anyone except Jeremy.'

When her father had died five years ago, she had thought she would look after her mother for the rest of her life. But her mother had had other ideas. 'She was much younger than

Papa, you see, and still beautiful. She quickly remarried, and they made it plain they didn't want me with them. Papa had left me financially independent, so I decided to live on my own.'

'Didn't that cause a scandal?' Nina asked.

'Oh, yes. Various aunts and godparents said it was out of the question, but eventually they fished up a widowed cousin to live with me and make it all respectable, and insisted I lived near my mother, however little she liked the idea. But when Maria died, last year, and they tried to make me take on another chaperone, I put my foot down. I have our family's butler, who is tremendously loyal and watches over me, and my maid, who used to be my nurse and is very fierce. So I looked for another house, somewhere nobody knew me – and here I am.'

On the day after that, Bobby invited both of them to tea at Welland Hall. Bobby's children were in attendance, and seemed as instantly attracted to Clemmie as Trump had been, and like him wanted to climb all over her. 'I love children,' Clemmie said and, unlike many people who claim to love them, did not only do so at a distance. She ended up crawling on the floor with them playing bears, and since her clothes were sensible and her hair securely pinned, she rose only slightly dishevelled when Adam arrived to join them for tea, and the children were spirited away to the nursery.

Clemmie seemed a little reserved with Adam just at first, but he had Bobby's lack of self-consciousness, and soon drew her out. The four of them made a good tea, and talked great volumes.

Nina finally managed to ask the question that had been on her mind for two days. 'Why did you choose Market Harborough when you came to move away from home?'

'As I mentioned, I wanted to go where nobody knew me. I looked at some guide books, and visited the towns it said were attractive.'

'Such as?'

'Oh, Stamford, for instance, and Norwich. I did think hard about Norwich, because of Caley's chocolate factory, but in the end I decided it was too big. And then I came here, and found not only a delightful town, but one with a factory right in the centre.'

'What,' Adam asked for all of them, 'was the significance of the factory?'

She turned her pale, earnest eyes on him. 'I am interested in the conditions of workers in factories – particularly women workers.'

'Are you, indeed? Did you know Nina's husband owns that factory?'

'I didn't at first, but I did learn it yesterday.' She smiled at Nina. 'I'm sure your husband is an enlightened employer.'

'I couldn't say,' Nina said. 'He only recently bought the factory, so I don't know whether he's concerned himself with the workers.'

'I'm interested in women's prisons, too, which need a great deal of reform,' Clemmie said. 'And the thing that underpins it all – the women's franchise.'

'Votes for women?' Adam said, and laughed. 'You remind me of my sister – she always picks the hardest fight.'

'Oh – what's your fight?' Clemmie asked with interest.

'Cross-saddle riding for women,' Bobby said. 'So far there are only two and a half of us in the area, but I shan't give up.'

'Two and a *half*?'

'I'm the half,' Nina admitted. 'Bobby had me try it and I like it so much better, but my husband doesn't approve.'

'Poor Nina fell victim to one of the local tabbies,' said Bobby, 'who gathered a yowling of other tabbies and frightened poor Mr Cowling off. But we don't despair, do we, Nina? He loves her, you see, Clemmie, and once he thoroughly grasps how much safer riding across is for women, and how much better for their health, I expect he will have a change of heart. Do you ride?'

'I have ridden, of course,' said Clemmie, 'and the country round here looks so fine, I did think once I was settled in that I should take it up again. But I've always ridden side-saddle – though I know quite a lot of suffragists regard it as part of the struggle for women's rights.'

'Then let me persuade you to join us,' Bobby said. 'The whole town is tremendously interested in you at the moment. If you were seen to be riding astride, it would be a great fillip to our movement.'

'Dearest, you can't call you and Mrs Anstruther a "movement",' Adam laughed.

'Every journey begins with a single step,' Bobby said solemnly, and then she laughed too. 'Even if we're not a movement, we can recruit to our cause, can't we?'

'I shall certainly try to recruit you to mine,' said Clemmie. 'I am having a visitor next week, a Mrs Albertine Crane, who was an active member of the Women's Franchise League – sadly now disbanded. If I can get an audience together, she has agreed to give a speech. She wants there to be a new organisation, like the League, but bigger and more ambitious. She and other League members were pinning their hopes on the Independent Labour Party, but they don't really speak for women – and, in fact, some of them are quite hostile to the idea of the franchise. Now,' she looked around them hopefully, 'do say you'll come and listen to Albertine. She is a most inspiring speaker – you won't be bored.'

'Of course we'll come,' Bobby said, in her warm, impulsive way. 'You too, Adam! And we'll bring lots of friends and applaud mightily at the end. And then, if you like, I'll make an impassioned speech about the dangers of side-saddle riding, and you'll endorse me, and tell everyone you'll be riding across with me in the near future.'

Clemmie smiled, and said, 'You're so full of energy, I wish

we'd had you in the League. With a hundred like you, we could move mountains.'

'I've just had a wonderful idea!' Bobby exclaimed. 'We should have a horseback rally – all women, all riding across, and carrying banners demanding votes for women! Two birds with one stone!'

'Can I come, in disguise?' Adam asked. 'In a dress and a wig and a veil over my face.'

'You shan't even come to the talk unless you take it seriously,' Bobby said sternly.


The larger Tabby grew, the more nervous she became. 'You've got to hurry up,' she told William, when they met in the barn behind the Dog and Gun. 'If you can't get a job, you'll have to marry me anyway. I'm not having this baby unwed, and we've not got long.'

'How long?' William asked. 'When's it coming?'

'Never mind. We've no time to waste, that's all,' said Tabby irritably.

'So – but how long *does* it take to grow a baby, then?' William asked.

'Why you asking that?' Tabby asked, her eyes narrowing.

He looked embarrassed. 'My ma would never talk about stuff like that. If ever I asked anything about baby stuff, she'd fetch me such a clout, it made me ears ring. D'you know how long it takes, Tab?'

She hesitated a moment, looking at him thoughtfully. 'Well, I've never had one before,' she said at last, 'but according to what my ma says, it's about six months. Or it might be five.'

'Same as sheep, then?' William said seriously. 'That's five months.'

'Yes, that's right,' Tabby said, getting into her stride. 'But my ma says some women don't take so long to make a baby as others. In my family, women gen'ly do it quicker than average. So this baby might be coming Feb'ry time, or it might even be Jan'ry.'

'You're right then,' William said, securing her hand, which was warm and a little damp. 'We got to get spliced soon as we can. You nervous, Tabby?'

'Course I am. Wouldn't you be?'

'Don't be ascairt. I'll look after you. Didn't I say I would? I love you, Tab.'

'Gerroff, you soft ha'porth,' she said gruffly. But she let him kiss her even so.

# CHAPTER TWENTY-THREE

'We have guests coming to dinner today,' Mrs Webster said at servants' breakfast. 'Friends of his lordship, a Mr and Mrs Talbot Arthur, and they'll be staying the night. We'll put them in the Jade Room – Rose, see it's prepared, please. Do what you can about flowers.'

'Yes, Mrs Webster.'

'And they won't be bringing servants with them. So will you look after Mr Arthur, Mr Crooks?'

'Certainly, Mrs Webster. It will be my pleasure.'

'And, Rose – you'll maid Mrs Arthur?'

'Yes, Mrs Webster.'

'They're on their way to Egypt,' Speen commented, 'where they'll live in a tent and eat God knows what – beetles, probably, and scorpions – so they won't need much looking after. A real bed instead of a blanket on the ground will be luxury to them.'

'It's not for you – or any of us – to pass comment on guests in this house – and close friends of his lordship into the bargain,' Moss said sternly.

'If anyone thinks *any* guest in this house is to be treated with less than full attention, they'd better tell me so now,' said Mrs Webster. There was a dutiful silence.

Then Ada remarked to Ellen, 'I shouldn't like to live in a tent. All grass and insects and such. I went on a picnic once, and a caterpillar fell down my neck.'

Moss heard her – he was always sensitive to her voice. 'A tent may be humble, Ada, or it may be very grand indeed,' he pronounced. 'When King Henry the Eighth met the King of France, all the tents were made of cloth-of-gold. When a tent is so rich and sumptuous, it is often called a pavilion. And Queen Cleopatra, the Bard tells us, lay in a pavilion of tissue of cloth-of-gold. "The barge she sat in, like a burnished throne, burned on the water."'

*Cleopatra again!* Mrs Webster thought, with a silent roll of the eyes. 'Never mind tents—' she began.

But Speen had picked it up and spoke over her. 'Burned, did it, Mr Moss?' he said innocently. 'I expect someone'd knocked over a lamp – like Mr Hook did the other day. Awful mess, wasn't there, Mr Hook? And flaming oil is a real danger, especially on those old wooden boats – they'd go up like tinder. I suppose she had to jump into the water, this queen?'

Moss drew breath to correct some of the many misapprehensions, then thought better of it, and said instead to Mrs Webster, 'A good dinner, I presume, will be ordered?'

'I spoke to Mrs Terry about it yesterday,' said Mrs Webster. Now that Ida was properly the cook, she was called by her surname, and was 'Mrs' by custom. 'Caviar, julienne soup, cold salmon, pigeons, saddle of mutton, plum tart, and anchovy savoury and cream cheese.'

'Excellent,' said Moss. 'They should carry away a good impression of Ashmore Castle.'

Hook was furious that Speen had referred to his lamp mishap, especially in front of the lower servants. He was seething as he strode along Piccadilly, and bumped hard into William, coming out of the boot-room and moving with a particularly under-water sort of languor, like weed swaying in a gentle current. 'Watch where you're going, can't you?' he snapped.

William didn't even react, only stared at him, and then said, 'Sorry,' as if his mind was far away.

401

Hook knew that look. 'Mooning about your girl-friend, are you? I don't know how you can be so daft as to be taken in by a female like that.'

William was jerked from his reverie. 'Don't you say anything about Tabby,' he said. 'She's the woman I love.'

'Huh! You and every other man in the county!' said Hook.

William didn't get the jibe. 'She's always been popular, and why not, so beautiful as she is? I'm lucky it's me she wants to marry, when she could have anyone.'

'Gawd! You get softer in the head every day! Have anyone? She's already *had* everyone!'

'What are you talking about?' William began to burn slowly, sensing at last that Hook was being insulting.

'She's only marrying you 'cause she's got a bun in the oven. And you fell for it.'

'I'm standing by her, as any decent chap would,' William said, reddening.

'It's not your bun, you dullard! Can't you count?'

'I don't know what you're talking about.'

'When's the baby coming?'

'Jan'ry or Feb'ry, she says. Why?'

'You and her got together in August, at the fair, right? And babies take nine months, start to finish.' Hook watched as William, frowning, counted in his head.

'She said it takes six months to grow a baby,' he said at last. 'Or five. She said—'

'Nine months. Everybody knows that. I'm not making it up. You ask anyone you like. She was up the pole before you ever laid a finger on her. And who was she seeing before the fair? Speen, that's who – our own roving tom-cat. Quite the Lothario is Mr Edgar Speen. Women can't resist him. O' course, to be fair, Tabby never *tried* to.'

William's face was red. 'That's not true! You take it back! She loves me, we're getting married, she'd never – she'd never—'

402

'She never stopped seeing him, you bloody idiot! She's got him for fun, and you for the serious stuff, like bringing up his kid.'

William's hands bunched into fists. 'You're making it all up,' he said. 'And you're a dirty dog for saying stuff like that. I could smash your face in for talking about my Tabby.'

'You're getting mad at the wrong person, cully. Speen's your man. He's not on duty tonight – where d'you think he is?'

William stared a moment with his mouth open, then walked abruptly away. He was too easy a target, really, Hook thought. It was like teasing a puppy. And a puppy that didn't bite, at that. William might talk big, but he'd never actually do anything. Still, at least he'd shaken him out of his languor, Hook thought: he was moving quite briskly now.

Giles came into Kitty's room, where Hatto was fastening her necklace. 'Nearly ready?' he asked.

She turned her head. 'The bell hasn't gone yet,' she said. Her eyes caressed him. 'You look so handsome in evening dress.'

Hatto picked up a few things for washing and slipped out of the room. Kitty turned back to the looking-glass and began to put in her earrings, watching him in reflection.

Giles moved about the room, fidgeting with things.

'Is something wrong?' she asked at last.

He opened his mouth and closed it again. She waited, thinking he was about to tell her something; but in the end, he said, 'No, nothing. Of course not. Why do you ask?'

'You seem – uneasy.' It wasn't quite the right word.

He knocked over a small vase on one of the tables and righted it again. 'It's probably the phase of the moon,' he said. 'Full moon tonight, isn't it?'

'That's women,' Kitty said. 'And cats. Men aren't affected by the moon.'

'What about lunatics?' he objected. 'Well, it's windy tonight. Horses get nervous when it's windy.'

Kitty turned to look at him again, wondering why they were having this conversation. 'Giles, if there's something you want to tell me—'

'It's nothing. Are you ready? Then let's go down. It would be bad form for our guests to wait for us.'

'Uncle Sebastian would look after them. He's always down early,' Kitty said, but she got up obediently and went with him.

'Where's William?' Moss asked agitatedly. 'Has anyone seen William?'

'I think he's gone out, Mr Moss,' Hook said.

'*Out?*'

'I saw him with a coat on a bit since.'

'It's not his evening off!' Moss cried in outrage. 'How can he go out? *Where* has he gone?'

'I don't know, Mr Moss. I didn't ask him,' Hook said.

Moss looked about him, a little wildly. 'But we have a big dinner tonight. With guests! I can't serve it just with Cyril. Sam has a boil on his chin – he can't go into the dining-room.'

Hook toyed for a moment with the idea of tormenting the butler, but decided to put himself on the side of virtue for once. 'I'll give a hand, if you like, Mr Moss. I don't mind.'

Moss looked at him almost with love. 'Would you? Thank you, James! That would be most gracious of you.'

'Glad to help, Mr Moss.'

'You can draw a coat and waistcoat from the wardrobe. Oh, my goodness, what a relief! Why people have to do these things, just when we have guests – getting boils, and going missing . . . I shall speak to William when he gets back,' he

404

added menacingly. 'He'll be docked a week's wages for this little spree of his! At least.'

He walked on down the passage, muttering.

The dinner was good, the conversation fluid and wide-ranging, and Kitty was glad to see Giles eat enough for once, probably due to a combination of the two. She liked the Arthurs, and was particularly touched by their obviously close relationship. Talbot Arthur had been at university with Giles, both studying under Flinders Petrie, and Mary Baxter had been a librarian at the college at the same time. Talbot and Mary had fallen in love, and since Talbot was a man of independent fortune, they had married as soon as he had taken his degree, had spent their time since then travelling, and Mary went with him on all his digs, and acted as secretary, taking and keeping his notes, and ordering them afterwards for publication.

'It must be lovely to have so many interests in common,' she said to Mary at one point.

Mary smiled fondly at her husband, who was in animated conversation with Giles. 'My father always said we were more like brother and sister than husband and wife,' she said. 'I was never sure if he meant that kindly – but he agreed to our marriage anyway.'

'And you enjoy all the travel? Strange food and living in tents. And what about the danger? I suppose some of them are rough places.'

'I never mind anything as long as we are together. The only time I ever felt ill was when he left me behind in Winchester while he went to Greece – though perhaps that was partly because I was expecting at the time.'

Kitty was surprised. 'You have a child?'

'A boy, Ptolemy. He's five now. He stays with his grandparents while we're travelling.'

'How can you bear to leave him? Oh, I'm sorry, that was

rude. I didn't mean to be – but when I think of my little Louis . . .'

'It's getting harder to leave him,' Mary admitted. 'I don't care much for little babies, but he's getting to be more interesting now, and I do miss him when we're away. But he's always so glad when we come back, and wants to hear all about our finds. He wants to be an archaeologist too, when he grows up. In the summer, he did a very neat excavation of the kitchen refuse heap, and laid out all the bones very nicely.'

Giles, while listening and responding to Talbot, watched Mary talking to Kitty, and thought how wonderful it must be to have a wife who was everything to you in that way – a constant companion who shared your passions and your thoughts. Mary was lovely and bright and well-educated, and quite fearless on their trips: Talbot was fond of telling how they had been set upon by brigands once, and she had scared them away by firing her rifle over their heads. He joked that if they hadn't turned tail, the next shots would have been *at* their heads. She was the sort of woman one met only once in a lifetime. Giles thought of Nina. He imagined she would have relished the challenge of a nomadic life, too. If only he hadn't inherited his father's bankrupt estate, and the responsibility thereof, he might have had a life like Talbot's.

'William's back,' Wilfrid reported to Mr Moss as he darted past with a pile of dirty plates for the scullery. 'He's just come in the lobby.'

'Is he indeed?' Moss said and, with untypically rapid steps made his way to the rear lobby, where William was just taking off his coat, his back to the butler.

'Where have you been?' Moss demanded.

William turned. His face was white, with a long, nasty-looking scratch down one cheek. His hair was dishevelled, and either he had dirt round one eye, or the beginnings of a black one.

'What the dickens have you been up to?' Moss exclaimed, diverted from the simpler question. 'Have you been fighting?'

Fighting was a sacking offence.

'No,' said William woodenly. He seemed in a state of shock.

'Well?' Moss demanded. 'Answer me! What have you been doing?'

William swallowed. 'I – I fell down.'

'*Fell down?*'

'I slipped, going down the hill. It's muddy. I fell into a ditch.' He put his hand up nervously to his face.

Moss caught the hand to examine it. There were scratches across the back. 'What's this?'

'Getting out of the ditch. I kept slipping. Couldn't find anything to hold on to.' He was talking almost as though hypnotised. 'I must've – got tangled in some briars.'

Moss reverted to the principal point. 'Where have you been? It is not your evening off. How dare you leave the house without permission?'

'I – I got a message,' he said, staring at nothing. 'My ma – she had one of her turns. I had to go. She's all right though. She was better by the time I got there. But it could've been bad.'

'What message? Who brought it? Where is it?'

'Not writ down. A boy came,' he said. 'A neighbour sent him. Said it was urgent. I had to go, Mr Moss. My ma, she gets these turns. Anything could happen. That's why the neighbour sent for me. And then, and then, coming back in the dark, I slipped on the path and went into a ditch.'

'You should have asked permission,' Moss said. 'In such a case, an exception can be made. I am not an unreasonable man.'

'No, Mr Moss.'

'But you do not walk out of the house without telling anyone. There was an important dinner tonight. You put everyone to a considerable deal of trouble. I shall have to think carefully about what punishment is appropriate. Go and get cleaned up, now. And see Mrs Webster about that scratch on your face. That's all we need,' he added angrily to himself, 'another footman who can't appear upstairs!'

'What's that?' William said vaguely, putting his hand up to his cheek.

'Pull yourself together!' Moss said irritably. 'Anyone would think you'd been knocked stupid.' Tears gathered in William's eyes. 'And don't you dare start crying!'

'Sorry, Mr Moss,' William muttered, and wandered off, head down.

Kitty sent Hatto away, and went to look out of the window for a moment. The wind had blown the small clouds into elongated strands of silver fleece; above them, the cold moon polished the sky around it. It was almost bright enough to read by.

Then Giles came in, and crossed the room to stand behind her. 'Beautiful, isn't it?'

Kitty turned her head to look at him, and smiled, delighted by his presence – he had not visited her bed for a long time – but a little apprehensive. He had come in before dinner, too, which looked more like having something on his mind. Something he had not felt able to tell her at the first attempt.

But she wasn't going to waste an opportunity. She turned on the spot and put herself into his arms. He closed his round her absently, his mind obviously elsewhere, so she stretched up on tiptoe and kissed him on the lips.

He kissed her back, and then looked down at her quizzically. 'What's all this?'

'If you've forgotten, I can remind you,' she said. 'Come to bed.'

Long ago, on their honeymoon, her directness, so surprising in someone usually so diffident, had excited him. It did so again. He felt his body stirring in a familiar, half-forgotten way. 'You shameless wanton,' he said.

'I am, aren't I? You used to call me your little pagan.'

'Oh, Kitty!' he said. It was half laughing, half sad. But he let her draw him to the bed, and once in, stretched against her warm softness, his instincts took over. His body, long neglected for things of the mind, wanted its way, and she responded to him so passionately that he was carried away on a flood of sensation.

Afterwards, he made as if to get up, and she tightened her arms round him and said, 'Don't go. Stay with me – stay all night.'

'You *are* a wanton.'

'I love you.'

The words broke the spell. He felt the chains fastening round him – like her arms, like her touch, soft as cobweb, strong enough to choke him. Her curly head was under his chin, her warm body curled bonelessly into his. She had always made it easy for him, not demanding anything of him, seeming happy with her own little circle of life, her own concerns. But she loved him, and that love was another burden. He was tangled in responsibility, like a wild creature caught in a wire, so that even to struggle against it was to hurt himself.

'Kitty,' he said.

'Yes,' she said; and he knew from the tone of that one word that she had guessed why he had come to her room before dinner, why he had come back again. She knew, and her knowing was coals of fire.

'I'm going to Egypt,' he said. At the last minute, he didn't say, 'I want to go,' because that would have been to suggest she could argue him out of it, and he didn't want to prolong her pain.

In the long, long silence that followed he could almost hear her going through the arguments and pleas inside her mind, and rejecting them all. She knew why he had phrased it that way. In the end, what she asked was, 'How long for?'

'I don't know,' he said. Her kindness hurt. He wished she

409

could have been angry. 'A few months.' She digested that in silence. 'Markham can look after everything. And Richard – it will do him good to take responsibility. They can run the estate between them.' She said nothing, but as if she had protested, he cried softly, 'I'm suffocating here! I can't help it, Kitty. I feel as if I can't breathe. I *have* to go.'

'When?' she asked in a small voice.

'Soon,' he said. 'Next week.'

She said nothing for such a long time that he thought she had fallen asleep, until she nudged closer, pushing her body into him. He stroked her head enquiringly, and she lifted her face to be kissed. And kissing, she caught fire, and her passion lit his, and they made love again; more slowly this time, as though they had been told it was the last time.

'Here's a queer thing,' Richard said in the morning at breakfast. He'd cornered Giles at the sideboard and spoke quietly, so the Arthurs would not hear. 'My man's gone missing.'

'Missing?'

'Went out last evening and didn't come back. I had to undress myself. Didn't bother to ring as it was late. But this morning, in comes old Crooks with my shaving water, looking very furtive, and says no one knows where Speen is.'

Giles frowned in thought, taking his time over silver tongs and kidneys. 'Does he drink?'

'Oh, I'm sure he does. Crooks mumbled something about the Dog and Gun – that's where the male servants go on their evenings off.'

'Well, he probably got drunk and went to sleep in a barn or something,' Giles said. 'He'll come back with a sore head. But we'll sort it all out later, when Talbot and Mary have gone.'

The carriage had departed for the station, the females of the household had withdrawn, and Giles summoned Moss before himself, Richard and Sebastian.

410

Moss was almost wringing his hands. He knew this was a judgement on his running of the below-stairs. His authority there ought to be absolute. That someone had flouted it so obviously – and in such a way that the Family had to know – diminished him.

'But where was he going?' Giles asked impatiently.

'No one knows, my lord. I don't think anyone actually saw him leave.'

'So he could still be in the house?' said Richard.

'I have, of course, undertaken a search. He is nowhere on the premises.'

'Speaking of premises: did he go to the pub?'

Moss's eyes slithered away. 'There is some talk that he went to the Dog and Gun, my lord, but when he did not return this morning, I took the liberty of sending a boy over there, and the landlord says he did not see Speen there last night.'

Richard looked at Giles. 'Well, that's the most likely scenario scotched.'

'There are plenty of other pubs,' Giles pointed out. 'He might have gone down to the village.'

Sebastian spoke. 'Is there bad blood between Speen and anyone else in the house, Moss?'

Moss swallowed. 'There are always little frictions, sir, as is natural in a staff, but nothing serious.'

'Not so as to make him want to quit?'

'Oh, you're thinking he's hooked it?' said Richard. 'But I can't see him being bested by any of our people. He's a crafty Londoner, the sort that always comes out on top. I can imagine him leaving because he's bored with country life, but if that was the case, why wouldn't he give his notice in the normal way?'

'I beg your pardon, sir,' Moss said 'but we checked his room first thing, and there's nothing missing, not more than he might be wearing or normally carrying.'

'Well, then, the most likely thing is that he's had an accident,' said Giles. 'Though since you don't know where he was going, it's hard to know where to look. But we had better search, in case he's lying helpless in a ditch somewhere.'

Moss's mind tweaked painfully at the word 'ditch', and he thought briefly of William. He had been out at the same time, and come back with scratches and a bruise to the cheek. Had they met? Could there have been a fight? But as Mr Richard said, Speen was canny and hard, and in any fight would surely put William down with one hand tied behind his back. In any contest, Moss would back Speen to come out on top, so where was he? Besides, Corbie at the Dog had said he hadn't seen William either. Moss had asked, in the note he sent by the boy.

Giles made his decision. 'The grooms and boys must search the estate. Those who can be mounted can start at the far boundaries and work back, those on foot starting here and working outwards. And when they reach the farms, they can ask the tenants to use their own men to help cover the ground.'

Richard cocked his head. 'From the tone of your voice, you don't think they'll find him.'

'I think if he was going to be found, he'd have been found already. All these tracks are well-used. And I can't see a town-bred man like him venturing off the paths or into the woods. No, I think that for reasons of his own, he's flown the coop.'

'And not taken his clothes with him?' said Richard.

Giles met Moss's eyes, and a painful thought occurred to both. 'Better find out what he *has* taken,' said Giles. 'But do it discreetly. No need to blacken a man's name without evidence.'

'I certainly would not do that, my lord,' Moss said, shocked. Theft, in a house like this, was a horrible thing.

Moss was at the door when Sebastian had a thought. 'Has Speen any family? Who is his next of kin?'

412

'I have never heard him speak of any family, sir. But I will enquire of the other servants.'

Mr Cowley was delighted with Nina's new friend. He had been acquainted with Lady Clemmie's father, having met him a couple of times at Marlborough House. He thought her manners particularly gentle and ladylike, a model for any young female.

He had been away again, and had asked Nina to arrange a dinner party for his return, and was glad Nina had invited Lady Clemmie. He was slightly less glad that she had invited Adam Denbigh, though he acknowledged the need for a single man to balance the numbers. And Adam was lively company. The other guests were Sir Bradley and Lady Graham, Colonel and Mrs Cazenove, and Lord and Lady Kelgrove, so with the Wharfedales they were twelve at table – a nice, comfortable number, he thought, and not too much for Mrs Deering to manage. The party went well. While Lady Wharfedale was animated and amusing, she did not stray onto any contentious subjects, and Lady Clemmie added a metropolitan dimension, having moved in wide circles through her diplomat father. She behaved very prettily to Mr Cowling, and coaxed anecdotes about the King and his circle from him, so by the time the evening ended, he was in a mellow mood.

'A happy evening,' he said to Nina, as they went up to bed. 'What was young Denbigh talking to you about so earnestly in the drawing-room over coffee?'

Adam had placed himself beside Nina as soon as she sat down, and had told her about a dreadful dinner party he had once attended, caricaturing the guests in such terms she had struggled to conceal her laughter, knowing her husband was watching her. She had been forced, breathlessly, to make him change the subject. 'It's so unfair to make me laugh.'

'Then I shall be very sedate and bore you with horticulture,' he had said. 'That's safe enough, surely?'

'Gardening, mostly,' Nina said now. 'When he inherits the title, he means to make a fine garden at Kibworth. He told me some of his plans.'

Cowling was unconvinced. 'I don't see that young rake having a turn for gardening. He's altogether too light, to my mind. I hope Lord Kibworth makes old bones, and keeps him out of the title till he's grown up a bit. But Lady Clementine, now, she's a real lady, just the sort I should like you to have for a friend. Nothing against Lady Wharfedale, mind, but she lacks . . .'

'Gravitas?' Nina offered.

'That's right. She never has a thought that's not frivolous. Whereas Lady Clementine thinks seriously about things, you can see that.'

Nina agreed. 'She wants to interest me in her causes.'

'Well, she can't but have a good influence on any young lady,' said Mr Cowling approvingly. They had reached her bedroom door. He looked down at her with love, and briefly stroked her cheek with his big, hard hand. 'I won't say goodnight yet,' he murmured, and she knew from that that he meant to visit her in bed.

He did, and she did her best to make him welcome, but it was another failure. She wished with all her heart that he could succeed, because he was a good man and she was fond of him, but there didn't seem to be anything she could do about it.

The search of the estate uncovered no trace of Speen, and no one claimed to have seen him either.

'I can't waste any more manpower on it,' Giles said to Richard. 'The man's obviously absconded, and the why and the how of it are of no concern. If he comes back while I'm away, you can deal with it as you see fit. What will you do for a valet?'

'Oh, I don't really need one. Old Crooks can look after

me as well as Uncle Sebastian while I'm here. And one of Aunt Caroline's fellows when I'm in London. I'm not a dandy, like you, Giles – I don't need a dedicated wardrobe-master.'

'Ha ha,' said Giles stonily. 'Where did you learn such wit?'

'You're really going, then?' Richard asked seriously.

Giles resisted the tacit demand to explain himself. 'I really am. And you, little brother, will take care of everything while I'm gone. I have absolute faith in you.'

'Then I suspect your judgement in more ways than one,' said Richard. 'But do I have full powers? Or am I simply stopping the house from burning down?'

'Why? Are there things you want to do?'

'There may be. Who knows what might come up? A business opportunity that needs to be acted on? Our friend Cowling says a man must be nimble to seize the advantage, but if I had to wait for a message to get all the way to darkest Africa and back . . .'

'You have full powers,' Giles said. 'I trust Markham to keep you on the straight and narrow.'

'What you mean is that you don't care,' Richard said, with a hint of criticism. 'If I did destroy everything, I suspect you would merely shrug, and feel a guilty relief. I know where your heart is, brother mine, and it's not here.'

Giles looked bleak. 'I wish I didn't have a heart,' he said. 'Life would be so much easier if one weren't torn two ways. I wish I had no feelings at all, like you.'

'Is that what you think of me?' Richard said. 'I am lucky, am I not, to care for nobody? No wife and child to tie me down – not that yours are tying you.'

Giles turned away abruptly. 'You'd better have Speen's chattels packed away, in case some relative turns up and asks for them.' And he left the room.

William was smoking in the backyard, when Hook sidled out

to lounge beside him. William gave him a nervous sidelong look, like a sheep that's spotted something moving in the bracken.

'So, William, I see your black eye's nearly gone. And that scratch on your face. How *did* you get 'em, by the way?' Hook asked insinuatingly.

'I told Mr Moss—' William began.

'Oh, I know what you told him. But it doesn't cut the ice with me. I been in enough fights to know the signs. You went after Speen, didn't you? Question is, did you find him? Or, more to the point, how did you leave him?'

'I don't have to answer your questions,' William said. 'Mind your own business.'

'Oh, William, don't make an enemy of me,' Hook said silkily. 'You might need all the friends you can get. What if the police take an interest?'

'I got nothing to say to the police. I wasn't in no fight. And I never saw Speen.'

'You went off after him, hot-footed, when I told you the truth about him and Tabby. Doesn't look good, does it, him going missing right after that, and you turning up with a busted face? And how is the lovely Tabby, by the way?'

'Don't know. Her and me is broken up,' William said sullenly.

'That's terrible. The poor girl, left to bring your child into the world all alone.'

William turned, his fists bunching. 'You leave me alone, you devil, or I'll—'

'You'll what? You'll kill me, like you did Speen? Where did you hide the body, then, Billy boy?'

William threw down his cigarette and stalked into the house. Hook picked it up, examined the end, and put it between his lips, leaning against the wall with one foot up behind him. Of course he didn't really think William had fought Speen – if he had, he'd have come off a lot worse,

416

and it would have been Speen who came back and William who went missing. Hook would back Speen every time to knock William down without a finger being laid on him. William had had a scrap with *someone*, all right, but it wasn't Speen.

But it was fun to tease William, the little twerp. And – his mind started to work – maybe there was profit to be made out of the situation. Naturally, all the servants had quickly learned that Mr Moss was checking to see if Speen had stolen anything. It was meant to be a secret, but there were no secrets in a house like this. Now, with Speen missing, it was a good opportunity to lay a lot of sins at his door. He must see what he might safely lay hands on, anything he could dispose of easily and safely.

And it might be fun to drop an anonymous line to the village constable about William (who *had* he been fighting with, anyway?)

As to what had happened to Speen, Hook reckoned he had just run for it, probably because something he was up to had been found out, or was about to be. He wouldn't be surprised if Speen hadn't had a lot of irons in the fire all around the village. As for leaving his kit behind, there wasn't anything of worth there – Hook had checked. No doubt he kept anything worth having hidden somewhere, and had made sure to take it with him. They wouldn't see Speen again, Hook was sure of that. And he didn't care, either. Good riddance to bad rubbish, was his view.

# CHAPTER TWENTY-FOUR

Giles came into his bedroom looking for his pen, and found Hook there, packing his trunk – or, rather, staring with a frown at the items laid out for packing. He gave his servant a sharp glance but had no intention of engaging in conversation. But Hook first cleared his throat in a significant way, and finally, as Giles bent over a bedside drawer, said, 'I beg your pardon, my lord.'

Giles straightened. 'Yes?' he said irritably. When a valet began with, 'I beg your pardon, my lord,' no good thing ever followed.

'This trip, my lord, to Egypt, I presume . . . That is to say, I suppose . . .'

'Oh, spit it out, man!'

'Your lordship will be staying in Cairo? In a hotel?'

'For the first night. Then it's out to the dig. The Valley of the Kings,' he elaborated. 'Why?'

'In the Valley, my lord, of the Kings, I suppose there is a hotel for all the English gentlemen?'

'Why the devil should you suppose that? We live in tents. There are no towns nearby.' He narrowed his eyes as Hook shifted uncomfortably from foot to foot. 'What's wrong with you? Why are you asking stupid questions?'

Hook had not really believed what Speen had said about living in tents and eating scorpions, but from various snippets he had overheard while serving dinner to the Arthurs, he had begun to wonder. And then his lordship had vetoed so many of the things he had been intending to pack for him, saying he wouldn't need them . . .

'It's just that I'm not sure I'll be able to look after you properly, my lord,' he blurted, 'in a tent. The fact is, I've never—' He intercepted Giles's glare and descended into a mumble. 'It isn't . . . I can't . . . Not really an outdoors person—'

Giles breathed out hard. 'Let me understand you – do you refuse to accompany me to Egypt?'

The word 'refuse' silenced Hook for a moment. But the vision before him was too awful. 'I don't see that I would be much use to you, my lord,' Hook said in subdued tones. 'Not in a tent.' He didn't mention the scorpions, but they loomed large in his imagination.

'Then you had certainly better not come,' Giles said. 'I have little enough need of a town valet on a dig – of an unwilling one, none at all.'

'Thank you, my lord,' Hook began.

Giles held up a hand to silence him. He was furious at the impertinence – the man's presuming to choose when he would deign to do his duty and when he would refuse! His first impulse was to sack Hook out of hand, but a second thought suggested a punishment that would make him suffer more. 'You are no longer my valet. You may return to your former position of footman, at a footman's salary.'

Hook's mouth opened and closed – for once he was lost for words.

'Or, if you prefer,' Giles went on with poisonous kindness, 'you may leave my employ entirely. A month's notice would not be appropriate, since I shan't be here, but you may take a month's wages in lieu and go at once.'

Hook's nostrils flared as his temper rose. Nobody dismissed James Hook! But go back to footman? It would be humiliating. He managed to swallow the words that sprang to his tongue.

A month's wages wouldn't go far, and what if he didn't get another place right away? He was used to his comfort – he didn't want to pig it in cheap lodgings while he looked for a place. And he hadn't had time to carry out his plan of take-stuff-and-blame-Speen yet. Better to take a month or so as a footman and leave at a time of his own choosing, than have everyone say he was dismissed. He'd find some way of making it seem as if he'd been clever, getting out of going to Egypt.

'Thank you, my lord,' he said with an effort. 'I'll serve as footman, if you please.'

'You may go, then. And ask Crooks if he'll come and finish my packing.'

'M-my lord?'

'It is a job for a valet. You are no longer a valet.'

Hook swallowed, bowed, and backed out.

Giles felt a moment of satisfaction, but it quickly faded. Petty triumphs over servants did little to assuage the pain of a torn mind.

The presence of a policeman below stairs was disturbing. PC Holyoak was darkly handsome, and had a commanding presence. The maids found a surprising number of reasons to scuttle along Piccadilly and past him in the minutes he was waiting there. His head was politely bare, and his dark hair, curly as a ram's fleece, almost brushed the low ceiling of the passage. He was altogether thrilling. Even the kitchen staff peeped out, and Brigid made so bold as to offer the young Dionysus a cup of tea – which he politely refused.

Moss was apprehensive when Holyoak was shown into his room. A visit from the police is never comfortable for a butler. It never meant good news. The last time, it had been to announce that Mr Richard had been in a motor-car smash and was close to death.

'How can I help you, constable?' he asked.

'You have a footman here, name of William Sweeting?'

'Yes – yes, we have.'

'I'd like a word with him, if you please.'

'He's a good, quiet lad. A good worker, never any trouble. What is it about?'

'I have received information that he may have been involved in an incident. Would you send for him, please? I'd like a word with him.'

Moss got up and went to the door. There was no difficulty in securing a messenger – all too many people were hanging around innocently engaged in nothing very much. In the following interval, the policeman waited with positively geological patience, which made Moss feel fidgety and ill at ease by contrast – a mayfly beside a mountain. When William appeared hesitantly in the doorway, Holyoak said, 'I'd like to speak to the young man alone, if you don't mind.'

Moss felt he was on firmer ground here. 'But I do mind. I am in loco parenthesis to all my staff, particularly the younger ones. I must be present.'

Holyoak looked questioningly at William, who blushed under scrutiny and managed, with an heroic effort, not to put his hand to his face. The scratch had been a deep one, and the healing line was still visible. 'I don't mind,' he mumbled. 'I'd like Mr Moss to be here.'

'Very well, then,' said Holyoak. He took out his notebook and consulted it – not that he needed to, but people expected it. It impressed them. 'I have received information that you were out of the house on the evening of Wednesday, the fourth of November.' William's lips moved as he calculated the date. '*Last* Wednesday. Where did you go?'

William glanced at Moss as if he might answer for him, but then was captured by the mesmeric gaze of the policeman. 'I went to see my mum.'

'It was your evening off?'

'No, I had a message she was ill. One of her neighbours sent for me.'

421

'What neighbour was that?' Holyoak appeared to be writing down what William said, which disconcerted him.

'I don't know,' he said. A burst of inspiration came to him. 'Ma lives in Acres End Row. She's got lots of neighbours. They all look out for her in the Row. She – she has these funny turns. But when I got there, she was all right again. So I come back.'

'And did you see this neighbour, at your mum's house?'

William had to think. 'No. No, she'd gone home. 'Cause my ma was all right.'

'Did she mention which neighbour it was who helped her?'

'She never said. Or I don't remember. I was a bit upset. I was worried about her. It's all a bit muddled in my head.'

'I see. And what happened on the way back?'

William chewed his lip, his eyes fixed desperately on the dark, handsome face. 'I – I fell into a ditch in the dark. It was all brambles. I couldn't get out. I kept slipping in the mud. I got all scratched.' His hand got halfway to his cheek this time before he dragged it back.

The constable's pencil moved implacably across the page. 'Did you meet anyone else on the way there, or on the way back?'

'No,' William said. He chewed his lip.

The pencil stopped. The dark, steady eyes looked up, into William's, straight through the back of them and into William's head. 'Are you quite sure? No one at all? No man, woman or child?'

'I never met no one,' William said.

Holyoak moved his feet slightly more apart, making himself even more unrockable. With his weight spread and anchored into the ground, an earthquake would have had a job knocking him off balance. 'Now, I want you to be quite clear about this, William Sweeting. Did you at any point on that evening meet, or see, or speak to, or have any dealings with Edgar Speen, valet in this house?'

'No! I never seen him. Why you asking me this?' William said, a little wildly. There was a bead of sweat on his upper lip. 'I never done nothing. Tell him, Mr Moss! I've never been in trouble.'

Moss opened his mouth to speak, but Holyoak stopped him with a glance. 'That's all right, William. You can go now.'

When they were alone, Holyoak turned to Moss and folded over a new page in his notebook. 'Now, Mr Moss, when that young man got back on Wednesday evening, you went to meet him at the back door, is that right? Why did you do that?'

Moss bent his brow in apprehension. 'It wasn't his evening off. He shouldn't have gone out. I went to reprimand him and ask where he'd been.'

'And he told you the same as he's just told me.'

'Yes,' said Moss. He thought of something, hesitated, then said, 'Yes,' again.

'And what was his condition?'

'Condition?'

'Was he agitated?'

'No, I can't say he was.'

'You noticed a scratch on his face?'

Moss stirred. 'How do you know all this? Who told you about William being out?'

'Information was placed before me,' Holyoak said. 'What about the scratch?'

'Yes, I noticed a scratch on his cheek and some on his hands. He'd got them on the brambles, trying to get out of the ditch. Like he just told you.'

Holyoak wrote in silence. Then he looked up. 'Have you heard anything from the valet, Speen, since that evening?'

'No.' The dark stare was like a vortex; it drew words out of you into it. 'He was a strange man. A difficult servant, clever, but satirical. Had an odd sense of humour. And secretive. No one knew anything about him. Frankly, I'm not

423

surprised he took off. He wasn't suited to country-house life. He was a town person.'

'That's what you think, is it? That he just took off?'

'I'm sure that's it.'

Holyoak nodded massively. 'Very well. If you think of anything else, you'll be sure to let me know, won't you? And now I'd like a word with Mr Richard Tallant – Speen valeted for him, didn't he?'

'I shall enquire whether Mr Richard is at home, and can receive you,' Moss said, being massive himself, now he was back in his own sphere. 'Wait here, please.'

Richard received Holyoak in the morning-room, and answered his questions, though there was little he could tell him. 'He never mentioned any family to me. I always assumed he was a lone wolf. I've no idea what he did in his time off. I suppose he had friends, but it's not something one discusses with a servant.'

'Was he a good servant?'

'Satisfactory. I wouldn't say he was a born servant – hadn't the attitude for it. Too independent. But I don't need much looking after, and I was used to soldier-servants, who don't have the attitude either. I imagine he just got bored with life out here. He was a Londoner, probably missed the bright lights. But what's brought you out here, constable? You're not suspecting foul play, surely?'

'I received an anonymous note, suggesting that one of your footmen, William Sweeting, knew something about Edgar Speen's disappearance, and it was my duty to follow it up. Sweeting had scratches on his hands and face, and a black eye, suggesting he'd been in a fight.'

Richard's eyebrows rose. 'Dear me, you can't be thinking William beat Speen to death? He's as soft as a blancmange. Besides, we'd have found the body – we've searched the whole estate, just in case Speen had had an accident and was lying hurt somewhere.'

'Quite, sir. I didn't say I thought anything of the sort, but it was my duty to make enquiries. Sweeting says he got scratched falling into a ditch in the dark, and there seems no reason to think otherwise. Unless any other information comes to light, we must assume Speen has absconded voluntarily.' He closed his notebook, gave Richard one more thoughtful look, and departed.

Richard did not propose to waste any more thought on his former valet, for whom he had never developed any fondness. It did just cross his mind, though, that the moon had been almost full on Wednesday night – full moon was in fact Thursday the 5th – and it had been a clear night: he remembered there had been a sharp frost on the Thursday morning. So it was a little odd that William said he'd fallen into a ditch in the dark. Still, most people got flustered when the police asked them questions, and said the first thing that came into their heads. He didn't propose to waste any more thought on William, either.

Mrs Albertine Crane turned out to be a brown, hard little nut of a woman, the widow of a doctor of the more lowly sort, not a grand physician to the carriage class, but the kind that just made ends meet tending the needs of the less well-off, and running a free clinic for the really poor. She was neatly dressed in clothes bought to last, and made an odd contrast with Lady Clemmie, but they were obviously old friends.

And when she talked, it seemed to make the air crackle as though with electricity. Nina was held rapt the whole time. It was interesting, she thought, that Bobby was evidently impressed, to the extent that when they gathered round afterwards with cups of tea, she was largely silent.

In fact, it was Nina who said, 'I do think you ought to hold a public meeting, Mrs Crane, and address a larger audience.'

Mrs Crane twinkled. 'What a splendid idea, Mrs Cowling.

And indeed I should like to, but it must be when I pass this way again. I am off to London tomorrow, for some very important meetings. But I shall return.'

'And you will stay here when you do?' Clemmie said.

'Thank you, I shall. Meanwhile,' to Nina, 'I see I have lit a spark – don't let it go out!'

'I won't,' Nina said. 'You've given me so much to think about.'

The trunk was corded and labelled and sitting in the hall. Tiger and Isaac circled it unhappily, then Tiger lay down as close to it as he could manage, while Isaac wandered about the hall as if he had lost something. Upstairs, in his room, Giles was packing the last few items into his leather Gladstone, while Kitty watched.

'How will you manage without a servant?' she asked, for something to say. She wanted to hear his voice while she still could.

'I've no need for a proper valet out there. I never had one before, you know, just a native servant to keep the tent tidy and wash my linen. We live very simply.'

'But what if you get ill? Who will look after you?'

'I shan't get ill,' he said. 'And I have a good medical kit in my chest.'

'Why do you need that, if you're not going to get ill?'

He snapped the clasp closed and went over to her. She stood as though frozen. She seemed very pale, too. He half thought that if he touched her she would shatter like ice. 'I'll be all right,' he said kindly. 'I've done this before.'

She looked up at him intently, as though memorising his face. 'You will come back?'

He tried to smile. 'What sort of question is that? Of course I will. I'll just be a few weeks. I have to get away, Kitty. You understand, don't you?'

'No,' she said. Everything she loved was here. She had no

need to go anywhere else. 'But I know you *will* go. Just promise me—'

He didn't want her to complete that sentence. There were things she might ask that he couldn't promise. He took hold of her by the upper arms and stooped to kiss her. Her lips were eager under his. When the kiss ended, the words had stopped, and there were tears on her eyelashes.

Alice appeared in the doorway. 'The carriage is here, Giles.'

Giles looked down at Kitty. 'We must go down,' he said. It was almost a question.

Kitty released herself. She looked around. 'My hat,' she said vaguely.

'No,' he said. 'Don't come to the station. No more good-byes. It's only for a few weeks, goose!'

'A few weeks?' Alice asked from the door. 'Does that mean you'll be back for Christmas?'

'Well, perhaps not *that* few,' Giles said. 'Remember it takes a couple of weeks to get out there. And then there's—'

'He'll come back when he's ready, Alice,' Kitty said loyally. 'It's not for you to question.'

Sebastian had asked Kitty if he could borrow Dory again. They travelled separately on the train, as was proper, but Sebastian directed her into his cab from the station to Wisteria House. 'I expect you're wondering what task lies ahead of you,' he said. 'I've made some changes, and I'd like your opinion on the result. And perhaps to ask you to arrange things nicely – whatever it is women do to make a house look like a home.'

'You mean, provide a woman's touch?' she asked, amused.

'Precisely.'

'I will, of course, do anything you like, sir, but don't you think she'll have her own ideas?'

'Who?' he said vaguely.

'The lady you're doing it all for,' she said. He looked at

her with one eyebrow raised. 'You've lived in that house for years and been content with it. And you wouldn't have needed to consult anyone about your own taste, would you?'

'No, I wouldn't. That's logical.'

'Then perhaps you should wait and let her do it when she comes.'

He thought a moment. 'Well, she can change things round if she doesn't like them. In fact, I expect she will, anyway. Don't ladies like to rearrange everything on a regular basis?'

'Depends what else they've got to do,' she said. 'I think it's mostly bored ladies who have the furniture moved about.'

He smiled, and turned away to look out of the window, ending the conversation.

At Wisteria House, Dory was greeted warmly by Mrs May. 'We've had so many changes since you were last here, dear,' she said. 'The house done up from top to toe. I'm sorry there's a smell of paint still. I've done my best airing the rooms, but it does stick. Does it bother you?'

'It's rather nice, in a way – a clean smell.'

'I'm glad you think so. I must have used a gallon of lavender wax but it doesn't cover it. No Mr Crooks this time?'

'Apparently not. I suppose Mr Sebastian's not staying long.'

'Oh, well, he's always managed before. Quite an old campaigner, I always say. What does he want you for this time, dear?' Dory told her. She looked blank. Then she shrugged. 'The gentry have their funny ideas, don't they? Time for a cup of tea first? I hear your master has gone off to foreign parts,' she said, when they were sitting at the kitchen table.

'How did you know that?' Dory asked.

'Our rector's a friend of your rector, and mentioned it in a letter. And our rector's maid is first cousin to our Olive, so she heard it from her. A bit of a surprise, isn't it, his lordship going off like that to dig up old bones and such, and in them nasty foreign places, all flies and dirt and disease? Whatever does he do it for?'

428

'It's not old bones, as I understand it, but vases and statues and so on, and lots of gold and jewels.'

'Oh, well, that's different, then. How does her ladyship like it?'

Dory reflected how Rose had said her ladyship had wept all night for two nights; and she herself had seen the swollen eyes, not sufficiently brought down by cold water and witch hazel, when she had happened to be in the nursery while her ladyship was visiting little Lord Ayton. And Mr Richard had seemed to be hovering around her the first few days, as if to be on hand if she collapsed. But it seemed she had made a determined effort, stiffened her spine and was showing a brave face. No collapse was likely.

'Oh, she's all right,' Dory said.

The bell rang. 'Parlour,' said Mrs May. 'Funny to see that bell rung, when it's always been empty. That'll be for you, I don't doubt, dear. D'you want to go, or shall I send Olive?'

'I'll go. I want to see how the place has changed.'

'It's all very nice, to my mind. Bar the smell of paint.'

'What do you think?' Sebastian asked. 'Did I get it right?'

Dory turned slowly on the spot, taking it all in. The walls were now covered with a pale green silk wallpaper, the floor with a green-and-white Chinese carpet, and there were soft voile curtains at the window. There was a round table in the window, of rosewood, with four pretty chairs upholstered in a darker green silk. There was a dainty French ormolu clock on the mantelpiece and parlour palms in big pots softening the corners of the room. There were comfortable armchairs by the fireside, and beside one of them a nice little sewing-table with a pleated silk drum. And on the walls, there were watercolour paintings of landscapes. It was restful, feminine, inviting – and she loved the sense of the green of the garden making its way in, as if there were no barrier between inside and outside. In the summer, with the windows open . . .

'It's perfect,' she said, with a sense of sadness. She made herself smile at him, touched by his eagerness to please this unknown woman. 'There's nothing for me to do here. She'll love it, sir – or if she doesn't, she's a very strange person indeed!'

'She isn't strange. But she is remarkable. The most remarkable woman I've ever met.'

'Well, sir, if I might presume, I hope you'll be very happy together. Just be sure to have lots of flowers everywhere when she arrives as your bride. Have you fixed a date yet?'

'Not yet,' he said.

'I'd be happy to come and do the flowers for the occasion, if you wanted. Oh, but Mrs May can manage them just as well,' she corrected herself, feeling foolish.

'I'd like you to do the flowers,' he said. 'I'd like you always to do the flowers.' He took a step towards her, and she looked up, and met his eyes with a sense of shock deep in her stomach. Suddenly, he was much closer than mere geography. 'Haven't you guessed?' he said quietly. 'You're usually so quick on the uptake. I did it for you, all for you. That's why I asked you, so that it would be how you like it.'

Dory stared, unable to believe what she was hearing. But it was all there in his face, more love than she had ever seen in her life.

'I'm asking you to marry me,' he said. 'I think I loved you from the first moment I met you. Our times together have been so precious to me. You amaze and delight me every day: your mind is like a box of treasures. I've talked to you more in the past year than I've talked to anyone else in the whole of my life. I feel as if we are very alike, as if you understand me. All I need to know is whether you can also love me.'

She didn't answer, staring at him, trying to make sense of this new information. She felt dizzy, shocked, excited and desperately sad all at once.

His smile wavered. 'You – you don't care for me? I thought I had detected a fondness in you towards me. Did I imagine it? I know I'm older than you, and I suppose I'm no great catch – but I am rich enough to support you handsomely, and if devotion, if unwavering love means anything—'

'Oh, please, don't!' she cried. 'Don't say any more!'

She saw she had hurt him. A spark went out. 'I'm sorry,' he said. 'I presumed too much. I've put you in a dreadful position. Please forget all about it. I shan't refer to it again. It will be as though this never happened. The last thing in the world I want is to make life difficult for you. I wanted to see you happy and settled and comfortable, and in my old man's folly, I imagined—'

'You didn't imagine!' she said urgently, catching his hand. It was strong and warm, the fingers flexible; it was a source of life. 'You didn't imagine it! I've loved our time together too. I never felt like a servant when I was with you. It's strange, but I always felt like an equal, as if we were – made from the same cloth.'

'It's my age, then,' he said sadly. 'You think I'm too old to marry.'

'You're not old!' she protested. 'You mustn't ever say that. I would be honoured to marry you. There's nothing would delight me more than to say yes—'

'Then say it,' he said. He stepped right up to her and took her in his arms, and she tilted her head up, longing just for an instant to be kissed. 'Never mind what anyone else thinks. Marry me, and say to hell with them all! And we'll show them what real married bliss looks like.'

With a huge mental effort, she made herself reach behind her, took his hands and unclasped them. 'I can't,' she said, taking a half step backwards. 'I wish I could, but I can't.'

He regarded her for a long moment. 'I think you have at least to tell me why. I think I deserve that.'

'Because I'm married already,' she said, and the words were like frost falling on roses. 'I'm sorry,' she said softly.

★ ★ ★

431

Kitty had wept when Giles was gone, wept for the loss of the golden dream of her growing-up years, of the prince on the white horse and the happy-ever-after. Her dream had seemed to be coming true last year – to marry the man she loved and, on their honeymoon, to discover in the most practical and unexpected way, that he loved her. She had never imagined physical bliss of that order could exist. Then had come the castle, the riches, and the young princeling, her perfect, adored baby.

But Giles had gone to Egypt because, he said, he felt stifled. None of this had been his dream. Underneath all the pink clouds of her happiness, she had always known he had married her for her fortune. But she had believed there could be love as well. Why should one preclude the other? Now she knew: he didn't love her. He didn't love her. He didn't love her. The agony of it, and the longer sorrow of the lost dream, made her weep. She wept as an exile from a dear land that she could never go back to.

But after two days, she had found the courage to pull herself together. She still had her duty to do. And whatever else was true, he was still her husband. *Hers*. He had married her, they were married, and there was nothing he could do about that. He might run away, but he would always have to come back, because he was tied to this house and to her by an unbreakable thread, and it would always bring him back.

So she had to make the best of things. And he had left her with something to do – a house to run, a kingdom that needed a queen while the king was away.

She would have things the way she liked them now, she thought with a queer satisfaction. And she would entertain! She would fill the house with guests, with life, with fun. She would hunt – she had been pregnant last season and hadn't been able to take Apollo out once. She would hunt him, and they would have hunting weekends, and neighbours for dinner, and balls. Rachel would be coming home soon, and

Rachel and Alice would enjoy the balls. A house with young ladies in it couldn't be dull.

And her mother-in-law had better not try to get in her way. She would not be told any more – or told off.

She splashed cold water on her face, inspected her reflection for a moment in the glass, then sat down and drew a sheet of paper towards her.


'What do you think really happened to Speen?' Alice asked Richard, as they came back from a ride.

'Don't know,' Richard said. 'Legged it, I suppose. I never did know much about him – picked him up when I came back from South Africa and lost my soldier-servant.'

'But he left his clothes behind,' Alice said.

'He probably had some more stashed away somewhere. He's the sort of bird who'd have a little hideaway in London to go back to. He had a lot of free time when we were in London, and I never knew how he spent it. I wouldn't worry about him – he's the sort who always lands on his feet.'

'Oh, I wasn't worried,' Alice said. 'I just wondered.'

Richard gave her a canny look. 'Now, what's the griff? You can't fool me, Alice Tallant. You've got something on your mind.'

'I hear the servants talking. Something about a fight between Speen and William over a woman.'

Richard snorted. 'If those two'd had a fight, it would have been William who'd come off worse. He'd be the one to run away.'

'That's what I thought,' Alice said. They turned into the stableyard. 'Oh, the greys have been out,' she said, seeing them being led into their stable. 'What's happening?' she asked Giddins, as he came towards them.

'Her ladyship's back, and Lady Rachel,' Giddins said. 'Just fetched 'em from the station, my lady.'

'Oh, lor,' said Richard. 'Mother's back. There goes our peace and quiet!'

Alice put the foot she had freed back into the stirrup. 'I'm not ready for that yet. Let's go out again.'

Richard had already dismounted. 'Can't,' he said.

'Well, I can,' Alice said, turned the surprised Pharaoh and with a sharp kick sent him careering out of the stableyard, ignoring the shouts behind her. She'd get into trouble later, but later was later. And maybe it wouldn't happen.

When Maud brought Rachel home for the hunting season, Giles had been gone five days. She was furious.

'How could you let him go off like that?' she demanded of Kitty. 'You should have stopped him.'

'That was not possible,' Kitty said unsteadily.

'*I* would have stopped him if I had been here,' said Maud. 'Why was I not informed of this ridiculous, this *unseemly* plan? It was one thing for him to go digging in ruins when he was Lord Ayton, unmarried and without responsibilities, but for the Earl of Stainton to run about in that fashion! There has been some mismanagement here. He would not have gone if everything was as it should be. You have driven him away!'

'I didn't want him to go,' Kitty said. 'I had no idea until the last minute that he was' – she almost said 'unhappy', and changed it at the last moment to – 'restless.'

'Restless!' Maud snorted. 'It is pure self-indulgence on his part. A dereliction of duty. It is only a step from this to gaming and extravagance and – and other things. I blame *you*,' she said, fixing Kitty with a gimlet eye. 'You have allowed him to become unregulated. Who knows what the consequences will be?'

'It wasn't my place to stop him,' Kitty said.

'Milk-and-water nonsense! Well, I am here now, and I shall take charge of everything in his absence. We will continue with the hunting season as usual. We will entertain as if nothing had happened, and our entertainments will be so splendid people will forget the earl is absent. Richard can act as host in his place – I will make him behave himself. I shall arrange it all. First we must—'

'I beg your pardon,' Kitty interrupted her, with an unusual steel to her voice. Maud looked at her in surprise, as if a mouse had barked. 'We shall entertain at Ashmore Castle. That has already been decided. But *I* shall see to the arrangements.'

'You?' Maud said. 'Nonsense!'

She turned away; and Kitty actually caught her arm, her fingers biting. Maud stared in shock at being touched. 'Remove your hand at once. How dare you?'

'No, Mother-in-law, how dare *you*? *I* am mistress of Ashmore Castle. Orders given in this house will be given by me. Any guests invited to this house will be invited by me. Everything will be arranged as *I* like to have it done. You are welcome to stay here for as long as you wish, but it's *my* house, and if you can't accept that – well, there's the Dower House in the village.'

Maud opened her mouth, and shut it again. It was a different Kitty who was staring her down. Something had happened. Her previous rebellions had been those of a child half-scared with its own daring. Now there was no passion in the stare, only steady determination. And, unwillingly, Maud felt a stirring of respect. 'Mistress of Ashmore Castle is not a title you take, it is a title you earn,' she said.

'I disagree,' Kitty said. 'It is simply a matter of fact.'

'You are very bold,' said Maud. 'But we shall see. I shall step back and watch you dig your own grave. And when you beg me for help, I shall step in and take back what was always mine.'

'Thank you, Mother-in-law,' Kitty said, with irony.

'And don't call me Mother-in-law,' Maud snapped, and walked away.

Only after she had left the room did Kitty allow herself to

tremble. It was not fear, but the unfamiliar sensation of triumph

Axe came out from his cottage, wiping his hands on a cloth. He looked at Pharaoh in surprise. She hadn't come on horse-back since Josh had forbidden her to ride alone. He sensed trouble ahead.

She had halted and freed her foot, and he had to hurry to jump her down, or she'd have jumped by herself, and he didn't think jolting on the ground like that was good for young ladies.

'Something wrong?' he asked, taking Pharaoh's rein. The horse nuzzled him, happy to renew old acquaintance.

'Not yet,' Alice said, 'but there will be. Mother's back from London. They were just leading the greys in as I got home, and somehow I couldn't face seeing her right that minute.'

'So you ran away?'

'Don't make it sound bad. You'd run away from her if you could, in my position. She's bound to be in a bad mood.'

'Will she be in a better one for you running away?'

Alice narrowed her eyes. 'Oh, you always talk such horrid good sense! I know I'll get told off, I just wanted a bit more freedom first. Can I have a cup of tea before I go back?'

'Just finished one,' he said. 'I'll make another pot.'

It was growing colder, and the clouds were heavy, as if it might snow soon. But the cottage was lovely and warm, and Dolly and two cats were jumbled up together in a furry mass on the rug in front of the fire. Dolly lifted her head and wagged her tail, but was too comfortable to get up and do a proper greeting.

Axe put the kettle on the trivet and pushed it back over the heat. 'Won't be long warming up. I only just finished my cup.'

He straightened up and stood looking down at her. 'You'll get into trouble,' he said. 'What'd they think if they knew you were here?'

436

'They can't possibly find out. Nobody comes here – nobody from the house.'

'Going to snow soon. I can smell it.'

'I'll go as soon as I've drunk my tea,' she said with a sigh. 'Anyone would think you don't like me visiting.'

''Snot that,' Axe said. 'And you know it.' She'd grown taller again, he thought. She wasn't that much shorter than him, now. He wouldn't have to stoop very far if he was to—

He stopped his thought, shocked with himself.

'What?' she asked. 'You just thought of something.'

She was too quick at reading him. 'Just worried about you getting into trouble,' he said.

'But your face went red,' Alice persisted.

'Heat of the fire,' Axe said. She was staring up at him intently.

She was so lovely, he thought dispassionately. He didn't understand why they didn't notice it up at the house. He knew from her conversation and things overheard that Lady Rachel was 'the pretty one' and Lady Alice was shrugged over. But there was far more character in her face, to his mind. She was more beautiful than her sister in the way that an Arab horse is more beautiful than a kitten.

'You shouldn't be here,' he said, his voice suddenly husky. 'It's not safe.'

'How could I not be safe here, with you?' she asked, as if it were a simple question. But then the focus of her eyes changed, and they seemed to darken. The fire spat a little, the kettle hissed quietly, and Dolly stretched out her hind legs and groaned with comfort.

Axe could not look away from Alice; their eyes seemed locked disastrously together. He bent his head, slowly, as though trying to resist a terrible power; the muscles of his neck almost creaked with the effort. Her face, rosy in the firelight, grew closer; her sweet breath touched his face.

'What do you really come here for, Lady Alice?' he asked softly.